Neverland

Neverland

DOUGLAS CLEGG

Interior Illustrations by Glenn Chadbourne

Vanguard Press
A Member of the Perseus Books Group
New York

Published by Vanguard Press
A Member of the Perseus Books Group

Designed by Brent Wilcox
Set in 11 point Adobe Caslon

Library of Congress Cataloging-in-Publication Data
Clegg, Douglas, 1958-
  Neverland / Douglas Clegg.
    p.   cm.
  ISBN 978-1-59315-541-4 (alk. paper)
  1. Boys—Fiction.   2. Islands—Fiction.   3. Family secrets—Fiction.
4. Demonology—Fiction.   I. Title.
  PS3553.L3918N48 2010
  813'.54—dc22

                                                        2010002330

Vanguard Press books are available at special discounts for bulk purchases in the
U.S. by corporations, institutions, and other organizations. For more
information, please contact the Special Markets Department at the Perseus
Books Group, 2300 Chestnut Street, Suite 200, Philadelphia, PA 19103, or call
(800) 810-4145, ext. 5000, or e-mail special.markets@perseusbooks.com.

10 9 8 7 6 5 4 3 2 1

⇥ FOR **R.S.** ⇤

Acknowledgments

With thanks to Glenn Chadbourne, Matt Schwartz, M. J. Rose, Bentley Little, Francine LaSala, Amanda Ferber, Roger Cooper, Geórgina Levitt, and everyone at Vanguard and the Perseus Group.

To the reader

Be sure to drop by Douglas Clegg's website at
DouglasClegg.com for bonus content.

Prologue

No Grown-ups.

    Among other words we wrote across the walls—some in chalk, some with spray paint—these two words were what my cousin Sumter believed in most.

    There *were* other words.

    Some of them were written in blood.

⊰ 2 ⊱

No child alive has a choice as to where he or she will go in the summer, so for every August after Grampa Lee died, our parents would drag us back to that small, as yet undeveloped peninsula off the coast of Georgia, mistakenly called an island.

    Gull Island.

    We would arrive just as its few summer residents were leaving. No one in their right mind ever vacationed off that section of the Georgia coastline after August first, and Gull Island may have been the worst of any vacation spots along the ocean. Giant black flies would invade the shore, while jellyfish spread out across the dull brown beaches like a new coat of wax. It was not, as sarcastic Nonie would remark, "the armpit of the universe," but often smelled like it.

The Jackson family could afford no better.

We were not rich, and we were not poor, but we were the kind of family that always stayed in Howard Johnson's when we traveled together, and were the last on the block to have an air-conditioned car and a color television.

Daddy jumped from job to job, trying to succeed in sales while he also tried to overcome the bad stammer that had appeared when he'd attempted to sell his first piece of commercial property. We could not afford the more fashionable shores of the South, nor would my mother consent to go to the land of the carpetbaggers, as she called Virginia Beach. So we would go to what was called the "ancestral home" on Gull Island.

It was there—at the edge of my grandmother's property—that we were first introduced to a clubhouse inside which my cousin, Sumter Monroe, ruled, and through which our greatest nightmare began.

The shack, really just a shed, was almost invisible were you to walk into the woods and look for it; it blended into the pines that edged the slight bluff rising out of the desolate beach.

There was a story that it had belonged to a dwarf who had been a ship's mascot all his life and had built it there so he could watch the boats come in. Another story was that it had been built on the site of an old slave burial ground.

But my mother told me that it had just been the gardener's shed and "don't you kids make up stories to scare each other, I will not have my vacation ruined with nightmares and mindless chatter."

Sumter was fascinated by the shack—and terrified, too.

The first three Augusts my family spent on the peninsula, my cousin Sumter would not go near that rundown old shack, nor would he allow any of us others to venture through its warped doorway.

He acted like it was his and his alone, and none of the rest of us cared enough about that moldy old place to cross him.

Aunt Cricket, wiping her Bisquick-powdered hands into her apron, would call after him from the front porch as we all trooped toward the woods, "Sunny, you be careful of snakes! You wearing your Off! spray? Don't you give me that look young man, and don't spoil your appetite for lunch. And Sunny, never, never let me catch you around that old shack! You hear me? *Never!*"

The fourth summer he entered the shed and he named it.

He called it *Neverland.*

Blood Oath

ONE

Arrival

⇥ 1 ⇤

All summer trips in the Jackson family began with one form of crisis or another.

The trip that last August to Gull Island was no exception. Our spirits had begun high enough: Nonie led us in singing "A Hundred Bottles of Ginger Beer on the Wall," the Mom-approved version of the popular school-bus song, and Nonie herself drifted off to sleep by the time we'd crossed the North Carolina border. Governor, the baby, only screamed intermittently. I had brought along dog-eared copies of *The Martian Chronicles* and *My Side of the Mountain*, although my mother insisted I should be moving up in my reading to the classics. I had read both books a zillion times and could read them a zillion more times. We kept the windows down all the way, and when we stopped at a motel the first night, I think we all fell asleep without much fuss.

I had one of my dreams that night. I dreamed I was drowning in the sea with small fish nibbling at my skin. The next day in the car I said to Mama, "I had a dream."

"Tell me it."

"I was in the ocean. I couldn't swim."

She said, "Well, Beau, that must mean that you shouldn't go in the water this summer. At least not past your knees."

But I didn't tell her the worst part of the dream.

In the dream, one of the nibbling fish was all scaly and silvery, but his eyes were large and round and human and belonged to my cousin Sumter.

RIDING in the station wagon all day, it was easy for us kids to alternate pouting. First Nonie, then me, then Nonie, then Missy—but Missy took the prize. She quickly became the malcontent of the trip, and it was over her hamster, which she had smuggled into the car. It was supposed to be left at home to be cared for by our usual babysitter, Lettie, who was going to water the plants and feed and walk our dog, Buster. But Missy, not wanting to part with her dear Missus Pogo, put it in an airhole-punched shoe box and thought it would survive the first day's ride alongside the spare tire beneath the backseat of the station wagon.

Missy, two years older than me, had a rare lack of foresight for someone her age as well as an unlimited capacity for suffering. She said she didn't think the spare-tire area would be any hotter than the rest of the station wagon, and she *had* jabbed holes in the shoe box with a ballpoint pen and left some lettuce and sunflower seeds in there for the hamster.

But Missus Pogo was dead on her back, her tiny ratlike feet curled into balls, dead as I'd ever seen any animal be dead before. Missy cried her eyes out, then pouted, then kicked her feet against the back of the seat, then wouldn't talk to anyone. Daddy had wanted to bury Missus Pogo right there on the North Carolina border, but Missy screamed some and made ugly faces, so Daddy put the dead hamster and its Buster Brown coffin back in the car. I swore you could smell it every time we hit a bump. "Never liked that hamster," I said, "not since she ate her babies."

"Just shut up, Beau," Missy muttered, "she didn't eat them on purpose. Missus Pogo would've been a good mother."

"Something sick about a mother who eats her babies, is all. I don't exactly call that a good mother. Mama, you ever want to eat your babies?"

Mama shot me a look that meant she was about to turn and slap my knee if I said another word about the whole business, so I just clammed up for a while.

"You know where Missus Pogo's gone on to?" Daddy asked Missy.

Missy shook her head. "Didn't go nowhere. She's just dead."

"She's gone on to God, sweetie. It's where we're all headed." It was the one sliver of religion shining through his weary eyes.

But no one in the family was buying it, least of all Missy—and I knew that no hamster who ate her own children was likely to make it to the pearly gates. My father was as defeated as a man could be when it came to his wife and children; he could not fight us, for he would never win.

My mother clucked her tongue, "Jesus, Dab, she'll be crying the whole trip now. Missy," she reached over and grabbed my sister's hand, "Missus Pogo's just died, perfectly natural. Hamsters don't live all that long. It hurts when something you love dies, but you have to remember that they don't hurt anymore."

"Not if she went to Hell," I whispered, "then she's gonna burn eternally for eating her babies."

"Beauregard," Mama snapped, "is this the way you're going to behave the whole vacation? Well, I won't have it. You just be your good self and keep that bad part put away for at least this trip. Beau?"

I sighed, "Yes'm."

A DEAD hamster probably doesn't exude any kind of smell, at least not for several days, but we began to imagine that it did, until finally Daddy agreed to pull over and bury Missus Pogo on the edge of the highway. He did a piss-poor job of it, using the plastic ice scraper as a shovel and only digging down in the gravel deep enough for the small body.

Missy opened the box again to get one last look at the hamster. "Lookit," she said, poking around with her fingers, "she's all squishy, her eyes are open and sunk."

Nonie and I peered at the furry corpse, and each of us got to touch it. Nonie said, "I bet in a week ants'll've eaten all the skin off so's it's all bones. Probably already's got worms in her innards eating away. Worms'll eat just about anything."

"Naw," I said, feeling the hamster's soft, still fur—it was creepy and beautiful and mysterious because it felt so different from when the animal had been alive. "Some stray cat's gonna dig it up and eat it—just like it ate its babies, something's gonna eat it." As soon as the words were out of my mouth, Mama's hand came out and whapped me on the behind.

"Speaking of food, I'm *starving* again." Nonie licked her lips over the hamster as a joke.

"You children are being revolting," Mama said, and turned to get back in the car.

My sisters and I giggled, knowing what all children know: Sometimes it's *fun* to be bad and gross.

I heard Missy mutter as we got into the car again: "Now I wish we coulda kept Missus Pogo to see how fast the worms would come out."

⊰ 2 ⊱

Mama said to Missy, "See how many different license plates you can count, honey." We were back on the interstate and had not yet seen the ocean, and Governor kept screaming whenever Daddy hit a bump on the road. Missy had drawn a line with her finger down the backseat and told me that if I crossed it with my knee, she was going to scream like Governor.

"Scream your head off," I told her, sliding my knee over to her side. My leg had, as usual, fallen asleep, so I barely felt it when she scratched me on the thigh with her cat-claw fingernails.

Nonie, whose mood had also turned sour, pretended we were not related to her. When other cars passed near us, she smiled at the strangers as if to indicate that she would like them to adopt her. Nonie was, after all, a born flirt, and I knew that the real reason she was eager to get to Gull Island was so she could wear her two-piece and lie on a rock and thrust her chest out.

She and Missy were twins, but miles apart in most departments: Nonie was a tease and walked in such a way that men of whatever age watched her; Missy was withdrawn, sulky, and didn't seem to like boys at all—on the beach she wore a long T-shirt over her bathing suit, and unlike Nonie, she did not stuff wads of Kleenex into her training bra. Friends used to ask me which of the two was the evil twin—because there is always good and evil—and I would tell them that they were both evil twins, each in her own special evil way.

"Lord, how much longer?" Mama asked, and Daddy just thrummed his fingers on the dashboard when we pulled over at an Esso station for gas. I went into the station to get a Yoo-hoo chocolate soda and some Mallomars for the road. They were the last things I needed; we'd stopped at every Stuckey's from Richmond on down, and I felt green from eating chocolate-caramel turtles and pecan logs.

There was a map machine, and I had a couple of dollars in quarters, so I dropped some in and got a map of Southern California. The man behind the counter said, "Your daddy probably wants South *Carolina*."

He thought I was retarded, I guess, so I started playing retarded and stared blankly back at him and began drooling.

"You okay, little boy?"

I hadn't had anyone call me little boy since I was four, and I wanted at that moment to cuss a blue streak, but I was sure Daddy would come in at any minute. "Jes fahn," I drawled, sucking up drool back into my mouth. At that moment Mama came in, carrying Governor under her arm like he was a pig going to market.

"Pardon me, sir," she said, glancing over at me as if she and I did not belong together, "which way to the ladies'?" The farther south Mama got, the thicker her accent; I could barely understand her.

"Just t'other side of the water fountain, and you don't need no key, but knock first, if you please."

She rubbed my head as she went by, and Governor stared at me wide-eyed the way he did when he watched TV; I was afraid that the way my mother carried him, he would fall on the soft spot of his head, and I didn't want to be around to see that. It had been rumored that my cousin Sumter had been dropped repeatedly on his soft spot when he had been a baby, and I knew what that had done to Sumter. I unfolded the map of California and then refolded it.

"Listen," the man behind the counter said, "your daddy's gonna be mad because you got the wrong one, so I'll just give you one for South Carolina and it'll be our little secret." There was something in his smile that reminded me of what Mama had always said—*Don't talk to strangers, and don't take things from them*—something spooky and leering, like he wanted something from me, only I didn't know what. "It'll be our little secret, huh, little boy, just you and me," he said, and I grabbed the map and got out of there as fast as I could because grown-ups scared me more than anything else when they were like that.

⊰ 3 ⊱

"You had to be a smart aleck," Mama said when we were on the road again, and she reached back and pinched my knee hard. I held my breath and pretended it didn't hurt—at ten I was getting too old for the traditional modes of punishment: knee-pinchings, butt-slappings, my grandmother's natural bristle brush on the back of my bare leg. "You couldn't've gotten a map of Georgia, now could you?"

I began unfolding the map of Southern California across my lap, and handed Missy the one of South Carolina.

Missy said, "There's a little bit of Georgia on mine."

"Georgia on my mind," Daddy began singing, but because he never could remember the words to a song, he hummed the next line and then let the tune die in his throat.

"Why don't we ever go to Disneyland?" I asked.

"If I ever get your Daddy to take me to California, I can guarantee Disneyland will not be one of our stops. Don't you like the island?" Mama asked. "Maybe Sea Horse Park'll be open this year."

But the amusement park on Gull Island was a collection of dinosaur bones: a run-down roller coaster, a lopsided carousel, several kiddie rides, a dried-up tunnel-of-love ride, and a swampy flume. From the time I'd set eyes on Sea Horse Park, my first visit to the peninsula until this ride out to Grammy Weenie's, the place had never been open, and from the decrepit looks of it, it would never pass any kind of inspection. There was about as much chance of that place being open when we arrived as there was of pigs flying, and I would've been less surprised by the pigs. I looked out the window of our Ford station wagon. It seemed then like we'd had that station wagon forever. It was a pale green and had what the car salesman had called "beaver sidings," which made my sister Nonie laugh out loud whenever someone said it. "We never even go to South of the Border."

"Hey, Mommy," Missy yelped.

"Hay is for horses," Mama said. She always said this, and we always groaned when she did.

"I just thought of something."

Daddy winked at me from the rearview mirror.

"What's that?" Mama asked.

Missy said, "At the gas station, you left your purse up on the roof."

⊰ 4 ⊱

As always, we arrived at the peninsula by night.

My father would be playing the radio softly, a Muzak-type station, and my mother would sleep in the middle seat, curled impossibly around the baby's carrier while Governor gave us a few hours of silence. The twins would be asleep in the very back of the wagon, having made beds for themselves out of the sleeping bag Daddy kept back there.

I sat up front, the naviguesser for the evening, poring over the map of the Georgia coastline.

"Snug," he'd say, and that was my nickname from earliest memory, although only my father and mother would use it; Missy and Nonie dared not say it, because their nicknames, Mutt and Jeff, seemed a hundred times worse to them. I was too old for that nickname—I had been too old for it for a good while—my name is Beau. But sometimes when I felt the coldness of the world, I didn't mind it. "Snug," his voice weary and kind, "see the lights down there? That's the bridge."

I would peer over my map, crinkling it up and tossing it on the floor. In the dark, the peninsula was beautiful, and it was like driving around and seeing Christmas lights: Yellow and dim-blue lights studded the bridge over the bay, which my grammy Weenie called the "tiara."

It dipped into a flat end of Gull Island, but low hills rose up beyond, specked with more flickering, wavering lights, as if the place were held hostage by lightning bugs.

"Nighttime's a wonderful thing," Daddy would say as we drove down the hill to the tiara bridge, "it makes things prettier than they are."

And, waking perhaps even the dead, I would turn around and shout, "Hey-ey!" to my mother, my sisters, and now my baby brother, too. "We're almost here!"

⊰ 5 ⊱

Gull Island was as small as my thumb from the bridge, and only two hundred people ever occupied the peninsula at any one time. It was too marshy for much in the way of development, and it would be too expensive to fix up. (At that time its reputation was at an all-time low, no one to speak of ever went there for vacations, and even the people who lived there year-round tended to head for other beaches down the coast by August.)

Arrival to Gull Island meant crossing through the West Island—the *bad* part of the peninsula. Stories abounded about pirate treasures sunken in the marshes, which glowed with firefly light and will-o'-the-wisp and smelled like rotten peaches and baby vomit; the Gullahs had a graveyard they kept decorated with colorful flowers, and Nonie had started a tradition in my family that, when we passed the graves, we had to hold our breath or a ghost would get us.

"Leonora Burton Jackson, you stop that right this instant or your face'll freeze that way," Mama said.

I looked from the front seat to the back to see Nonie turning blue.

She let out what could only have been a honk when she finally could no longer hold her breath. She glared at me. "A plague on *both* your houses," she hissed. In seventh grade she'd fallen in love with Shakespeare and was fond of quoting and misquoting her favorite lines.

Missy, the less avid reader of the two, chimed in, "Bloody bones on the first step."

"Stop that," Daddy interrupted, "right now."

"We can't have him wetting the bed again." Missy couldn't resist this stab at my machismo.

Okay, I confess. I was the kid who wet the bed, and although the damp sheets had ended when I was eight, my sisters still used it as leverage, particularly when it came to blackmail, and would probably continue to do so until I turned ninety. The root of the bed-wetting, according to a friend of my mother's who was up on such things, was my hatred of my mother, which I can tell you did not go over well in the Jackson household. But the true reason was simpler: My sisters would take great pleasure in telling me horror stories, and lying in bed at night, I would be too scared with nightmares to set foot on the floor of my dark bedroom. So the natural thing to do was to just relieve myself in my jammies and then sleep *around* the spot—a habit from which I broke myself by simply moving my bed closer to the door and the light switch.

But in the station wagon, on the way to the Retreat, such petty assaults as bed-wetting reminders were common. Most brothers and sisters say they love each other even if they fight, but when I turned back around to face forward again, I remember thinking that I hated the twins more than I hated school and more than I hated farts.

When the Retreat came into view, its jutting geometry pushing at the luminescent drifting clouds behind it, I reached over and pressed my hand into the horn and Dad swore, and I heard Mama whisper tensely, "Starting in already." I didn't take offense when my mother began scolding us— there was some magnetic field around Gull Island, at its strongest at the Retreat, with its epicenter dwelling in Grammy Weenie herself. The closer Mama got to *her* mother, the more wound up she became.

⊰ 6 ⊱

Rowena Wandigaux Lee, no relation to Robert E. or Harper, although she claimed to be kin of anyone of note, had inherited the house and the land from her parents. After a few decades of renting the property out, the place was completely unrentable, and now Grammy Weenie lived there most of each year. She was a dethroned princess, riddled through like a Swiss cheese with the slings and arrows of outrageous misfortune. "My daddy invented a most curious elixir," she'd say, her powder-white, liver-spotted fingers picking lint off our Sunday-school clothes, "and we would be doing quite well now, if that *pharmacist* hadn't stolen it." And we all knew she was referring to Coca-Cola, a drink that would never touch her lips; or, "Your great-great granddaddy was a wealthy man before the war"—and needless to say, the war she meant had ended in the

1860s. When Grammy Weenie kissed us, we smelled a mixture of bourbon, Isis of the Nile perfume, and something sour and yeasty; all of us children agreed that it was like having to kiss a toad, and my cousin Sumter tried to prove us wrong by kissing an actual toad, but our opinion could not be swayed.

So the big house on Gull Island was yet another albatross for Grammy Weenie, and none of us was surprised when we learned that Great-Grammy Wandigaux used Confederate dollars to purchase it back in the long ago—and it looked like it. The house sagged as if it were beginning to sink into the ground. It was always sweltering in August, and the Retreat, which was the name of the place, had warped steadily year by year since early in the century, until it was bowed like a grounded ship. A poorly conceived Victorian mess, the Retreat had lost its color through tropical storms and lack of care: It was a muddy khaki hue, like the oversized shorts Sumter's mother forced him to wear around the house rather than the cutoffs the rest of us ran around in. Aunt Cricket would sniff, "In a classless society there's always going to be folks without class," and my father would do his best to belch at such moments. The house was sturdy, however: It had survived four tropical storms, two hurricanes, and three fires set by locals at various times in its long history.

Most of the islanders were black and considered by my Grammy Weenie to be quite backward and filthy. To her, they were always going to be lower-caste victims of their own lack of civilization and cultural advancement, stemming back from their origins in the Dark Continent. *Coloreds*, which Grammy Weenie called any race other than her own, were very much like children themselves and needed watching over. Grammy Weenie was what you might call—if you felt charitable—an unrepentant racist who believed it was a white woman's duty to uphold such bigotry in the face of the modern world's loss of values. She would be equally vocal in her denunciation of groups such as the Klan, and if you were ever to point out how similar her prejudices were to theirs—as Daddy often did—she would tell you point-blank that you were just too young to understand the beauty of paradox.

But the Retreat: From the road up, even at night, it looked misguided and senile and ready to drop. And ugly—even the surrounding trees wanted to get rid of it; they pushed against the long windows, and poked the gambrel roof. The screen of the front porch was torn and tattered, so if you sat out there at night, you'd get eaten alive by mosquitoes. *Skeeters*, Grampa Lee used to say. After his death, Grammy Weenie would continue the tradition and say, "Like Old Lee used to say, 'Skeeters,'" while she swatted at the bloodsucking menaces.

⊰ 7 ⊱

Helping us unpack the car, Uncle Ralph—smelling of Bay Rum and bourbon and Coke—slapped me on the shoulders and said, "Either you're gettin' in some whiskers on that upper lip, boy, or two caterpillars're matin' right under your nose." I didn't think it was funny, and Daddy offered me a smile as he pulled the big hard brown suitcase out of the open back of the wagon. The smile was meant as a "Yeah, Beau, he's a jerk, all right, but it's okay, you're not related to him by blood."

Missy and Nonie ran ahead to where Grammy Weenie was sitting on the porch, and I heard my mother say to Aunt Cricket, who had run out to coo at Governor, "Why isn't Mama coming down?"

Aunt Cricket whispered so loudly that all of us could hear it, shooting the words out a mile a minute. "Oh, Evvie, Mama's just not the same without Daddy. Don't *I* wish he was with us, the way she's been driving us all up the walls the whole week and getting after Sunny for just being a healthy boy . . . and it wasn't much of an accident, she just gets, you know, *dramatic* when she wants attention."

Sumter was noticeably missing. Last I'd seen him, summer before, he was still embedded in Aunt Cricket's shadow.

Uncle Ralph mumbled to Dad, "Sumter *was* the accident."

My mother passed Governor to her sister and went running up to the front porch, where Missy and Nonie circled around Grammy Weenie as the old lady leaned forward in her wheelchair; the wheelchair was new—and directly related to the Sumter accident.

Uncle Ralph tossed me a small bag to carry. "Think quick!" He lifted the twins' two small pink suitcases and walked alongside my father, and I followed behind. The ground was muddy from a recent rain, and because my shoes got sucked down an inch or two with each step, I made sure my footsteps stayed within my father's well-ground-in enormous steps.

"What's the story here?" Dad asked. His typical question: *What's the story, young man?*

Uncle Ralph glanced over his shoulder at me, and I was afraid he'd say, "Little pitchers have big ears," but he didn't. He turned back to my father, both their steps slowing. "The old witch claims Sumter tripped her on the stairs, and Sumter says he didn't mean to leave his Slinky lying there—all that crap kids give you. To tell you the truth, Dab, it's been like living with Gramma Adolf Hitler for the past month—maybe she won't be so high and mighty now."

"That's Christian of you, Ralph."

"Not you, too, Dabney? I'm gettin' it from all sides this summer. I thought at least a *guy* would know what I'm talkin' about."

"I know what you're talking about."

They walked the rest of the way up to the house in silence, and I tried to stay within my father's muddy footprints, but I heard a noise above me and almost fell in the mud when I looked up.

It was Sumter at one of the upstairs windows. He looked like he thought he was a preacher blessing us: He was flipping the bird, although as in all things he did, he didn't have it quite right. His middle finger was extended all right, but rather than having the back of his hand facing me, he'd turned his palm outward. I wanted to remember to tell him that it looked like he was flipping the bird at himself. I set my suitcase down and waved to him because I knew he meant it as a gesture of welcome.

Once inside, Mama immediately pulled Grammy and Aunt Cricket into the den. Daddy rolled his eyes and sat down on the largest suitcase.

Uncle Ralph said, "We have some bourbon, Dab."

Wearily, my father nodded to this offer.

"I'd like a Coke, please," Nonie said.

"No Cokes in this house."

"And no soda this late," Daddy said. "You kids can go in and have some milk or water if you want, but no sodas."

Nonie and Missy trooped into the kitchen after Uncle Ralph.

I sat down on the sofa next to the big front window. I was dog-tired and longed for a soft bed, but knew I would have to wait until the girls had finished their milks and Mama had finished her first "discussion" with her sister and mother.

The voices in the den were gradually rising until it was just like the walls were talking. Grammy's was the first to rise into the audible range. "You know what they did to Babygirl? The doctors ruined her. And to your daddy?"

"They helped his pain, don't be foolish."

"One does not *help* pain. Doctors never brought anything into this world except drugs and knives, cut and paste and make you feel good while they take all your organs out. Well, no thank you, no thank you."

"Has she been this difficult all summer?"

"Stop talking about me as if I am not here. I'm your mother, and you show me some respect or I swear when I do go, you will have me haunting you for the rest of your lives."

Then there was a pause. Daddy and I pretended we were not listening in at all. From the kitchen came the clicking sounds of Nonie and Missy snooping through all the cabinets.

"Well," I heard my mother say, "I just think you should see some kind of doctor. You need to get X-rayed . . ."

Uncle Ralph returned from the kitchen with two large glasses of rusty liquid: bourbon and Seven. He handed one to Daddy. "Sumter's probably in bed already, otherwise I'm sure he'd come down and be social. We've been here six days and already he's in trouble, but I suppose it's good for boys to get in a little trouble. Long few weeks ahead, though."

"There's always fishing," my father replied. He took a sip from the glass and sighed. "You're gonna be a good boy for me, Beau?"

"Naw, I think I'm gonna set fire here 'n' there and rip off a few Piggly Wigglys and maybe axe down a few locals."

"Like father," Daddy said as he raised his glass, "like son."

"Sometimes," Uncle Ralph said, looking at me and trying to be good-natured when I knew he was just being mean, "you're kind of spooky, you know? Hey," a dangerous word from my uncle because it meant he was shifting into an unknown gear, "how's your, um, little medical problem going?"

"*Ralph*," Daddy moaned, shaking his head and offering me a dopey grin.

"Just fine, thank you," I said as icily as I knew how. My sisters made fun of my early bed-wetting, and my uncle made fun of my bad circulation. "It's nothing to have a cow about."

Mama came back out of the den without Aunt Cricket or Grammy. Governor looked like he was off in baby dreamland. She called to the girls, "Come help me with the linens, and Beau, you and your sisters make your beds and then lights out, and *no*, I repeat, *no* reading under the covers. Lights out, understand?"

"I *HATE*, absolutely *hate* family vacations," Nonie said as she tossed the sheet across the length of one of the twin beds in the girls' bedroom. "Gawd, we have to be *nice* to these people. Well, all I can say is there better be good TV shows down here this year."

"You mean good reception," Missy said, flattening the edges and tucking them in between the mattress and box spring.

I wasn't helping at all, but then, I never did. I always watched my sisters make the beds and then did a haphazard job on my own. "I wonder why he hasn't come out."

"He's uncouth," Nonie shrugged.

"I think he's just plain common."

"Melissa Jackson, if you were as smart as you think you are, you'd know being uncouth *is* being common. Anyway, he's weird."

"Yeah, he's so weird he smells. Don't you think he's weird?"

"Uh-huh, yeah, but he's always up to something," I said, and could not explain further why I sought out my cousin's company on these trips to the Retreat. I usually got in trouble for things he did, and he wasn't anything like the kids I made friends with back in Richmond. Mama always said that blood was thicker than water, and I guessed at the time it was true, because, in spite of Sumter's oddness, there was something familiar about him, and he was the closest thing to a brother I had, if I didn't count Governor.

I HEARD a noise in the hallway and went to investigate. Sumter was probably spying on us. But the only thing there, sitting against the banister, right outside the bedroom door, was Sumter's raggedy brown teddy bear, Bernard. I swear he'd had that bear since he was three years old and had yet to relinquish it. It had been spit up on and dragged through prickers and mud and sea; half of one of its ears was torn off, and stuffing leaked from its behind.

Figuring I'd flush Sumter out, I greeted the bear. "Well, hey, Bernard." But I got no reply from either bear or cousin.

TWO

Where You Ain't Supposed to Go

"You seen him yet?" Nonie asked me, sliding my bedroom door open, rapping on its frame at the same time. Sumter and I should've shared that room, as tiny as it was, but because of the fracas over what would become known as the Slinky Misunderstanding, my Aunt Cricket had moved him into her room.

My sister went over to the window and drew the shades. Sunlight hit me like a bully in a schoolyard: I was down for the count. My limbs were like rocks.

Morning.

"I think I'm paralyzed like Grammy."

"You're not. And she isn't paralyzed, either. She hurt one of her hips, and you got two of those anyway. I asked you a question."

"I can't move."

"I couldn't care less. You seen him? I think they *killed* him."

"I saw him last night," I said, needles and pins pricking at my arms as I finally managed to lift them. "When we came in, he was at the window in Grampa Lee's old room."

"Grammy said he should get more than a talking to. She wants to take the *brush* to him." Grammy Weenie's silver-backed all-natural bristle brush was legend in two generations of Lee descendants. It had touched not only my mother's and my aunt's and my sisters' and my hair, but also all our behinds at one point or another. Only when my father finally interceded did that form of punishment stop. We lived both in fear and awe of that brush, and whenever Grammy Weenie asked one of us to bring it to her, even though we felt safely beyond the age of spankings, I have no doubt that my sisters, my mother, my aunt, and my cousin all relived for a moment some shuddering memory from early childhood.

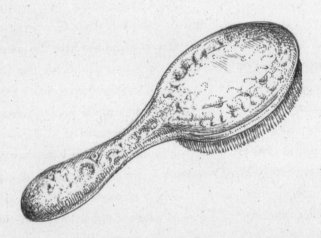

I sat up in the lumpy bed, the feeling coming back into my toes. I had bad circulation according to the family doctor, and my mother said it came from Daddy's side of the family, but I knew *that* because it was *bad* circulation and not *good* circulation. All bad things seemed to come from Daddy's side of the family.

Aunt Cricket appeared in the doorway, arriving in miraculous silence. I was used to hearing her block-knocking footsteps as if she wore Dutch wooden shoes, but this time she was at my door without prior warning, possibly because Uncle Ralph was sleeping through a hangover and she had learned to keep her clopping to a minimum. Her face was like a tapioca pudding, wiggly and *still* self-contained, her eyes two small raisins, and she whispered, "Get down to breakfast. Grammy's got someone she wants you to meet."

Grammy Weenie had hired a black girl as a nanny for us kids so that our parents could have most of their days free. Grammy Weenie sat at the breakfast table and introduced us to Julianne Sanders, who was sixteen and looked us over like we were stinkbugs that needed squashing. Sugar, the housekeeper we were used to dealing with, was pregnant, and as Grammy Weenie said, "At her age she's got to take things slow because you never know ... Emily Pinkham had an idiot when she was forty-two, and they say it's got to be either that or a brain surgeon, and between us, I find it extremely doubtful that Sugar Odell is going to deliver a doctor on her living room rug."

Julianne kept her eyes mostly on the twins while Grammy babbled on about monster babies born to women who did not have the good sense to lock their husbands out of the bedrooms at a decent age like she'd done with Grampa Lee—"and there was Holly Skinner, remember that woman from Macon? She had one of those children with the big heads like a piñata, what do you call them? Hydras?"—and Mama sat there with Governor, trying to make pleasant eye contact with our nanny. She quickly gave up the effort, seeing that Julianne was waiting for one of us to step out of line.

Sumter was conspicuously missing from the table. While Aunt Cricket and Mama talked family talk, and Uncle Ralph and Daddy tried to be pleasant to each other, Missy leaned over to me and whispered, "He tried to kill Grammy last night." I swatted at her like she was a fly; her breath was all scrambled eggs.

"I know that." I didn't bother whispering.

Nonie, sitting on the other side of Missy, whispered to her, "He did not." Grammy Weenie kept right on talking. It wasn't so much that she believed children should be seen and not heard, but just that she didn't hear what she didn't want to.

Julianne clapped her hands. "Sharing secrets at the table ain't polite, yes, I am talking to you young lady, and if you have something to share, you can just go ahead and tell all of us."

Missy looked up at her, shocked by this intrusion. No one ever told Missy Jackson what to do, particularly not the hired help; she had a bit of the Bad Seed in her. But her astonishment was momentary. She whispered a bit louder, "He says he didn't. *He* says his Slinky tripped her on purpose, but he was upstairs in his room."

Again Julianne clapped her hands, but this time on the table so that everyone was rattled. Julianne was skinny and dark; she looked to me like one of the naked women in *National Geographic* even though she was wearing a V-neck T-shirt, beneath which I glimpsed the top of a bathing suit. Her eyes were deep brown and soul-piercing, and her voice sounded like she had a sore throat; it hurt to hear her, like she was scraping at the words with her teeth before letting them out of her mouth. "You just lost a day at the beach for that kind of insolence, little miss."

"That's *Missy*," my sister said defiantly, but there was an edge of fear in her voice. A day at the beach was high on the list of bearable activities on the island.

"Once had a dog named Missy," Julianne said as if it were meant as a passing comment, "put her to sleep when she got too proud."

I heard Aunt Cricket whisper to Mama, "It's all that Civil Rights stuff, it makes them think they're better."

"Enough, Crick," Mama said, and turning to Missy, betrayed us all by adding, "and you obey Miss Sanders or you will not be enjoying this vacation at all."

2

"Is the bitch gone?" Sumter asked.

I had never, until that moment, heard someone my own age use language that would be described by my parents as common. The B-word was one of the many forbidden words—taboo to children, but regularly in use by the grown-ups.

Sumter, whose Southern accent tugged at vowel sounds as if for dear life, clipped this one word the way my uncle Ralph snipped his cigars. I had just gotten my swimming trunks on and grabbed a towel out of Grammy's linen closet. I closed the closet doors, and there was Sumter. He had changed. I knew that. Not just that he'd grown slightly taller, although I swear I thought he was going to be a dwarf most of his natural-born days. He had *changed*. Oh, he was his usual pale, wormy self, and his snow-white hair was ragged from one of Aunt Cricket's bad cutting jobs (at their home in Savannah they had three dogs, and Aunt Cricket used the dog-clipping shears on the pets and on her child—the results were usually choppy). He looked the same on the outside, but in the *eyes*—that one place in all living creatures that lets you look right down into their most secret places—*his eyes were different*. The only thing I could think was maybe he'd stayed up all night brooding over things.

He squinted them so they turned into slits. One thing about Sumter, however: He was always an immaculate dresser, which I never could comprehend because he was such a walking disaster area in every other respect. He wore a clean-pressed white oxford cloth button-down shirt and khaki shorts, a pair of white socks beneath his sandals.

"You hear me, Beau? She gone?" He began twiddling his fingers across the stains on Grammy Weenie's faded wallpaper—the stains had been made by us kids over various summers, and although Grammy always had help to do the cleaning, no one ever thought to scrub the walls.

"Hey, Sumter."

He brought his thumb back from the yellow paper, licking it. "Peach preserves." He held his fingers up; they were covered with a dark amber goo. "'Member that time you stole 'em from Grammy's cupboard? You ran along here and threw one of the jars at the wall. Still tastes like what Gummi bears would do in the woods." He had a laugh that went "Haw Haw Haw," just like he was faking it.

Sumter himself had broken the jar by throwing it. I know because I was there and the jar narrowly missed my head—three inches, if at all—and running barefoot across the landing, I cut my feet on the glass. I reminded Sumter of his participation in stealing the preserves; he was always making up stories to suit his version of things.

He smirked, flicking the last of the preserves in my direction. "You're getting more and more like the old Weenie, but my mama says that you're all doomed because of the alcoholism that runs on your daddy's side."

I was not witty or clever enough to say what I should've, which was, "Seems to me your own folks knock back their fair share of booze." Even this wouldn't have gone over with Sumter, because there was a popular mythology among the Lee side of the family that other people couldn't hold their liquor, but the Lees had no problem. How many times had I heard Aunt Cricket say, "Lord, I hope I never become an alcoholic, 'cause then I couldn't drink anymore."

What I did say was, "I hear you tried to kill Grammy."

"It wasn't me. It was my Slinky going down the stairs that got her. If you don't believe me, the old witch knows the truth. Ask her."

"How can a Slinky attack somebody?"

"Don't ask questions you don't want answered."

"You coming to the beach?"

He grinned—Sumter didn't have an open, friendly grin. He always looked a little sour, even at his best. "I got more important things to do."

"Like what?"

"Like I'm not gonna tell you."

"Oh, come on."

"If I told you, you'd be a blabbermouth, you'd tell Missy and she'd tell Nonie and she'd tell Aunt Evvie and she'd tell the Weenie."

"You don't have anything to do. You're a big fat liar."

"I'm holding something ransom."

"Kidnapping?"

"You tell anyone and you're dead."

26

"Tell me."

Sumter shrugged. Julianne started yelling for me to come down because it was time to go to the beach and if I wasn't down by the count of five I may as well not come down at all. Already I could hear the big horseflies buzzing and whapping into the screens on the windows.

"Wait," he said, grabbing my arm. "Don't go."

"I *want* to go."

"Don't go and I'll show you. What I got."

"Where is it?" I asked while Julianne counted to five and then ten and then fifteen on the floor below.

"I keep it someplace. Someplace where you ain't supposed to go."

⇥ 3 ⇤

On Gull Island we went barefoot. It didn't matter that Aunt Cricket would be there warning us that hookworms were no laughing matter and that broken glass grew like kudzu along the shoreline; it didn't matter that the summer before, Nonie had sliced a neat wedge from her heel when she came down on a fancy fishing lure that had fallen out of my Daddy's tackle box; nor did it make any difference whatsoever that we would all, on occasion, slip into a fresh pile of dog doo and have to not only hose the flats of our feet down, but put up with endless ribbing and the uncertain feeling that somehow the stuff was never completely washed away.

As Sumter and I stepped down off the front porch into the fat slab of mid-morning sunlight, I noticed that my cousin was still wearing his sandals and socks. "Hey," I said, pointing to his feet.

"She'll go into conniptions," he whispered. I didn't know why he was whispering when no one else was outside with us, nobody was on the porch, and, as far as I knew, our mothers were upstairs with the baby and both our fathers were down at the Footlong Nightcrawlers–Live Bait store over to the West Island; Grammy Weenie couldn't hear much, and Julianne and my sisters were already halfway down the steep path that ran down the bluff to the shore.

But Sumter kept his finger pressed against his lips to shush me until we were farther into the scraggly woods. .

"The Weenie lets her mind roam," he said. "She knows what I'm gonna do before I do it. My mama bought me a new croquet set, and the Weenie yelled at me through one whole game because she knew I was up for cheating."

"You mean like a mind reader, like Kreskin?"

"I mean like a witch. In olden days they would've *burned* her. Oh, how I wish these were the olden days!" He plopped himself down on a stump and began removing his sandals. "Something about the Weenie—if I'm anywhere within a mile of her, she knows *everything*."

I could hear Julianne crying out to my sisters to stay away from the rocks. The air smelled of dead sea creatures and leftover bacon brought by a breeze from the house. The cluster of trees we called the woods was that deep rich odor like when my father used to unroll his tobacco pouch when it was new and I'd lean into it and breathe it in until bits of dark tobacco flew up my nostrils. But even so, at Sumter's suggestion I could almost *smell* Grammy Weenie's Isis of the Nile perfume. "We're not even a mile away," I said, looking back at the Retreat through the spiky line of trees.

"You know the shack," he said after he'd wadded his socks up and stuffed them with his sandals into the rotted hollow part of the tree stump.

I nodded.

"That's where I keep it."

"What is it?"

He looked to his left and then to his right; he looked up in the branches of the tree; he looked down at his wiggling toes; he looked at my face for signs of betrayal. He whispered, "It's *god*. And it's in *there*."

He pointed to a place I had always seen and never noticed, as if it had been a blank spot, a hole in the world. Even though I knew the place had existed there every summer we'd come up to the Retreat, I had no curiosity about it, I had no thought for it.

"In Neverland," Sumter said.

The shack was falling apart. When I was younger I thought that it was some kind of old outhouse given that it stood within a quarter mile of the Retreat, hidden back among the trees, and it looked and smelled pretty bad. I had never been inside it before. The windows were caked with dust, and when you tried to look in, it was full of nothing but old tools and cans of paint.

Grammy Weenie had hired a caretaker years before I was born, back when she didn't spend most of the year on Gull Island, but the man had gotten some local girls in trouble and had to be let go. The shed had been his, and when he'd left the peninsula, no one bothered to take it down. This was when the surrounding trees still were seedlings, my mother told me, when the view from the Retreat to the sea was clear, when she and Aunt Cricket and my other aunt, the one they called Babygirl, would take Grammy's Victorian doll collection out to the bluff and play tea party and watch pelicans glide like winged horses over the shoreline.

I had never known Gull Island to be a beautiful place. As far as I could tell it was a sweaty, sandy stretch of family arguments.

And the shack: I had tried to look through the dusty windows before but never dared to go inside it. Just as Sumter had said, it was "where you ain't supposed to go."

And I never went places where you ain't supposed to go. Before this particular summer I had always stayed to the paths, I had always been under the shadows of grown-ups, and I had always been a good boy. I was tired of it. As we headed toward the door, I began to see nothing but Neverland and the piney bluff it rested on, the sea below.

The house behind us was nearly invisible from the stand of trees that guarded the shack. The trees were wiry and thin but clumped together, like fingers along the rim of Neverland. There was something like an irresistible smell emanating from the place, or like a high-pitched whistle that only

Sumter and I could hear. I wanted to go inside that place at that moment more than anything in the world.

There was a lock on the door, too, but when Sumter took me up the threshold, he unlocked it with a key.

"How'd you get that?" I pointed to the key.

"Nobody *gave* me it. I took it. You want something, Beau, you just *take* it. If I waited for folks to *give* me things, well, where would I be?" From the way he said this, I knew it was something his daddy had said.

"Welcome," he said, flinging the door wide, "to Neverland. If you tell anybody about this, Beauregard Jackson, I am warning you, it's gonna be the end."

The door, as it opened, scraped across moldy earth and broken clay pots. I got a whiff of something like old socks and detergent and dead sea creatures. For a single moment my curiosity was replaced by dread and I did not want to venture inside.

But I went with my cousin because we were both boys, and boys will always go where they know they shouldn't.

On the back of the door was spray-painted this warning:

fuck

Fluorescent orange spray paint, curved into curlicues and raggedly connected at the tail end of the *k*. I knew then that no grown-up had been in here in a while, because this one word above all others marked the territory of taboos. This was the road sign.

I felt as if I were about to enter the Holy of Holies. I crossed myself as a form of protection. The dirt beneath my toes was cold and crumbly.

I peered through the doorway and glanced back at my cousin.

Sumter grinned. His teeth were hopelessly crooked and canine, and his overbite made it seem like he was about to take a chunk out of his lower lip.

"Wait'll you see what I got in here. Watch out, watch out—" He pointed to bits of broken green glass from Coke bottles that had once been stacked

near the door. "Jinx on a Coke, I just saved your life, cuz, so you owe me. I'm always saving your life, ain't I?"

I couldn't stop coughing on my first visit within those hallowed walls. You could see the dust hanging in the air—you could practically cut off a hunk of it and bite down.

"Smells like the shower at the YMCA at home," I said, pushing my way through the gray light, tiptoeing between the thick chips of glass the way I'd seen Indians do it in a Disney movie.

The two windows on the side walls had a skin of dust and grime, and surrounded by trees as the shack was, it gave the effect of being in some dark, underground tunnel. I watched dark spiders run madly under the sills as I tried to wipe away at the glass. I spread layers of dust upon dust. My fingers painted dirt circles without ever cleaning a way to the daylight.

Sumter pointed out a stack of dirty magazines: old *Playboys*, women's lingerie catalogues, and—his pride and joy—a cutout in the form of a pair of glasses, but these were a woman's breasts. He picked up the cutout and draped them across the bridge of his nose. "I *see* you, Beauregard Jackson, I *see* you."

Despite the fact that the *Playboys* had the most female nakedness on display, Sumter's prize dirty pictures had been culled from the pages of *National Geographic*: endless clippings of topless African women with their lips extended, with a dozen metal rings around their necks, a look in their eyes as if they were not even aware of their nudity. Sumter waved a page in front of me; he pressed the page up to his face.

"You're gross," I said.

Ignoring me, he smooched with the photograph before tossing it down onto the rest of the clippings.

"Hey," he said to no one. He glanced about, kicking up some dirt around his magazine collection. Then he knelt down and scratched around in the debris. He squinted, sniffing the air. "Something's changed."

I looked around. Three old tires leaned against a rusted-out wheelbarrow in my path. Brown-red flowerpots—some cracked, some whole, some in the process of breaking down into bits of earth and clay—defined a path between the jumble of hacksaw, a manual lawn mower, and miscellaneous souvenirs of yard work.

"Someone's been in here." He rose and began wading across the floor. "Who'd be in *here*?"

"The witch. The Weenie. She's jealous 'cause I got the key."

"She wheel in here on her own or'd somebody help her?" I pumped sarcasm into every word.

"I know she did," he said, clenching his fists tight, closing his eyes as if it hurt to admit this. "She's so *mad*, she's so *jealous*, she's so *jealous*! Why does she *hate* me so much?" He stomped one foot on the ground, and when he did this I thought I felt the ground shaking, but it was only the rattling of paint cans as he kicked one of them. He punched one fist into the other—it looked like it hurt—and when he opened his eyes they were full of tears. His face was red like one of Grammy Weenie's neck boils. He wiped at his eyes.

Sumter never scared me when he acted like this. In fact, he only terrified me at his quietest, because it meant he was scheming. But when he went into one of his tantrums, he seemed pathetic and silly, and I always had to suppress the urge to laugh out loud. "Where's this god thing?" I asked impatiently.

He calmed down a bit, and when he spoke again it was as if nothing had happened. His eyes were dry, his hair only slightly ruffled from the exertion. He wiped the palms of his hands across his shirt. "All the way to the back," he directed me. He returned to the door, closing it.

With the door shut, Neverland was twilight dark, even though I knew perfectly well it wasn't even eleven in the morning. Colder, too, and somehow larger, longer—its very geometry having changed with the closing off of its only exit. Sumter went around me, complaining that I was too slow, but my fears of things like black widow spiders and coral snakes—even though I was never sure if they inhabited Gull Island at all—kept me moving carefully amidst the debris.

Sumter bounded over all of it, and when he got to the back corner of the shack, he dragged a plank off the top of a crate. It had pictures of peaches on the outside of it. He lifted the crate up a few inches off the ground and carried it over to where I had stopped walking.

"You keep god in a crate?" I snorted.

I peered into the shadows of the wooden box and thought I saw something move. I was almost frightened, but Sumter was always such a liar and sneak that I knew there wasn't any god in there. The thing in the crate was in the light. For a second I knew what it was and said, "That ain't god, that's a horseshoe crab. How long you been keeping it in here?"

"Three weeks so far." He was grinning at me like I was about to get a good joke, only I didn't know it.

"Three weeks! It would be dead by now."

"Believe what you want, I don't care." This was the first time I'd ever heard him express this viewpoint. Normally he begged to be believed, threatened to be believed, threw tantrums until you believed his lies. "If something *is*, it don't matter if you believe it or not, 'cause it *is* what it *is* anyway."

"Well, that *ain't* what it *ain't*. It'd be dead."

He brought the crab out of the crate and set it down in the dust. It didn't move, and I figured it must really just be dead. It smelled like it was dead. I prodded it with my toe, and maybe it moved a little, but I figured it was just 'cause I'd touched it. I picked the crab up and shook it, and its innards rattled. Sumter grabbed it from me like I'd offended him and he set it gently back in the crate.

He said, "I got something else, too."

He reached into the crate, and I was reminded of a magician reaching into a top hat. The creature had probably starved for days before it died, landlocked inside this dry shack. I began to realize how cruel all of us children were with our pets, how we were all cruel small gods, killing our animals, our guinea pigs, our hamsters, our chameleons, our frogs, our salamanders. I was getting physically sick. I remembered seeing a dog that had been flung out of the back of a truck as it drove down a highway, and, upon hitting the road, the dog had been transformed from a living thing into a piece of butcher shop meat, one half of its fur skinned completely off, and my father saying to me, "Don't look, Beau, nothing we can do for it." Who thinks of crabs? I'd seen sea gulls carry them up over concrete and drop them down so the birds could feed more easily on them, but somehow this seemed different. This seemed unfair, that my cousin Sumter would trap this thing in a dark crate for his own entertainment.

Sumter caught my attention, his hands a blur of movement as he leaned back into the crate. He had extracted something small and yellow and round from the crate.

A very small human skull, one that seemed too tiny to be real. I thought he'd bought it at a magic or joke shop: It was too perfectly deformed, too finely crushed along where the left ear would've been.

As if reading my thoughts, he said, "It *is* real."

"If it's real, where's the rest of it?"

"I left it where I found it. This was all I needed. See, she got murdered. Right here." He grasped the skull like it was a bowling ball, his thumb and forefinger thrust in the eye sockets. "And this is all that's left of her."

"Her?"

"Yeah, her name was Lucy and she was in love with this man, and she was going to run off with him, only he didn't love her. So they met right here, at midnight, and when he kissed her, and she shut her eyes, he placed his fingers around her neck and strangled her. Her eyes popped open in terror and the killer says to her, 'You will never leave this place. Ever.'"

Sumter had a way with the spur-of-the-moment story, and I've got to admit I was taken in for about a minute as he spun this melodrama, but then I knew, like all of Sumter's stories, this was something he just made up. He had a half-smile that was the tip-off: He enjoyed the company of gullible people.

"If she got strangled, how come it's smashed in?" I pointed to the left side of the skull, which had large chunks missing.

He gave it up. "Okay, okay, wise-ass. My daddy says there's this big old grave where these dead slaves were buried right around here, and I guess when they dug out this shack, this," he practically shoved the skull in my face, "must've just been in the dirt. Found this, too." Again he reached into the crate, and brought out what at first seemed to be a thick twig with several prongs at the end. It was a small animal paw. "Like that story, 'The Monkey's Paw.' Only I don't think it's a monkey or anything. Maybe the missing link." He dragged the edge of the paw along my arm and it tickled. The skin was dried right onto the bone. "Maybe it was some little dog's. Like someone cut off this dog's foot. Yeah, they cut it off and hung it up to dry. You see any three-legged dogs, you know we got its foot."

"I bet you dug those things up. I bet you stole them or something. I bet you weren't supposed to."

Now he looked perturbed—he'd been found out. He tossed the skull down on the ground. He lifted three of his fingers up and said, "Peel the banana." But he peeled it himself, bringing two fingers down around his middle finger, once again flipping the bird, his favorite form of greeting.

"I bet you took those things from somebody and you're gonna be in trouble for doing it."

Guilty as he was, he managed to make me feel guiltier for having seen right through his stories. "If you squeal . . . " Sumter didn't complete his threat. You may wonder how anyone could feel threatened by someone as apparently sissy as my cousin Sumter, but let me tell you, if you were a kid, you could *smell* what was wrong with him. His stink wasn't like any other kid's stink. Grammy Weenie always said you could tell the races just by their smells, and let me tell you, Sumter himself must've been from another planet, because he had a smell that was not like anybody else's, and it came out when he made threats. It was like his juice was switched on electric, and if you touched him, you'd get a blinding shock. I guess I thought then that he was kind of psycho and weird, and I will tell you plainly that I did not like to cross him if I could help it. "If you squeal . . . " His small fist was raised in the air.

"I wouldn't *squeal*."

A shower of pebbles hit the window.

"What the—" Sumter motioned for me to duck down. He dropped to the ground and crawled over and around all the rubble. He popped up beneath the window like a jack-in-the-box. "Spies!" he shouted.

"It's probably just Nonie."

"Nope, it's white trash. They're yellow and running scared."

I stood full up and looked over his shoulder. "I don't see nobody."

"That's 'cause they *are* nobodies. Dang it if this island ain't full of the trashiest sorts. If I was to catch one, I'd turn him into rump roast."

We both heard the scraping at the same time, and Sumter returned his attention to the crate.

"Look here," he said. "C'mon, Beau, look here."

When I looked again into the shadowy interior of that crate, I thought I saw:

A creature with a human face, with legs like crab pincers, with a tail like a lizard, with the cold staring eyes of a bluefish, its mouth opened wide, gray shark's teeth thrusting out of bleeding gums.

Sumter began giggling, and before I could stop him, he reached down into the crate and punched his fingers into the monster's round fish eyes.

When he withdrew his fingers, the face of the thing changed, melted down like wax and reformed—it was the face of something I had never seen, and yet it was closer to being human than it had been a second before. The eyes still had the dull rounded stare of a bluefish, the mouth its jagged teeth, but there was a wisdom and a horror that brought to my mind an image of suffering. It was the ugliest, most hideous face I had ever been witness to—it was what they told us in Sunday school was *unclean*. I could not tell if the thing was male or female, child or grown-up; its skin was covered over with gray-green sores, and its lips were in shreds from where its own teeth dug into them.

And then, as if it were being stripped of its disguises, again the image changed, its skin dripping down around its eyes as if it were weeping, and what I saw beneath the liquid flesh was just the turning earth, ripe with nightcrawlers, thick with roly-poly bugs and albino grubs, feeding, feeding, feeding on the pungent and rotting vegetation—and even *this* was a face.

Every cell in my body seemed to rebel against this image, and it was like hitting a sudden high fever or like a dream where I would fall from a great height down into the sea. I had no breath, I had no muscle, I had no *life*. All around me I smelled—not the sea, not the clean air—but the mustiness of rotting, damp leaves, of just-turned earth, of places beneath stones where creatures moved slowly on their dark paths.

As if in a distant world, I heard Sumter's voice, "The face of god. You saw it, didn't you? I know you saw, I *know* you did."

I blinked and it was gone. That vision, that face from a nightmare no longer existed—only a lingering sense of dampness and rot, which even then faded like a half-remembered dream. As I turned to the sound of his voice, Sumter's face was red and shiny, as if he'd undergone some great exertion, like rolling an enormous boulder up a hill.

I had goose bumps all up and down my arms—Mama always said that it meant someone was walking over my grave. I had had my waking dreams before, but I was sure this was no dream. I could've sworn that I *saw* what I *saw*. I gasped, "How'd you do that?"

He looked all innocent. I could never tell if he was lying or not, although I always strongly suspected he was. "Huh?"

"What I just saw. Jesus, Jesus."

Like I said, Sumter always scared me the most when he was quiet, mainly on account of he wasn't quiet a whole lot, and when he *was*, he looked like a different kid. He looked like he wasn't my cousin at all, but somebody I never met and would never want to meet. Sometimes I couldn't believe we'd come from the same blood. Here he was being the most quiet I'd ever known him to be, and I got the shivers. I could just about feel my face turning from deep red to white and back again.

"You saw the face of god," he said in the tiniest voice, so I had to strain to hear him. "It's a god that eats, and you got to feed god so's it won't eat you first."

I could smell his bad breath, just like he'd been vomiting candy all morning: sweet and sticky and warm. I just couldn't bring myself to look back at the dark opening of the crate. Sumter's eyes rolled up a little, so I could only see their whites, and he gave out with a little gasp like someone had surprised him—he was making some motion with one hand over the other. He had used the metal edge of the soda-pop tab and sliced down on the flesh that ran between thumb and forefinger of his left hand. He used his other hand to milk the blood out of it—a few droplets of red hit the edge of the crate. Something smelled funny, and I noticed he had a growing wet stain down around his zipper.

More drippy blood spat from his hand to the opening in the crate.

He let out a long sigh just the way Grammy Weenie did in her sleep when I thought she was giving up the ghost, and then his eyes rolled down into their normal places.

I had goose bumps just about everywhere on my body I could admit to, and I heard the thing move in the crate as it came toward the few drops of blood he'd squeezed out.

Someone said, "*Good, good.*"

I looked at Sumter again. Had he just said that?

I didn't want to look back in the crate and take the chance of seeing that gross face, but I did, and there was nothing like it within a mile: In the crate was what I thought I had seen at first.

A horseshoe crab.

Only now it was different.

Now, it was *alive*.

Its helmet-back dull and dusty, its dozen legs scraping and clacking against the splintery wood, its spiny tail rising and falling. The thing seemed bigger than life, larger than Sumter's hands put together as he hefted it up out of the crate, its tail whiffling through the air, its tiny claw legs slicing across one another.

"You feed it *blood*? Jesus, you feed it *blood*?" I took a step back and practically tripped on a clay pot. "Jesus, it's alive, you . . . blood . . . feed . . . "

"*Yeth*," he lisped, inhaling deeply, and he did something then that seemed so horrifying to me—more than the blood on the edge of the crab's shell, more than my growing sense that there was something else, something *almost human* in the shack with us. He brought the crab up to his face and pressed its underside to his lips. The spiny tail flicked straight up and down, and its legs clung to his cheeks, and a noise came out of my cousin like I'd never heard, a wheezing noise like Grampa Lee made on his deathbed, like Grammy Weenie when she was snoring away, but mostly like Sumter was feeling a kind of pleasure I had never seen another human being feel. Like an expiring sigh.

"Jesus, Jesus, Jesus!" I screamed and leapt forward and grabbed the crab off his face; I heard a sound like a sheet ripping in two.

As I pulled the creature from his face, his skin came with it.

His face was just a mass of black dripping muscle and lumpy fat and bone, and in my hands—the other side of his skin, a perfect mask of Sumter.

"*Good, good*," someone said, and it was Sumter's skin stuck to the crab, flattened like a pancake, torn lips smacking.

My hands were shaking so much that the horseshoe crab rattled, but I could feel it trying to pull my hands, and it, toward my own face, and I felt a calm the way they say drowning people feel, and even I wanted to bring that crab with the flapping human skin to my face and feel the pleasure Sumter felt.

"*Good*," the faceskin smacked.

As hard as I could, I smashed the crab down on the edge of the wheelbarrow, and when it hit the ground I stomped my bare foot hard on it, again and again and again.

When I was sure it had been completely destroyed, and my feet were cut and bleeding from where they'd cracked the shell, I felt his hand on my shoulder and jumped at his touch as if I'd just been given an electric shock.

Sumter was whole; his face was intact. I couldn't believe it; I kept half expecting the skin to be ripped away again, but it remained.

He was mad as hell.

"You fool," he snarled, "it was a trick, it wasn't real, goddamn you, that wasn't even god, you moron, I was just testing you, and you failed, Beau, you failed big-time. Get out of my clubhouse and don't you ever come back here, ever. You just think you're so smart, but I just showed you, didn't I? I just showed you! Don't you ever dare come back here again!"

⊰ 4 ⊱

I wandered the bluffs for hours, confused by what I'd just seen. It hadn't been like any dream I'd ever had: I really believed that I had seen his face ripped off. I had no desire to ever set foot back in that shack again. I heard the blood pumping through my body, and the sun felt good on my face and neck. *I am alive, nothing happened. Just scared.* The world seemed like it had been just polished; I noticed the bark on trees and the birds in them, chattering away. The sea air almost took my breath away, it was so strong and thick. *Just scared.* I decided then and there that I would not play with Sumter at all anymore, that he was too weird, and his Neverland was just an awful bad place. I would never go back inside there as long as I lived, and he could just go and sell his soul to the Devil for all I cared, but I was well out of it.

But as I passed the shack on the way home in the afternoon, I picked up its scent, like just-turned earth in a garden, and I told myself that it had been my imagination or a trick, like Sumter had said. How had he done that? *I don't care, he's just perverse, and I'm not gonna be part of it.* Maybe he'd used a Halloween mask. It must've been a pretty neat one, too. It looked real, but maybe if I hadn't been so scared (*you're a fool*), I would've seen the seams or the wires or where it didn't fit over his face right. They always advertised masks like that in the back of comic books; maybe he'd sent away for it. *I don't care. He's just perverse, and I'm never gonna go in there ever again as long as I live. Never. Cross my heart and hope to die.*

When I got home, Daddy was snoozing on the grass while Mama and Uncle Ralph were setting up Aunt Cricket's croquet set on the side lawn, trying to be careful to avoid stepping on the flower beds that Aunt Cricket guarded over while she stayed at the Retreat. They were being mindful of stepping over the wickets, too, and not tripping on the balls and mallets, because Uncle Ralph and Aunt Cricket and my parents had been having early cocktails—it wasn't yet four—and they all smelled like gin-and-tonics.

"I got to talk to you," I told my mother.

She was smiling, but a kind of tense smile the way she sometimes did around my aunt and uncle. "Honey?"

"It's about Sumter," I tried whispering, but Aunt Cricket heard me and clomped over to get in on it.

"What do you have to say for yourself?" Aunt Cricket asked suspiciously.

"Oh, Cricket, let him say what he wants," Mama said. She swung her croquet mallet back and forth idly.

"He's doing strange things," I said, ashamed that I was so close to squealing. I couldn't bring myself to say it. I tried, but it came out all wrong. "I saw like this monster and it ripped his face off and it had shark's teeth. He has this skull, and he feeds it blood. But it may be a mask or something. Like those things on *Creature Feature* with the skull sticking out, sorta."

Mama sighed, and ignored me then, the way she did whenever I told her a particularly strange dream. I knew she must wonder if I was a little crazy. "No more horror movies late at night," she said. "I don't care if it is summer, no more horror movies. Beau, you're too impressionable. You'll be wetting the bed all over again."

I felt my face go red with embarrassment.

Aunt Cricket sipped her drink. "Seems to me you're the one doing the strange things," she said. "He told us all about it. Frankly, I don't care about one of them ugly old crabs, but it wasn't too nice of you to smash up his pet, now, was it? He caught it and he was taking care of it, and what kind of little boy goes around stomping on horseshoe crabs, I wonder."

⇥ 5 ⇤

Lying is a trait common to children, but we are never good at it. Sumter had gotten home first and had lied to save his skin.

I wiped my feet on the bristly welcome mat on the porch when Grammy Weenie's harsh voice called out, "You been up to no good, Beau? You been with that cousin of yours?" She punctuated each word with a phlegm-laden cough. The wheels of her chair scratched noisily against the warped floor of the front hall as she slid to the open doorway. Aunt Cricket's black-and-yellow crocheted throw lay across her lap, and Grammy picked at the flower pattern with her bony fingers. There, amidst the flowers, rising between her knees, was the dreaded silver-backed, all-natural bristle brush.

The brush put the fear of God in me, but I didn't want to go through the humiliation I'd just endured at the hands of the other grown-ups. Grown-ups never wanted the truth, anyway; they only wanted to hear what they wanted to hear. I lied, "Ain't seen Sumter since this morning."

"'I haven't seen Sumter since this morning,' you mean."

"I haven't seen Sumter since this morning. Yes'm."

"You got to practice, Beau, you're not very good."

"Ma'am?"

"Prevaricating."

"Ma'am?"

She squinted her eyes and leaned forward, clutching the brush by its handle, lifting it up and slapping it down lightly on the top of her leg. *"Don't you 'ma'am' me, young man."*

I never knew how to respond to Grammy Weenie. She could be sweet and smooth as molasses sometimes, and then she could be sharp and mean and cruel. My reaction was always to play dumb in these cases. "I don't know what you mean."

"Close your mouth, boy, you look feeble-minded like that. Planning on eating flies for lunch?"

I was too scared to look her in the eyes, so I watched the silver brush in her hand and the small pink squiggly veins that ran around her knuckles and under the ruby ring she kept on her thumb. Her fingernails were chewed down to the soft white flesh; the cuticles were shiny half-moons.

"A prevaricator is a young man who lies. You love your grammy?"

I nodded.

She shook her head slowly, leaning back in her wheelchair, letting out a rasping laugh. "No you don't, Beau, you will never be a liar, so don't even try. You hate me, all children do, all children do because I know what children *think*, I know what you're up to, all the time. So when I die, you just grab some sliced lemon from your iced tea and rub it around your eyelids and then you can pretend to cry and people will think you loved your grammy. What people think is all that matters in this world."

"I don't hate you, Grammy."

"I don't care if you do, young man. I'm your grandmother and you can hate me or like me, but I won't have you lying to me. Now, come over here."

I could've stepped backward and run away. The old woman was in a wheelchair, after all, and it wasn't likely that she would jump out of it and chase after me into the woods or down to the shore. If I were my cousin, I would've done it. But I wasn't Sumter, and I had never disobeyed the grown-ups except when they weren't around to find out about it. My feet began tingling, and I knew that if I didn't step toward her, I would not be able to move, I would take root right there, my toes would sink into the floorboards and tangle around beneath the house and then they'd have to cut me down. I padded over to Grammy Weenie, and she had me sit up on her lap, the silver brush still in her hand. Long strands of her white hair hung down from its bristles like tentacles from a Portuguese man-of-war. She raised it above my head, and I was sure she was going to bang it against my shoulders, but instead it came down softly on my hair, and she gently brushed through my scalp. I looked straight ahead, out onto the road, the trees, the sky, and could not see Neverland, could not see Sumter. All I could smell was Grammy's Isis of the Nile perfume and her sour breath.

"You're a good boy, Beau, I know you are, I can see your soul, and it's a good soul. But everything can become corrupt. It's nature, and all nature must be fought. Nature is evil because it corrupts. Flesh is corrupt, child, and spirit is pure, and all of life is a struggle between spirit and flesh, and flesh must never be allowed to win. *Never*."

The effect of her voice, a moment ago raspy and terrifying, transformed into this lullaby, this soft monotone, as she brushed gently, gently, in careful, even strokes along the ridges of my crewcut, was hypnotic. "Flesh and spirit, child, always at war, the demon and the angel fighting, but always the spirit will seek the higher ground, always we must seek the higher ground, flesh is our prison, but always we strive to break free." I felt her silver brushing in the drawers of my mind, her words repeating themselves over and over, and I was no longer frightened, just sleepy, and soon I closed my eyes, her brush calming my blood.

Somewhere in my falling sleep I heard her ask, "*What did he show you there, child? What was it?*"

And in my dream in the dark of my head, I told her, and it didn't hurt to squeal, it felt like a peaceful bed into which I was sinking.

A fragment of dream began tugging at me: *two figures, they were shadows, but one was a woman, and she was saying, "Go ahead and do it, see if I care, I don't care," and the other one, sounding like my father, was saying, "I don't know why you make me do these things," and then she was choking and he was crying like a baby.*

I awoke in the upstairs bedroom, thinking I had screamed. I sat up in bed. How the heck had I gotten there? Who had carried me up? I had not lost the feeling in my arms and legs completely the way I usually did, although it was a few minutes before I felt steady enough to step down on the floor without falling. The clock on the shelf read 6:30, and I was so disoriented I thought it was early morning. I didn't know what I had done between the day before and now. Had I slept the whole time? Sunlight lay like butter across the damp sheets—I'd been sweating. I got out of bed, fully clothed, and walked down the hallway to my parents' room.

My mother lay on her back, diagonally across the bed, her right arm draped across her forehead, her left on her stomach. She wore a skirt; her blouse was unbuttoned to reveal her white bra. I tiptoed around the edge of the room, pausing as if every creaking board were painful, until I could look into the crib. Ever since I'd heard of crib death, I would check on my little brother every now and then to make sure he was still breathing. The baby was sleeping peacefully. It was the only time I adored him, when he was asleep, the only time I was happy to have a little brother for competition. He was definitely breathing: His small bean nostrils flared and flattened. He had a body like a fat little buddha, and his face was a ripe peach. I tickled his toes with my fingers, but he didn't stir. Governor was off in a more peaceful dreamland than the one I had just visited.

"Beau?" Mama asked, and I glanced over to her. She lifted her arm away from her eyes, brushing her hair back. She was already pulling her blouse together with her left hand. "It's so hot in here. I wish she'd put in air-conditioning. You okay, sweetie?"

There were times when I didn't think my mother recognized me, and this was one of those. The word "sweetie" was the tip-off: She only said that after a stiff drink. Not the gin-and-tonic of the cocktail hour, but bourbon, straight up. And she only had a stiff drink after an argument with my father, and she only argued with my father if he was drinking, too. An entire situation presented itself to me: My parents were guzzling bourbon at six in the morning. But it was too hot to be dawn, and I smelled supper downstairs, so they'd had their bourbons, and a row, and now Mama was recuperating while Daddy was out back somewhere, walking off steam.

"I had a nightmare," I said to my mother, who smiled sympathetically. But her mind was on other things, and her words seemed perfunctory. "Did you. Well, it's only a dream, sweetie. You like scary movies too much, don't you. Oh, well. Want to tell me it?"

"Nothing special. It was just scary."

She stood up, buttoning her blouse—in the humidity and heat of Gull Island it was normal to always be half-dressed, to see bits of slips, of undershirts, a white lace hem, a sweat-mottled edge of boxer shorts. She began a series of sighs, and I sniffed for the whiskey, but there was none. "Aunt Cricket's loaf must be done. Go wash up and call your sisters, will you, Beau? And tell Miss Sanders that your daddy won't be joining us tonight at the table."

⊰ 6 ⊱

"How could you nap through it?" Missy asked, grabbing me and pulling me into the twins' room as I went by. She shut the door, and Nonie, who was in a corner checking the tan line around her shoulder straps said, "Try being a little blasé."

"Blasé?"

"You don't have to get excited every time it happens, just because they don't love each other. They've never loved each other, they've only been staying together for the children. That's why people get married at all. Nothing to go hysterical over."

"*God*, Nonie, they were at each other's throats."

"Exaggeration."

"Didn't you hear it?"

I shook my head.

"Daddy said he didn't know why we came on this trip, and Mama started crying, and then she threw the lamp at him. *Gawd*, Beau, how could you not hear it? Governor was bawling, and the lamp broke in a million pieces and I think they're getting divorced."

"Such a little actress," Nonie sneered. "They were only being foolish and drunk. Mama had her julep. It was an ugly lamp, anyway."

"Mama says we should go downstairs now."

Missy waved her hands in the air the way I'd seen charismatics call down the holy spirit into their scalps. "How can we *eat* after what just went on?"

"I'm so hungry, I'm *ravished*," Nonie said, adjusting the red-and-yellow beach towel more tightly around her waist. Her bathing-suit top was almost flat against her chest, but when she wore it she sucked in her tummy and pulled her shoulders back so it looked like she had breasts.

"You're wearing that down to supper?"

"So what?"

"Hey-ey." Someone banged on the windowframe from the outside, which was quite a feat as the room was on the second story. It was Sumter. "You look like Lady Godiva," Sumter said. He shocked us all: He was leaning over the window ledge from the outside, his arms hanging in, his face pink with sun and effort.

"You climb all the way up here?"

"No, you dumb bunny, I *flew*. 'Course, I shimmied up on the drainpipe, and *you*," he pointed directly at me and I felt my face going red, "I know what you did, squealer, and I told you I'd kill you and that's just what I'm gonna do." He raised something up from the outside ledge. It was yellow and oblong, a balloon. "Bombs away!" He lobbed it at me. I ducked down. The balloon sailed right smack into Missy's sunburned face. Both the balloon and her forehead seemed to burst open at the same time, and she screamed as water drenched her hair and dribbled down across her chin. Nonie laughed, wiggling her fanny as she walked around us and out the door. Sumter had already disappeared from sight. I turned to Missy to help wipe her face off, and she said, "Thanks a lot!" as if I were to blame for her being hit just because I had dodged the water balloon.

SUPPER was Aunt Cricket's Famous Meatloaf, which floated in greasy tomato sauce puddles, potatoes, and boiled kale. I wasn't all that hungry, which was unusual for me, but I felt vaguely guilty for having perhaps squealed on Sumter and his shack. Although I couldn't remember exactly what it was I'd told anybody—I was still so confused by what I thought I saw in Neverland. And I was mad at him for lying to them about the crab, but more guilty for the worst crime: squealing. I had fallen asleep in Grammy Weenie's arms and then awakened upstairs, but anything in between was fuzzy, like the floor underneath my bed.

The drone of the ceiling fan made all conversation sound as if it were underwater, and Mama sat next to her sister and kept rubbing water spots off the flatware with her paper serviette. Governor was sitting up in his high chair with baby slop running down his chin. Uncle Ralph was telling jokes, but I could barely hear him, and Aunt Cricket kept interrupting him with, "I don't mean to be such a wife, honey, but couldn't you please not put your elbows so far over on the table?" Or, "I don't mean to be such a nag, Ralph, but you could pass the potatoes to Grammy, if you had a mind." Missy was kicking me under the table, and Grammy Weenie sat near me at one end and did not look up from her plate while she ate. Nonie ate her food in a ladylike manner, chewing each bit a thousand times; she ignored the rest of us.

Sumter dug into his food with relish. "Mama this is the absolute-lee best meatloaf you ever did cook."

"You ready for seconds, Sunny?"

Sumter nodded greedily. "Am I ever."

"Big appetite," Uncle Ralph nudged his wife, "for a big mouth."

"I'm just hungry, is all," Sumter's voice was smaller, thinner.

"He's a growing boy, Ralph."

My mother stood up so quickly, pushing her chair back, that even Grammy Weenie looked up from her plate. "I don't know why you men are so inconsiderate to the people around you. It's not like anyone *needs* you for anything."

Missy stopped kicking me under the table. Nonie began scratching her neck; she always did that when she was nervous. She rolled her eyes and whispered, "Here we go."

Grammy Weenie waved her fork around in the air. "All I ever ask for is peace and quiet at the table, and this is what I get. Well, thank you very much for this scene, Evelyn, and may you burn this quotation into that mind of yours: 'Behave like a nut and you will soon become one.'"

Mother squinted her eyes and leaned forward, her palms slapping down on the table. "And I have one for you, too, Mama, and it goes, 'The *nut* doesn't fall far from the tree.'"

Grammy smiled and took my hand up in hers. "Your mother, dear, was always a high-strung child. I thought I was raising daughters, but I have since discovered I was raising demons." The ring on her thumb scratched against the back of my hand.

⇥ 7 ⇤

After we'd finished eating, I found my father smoking a cigarette out on the front porch.

"I wasn't hungry," he said when he saw me.

"It wasn't very good. Mystery loaf."

"Want to sit?" He made room on the porch swing next to him.

I shook my head. "I just didn't know where you went."

"I was here. I'm your daddy, Snug. I'll always be here, don't you worry about that."

"I wasn't. And I'm too old for Snug. And I wasn't worried."

"If you ever think you might be, you'll see. I'll be somewhere nearby."

Mosquitoes pecked at my neck and ears, and the sky was murky with oncoming night. The sound of the ocean was like trucks out on the highway near where we lived in Richmond. I could see no stars, not because there weren't any, but because I had closed my eyes and was wishing that we were back there in our small house with our dog Buster. And if I opened my eyes after I counted to ten, I would be there, in my room, and the stars and the dark would be different than what hung over Gull Island, because this night was a wall that I would not be able to see over.

I AWOKE in the middle of the night with someone standing over my bed.

"Beau? You awake?" It was Sumter, although I could not see his face because of the dark.

"I am now."

"I can't sleep. Everybody's snoring except you."

"You can't sleep here. Not enough room. And I'm mad at you. You lied about the crab."

"I'm mad at you, too."

"Oh."

"I lied 'cause if I didn't lie they'd tear Neverland down."

"Oh," I said.

"It didn't hurt you, anyway. And you squealed."

"I did not . . . well, nobody believed me."

After a moment he said, "I could sleep on the floor."

"I guess."

"Beau?"

"Huh?"

"'Member Grampa Lee? When he was alive?"

"Only way I *do* remember him."

"He seems like a shadow to me. I can't even remember his face. 'Member his stories? About W. W. Two?"

"About the Pacific?"

"Uh-huh. And the beautiful bomb. How people just disintegrated and it went down *whoosh* and then went up again like a giant mushroom up above Japan. He said it was a good bomb 'cause it stopped worse things. You think that's true? Things being good just 'cause they stop worse things?"

"I am so sleepy I can't even think straight. Go to sleep."

"Grampa Lee said it was 'Lights out for the Rising Sun.'"

I was just falling asleep when I realized he was still talking, droning on. "That's what I feel like, sometimes. Like I just want it to be Lights out. Lights out and no sun to come up, no sun 't'all. You think if there's a god of light, there's one for the dark, too? I mean, you know, let there be *dark*, and it was *good*. Just like Lights out."

SOMETIME later, as I was struggling through some intense but forgotten dream, I felt Sumter climb up into bed and press his sweaty back against mine. It almost hurt to wake up, and I was too tired to protest and tell him to sleep on the floor or back in his folks' room. Instead I moved over closer to the window and dropped down again into sleep, the left side of my face pressed against the rough, cold wall.

THREE

Rabbit Lake

◄ 1 ►

I knew it was morning because it was still dark but the damn mocking-birds were already singing outside my window. The pane was stuck three quarters of the way down, and there was no way of shutting out that hel-lacious warbling. The air was still and moist, and it felt like I was stuck in some kind of limbo. I was pushed up against the wall and knew that I'd be aching from sleeping in such a strange position. Sumter had ap-parently taken up most of the bed. I turned to shove him over, but he was not there at all. I was alone in the bed, and my cousin had gotten up some-time in the night and gone back to his parents' bedroom to sleep. I won-dered if he had really come into my room at all or if I had just been dreaming.

I lay in bed for a while longer, trying to figure out my dreams, waiting for the mockingbirds to shut up and for the light to appear outside, when I heard a soft rap at my door. It was my father. In early morning, before any other soul was up, he always looked refreshed and ready for the day. It must have been a magical time for him, before the rest of the family could bother and worry him. He was wearing a sweatshirt and khakis and his clodhoppers. His hair was still wet from the shower, and it made him look shiny and new. He came in and sat on the edge of my bed, scruffing up my hair. "Beau, hey Beau," he whispered. "Uncle Ralph and I are taking you boys out to the lake this morning. Just us guys." I could still taste Aunt Cricket's Mystery Loaf in my mouth. Dad helped me sit up, rubbing my feet and my hands to help get the circulation going. My circulation was so bad some days it would take about half an hour to get me moving.

"Why does it always have to be me?"

"Beau?"

"I got crooked teeth and a sunken chest and bad circulation. It's like I'm a hundred years old."

"Those things don't mean anything."

"Yeah, *huh*."

"You've got everything in the world. Look at your cousin."

"Sumter does what he wants and gets what he wants."

"Getting what you want isn't much. Nobody knows what they really want until they've had it awhile. And some folks want things all the time just because they want to *want*."

"Well, I've had this circulation awhile and I don't want it and I don't *want* to want it. And don't tell me it makes me special. I don't want to hear it."

"Mr. Grump."

"And I don't really feel like going to a swamp at five in the morning to catch dirty old catfish."

"You want to stay and go to the mainland and go shopping with your mama and the girls?"

Shopping with my mother was a draining experience, more so than going fishing in the malarial swamp called Rabbit Lake, which was a freshwater runoff from the bay that the Gull Island peninsula encircled. Shopping or fishing: Either way it was a toss-up. If I'd had my druthers, I would've stayed home and watched TV, but that would mean dealing with Grammy Weenie.

"No," I replied in the smallest voice I had. The feeling came into my arms and legs, and I got up to dress. The day would be a long one, and by the end of it I would be bumpy with mosquito bites.

Two miles down the road from the Retreat, going Up Island, as we erroneously called it—as all things were misnamed on an island that was not an island, a retreat that was no retreat, a lake that was no lake at all—at the nearest edge of the bay was Shep and Diane's Nightcrawlers–Live Bait Shop—open all nite—Fireworx—Coca-Cola on Ice. It was the emporium of bait shops, and Shep Miller liked to brag that he had 400 different items on sale, each one multiplying 400 times a night.

There were long tanks, bubbling with minnows of all sizes—some fish that seemed too long to be properly called minnows, some that were too tiny to see. Huge fruit crates, reinforced with chicken wire on the outside, packed with dark pungent earth, wriggling with foot-long worms, some with their heads or tails (I never knew which) hooking out of the chicken wire like beckoning fingers. The boards under our bare feet were warped and splintery and unpainted, and beneath them the dark water lapped gently against the log pilings thrust like stilts into the shoreline. Tiny sea horses galloped in their own special tanks, surrounded by plastic deep-sea divers and gurgling treasure chests. Another tank was filled with hermit crabs, another with baby eels, and another brimming with armies of black translucent snails. Not all creatures in the shop were bait: Some were for pets, to be kept for the few days or weeks families spent on the island and then, no doubt, flushed down toilets or dumped out on the beach. The smells pervading the shop came up at you like you were coming up from the waves right into a wreath of bulbous seaweed, a dead fish caught in its center. The firecrackers were sold behind the counter, and kids were not allowed to purchase them unless their parents were with them.

Diane, Shep's girlfriend of twenty-four years, worked the cash register from two-thirty in the morning until noon, at which time Shep took over. I never truly believed they had any business between midnight and three a.m., but still they kept the shop open. The longevity of their relationship was attributable, Shep said, to their never seeing each other. This was also the reason why they never married, and yet they didn't live together because Diane was a devout fundamentalist and feared the fires of Hell with a capital H. She was a large woman with an unkind face and moles spotting her chin, always reading the Bible while she worked, and behind her on the wall she had framed a black-and-white photograph of Shep holding up several bluefish, beneath this a saying in large block letters: BE YE FISHERS OF MEN.

In spite of her religious fervor, on sale also behind the counter were *Playboy* and *Penthouse* magazines, but I never dared to sneak behind it and get a peek at them because Diane Cooper terrified me more than any god or devil ever could. She was wall-eyed, which gave you the feeling she was always watching you even when she probably was not.

Sumter was still mad at me for squealing, although I still wasn't positive I had told Grammy Weenie anything about going in Neverland. In the car on the way down to the bait shop, he didn't even glare or sulk; he just acted sweet as pie, which, with Sumter, meant he was mad as all getout. "I slept well," he said. "Something about sleeping near the ocean, it makes you feel well rested. You well rested?" he'd asked me. I was still in my grouch morning mood and didn't reply.

"You're full of beans this morning," Uncle Ralph told his son, beaming with fatherly pride, leaving me feeling that I had somehow disappointed my dad, who wasn't saying much.

Sumter grinned broadly, obnoxiously, and said in the unnatural cadences of a child who's trying to put something over on his parent, "Oh, yes, indeedy, it sure enough is good to be alive on a fine morning such as this. Beau, if you just act enthusiastic, then you'll *be* enthusiastic."

I wanted to punch him, but I was too sleepy.

Once out of the car, he raced into the shop, with me lagging behind. "Hey-hey, Miz Cooper, got any crabs?" Then he went: "Haw-haw-haw." He clomped around to the worm crates and lifted a handful of snaking earth, putting it near his mouth. "Spaghetti for breakfast, mm-mm, good!"

"Don't even *think* about it," she snapped from behind her Bible.

"I wasn't doing nothing," Sumter said, and his voice was light and sweet. He dumped the worms and dirt back into the crate.

"You never do nothing, way I figure, but what you ain't supposed to do." She may have been the only one on the island besides me and Grammy Weenie who could see through my cousin's games, and I wasn't always sure *I* could see through them. Turning to me she said, "Good to see you back, Beauregard, but I see you left your smile hanging up in your closet."

"It's early."

"You boys should be like the lilies of the field. They don't toil, they don't sweat, they just grow in God's sunshine."

"I'd trample 'em," Sumter said, "and then I'd pick them apart, petal by petal."

"They'd just grow up again."

"And I'd dig them up."

"You have a mouth on you, boy."

"That I do. The Mouth of the South." Then he began singing off-key, "Whoa, Big Mama, why'n't you turn your damper down?"

I was almost happy to see Sumter's nasty side start to come out after his earlier syrupiness.

"I said, whoa-oh, Big Mama, why don't you just turn your old damper down? 'Cause when you flap those big lips, just makes me wanta frown." He stomped his bare feet down on the boards, causing half the shop to rattle. Minnows scattered in spotty schools along the edges of their tanks, cutting through the water at right angles.

"The fire's eternal, Sumter, it don't just go out," Diane muttered, but returned to her scripture.

Sumter finished his song and dance, moving back around to the fish and creepy-crawlies. He pressed his face against one of the tanks and made fish lips. "Don't you feel sorry for these poor suckers?" he asked me, and now I knew he had at least momentarily forgiven me for whatever it was I was supposed to have done. "They wait here for someone to put a hook through their middles and while they're *dying* they get pecked at by snappers and catfish. But, on the other hand, if they were just swimming down at the lake *now*, they'd probably have been *eaten* by now." He shrugged.

The minnows looked to me like slivers of silver skin, moving together in perfect strokes as if they had not fifty fish minds between them, but one will.

"Daddy!" Sumter yelped. "I want a sea horse! Can I have one?"

Uncle Ralph snorted, and Sumter made a face at his father's back. My dad was looking at a set of fancy lures, and I heard Uncle Ralph say, "Dab, those are for pussies." My father looked back to see if I'd heard, and I looked back at the tanks and played dumb.

"You'd know," Dad told him.

"They got Caymans this year." Sumter grabbed my hand and yanked me over to one corner of the store.

There was a screen stapled down to the top of a wood-frame aquarium, scratched plexiglass all along the lower edges. Sumter and I leaned over it, and a stink came up like Don's Johns at campgrounds during sticky summers. "Take a whiff." Sumter gargled the air into the back of his throat and coughed it out. A thin layer of brown water coated the tank bottom; clumps of hairy moss floated lazily like unanchored gardens. A chunk of sepia-tinted hamburger was pushed up against a corner. There were two Cayman lizards: They were like baby alligators, but somehow more exotic because they were called Caymans.

"I want one of them," he said.

"They're neat."

"I bet they eat virgins for breakfast."

My only knowledge of virgins at that age was the Virgin Mary. Our neighbors in Richmond, the Antonellis, had a blue Virgin Mary in their garden, and I imagined her surrounded by hungry Caymans.

"I bet they eat fingers," he said, grabbing my wrist and slapping my hand against the top of the screen. I pulled my hand away from him. The lizards swished their tails, splattering the sides of the tank as they moved swiftly, practically burrowing under the floating moss. When they rested, their pop eyes came just above the water, the bumpy ridge of their tails like tiny spikes in a perfect trail behind them. "I bet they get real big."

"Yeah, huh," I replied.

"How much you think they are?"

"Ten dollars."

"I bet twenty."

"No way. Ten."

"It don't matter, anywho," he patted me on the back, "'cause I'm gonna get one for free."

"Yeah, *huh.*"

"If I have to kill fat old Diane to do it." He managed to undo one of the staples from the screen. He slipped his hand down into the tank, into the far corner, away from the resting Caymans. His fingers squished into the old raw hamburger and pulled it up. When he'd freed his hand from beneath the tank's screen, he lifted the hamburger to his nose. "Smells like a toad turd."

I wrinkled my nose. "Gross me out."

Sumter popped the disgusting meat into his mouth and swallowed, snapping his teeth together so they clicked. "I was getting kinda hungry."

⊰ 2 ⊱

I hated fishing.

But what I hated more than fishing were the stories Uncle Ralph would tell in the little dinghy we rented to go out on Rabbit Lake. We launched it into Rabbit Lake, our feet stinging with damp prickers, mud oozing between our toes. Sumter was up to his butt in the water before he leaned into the boat, head and arms first, feet last, sliding in, his teddy bear tucked under his arm.

When he got all settled in, he said to me, "Bernard doesn't like you."

"It's just a stuffed toy," I said, "and your daddy's right, you're too old."

"If you keep talking like that, I'll be mad enough to spit tacks, and Bernard'll eat you before you can blink."

"That thing ain't gonna eat nobody, it's just gonna lose its stuffing."

"A good bear can tear you limb from limb. I read up on grizzlies, and they're the meanest. Bernard is part grizzly and part something else."

"Yeah, huh," I said, reading the label beneath Bernard's tail, "part polyurethane."

"Quiet," Uncle Ralph whispered, swatting at the air. "You'll scare the *fish* away."

Uncle Ralph was an avid fisherman, wasting no time: The sun was almost completely up, it was nearly six a.m., and his bad jokes could wait no more. "There was this fella who goes to his doctor and the doctor says to him, 'I'm gonna need a urine sample, a stool sample, and a sperm sample,' and the guy goes, 'Well, hey, why'n't I just give you my underwear?'" Sumter laughed so hard he started hacking, and Uncle Ralph had to slap him on the back. Sumter hawked a loogie out the starboard side, and we watched it splash down and create ripples. A small sunfish came up to nip at it.

"Good one, Daddy, but tell the one about you know the guy who you know gets caught on a you-know-whatever of spit." Sumter tied a lead weight to the end of his father's line. Whenever Sumter played with hooks, I stayed as far away from him as possible. He had poked half a dozen hooks through Bernard's ears, and probably would've been just as happy to put them through mine, too. "You know, Daddy, that one about drinking spit. You *know*."

Uncle Ralph had a face like a moose, and his blubbery lips parted in a smile-snarl as he chomped down on a wad of tobacco. "Okay, there's this guy walks into a bar and he goes, 'Ain't got no money, but I'll do anything for a drink,' and the bartender goes, 'Howsabout you take a sip from the spittoon and I'll give ya a shot of bourbon,' and the guy goes—"

"Ralph, I think you should stop while you're ahead." When my father spoke to his friends or family, his voice was low and authoritative; the stammer he had in his business life never carried over into personal matters. I used to stand in front of a mirror and try to imitate that deep, unaccented sound, but never could.

Uncle Ralph paused momentarily, but went right on, "Reminds me of this one about this guy . . . "

We sat in muddy water, me in the very back—because I didn't want to be up with Sumter and Uncle Ralph—and my father baiting his hook.

I popped the top of a chocolate Yoo-hoo and took a swig. The drink was warm. I leaned back, resting my head against one of the life jackets, and gazed out over the small lake.

Dragonflies whizzed around us as mosquito larvae giggled in aquatic swarms around the edge of our boat. Cattails and reeds swiped at the oars, but we stayed still, and except for the droning sound of Uncle Ralph's voice and my father's trying to get him to shut up, we floated like the moss in the Cayman tank, waiting for something to bite. Every now and then Sumter would make a growling noise and pretend it came from his bear, and each time Uncle Ralph looked like he was ready to bite his own boy's head clean off.

Around eight we broke open the breakfast basket that Julianne had packed the previous afternoon: cold fried-egg sandwiches; cold blackened bacon; thick slices of ham, each with a generous lacing of fat around its edges; a thermos of coffee; and apple juice in bottles shaped like apples. After we'd devoured these, Uncle Ralph said, "Why'n't you boys go exploring? We can row you over to the island and you can play for a while." You could see through Uncle Ralph like a pair of binoculars: Sumter had been making too much noise out in the boat, and his father wanted to ditch him so he could catch some fish. Uncle Ralph was a glutton for catfish, and all morning he'd mutter under his breath whenever Sumter began shouting—things like "Land Ho!" or "Thar she blows!" Uncle Ralph didn't remember that he kept up his own steady stream of vocal noise by telling his off-color jokes. If anyone had scared fish off, he had.

THE ISLAND we jumped off at was barely an acre in size. I waved goodbye to my father and my uncle, but Sumter was already cursing his luck.

"Dang it all, I sliced my toe open." He plopped to the yellow summer grass, squatting in the mud, turning his foot over so he could view the damage. Blood had bubbled up onto his muddy foot. He plucked a hook out of it, tossing it onto the ground. He wiped his blood-muddy toe onto Bernard's shaggy stomach. "Sorry, Bernard."

"If you leave it here, somebody else'll step on it," I scolded, picking up the fishhook after him.

"Good," he replied. "Maybe it'll hook into you and get inside your greasy grimy gopher guts because you squealed."

"I did not." I brushed the fishhook off and caught it into the edge of my short-sleeved shirt, carefully twisting it through the cotton to dull the sharp point.

"I lied to my folks, but before supper the Weenie grabbed me and she went and slapped me on the fanny with that abomination of hers that she calls a brush. She said we were doing naughty things in the shack. What exactly did she mean, Beauregard Burton Jackson? What kinds of *lies* did you make up to get me in deep doo-doo? You tell her we were fornicating or somethin'?"

My face felt hot and red. The heat of the day was sneaking up on us slowly. "I didn't say *nothing*."

"Oh, *huh*, you didn't, you'd do anything to save your own skin. I bet she made you bawl out loud and you told her. That witch. Well," he said, calming, "I forgive you, Beau, because I know you knew not what you did."

"You're a blasphemer, Sumter."

"And I'm a rambling wreck from Georgia Tech and a helluva engineer!" He trumpeted, his fists up to his lips. He had mood swings the way Uncle Ralph had cans of beer: one after the other, no matter the time of day. He stopped singing, swatted his hands out like a referee calling foul, and said, "Beau, I think we got company." He pointed toward a crowded thicket of dried grass. He put a finger up to his lips. "Bernard," he whispered, "you stay here."

Something moved, there in the sprawl of dried-up grass and prickers. Two long, white, fluffy ears perked up, and a pink nose sniffed at us.

RABBIT Lake was so named because of the bunnies who occupied the small island we stood upon. These rabbits were here, not because they were natives of Gull Island, but because, over the years, when people vacationed on the peninsula around about Easter-time, the grown-ups would dump their children's pets out on that mound in hopes that either the animal would drown trying to get back to shore or live out its natural days there.

It must've satisfied a sense of what heaven was, for parents could row out with their kiddies and Mr. Flop-ears, let the bunny go, tell the kiddies how happy the bunny would be—much happier than in some crate down in the rec room eating kibble and being bored—and then row leisurely back. The myth would develop of Mr. Flop-ears, who would never die in their imaginations, but live on at the island on Rabbit Lake. The truth was that the bunnies did live on there, multiplying like, well, bunnies, but the small island in the lake became a stockade for the locals, the poor population of the island, the Gullah descendants, too, to whom the soft bunny meat was something of a delicacy. Sumter told me that he thought bunny meat tasted like chicken, "because every weird thing you eat is supposed to taste like chicken."

He poked me in the ribs as I came up beside him, tiptoeing even in the mud and grass. "They're made up of pure innocence," he whispered. The bunny was small and its soft, white fur was matted with burs and dried mud. Its nose twitched, and it rose up on its hind legs to inspect us before darting back into the high grass. "Pure innocence, the way babies are. Nobody's told them the way it is yet. Nobody's told that bunny that it's gonna be somebody's supper. It's living in bliss, Beau, pure bliss 'cause it don't know what's coming."

Because it seemed an intensely private moment—and therefore embarrassing—I didn't glance directly at my cousin, though I could feel his breath near my ear. But I knew he was crying, maybe not much, maybe just a few tears rolling from his eyes, but I knew he was crying. I pretended not to notice. I saw peripherally that his face was crumpling like rotten fruit. I thought he whispered something, but maybe he didn't, but it was something that passed between the two of us like a whisper, what was on his mind. "My Daddy wishes I wasn't ever born."

We spotted other bunnies in the next two hours, and we even tossed pebbles at some of them. Sumter did not come back to his usual obnoxious self; he was distracted. Finally, as if answering a question in his own head, he turned to me and said, "Give me that hook."

"Huh?"

He pointed to my arm: the hook he'd cut himself with. I plucked it from my sleeve reluctantly and handed it to him.

He stuck it against his thumb.

I winced, watching.

"Give me your left hand."

"Uh-uh."

"We're gonna take a blood oath."

"What for?"

"Because of Neverland. You and me, Beau, we're gonna be joined with blood so you never tell a living soul what you're gonna find there."

"I thought you weren't gonna let me in again."

"I changed my mind. And you can't tell nobody ever again about what's there."

"Not *much* there."

"If I told you something."

"Like what?"

"Like the Slinky attacking the Weenie. Neverland *made* it attack her. Neverland wanted to *kill* her. Like the horseshoe crab—it was a trick, but lotsa tricks happen in there. Like the skull of Lucy, my one true god, which speaks of what will come. And the Gullahs know about Neverland, Beau, they *know,* and they keep out, because of the god I found, and I am the priest of that god. Those dead slaves, they didn't just *die,* they *consecrated* that ground. But it's a god that don't just sit on its ass, cousin. It's a god of action, of retribution, it's a god of living bliss and destruction. It's the god of eternal hunger." His face was perfectly calm as he said this, and he didn't seem to move at all, but in the next second I felt the prick of the fishhook, like a needle of ice, thrust into my thumb, and he was holding our thumbs together, kneading the blood as it dripped out in shiny red pearls. *We are jars of blood.* I heard his heart beating in my thumb; I tasted something like the rusty metal of the hook in the back of my throat.

"Swear," he said, "*swear.*"

"No." I tried to draw back, but our thumbs were glued together. I had to breathe through my mouth because for some reason my nose didn't seem to work right. I wanted to be back home, or back in the boat. My whole head felt warm, and I felt Grammy's silver brush stroking through my crewcut. *Flesh is our prison.* I felt imprisoned then, wanting to get out of my body, which felt hot all over, which would not let me run away.

"Swear you won't ever tell, swear in blood."

"No."

Grammy Weenie said flesh is our prison.

"Swear."

Spirit and flesh constantly at war.

"No."

Angel and Devil.

"By your blood. Say it. Say it."

Something was pressing into me—not his hand clutching mine, trying to draw my thumb closer to the hook poised for jabbing—but something in my blood, like the tingling feeling I got whenever my circulation failed to kick in, the need of my bones and flesh to move, but my blood went from hot to freezing, icing around my veins, under my skin.

I shut my eyes to will this feeling away.

It was like the strokes of Grammy Weenie's brush, down through my scalp, creating some kind of electric field around me. Like that, but not, because whatever feeling this was, it was breaking down that field, it was invading my pores, it was turning me to rigid stone, a large block of ice.

"By my blood," I said and the pins-and-needles feeling crept across the backs of my legs.

"I swear."

"I swear," and my breath was frozen in the air.

"I will keep secret."

"I will keep secret." My jaws ached, my elbows creaked when I tried to bend them.

"All that is Neverland."

"All that is Neverland." I felt the hook penetrate my skin.

"Now our blood is mixed, cousin. Now I'm in you and you're in me. I will know if you break this, your most sacred vow."

When he let go of my hand, I heard the blood pounding in my thumb like waves breaking against some shore of night. I stuck it in my mouth and sucked at the drying blood as though I'd been bitten by a snake and needed to spit out the poison.

3

While I still pressed my bleeding thumb against my lips, Sumter cried out, "Look! *Gawd*." He pointed to a tamped-down patch of reeds. He waded through a stagnant pool and alongside some prickers, carelessly pushing them aside. I followed close behind, and the pricker branches sprung back at me.

He knelt down in the reeds, spreading them apart. When I came up behind him, he had a twig in his fingers and was poking at his find.

I squatted down, barely balancing with my hands on my knees.

Another bunny, but this one was dead.

Its black-and-white fur was matted with blood and crusted dirt. A gash ran down its stomach. While this wasn't the first dead animal I had ever seen, it was the only one with its guts hanging out. My usual death sightings involved roadkill or animals much lower on the food chain, and certainly none as sweet as a bunny. "Lookit," I said, my finger hanging just above the rabbit's head. Half of one of its floppy ears had been chewed off. When you're ten, death is less horrifying than it is fascinating. I would've been equally thrilled to have come across the corpse of a human being, and not in the least bit terrified.

Sumter industriously poked its guts back inside its stomach. "I bet everybody looks this way when they kiss off."

"I wonder what got it?"

"A dog or something. Maybe a raccoon. Or a Gullah." He dropped the twig and brought his hand down to the animal's belly. Its eyes were partially sunken in. Tiny ricelike maggots dripped from its nostrils. Sumter flicked at them with his fingers.

"Yuck. Don't *touch* it, Sumter, you can get all kinds of *diseases*." The maggots scared me more than the bunny. "What if we get *tapeworm* or something?"

"Then we get to drink chocolate milkshakes and cut the worm's head off with scissors. Anyway, these're just plain old grubs." Sumter went ahead and stroked the bunny's bloodied fur. "Not too warm, not too cold. Just died last night, I bet." He took his T-shirt off over his head and swaddled it around the dead rabbit.

"Gross. Whatju want to do *that* for?"

"We're gonna take it back to Neverland and see if Lucy wants it for a sacrifice."

"Oh, *neat*." I wasn't being sarcastic. I *really* thought this *would* be neat.

ALL THE way back home Sumter pretended he'd slipped in the mud and had taken his shirt off because of the slime. This satisfied both his father and mine, neither of whom were much up for questioning either of us as to why we looked so guilty. They had caught nothing all morning long and apparently had gotten along like yellow jackets. Sumter flashed me a smile in the car, keeping his prize close to his pale stomach, hiding it behind his teddy bear; later we would find bloodstains on Bernard's back. First chance we had, we raced out to the shed. Sumter tripped and would've gone splat down on the dead rabbit if I hadn't stopped his fall.

Inside Neverland he wasted no time. He went over to the crate and knocked three times on it. "Oh, Lucy," he said, "I have brought you a creature for your pleasure." He unrolled his shirt. It was completely brown and red, with some of the bunny guts on it, too. He lifted the animal up; blood trickled from the gash down on his forehead. I felt my insides heave. Blood grossed me out in a major way.

"Lucy!" he cried out. "A sacrifice for you, a victim for Neverland!" His voice was theatrical, like the preacher at the Baptist church in town.

Then he gently laid the corpse across the top of the crate.

I felt a little silly, although I didn't doubt that there was something to this sacrifice stuff. I was only a little scared, and more by the sight of bunny blood on Sumter's forehead than this invocation to the god Lucy.

"Lucy is pleased," Sumter said, opening his eyes again. "God feeds on the dead."

I couldn't even bring myself to look at the crate or the dead rabbit.

And then I heard the scraping from within the crate.

Along the sides of the wood.

An animal clawing slowly, slowly.

Then faster.

The wood splintered and cracked as it clawed.

"*Good, good,*" Sumter said.

It can't be.

It's just another trick, it's a Neverland trick.

The bunny had been dead when we found it, and dead when Sumter laid it before the crate. I'd seen some dead things before, I knew even a bunny couldn't be alive with its stomach ripped apart and maggots squirming up its nose and Sumter poking its red-brown guts back into it.

But the noise.

No longer scraping.

No clawing.

A sound from its throat.

It sounded the way I would imagine a bunny would sound.

If it were screaming.

FOUR

Island Lore

⊰ 1 ⊱

There are bluffs on only one side of Gull Island, to the northwest. Opposite them is a town called St. Badon, which is known mainly for its shopping malls. The southwest side of the peninsula is all gradually lowering slopes until you come smack dab into marshes and swamps.

The bluffs at the Retreat were our guardians against storms, and they cut our various paths down to the beach. They were not smooth, but corrugated with sandstone and chalk-white dirt. At dawn you could sit on the edge and watch the pelicans gliding just above the waves and then dropping into the black morning water as if reenacting some ancient struggle. In summers past, Sumter and I had thrown stones over the edge to occupy ourselves while domestic turmoil brewed back at the house. If you looked down to the south, you could just catch a glimpse of the top of the tattered roller coaster from Sea Horse Park, and if you looked to the west, beyond the tiara bridge and even St. Badon, you could see the place where the earth curved below the sky. But to the east there was only the house, the Retreat.

Often as not, the house was full of fights and squabbles. Usually it was Mama who was the angriest. She had a keener sense of injustice and untold truths and things just beneath the surface, at least when it came to her mother and sister and husband and brother-in-law.

Sumter once said to me, "Don'tcha just get pukey when your mama starts to caterwauling?"

I had no answer. I could mentally put myself somewhere else, off-island, in a country where mothers never got upset and fathers only rarely cursed and walked off. Sometimes I thought of stories I'd read or movies I'd seen, and I would just pretend I was in that world and not this one. But I knew it was just pretend.

My cousin knew no such boundary. He would tell me about trips he'd taken to the moon or the shootouts he'd had with cowboys or what Bernard, his teddy bear, had told him.

At night, before I fell asleep, he said, "I know where we go when we die, and it's a bad place. Lucy says we don't have to go there if we're faithful. Lucy says we can live forever in Neverland." And rather than scaring me, this was a comfort as I fell asleep, covering my head with my pillow while I heard Mama and Grammy sniping at each other downstairs.

And then I thought of the screaming bunny.

The nightmares all began the same way after that.

They all began with a woman I didn't recognize telling me that the bunny screamed, not because it was dying, but because it was alive.

⊰ 2 ⊱

Trips to Gull Island were never fun and games. Two years earlier we'd arrived during a tropical storm, which Mama was sure would end within a day or two, but instead lasted the whole two weeks we were in Georgia. The locals performed Gullah rituals, the evidence of which was scattered about the swamplands and down in back of the Holy Roller Church down at the West Side of the peninsula: dead chickens, their heads chomped off as if by geeks in a sideshow. Aunt Cricket tried to keep us from looking at the feathered carcasses, but Sumter kept piping up, "What's the diff if they're Kentucky Fried or Gullah Chomped?" The local newspaper, a one-page mimeograph usually tacked up in the general store on the West Side, carried the headline: animals sacrificed in ancient ritual. I was so intrigued by that headline, I stole the paper; the rest of the article was a protest from an unidentified Gullah holy man who swore on a stack of Bibles that no Gullah was responsible for the dead chickens, but something far older than Gullah, even, something that slept beneath the island and waited for its Great Awakening. I told Sumter that *he* was what had bitten the heads off the chickens, and it was *him* sleeping, waiting to be awakened.

All during that storm, Mama and Grammy Weenie fought—over the way they dressed, the way they treated their families, the way they were brought up, other people's mothers, all the things Aunt Cricket got as a child that my mother didn't get. They even argued over the brand of peanut butter Grammy had in her pantry. Daddy drank a bit more than he usually did and ran interference when he wasn't drinking by taking us kids to movies on the mainland when the arguments got too heated.

The second summer on Gull Island the weather was bad but not bad enough to stay indoors. Mama and Grammy Weenie were silent together, although you could see Grammy eyeing her when we all sat down to the table in the evening, looking for faults, finding them, and then keeping her silence. I used to think how happy we'd all be if Grammy Weenie just died. I didn't particularly love her, although she was at least interesting, if peculiar. When she talked of her long-dead daughter, she didn't call her Cindy, but "Babygirl." This was the oldest of the children—my mother being next, and then Aunt Cricket being last. We children called this aunt—who had died the year after I was born—the "Mad One," because she ended up in some kind of drying-out farm in North Carolina and died crazy. But she would always be Babygirl to Grammy Weenie. When Grammy spoke of her maternal grandmother, it was not as Leonora Bourgeois, but the "Giantess from Biloxi." Grammy Weenie was putting together a family history, although some days she said that her children and grandchildren weren't worthy of this record at all. She would read it to us at night, and we would yawn and stretch and fall asleep to her grumbling voice:

"Of all things I am most proud of, it is of being a Wandigaux—Daddy was from the New Orleans Wandigaux family, originally from France, persecuted for their religious faith, who escaped the wrath of the Papists of their native land. And when I think of that name, I am reminded we are wanderers. I am from a nomadic stock, and Gull Island has become the end of the journey . . . Wandigaux I am, and all that I am is Wandigaux. My husband was a Lee of Culpeper. We raised three daughters, my Babygirl, Evelyn Jane, and Cricket, and so the blood continues. I have regrets, as all mortals must, and I have done things that I ought not to have done, but we must all answer to a higher law than the law of man: There is the Kingdom of God to which we are accountable. All around us is that Kingdom; it is in the Garden in which we live. I am a poor humble and erring servant, and it is true that I have not always tended the Garden. But I have done what I have had to do. I have done what I must . . . "

The third summer on Gull Island we miraculously got along, and I completely attributed this to the fact that Sumter had been sent away to summer camp for the month we visited the Retreat. Aunt Cricket tended to cry every day because she missed her little boy, her "Sunny," but Grammy was pleasant and made gingerbread men and read from Charles Dickens every evening. When she went through *David Copperfield*, she said, "'I am born.' Isn't that marvelous? 'I am born.' Simple, direct, that Mr. Dickens knew how to *begin*, didn't he? Beginnings are all, and what is well begun cannot be undone."

Mama got a tan for the first time in years because she was finally able to squeeze into her bathing suit—she was never fat, but always said she was. Uncle Ralph and Daddy took us down to the Sea Horse Park, and although the roller coaster was still the unused dinosaur it had always been, and the Trabant and Whirligigs were closed, there were bumper cars and cotton candy. A long, thin black man with no arms and no legs rolled cigarettes with his tongue and then struck the matches that way, too. He charged a buck per rolled cigarette, but it was great entertainment. Still, as always, we had returned home at the end of August with mosquito bites and bad tempers from the humidity.

My dreams those summers were about going back to school, about my parents fighting, about my little baby brother who would be born shortly.

My dreams the last summer on the island made me scream.

⊰ 3 ⊱

The bunny screams because it is alive.

"Beau? You okay, honey?"

The bunny screams because it is alive.

"Beau?" It was my mother's voice that brought me out of the nightmare, not the face of that little black–and-white bunny, its whiskered muzzle stretched like an open sore, its eyes red with fury and knowledge of what was to come.

It was not quite daylight, but almost. She had turned on the lamp by my bed and sat next to me. With the palm of her left hand she felt my forehead. "You don't have a fever." I always smelled her hair first: It was like her shampoo, but also was like vinegar and lemon. The rest of her smelled like calamine lotion with only a hint of pine-clean gin laced in her breath. She'd been smoking cigarettes, which she bummed off Aunt Cricket, but only when she was very drunk. I liked that smell of ashes and gin from her lips. She was all smells that reminded me that she was my mother—I had known that perfume since the day I was born.

"I didn't wet the bed," I said.

"Honey, I didn't think you had. You're a big boy. I was in the bathroom and I heard you. You let out a big old howl. Was it bad?" Sometimes, and this was one of those times, Mama looked at me like she didn't quite know what to expect. I had always had dreams, and I had always told them. Sometimes they were about grades I'd get on my tests at school, sometimes they were about arguments, sometimes they were about storms that were on their way. *Was it bad?* she'd asked, as if she didn't really want to know.

"Don't laugh if I tell you."

"Dreams are just ways of sorting out messy thoughts—nothing to be frightened of. Come on and tell me it. I promise not to laugh unless it's funny."

"I can't remember," I lied. If I was to tell her the dream, I'd have to tell her about Neverland. And I could not break my blood oath. "What time is it?"

"Half past the freckle, eastern elbow time."

"Daddy's gonna be getting up soon. I have to go fishing again."

"You like it, don't you?"

I nodded. Two lies and the sun wasn't even up.

"Try to go back to sleep." She wiped her hand across my forehead and took with it some of my sweat. "Sweetie? Just close your eyes a little longer?"

Another nod, another lie. I was getting good at this.

Sumter and I were forced to go fishing for three days in a row, and each time Uncle Ralph would threaten to throw the teddy bear into the water.

Those same three days, Mama, Governor, Aunt Cricket, and the girls went to St. Badon to shop and wander, leaving Grammy home to read her Bible and scribble her memoirs in small black composition books.

We'd return from our daily trip, bumpy and sunburned, Uncle Ralph or Daddy with the one or two catches of the day, and Grammy would be sitting up in her wheelchair in the alcove of the living room, where the afternoon light came through the streaked window.

She wrote and wrote, faster and faster, as if she had to get it out, all her memories, now, now while she still remembered.

⇥ 4 ⇤

"It was all for the good," Grammy muttered, almost under her breath, as she sat up in her chair, and then she rose up.

"A miracle!" Aunt Cricket cried out as Grammy stood, wobbling, on her stick legs. "Praise Jesus! Alleluia!"

Grammy stood on her legs, "it was all for the good."

"Oh, Mama, the Lord shines his light on us, He surely does!" Aunt Cricket cackled.

"Spirit and flesh fighting, and always spirit must rise, must rise and conquer the decaying flesh, nature is all decay." Grammy pointed directly at me. "All that is natural is unnatural, child. All that can be made flesh can be corrupted."

"Praise His Name!" Aunt Cricket sang, clutching her boxy breasts through the cotton of her blouse like she was ready to give up her heart and soul to Christ right then and there—and by way of her nipples.

From the open doorway I heard the screaming rabbit. I went to shut the door, and when I got there it looked like a golden dust storm of yellow jackets was heading our way, and the locusts in the trees were barking, and behind me Aunt Cricket cried out, "Praise His name! And bless the fruit of His loins!"

And the one who walked in shadows moved among the great yellow swarms, his hands outstretched. Aunt Cricket pushed past me and ran out onto the porch and into the swarm to embrace him.

I AWOKE from this dream in the car on the way home from fishing, and I felt in a fever from sunburn. My scalp was sweaty against the vinyl seat. Sumter was whistling in the backseat, and Uncle Ralph was grumbling about not having caught anything. Daddy was driving and didn't look over at me.

As we drove up the road, the Retreat came into view, and I sent out a silent prayer that I wished I was home.

⊰ 5 ⊱

Julianne Sanders, our makeshift nanny and occasional cook for the brief holiday, snored when she slept. She lay curled into a fetal position on the front settee, her long legs impossibly drawn up in the least comfortable position imaginable, her face beatific in its calm. Her fluttering breaths were like distant foghorns calling out to each other. When we entered the house, the first thing Sumter did was go over to her and squeeze her nostrils shut until she started gasping. She reached up and grabbed him by the collar and shook him the way I'd seen mother dogs shake puppies, and my cousin let out a yowl to wake the dead.

"Sumter Monroe, you tell me how sorry you are you just did that" She was in complete control, smoothly coming out of her nap, leaning forward, her hands full of Sumter, shaking, shaking, just as if she'd planned on doing this.

"I ain't sorry."

Grammy Weenie, in her alcove, didn't even look up from her composition book; she scrawled another line across the top of a page.

Julianne kept shaking him, sitting up as she did this, and I was amazed to see that Sumter put up no resistance and, in fact, almost looked *defeated*. "You are sorry, Sumter, you are the sorriest little boy I ever did see." He was a rag doll in her hands, and I would not have been surprised to see the stuffing come out of him.

"Mama!" he keened.

"Your mama can't help you now. She's still out shopping, so you just take your medicine like a good boy and say you're sorry."

"Uncle! Uncle!"

"Not 'uncle,' *sorry*."

"Okay, okay, sorry, I'm sorry!"

She let him go.

He stepped back from her and said, "Hey, you're supposed to work for *us*, lady, not the other way around."

Julianne did not lose her smile. Her arm flapped out like a swinging tree branch and slapped him on the face. She said something in a language I didn't recognize. It sounded French, but at that age all I knew was *laploomdaymahtaunt* and I didn't even know what that meant. What Julianne was saying was a blur of *oohs* and *luhs*. Even though it made no sense to me, it meant something to Sumter, whose eyes grew wide, as if hearing obscenities. "We understand each other, then." She nodded and pinched his cheek, letting go and leaning back on the settee. She was all unshaven legs, dangly and bony, crossing over each other as she yawned and stretched. She saw me staring at her curiously and winked, "What *are* you ogling at, Beau? You never seen a Gullah girl with hairy legs before? *You* boys either go play and stay out of trouble till you get called to supper or you'll be peeling potatoes for this Gullah soon enough."

THIS was the first time she'd admitted she was a Gullah, and if I haven't told you already, I'll tell you now: I knew Julianne Sanders, *right then*, right at the moment she said she was a Gullah, I knew she wasn't a Gullah at all, because she said it like it was a lie. She said it like she was laughing at me on the inside for being so gullible. She was something else, part of some other thing besides Gullah. She was somehow more dangerous than Gullah, who were good people, who got life under their fingernails and lived it. But Julianne Sanders was something else.

She was what the folks on the island called *sinistre,* which is not to say she was sinister, but that she was a left-hander, which in Gullah parlance meant she lived to the west of the West Island. She was part of a select group of families who were feared by the Gullahs because they were descended from a god and a goddess according to the popular mythology. It was Sumter who informed me of all this, but he also added, "But you'd think if she was truly divinity she'd shave her legs."

He and I were tree-climbing up at the edge of the bluff. The day was growing late, and we'd taken our naps. The sun was slanting toward the mainland; the ocean trickled with piss-yellow light, as if schools of phosphorescent fish moved near the surface. Daddy and Uncle Ralph were playing cards out on the front porch. We could wave to them from our perch.

Julianne was in doing some cleaning under the supervision of the strictest of taskmasters, Grammy Weenie, scraping around the linoleum on her wheels. Mama, Aunt Cricket, and the girls hadn't returned from the mainland—it was near five o'clock, and if they were on their way, they were caught in the mild rush hour of St. Badon, the town just on the other side of the bridge from Gull Island.

"You can see the tiara bridge from here." Sumter pointed out through the veils of shimmering heat, across the peninsula to a curved bow. Cars like ants crossed over it. "I wonder if we can see the Chevy." Sumter held a pair of binoculars up to his eyes.

"Give me those." I made a grab for them.

"Ask and you shall receive."

"Okay, could I have those?"

"Pretty please with sugar on top?"

"Yeah, huh, *right*."

"What the hell." He hefted them over to me and I pressed the binoculars against my eyes and looked down at the bridge. The cars had grown, but only into larger ants. I tried to make out Aunt Cricket's Chevrolet, but it was all a blur of movement. Sea gulls fretted and cackled down along the shoreline over feeder fish that had been driven up near the shoreline by the fishing boats.

"I don't see them."

"You think Julianne hexed your mama and daddy? She's a *sinistre* and she talks that funny stuff. I think maybe she hexed me today, her and her leg hair."

"What'd she say to you, anyway?"

"Who the hell knows? But she looked like she was fixing me with whatever it was. She thinks she fixed me, anyway. She's a fixer, that crazy mama."

"You looked like you lost it."

"Yeah, well, I didn't lose it, bonehead."

"Toadhead."

"Nosehair."

"Toadhead."

"Know what?"

"What?"

"That's what. Sometimes you suck, Beau, you just plain suck. Now give me those binos and go play in traffic." He tugged on the binoculars, and my pulse pounded in my thumb where he'd stuck me with that fishhook out on Rabbit Lake.

The more he talked, the more I felt the blood break and crash within the confines of my sore thumb. "I hear the *sinistres* got a ritual where they are just like Catholics, only instead'a drinking the blood and body of Jesus in the form of wine and wafer, they use the genu-wine article, the flesh and blood, and you ask me, people like Julianne Sanders burn in Hell all the days of their life, and Mama says she'll be knocked up before she's seventeen with the way she sashays. But I don't know what Gullah's gonna get a boner for that hair on her legs. I think if I put my hand on it, it would feel like the Weenie's silver-backed all-natural bristle brush, don't you think? Bet her hair's stiff as a tack and twice as sharp. But, hell, I sure would like to see that flesh and blood ritual, know what I mean, jelly bean?"

Sumter was given to sudden transformations. Crouching up in that tree with him, I wondered what would spit out of his mouth next. Grammy Weenie was always saying that blood was thicker than water, "and some of it's so thick you need a knife just to get yourself a slice, and in this family we all have our knives and we all want our slices." But I was convinced that Sumter and I couldn't really be related. He was too spooky and unnatural, like an alien.

"Beau?"

"Huh?"

"You just looked funny for a second."

"I ain't been sleeping much. Bad dreams."

"Lucy'll take care of your dreams. Lucy wants to take care of all of us. You know that, don't you? Lucy's in and of the earth, she's our mother, she's the whole damn world. Don't you worry about stupid dreams. We'd never abandon you, me and Lucy. We should go," he said, bringing the binoculars down from his eyes. "Yeah, to Neverland. You coming? Don't be scared, 'cuz, it's our place. If you're gonna be scared, be scared of Grammy and *her* home. Now *that's* scary. Know what, Beau-Beau?"

"That's what."

"Nope. I was gonna tell you what that *sinistre* Julianne said."

"No you ain't."

"Yeah I was. Only now I'm not so sure."

"Okay, tell me."

"She told me she's seen my daddy."

"Big whoop. I seen your daddy, too. Half the liquor stores in Georgia've seen your daddy."

"Shows how much you know. *You* only *think* you seen my daddy, but I tell you, given her leg-hairy ways, I wouldn't put it past that girl. Scared the *be*-jesus outta me."

⊰ 6 ⊱

There was this woman who had nothing whatsoever to do her entire life because her husband died young and left a lot of money to her. She spent her winters on Gull Island and had, at one time, been neighbors with Grammy Weenie and used to come over and sit with her back in the days when Grammy was young. This woman began compiling a history of the island, which was pretty boring, mainly recipes from Gullah kitchens and Junior League barbecues back in the days when Junior Leaguers occasionally came to the peninsula. But this woman had a few screws loose, and she always repeated one of her favorite anecdotes about the island in each of her small self-published books—always on sale, even after her death, at the bait shop.

What a rich heritage our island is home to, what a luminous past, what an unmined treasure is Gull Island! And none so intriguing as the story of the slave-ghosts, a tale so lovely and peaceful that one can feel secure during the worst gale the sea has to give, if one is only at home on Gull Island.

The evil slavers, in their unquenchable thirsts for profits on human life, would arrive in the Caribbean with new prisoners from the Dark Continent, the most paradisiacal land then known, a place where man lived naturally and without aggression. Packed like rats together in the cargo holds of these ships, these good people prayed and died amongst themselves even before land was sighted. How hopeless must seem their plights to us as we sit here thinking of them! How unanswered their prayers!

But these good and primitive people believed that if they jumped from the ship, they could swim back to their sacred home, and if they drowned, their spirits would rise and return without need of the body.

One such ship sailed near the coastline, and more than a hundred slaves managed to jump together, bound with rope and chain, but no manmade shackle could bind their spirits. Men, women, and children, all swimming for their home, and all, alas, drowning, but dying without giving up hope, for their belief was strong.

To the horror of the few surviving escaped slaves who had made their homes on this brambled and twisted peninsula, full of quicksand lagoons and wild undergrowth, the bodies of dozens of the dead floated up onto the shores, groups often of ten or fifteen, shackled together, dead bodies. And the original Gullahs of this island, on finding their countrymen bound thus, blanketing the sand and surf, decided that this island must be the Paradise, the Guinee, the place where spirits dwelled. The place, they said, where the dead would dance. So it was sacred, and rather than a place of hopelessness, the island became the Place of the Gullahs, the home of the dead, the dwelling place of the soul.

Books such as this one fed our imaginations.

GLENN CHADBOURNE

In Neverland I sat on the edge of a rusted-out old wheelbarrow and thumbed through the *Playboys*. Sumter had gone through and sketched moustaches or broken teeth onto the girls' faces. Their breasts thrust out of the photos like grocery bags, their hair thatches were like hedges that needed trimming, their skin was soft and smooth. None of these girls looked like she had anything to do in life but be beautiful and still and waiting.

"Turn-offs: Insensitive people, people who don't like animals," he said in a high falsetto. "Turn-ons: People who like to have fun, people who love life in all its variety. Look at the bush on *that* one." He jabbed his finger over my shoulder into the pubic area of Miss June.

I slammed the magazine shut. "This is boring, I thought you had to do something."

"I do. But it's kind of a ritual, and maybe you shouldn't be here to see it. Maybe you're too young. Maybe it'll give you *nightmares*."

"I'm older than you."

"Emotionally immature, that's what Mama calls you. She says you're a hypochondriac and a neurotic and your mama and daddy are at the root of your problem."

"Your mama sucks."

"Is she wrong, Beau? Hmm? Is she? You and your circulation problems? They only come on when you can get the most attention. Do you think there's a connection? Hmm?"

I will admit that I wanted to hit him for saying this, and I wanted to cry, but I never cried. It was just one of those things I never did. Hit him, yes. That urge was harder to keep down.

"It's no big deal, cuz, honest, and the only reason I know is because, you know, the god Lucy told me it, and Lucy says you can be healed and saved and cured and all that. But only if you believe in Lucy."

"If Neverland's all around us, why can't I see it more?"

"If it's what you really, really want, but it gets scary. You sure you want to see?"

At that moment I almost said no. That small voice of conscience that my mother always talked about—that ghost of a voice in the back of my head—almost warned me away from this shack, this blood relation, this god of his.

But I said, "You bet."

"If you really see Neverland, Beau, you will never be the same. You've already seen the face of god, and now you want to see the All. *You will never be the same.* You hear?"

I shrugged.

"Feed it. In the crate." He held up a small safety pin, its sharp point gleaming. "Pray for what you want, and feed it."

Sumter led me back to the crate, lifting the lid. "Now open your mouth and close your eyes, and you will get a big surprise."

"I'm sure," I said between clenched teeth. I almost did not want to look.

"Close your eyes," he said softly. "And pray. You want to see the All, don't you?"

"Uh-uh."

"Close your eyes, Beau, and pray to see." His voice was like a rusty nail poked into my forehead, and for an instant I shut my eyes. I felt something tap at the back of my hand, almost tickling me, and then the sharpness of a pin. *Feed it.*

"Jeez," I gasped, opening my eyes to see a small dot of blood drop into the crate. Something like a chicken foot reached out from the crate and grabbed my left hand by the wrist. Its scaly talons pressed sharply into my skin and tugged me toward the opening, into the crate itself, and the wind was knocked out of me. I felt myself falling down a vast endless shaft, the way you fall in a dream, with no ground to come down to. Brilliant tongues of fire shot out all around me, turning to deep blue waves passing over my head. I saw what looked like a woman's face, screaming, only the skin had been eaten at, as if by fish. It was bloated and gray and chewed, but still the mouth was open and the sound that came out was like a child crying out without knowing words.

I was then on land, standing just outside the shack. All around me were colors I had never seen before, colors that I don't even have names for, colors that made me angry and worried, exploding around me like bombs. My stomach was queasy, my heart beat irregularly and slowly, my mouth tasted of dirt and mold. In the distance were figures dancing on a hillside, and there were cacophonous shrieks as if some tone-deaf person were singing in a language I could not make out. The sky was fragmented into sharp angles and octagonal clouds, and the entire universe's geometry had somehow expanded outward into shapes like strings of rock candy. Trees swayed in a strong wind, bending toward me, whispering; seagulls flew in great flocks with fish between their jaws, fish that screamed for release; the damp earth slithered and curled around my toes, its nightcrawlers and millipedes and pale white grubs chewing, chewing, chewing—as if they were inside my brain chewing on it. Somewhere among the trees something walked—I could only see its shadow, for the trees hid it well as they murmured their warnings to me.

Something walked there on all fours.

The sound of the trees became the sound of children laughing.

What walked there behind the thin line of trees, lit by the colors of madness, was not man or woman or animal.

And I knew that it was coming for me, with its hooves and claws and fingers and teeth—coming for me to do what only the savage god could do.

Feed.

I tried to scream, but had no voice.

I tried to scream because I did not want to be alive, because being alive hurt, because being alive meant *god would feed on my flesh*.

I heard Sumter's voice in my head whisper, louder than the chewing sounds, louder than the discordant voices: "The All. It's the All. Our father who is the All."

FIVE

Playmates

≒ 1 ≒

I opened my eyes not more than a second later, and I was lying in the lumpy earth of the shack, and Sumter stood over me laughing. "Fooled you, Beau, fooled *you*." Then, hearing a noise, he turned toward one of the filthy windows and said, "Dang, here come the island geeks."

I felt like I had gotten caught in some undertow and had almost drowned. I blinked several times to make sure that whatever I had just imagined I'd seen was definitely not there. I sat up. "What the hell," I gasped. I felt the earth spinning around me and wondered if I would be sick. I felt some kind of pressure beneath the skin at the base of my skull, like something pushing down hard from beneath the bone, trying to get out. When Uncle Ralph had his hangovers, he moaned about his head feeling like it would split, and this is what it felt like, but a hangover without ever having had a drink. "What was *that*?" I asked. I looked back at the crate, but it was just that, a crate. I thought for a second that I heard something scuttling around inside it, but it could've been my imagination. I thought I heard something *breathing* inside that crate. "What you got in there?"

But Sumter didn't pay me any mind. "Shh, Beau, I think we got *spies* outside." His attention was completely on the window.

I glanced up to it and saw faces pressed up against the glass: A girl and two boys were peering in.

THERE was one other group native to the peninsula besides the Gullahs. They were known as white trash, and they were almost a tribe. Gullahs were somewhat respected, even if in a condescending way. They tended to be employed and were more often than not smarter than the tourists. But the white trash were another story. They were drunk and raucous and filthy and just bad to know. To those of us from off-island, anyone who could be comfortably slotted as white trash were, in effect, of the lowest caste and untouchable. It was the meanest thing you could call anyone in the South, and on Gull Island they were like dirt beneath fingernails, people to feel superior to. The only group Grammy Weenie despised more than white trash were carpetbaggers, although I do believe that she might insist that these groups were one and the same.

These three kids peering at us through the window were definitely white trash. Grammy Weenie always said, "Don't you get involved with those white trash, just let them crawl back under the rocks from which they came."

Sumter went up to the window and growled at the white trash kids. "We shoot spies at dawn," he said, flipping the bird at them.

But the girl licked the dirty window, sponging her tongue in a snail trail across the pane. One of the boys ran around to the door to Neverland and pushed it boldly open, waiting for his companions before he would take a step in.

⊰ 2 ⊱

The girl's name was Zinnia, she told us in her almost unintelligible drawl, and she stepped through the door to Neverland as if she owned the place.

Her hair was lemon-juiced dirty blond, and she kept scratching at a place just above her forehead where her bangs curled down almost to her eyebrows. "Named for the flower, 'cause my ma tells me that I grow in the sunshine, and I seem to grow every five minutes."

"If you don't say the password, I'll cut your throat as soon as I look at you," Sumter snarled. He advanced on her with a rusty trowel, waving it threateningly. "No girls allowed." He aimed the trowel at her toes and threw it hard like a spear. It missed her toes by about ten inches, landing in the moldy earth.

But the girl was already inside, sniffing the air. "I come in here lotsa times. Don't need no password. This here's Goober and Wilbur," and the boys shuffled in behind her. All three wore shorts that ballooned out from their scrawny legs; the boys had no tops, but Zinnia had a sort of half top that exposed her small round belly and a series of moles like a connect-the-dot puzzle running along her back. She was ugly and pretty at the same time, which scared me. All three were dirty and sun-red and smelled just like the trash cans behind the house; I wouldn't have been surprised to see black flies buzzing around them.

"Hey," Goober said. He had a thick, greasy field of yellow hair on his head, practically growing out of his ears, and the biggest eyes I'd ever seen on such a small skinny face. His teeth were scummy yellow, and one of the front top ones was chipped.

Wilbur, dark and hungry looking, didn't say a word. He had mud on his feet up to his calves. Three scars were raked across his stomach.

"I know you put that word there," Zinnia said, tapping the back of the door. She traced her finger along the curlicue lines of the Day-Glo cuss word. "And I know what it *means*." Then she lifted her half top up to expose her mosquito-bite nipples and said, "I even done it before."

Drool spilled from the side of Goober's mouth as he said, "We all done it. You like her?"

I'd never seen Sumter so contained. "I *said* get out. And put those titties away, willya?"

"It's a free country," Zinnia sniffed, lowering her top again over her chest. She gave Sumter a face and then looked the two of us over. "You own this place?"

"We own this property, and you're trespassing."

Wilbur grunted, turning back to the door, but Goober grabbed his arm. "Ain't goin' nowhere."

"We declare war on you and your kind," Sumter said calmly. He looked at me, nodding. "This here's our clubhouse."

Zinnia shot me a blank stare. "That right? Can we join your club?"

"Trash is all you are," Sumter muttered.

"What if I was to show you something?"

"I don't want to see your mealyworm itty-bitty-toilet-paper titties again."

"I can do something. Like a trick."

"Baloney."

"Just watch." Zinnia scrambled around in the dirt, picking up old broken clay pots and tossing them before finding what she wanted. She held something small and shiny up to the light—a piece of broken glass. She turned it back and forth in her fingers and then placed it on her tongue, which she rolled up. Then she shut her mouth and swallowed the glass.

Wilbur began clapping, hopping up and down, a smile like a jack-o'-lantern slicing across his face.

"*Jesus.*" Sumter screwed his face up in distaste. "I told you they were *geeks.* You in a freak show or something?"

When Zinnia smiled again, her tongue was red with blood. "Zinnie's real good at tricks," Goober said solemnly. "She's gonna be on TV or something one day and real rich and famous and livin' in Hollywood."

Then Zinnia, clutching her throat, rasped, "Oh, help me, *help* me." Her fingers scratched into the skin just below her chin. But then she was laughing. "Just teasin' you, just teasin' you," and she held up the piece of glass, tossing it back in a corner. She hadn't swallowed it after all. "I can make coins disappear, too. All kindsa things."

Sumter sighed. "I just wish you'd make *yourself* disappear."

She turned to me. "Is he always so foul?"

But I was watching her mouth: Her teeth were red from blood. "How'd you make your mouth like that?"

"Oh," she winked, "easy. I got this one tooth that's sharper than a snake's, and I just bite down on my gums and it starts to bleedin'." She opened her mouth wide and pointed out the tooth. It looked like she'd chipped it on one edge. "Just was born with it."

"It's 'cause she's part snake," Wilbur said, scratching his scalp. These were the first words he'd uttered. His voice was low and deeper than most boys our age—for these kids weren't more than a year or so older or younger than us.

Zinnia nodded. "Ma sometimes picks up cottonmouths to prove that Jesus is King. They never bit her but once or twice. You ever touch a snake? You ever *want*a?" She reached over with both hands and grabbed me and pressed her lips to mine. I recoiled from her touch, but not before I tasted the blood on her lips. She pulled her face back and reached up with her left hand and slapped me on the forehead. "That's how my ma sends the Holy Ghost into you, with tongues of fire and a rap-tap on the head."

We heard ringing from far off: Aunt Cricket clanging the dinner bell. Zinnia, who was smiling from her forced kiss, looked back toward the door to Neverland and said, "Who's that for?"

"For you, white-trash girl, and don't you dare try to put the Holy Ghost in me neither." Sumter bent down and picked up a rusty rake and threatened her with it. Zinnia started caterwauling like some animal in heat, pushing Goober and Wilbur back out the door.

Sumter waggled the rake around, bashing it down into the ground. "It's the Devil ringing his bell for you, white trash." He held the rake up like it was a giant razor, shaving at the air in front of her face.

Zinnia ran out of Neverland faster than her two friends, racing out of there and into the scraggly woods, down to the edge of the bluff. The boys took off in opposite directions, one out to the main road, the other to the eastern side of the Retreat, their arms flailing out as they ran, hooting and hollering.

I watched Zinnia go, the first girl who had ever kissed me. She stopped at the chalk-white path that would lead her down to the beach. She looked back at me as I stood there, having come around the side of the shack to watch her. Her hair floated in wisps around her head; the sun was red behind her and it looked like a halo on an angel. I could not see the expression on her face, but she waved, and I could not help but wave back.

Sumter came up from behind me. "Don't encourage her." He grabbed my waving hand and brought it down. Then he returned to shut the door to Neverland, checking the lock. "I got to get a combination lock for this place or all kinds of garbage will find its way in."

As we walked back to the house, our feet getting sucked into the asphalt tar pit of the driveway, he curled his lips up as if he were sucking a lemon. "Yuck, I bet she tasted like a three-day-dead bluegill." Sumter laughed, swatting me on the back.

Her lips had tasted to me like nothing, but my own lips felt funny. My whole face felt funny. "I think I got bit by some bug," I said, scratching at the back of my neck. My whole scalp was itchy, but I figured it was mosquitoes. My mother had forgotten to hose me down with Off!, and we'd of course been eaten alive out on Rabbit Lake because of it. I generally preferred the mosquito bites to the smell of Off!, but it felt like all the bloodsuckers had aimed for the top of my scalp and nowhere else.

BACK home, while Sumter and I were washing up, Missy sat on the edge of the big old claw-footed bathtub and filled us in on the shopping trip. "We ate at the counter at Ruley's Five and Dime, and Mama kept talking about how Daddy was just a selfish so-and-so. All week she's been like this. And Governor just bawling his eyes out. Too, too much."

"I wish for just once in your life you'd get it right, Missy, just once." Nonie stood in the doorway filing her nails with a dull emery board. Her face was already peeling from the sun, but it was all mushed over with some of my mother's calamine lotion. "It was Aunt Cricket who said the stuff about Daddy, and I swear Mama was gonna slap her if she kept talking him down. That Aunt Cricket gets *nasty* when she wants, blah-blah Sunny this and blah-blah Sunny that, as if he's some little angel, and when *your* name comes up, let me tell you, she ain't got a thing good to say but how *sorry* she is that you're so *afflicted* with bad circulation and a melancholy temperament and *where*, she was wondering, *does all that come from?* Meaning *Daddy's* at fault on account'a her little precious ain't got nothing the matter with him. Aunt Cricket's a regular b-i-t-c-h."

"Can't help what my mama says," Sumter muttered.

Missy nodded, admitting her mistake. "That's right. Aunt Cricket said the bad stuff, but I think Mama is just fed up. And shoot, Beau, she must've bought up the entire store at Four Gals. She bought a dress that cost over a hundred dollars and then some."

"She wears such ugly things, it's about time," Sumter said, drying his hands off. "My mama says Aunt Evvie's got the worst taste in the world."

"Oh, huh, Sumter, yeah, huh," Nonie said sarcastically. "You believe everything your mama tells you, do you, huh?"

Sumter whapped her with the hand towel. "I believe things because I know 'em. Like today, we saw a girl take off all her clothes. She kissed Beau."

"He's a liar. She didn't take her clothes off."

"She started to. She kissed him."

"You got kissed." Nonie nodded her head up and down, amazed.

Missy began repeating "Wow" over and over to herself.

"She kissed him like this." Sumter poked his face against Nonie's and slathered his tongue across her lips. She slapped him and pushed him away, spitting his kiss into the sink.

"And he *liked* it. Beau got a boner."

"Did not. Just shut up," I said.

"Beau got a boner," he repeated, "and she was only white trash. Now we know what *he* likes. Now we know what *he* likes."

From the hallway Mama called out, "You children come to supper, now, or there won't be any left for you."

Uncle Ralph had only caught one catfish that day, and Daddy said it was hardly larger than the bait he'd used. "I felt bad for it." He grinned, sipping his beer. He patted the place next to him, between him and my mother, for me to sit at. "I was thinking maybe we ought to let it go. I think it was a newborn."

"It was big enough before it got cleaned," Uncle Ralph grumbled.

"You still smell like that lake." My mother wrinkled her nose at me as I sat down to the table. "Didn't you wash up like I asked?"

Grammy Weenie was distracted. Her eyes were like blue beads off of Nonie's costume jewelry necklace. She wore her thick reading glasses, and she had her little red Bible laid out in front other. I saw her from the side and noticed fine white hairs along her chin.

We had the tiniest catfish tidbits for dinner, and Sumter refused to eat anything except his corn. He nibbled at it the way cartoon characters did, like it was a typewriter and every time he came to the end of each side he'd make a noise like a tinkling bell: "Ding!" He wanted to sit his teddy bear at the table with him, but Uncle Ralph made him keep Bernard in the living room.

"But, Ralph, Sunny looks so sad without him," Aunt Cricket cooed. Her face was flushed and shiny, the way it always got whenever she spent the day shopping; it may have been the makeup she wore, or it may have been the thrill of the hunt. She'd pulled her hair back into a small Danish pastry on the side of her head, and this seemed to tighten the skin around her ears so that they looked pointy. "It's only a bear," she reminded my uncle, her pointy ears bobbing as she spoke.

Uncle Ralph looked at his son like he couldn't believe a boy like that could exist for very long under scrutiny. "I don't give a damn. I should've left that thing in a Dumpster back in Marietta when we had the chance. He's gonna be some kind of sissy if we don't get rid of that thing." Turning his attention to my father, he said, "I don't know what I did to deserve this. If he'd only take an interest in something, I tell you, something like bowling or even Matchbox cars, like a regular boy. I don't see your kid playing with dolls, Dab."

My father looked like he was about to say something, but held himself back. He winked at me. "Beau, you want to play with a Chatty Cathy, you go right ahead."

Grammy Weenie looked up from her Bible. She removed her glasses, holding them in midair. "Babygirl had an actual bear for a pet when she was a young girl. She'd found it as a cub and trained it, but in the end Old Lee had to shoot it. Babygirl was good with animals; she had sympathy for them. Not much interested in people, mind you, but bears and such . . . "

"Oh, Mama, really," my mother said, "why in God's name would there be a *bear* on Gull Island?"

"There was a *carnival*, dear, a *circus*, and there were *cubs*. You were only four, so how can you be expected to remember? Cricket was barely two. Babygirl was nine by then." Grammy sighed, seeing that my mother was ignoring her. "There was a *storm* and the *bears* got *loose*. It happens in the world, Evelyn Jane. Not everything is the way you remember it."

Mama looked at Aunt Cricket and then back down to her plate.

Aunt Cricket pretended she was interested. "I remember Babygirl talking about her bear. She had other pets, too, didn't she? She always went for long walks in the woods."

Under his breath Uncle Ralph muttered, "She was just an idiot, as far as I could tell. Making up stories like a gooney bird."

"Bernard would claw you up before you had your gun out and aimed," Sumter said. He reached up and parted the hair along his scalp. I assumed he had also been ravaged by mosquitoes that afternoon. He scratched furiously at the rim of his ears.

"How're your memoirs coming, Rowena?" Daddy asked.

Grammy Weenie made a sucking noise with her mouth; Sumter kicked me under the table; Aunt Cricket raised her eyebrows and I knew what she was thinking: *senility*.

"I am writing what I think happened," Grammy said. "Although one can never be sure if one is seeing things as an adult sees them or as they were seen as a child. And there is a difference. Big Daddy himself I barely remember, physically, and the Giantess from Biloxi is only a shadow and a voice. I remember not a shred of kindness nor mercy from either of them." She offered up a bittersweet smile, her eyes shining a bit in the light as if they held back tears. "My childhood seems terribly empty when I think on it. It was after I had children of my own that my recollections become better."

Then, brightening a bit, she laughed lightly. "Until I married Old Lee, I had no friends at all. But young ladies lived like that in those times. Then, my girls came along. Oh! How they were like flowers in a perfect garden! I love all my daughters equally, whether they choose to believe that or not, but because of Babygirl's sensitive temperament and the fact of her being firstborn, I suppose she and I were able to be the closest. She was always a child, even up until she died, always like a little girl, even in her twenties."

Then, that etching of sadness overcame her, the deep plunge that I often felt around my grandmother as if life were a precipice and, at any moment, she might fall from it. "Sometimes . . . I feel her. Tugging at my hands, brushing my hair. Those we lose are never really gone, are they? They are there, at least insofar as we remember them, and they have not really left us at all. Why, Dabney, it's just like she will walk back in that door and sit with us at the table. Perhaps if she had been home with us when she died, I might not remember her so clearly, but she left, you know, and went away, and there she died and there she is laid to rest. But it's as if she had never really done anything but walk out the back door one day. Perhaps, on another, she might walk right in through the front."

Grammy dabbed at her eyes with her grease-stained napkin.

Nonie, across the table from me, rolled her eyes. She hated Grammy's stories, particularly about Babygirl, our late aunt. None of us had ever met her, and we often doubted her existence, considering how many stories were spawned by her short life of thirty years. Grammy had been in her late thirties when she'd had her children, unusual for her day, and even stranger given the fact that Grammy often spoke on the subject of why women in their twenties should be the only bearers of children. "Anything can happen when you're older," Grammy would warn my sisters, "your babies can have all kinds of complications." Aunt Cricket would often remark that Babygirl was from Mongolia and that neither she nor Mama were much allowed to play with her. Grammy would say, "It was a tragedy, but sometimes I think she was lucky to have her life end so young—the indignities of age and a graceless family were never visited upon her." Grammy was most animated when telling death stories.

Mama clicked her fork on her plate. "I remember her, Mama, and the way she loved the dolls. I liked playing dress-up with her."

Governor made his *dit-do* noise.

"Dit-do," I said back to him, cocking my head to the side.

My baby brother looked at me like I was crazy.

Grammy Weenie continued her rambling. "About that bear, the bear had fur the same red color as her hair."

Aunt Cricket interrupted, "It was blond."

Grammy shook her head. "You only saw her in the summers when she'd been in the sun. I am her mother. Do you think I don't know my own daughter?"

"*Sometimes* . . . " Mama said under her breath, and then stopped herself.

Grammy continued, "Although y'all are just too young to remember. Her hair was like fire and ashes. Mine was always light, like Sumter's. Nobody's got that kind of hair, but it was beautiful, I can tell you. She wore it long, and once, as the story goes, she was brushing it at an upstairs window in the Biloxi house, she was only fifteen, and someone called the fire department because they saw the red of her hair reflected in the window glass and thought it was fire. As God is my witness, that's a true story. The whole town came out that day to see her hair. Of course, she was terrified of them, and never went to the window again. *People* she was never fond of. She loved children—but then, she was a child herself."

"She was not a redhead," Mama said, and then did what she always did when she was tense, which was to whistle in a way that was half "Camptown Races" and half whisper like she was blowing through bamboo. The dinner table was always the place for tension and frustration, and I glanced from Mama to Grammy Weenie to Daddy to Uncle Ralph to Aunt Cricket, and all the grown-ups looked just like little children, sulking and pushing their food around with their forks. Unhappy, spoiled children. Sumter, across from me, was grinning just like he'd won a bet, and his eyes got small and crinkly, his face all sunburned and shiny.

Hoping to get everyone out of their moods, I said, "Sumter's a toadhead."

"Son of a—" The words were barely out of Sumter's mouth when his father's hand was out and slapping him hard on the lips. The resulting whack silenced us all.

Aunt Cricket pretended nothing had happened. "Sunny's a *tow*head, Beau. Bright like sunshine. That's why I call him Sunny."

She stroked her hand through Sumter's wispy hair, but as she did this, she seemed distracted. She brought her fingers up, rubbing them together as if they were greasy. "Where you boys been today, anyway?"

"Fishing," I said.

"After that? You been around any dogs?"

"Huh?"

"They were playing in the woods," Uncle Ralph snorted.

"What is it?" my mother asked.

"*Dit-do.*" Governor said to me, his lips pursed together.

Something like a distant light washed across Aunt Cricket's face, her eyes squinting and then enlarging. As if having a sudden revelation from Almighty God—which Aunt Cricket occasionally had—she pushed herself up swiftly from the table and said, "You boys get away from the table right now and go into the bathroom and do not get near anybody or anything on your way!"

"Crick?" Uncle Ralph screwed his face up.

"Head lice," Aunt Cricket scowled, "Sunny has *head* lice, and now we all probably do." She pointed in my direction. "Who have you been playing with, what kind of mischief have you gotten my boy into?"

⊰ 3 ⊱

It had not been the Holy Ghost that Zinnia had slapped into my scalp, but hungry lice.

In all the time I was growing up, I'd never had head lice before, even when every other kid in elementary school had. I felt sure that by age ten you were immune to those little buggers. I will never forget the next day and night, the tar shampoo stinging my eyes, the itchy feeling of just knowing that I was crawling with tiny parasites all laying their eggs on my head, the scraping of needles on my scalp as my mother drew a fine-tooth comb through my gummy hair.

By the end of that first week on Gull Island, we'd all had head lice and we'd had to boil our clothes and practically burn our scalps with all the shampooings and combings. Sumter and I were the easiest to deal with because we had short hair.

As it turned out, Nonie and Missy also inherited the dreaded cooties. Missy held me personally responsible for the terrible haircut Mama gave her that summer.

⊰ 4 ⊱

I remember summers on Gull Island as being all begrudging mornings and afternoons that went on forever like a school day: hot and sticky and smelling like a stagnant pond.

Grammy Weenie sat among us beneath the big oak tree in the front lawn. I had Governor on my lap. I bounced him up and down and covered his eyes and said, "Where's Governor? Where did he go?" Sometimes

101

Missy would lean over, pressing her face into our brother's stomach, and make a fart noise with her lips. It made Governor cackle with joy.

The other grown-ups were going out for an early dinner, specifically without children. Julianne had just left for the day, and if the idea of spending the better part of the afternoon and early evening with our grandmother would not put fear in our hearts, nothing would. Grammy's legs were tucked neatly to the side, and her wheelchair was folded and leaned against the tree trunk. As always, in her lap was the silver-backed brush. Nonie had been trying to swipe it since we'd arrived, but with no luck.

Grammy read from the Bible and told more stories about Big Daddy and the Giantess from Biloxi. Occasionally she would refer to her black composition books to refresh her memory. "Big Daddy, your great-grampa, was an honest man, although he was not overly fond of children. Consequently, I was often left alone when I was very young, and I'm not sure that is good for a child. I was thrilled when, much later in life, Old Lee and I were blessed with our first child, my precious Babygirl, even with her afflictions. None of us knows the will of God, so we must submit to His mystery of creation. And then came Evvie, and then Cricket."

"Don't you know any *good* stories?" Sumter interrupted. "Like scary stories, or bloody stuff or outer space stuff?"

"You want me to make things up? You of all people, Sumter, should know the dangers of that. No good ever came from imagining; it's a trap for messy thoughts. Babygirl had a strong imagination, but her mind was too tender for it. Old Lee said she was too frail for the world. So she lived in a world of her own creation. She never saw what really *was*."

"I like her already. She sounds like somebody I'd like to know," Sumter said under his breath to his teddy bear. "Too bad she's dead, too bad it was her and not the Weenie." In defiance of what we were supposed to be doing, which was obeying Grammy, Sumter got up and, dragging his teddy bear, stomped off toward the woods.

Grammy continued her story about Babygirl's thinking that the world of nature was so much more beautiful than her homes on Gull Island and in Biloxi. The sun shifted, and shadows fell across her lap until she lost her place and set her composition book down. "You girls can go play if you like," Grammy said, "but Beau, you and Governor stay with me awhile longer."

My sisters gave me a look as if they thought I was in trouble. They were only too eager to get inside and hog the TV.

After they'd left, Grammy asked, "You love your little brother?"

I looked down at Governor's face. He was round and fat like a big puffy maggot, and he was actually asleep. I nodded.

"You take care of him, then. Keep him from harm. Cain asked the Lord, 'Am I my brother's keeper?' and do you know the answer, Beau? The answer is *yes*. Are *you* your brother's keeper, Beau? Are you?"

I nodded again.

"I have sensed that some harm will attach itself to us—all of us. You take care of yourself—and him, too. All along, I knew, and perhaps I should not have done what I did. But at the time—what was I to do?" She extended her hand out to me, and I flinched. Grammy gasped. "Are you scared of me, Beau?"

I shook my head.

"You are. All children are, but I won't hurt you." She beckoned me to her lap. "Just as children were drawn to my dear and doomed first child, so they have always been repelled in equal measure by me. But appearances can be deceiving. I have never done anything in my life without first thinking of what's best for the children."

"I want to go inside. I want to watch TV."

"Just for a minute, come sit with me."

Clutching Governor against my chest, I went and sat a foot from her. She patted the edge of her long dress. I scootched over another few inches.

Grammy Weenie brought her face near mine. Her breath was foul like an open wound. I could practically see through the blue-veined skin of her face down to her shrunken skull. She almost had no nose—just an impression of nostrils. "It's fine to play make-believe, but don't let it out. Once out, it cannot be put back. You know the truth of things, I can tell. Let things stay make-believe." She had a voice like a hammer coming down on a pillow, all soft and hard at the same time.

I would've jumped up and run away right then, but I was worried about maybe hurting Governor if I did that, so I just sat very still and nodded my head until Grammy let go of me. She had closed her eyes like I wasn't even there. Her black composition book had fallen open, but I couldn't read a word that was on the page because every single line was crossed out over and over again until the paper was itself just about ripped through with lines. And in the blackest ink, practically engraved into the paper, were the words, *Forgive me for what I have done*, at the top and bottom of the page.

With her eyes still shut she said, "The mother is gone, but the father is calling you. If you hear him, do not go to him, for he will never let you come back."

"Daddy ain't calling for me."

"Listen."

I held my breath and strained to hear, but all I heard were the gulls and the wind through the trees.

"He ain't calling, Grammy."

"I tell you he is." Her eyes popped open and scared the bejesus out of me, and she grabbed me around the neck as if she were going to choke me and she whispered, *"He is calling children, and you must not go to him. Even Sumter . . . You must never, never walk in his shadow."* I felt like I was seeing my grandmother for the first time, and that she was a stranger, that her dried and wizened features, her white hair, the smell of her curdling breath was something I had never truly beheld. I thought what so many children must think: Old people are from another species; they are not one of us.

Governor started crying, and I guess I hollered, because it hurt where she was holding my neck and I was about to lose my balance. Grammy Weenie let go, her hand curling into a fist and then dropping down into her lap. I backed away from her a few steps and waited.

"Tell your sisters to come help me into my chair, Beau." But she would not look back up at me, and I could not bear to look at her the rest of that afternoon.

⊰ 5 ⊱

After dark I went outside again. In the woods the dirt was fresh and moldy between my toes. I stepped around wood chips and knocked the heads off mushrooms and puff balls. I clicked my flashlight beam on and off like lightning. I heard some shrieking bird as it flitted from tree to tree, and my family seemed a million miles away. My folks were back at the house knocking back some liquor, and I was supposed to be in bed. But among two families of drinkers, it was easy to sneak out. I was on my way to Neverland, thinking about what Grammy had told me. I either was or wasn't supposed to be doing something, I wasn't really sure. *Don't let it out.* That must be whatever was in the crate. So Grammy Weenie knew about Lucy. The other stuff about going to Daddy was a bit more confusing, but then Grammy Weenie was always a little touched in the head.

"Hey." I heard a voice like a combination bird and girl.

I stopped in my tracks and glanced around. The trees were not whispering, and no one ran between them.

"Hey-ey," the girl repeated.

"Hey?" I asked, spinning around, trying to find out the source of the voice. These trees were so skinny they were impossible to hide behind, and unless this girl were hanging off the edge of the bluff, she'd have to be flying above me.

On that off chance, I glanced up.

She was there, not flying, but balancing on a limb that swayed each time she spoke. She was an inky figure of a girl, and I could not see her face at all.

"'Member me?"

"Zinnia," I said, recognizing the voice. I shined my flashlight up at her. She winced when the light hit her. "How'd you get up there?"

"Flew. Can you help me down?" She was wearing a plain and dumpy dress that might as well have been a sack. As I started to make my first feeble attempts to scale the tree, only barely able to hold the flashlight at the same time, I looked up again and was greeted by the pale roundness of her white fanny. She wore no underwear. "Don't look up there or it'll bite you."

I dropped the flashlight and tumbled back to the ground.

Zinnia scampered down between branches like a monkey. The last two yards she leapt, and her dress billowed up like a parachute, and my eyes went wide. Her underside wasn't much like the pictures in *Playboy*. She landed on all fours. "Help a girl up when she's down, why don'tcha?"

I offered her my hand, which she grabbed and practically tugged me down into the dirt, she was so heavy. "How old are you?"

"Almost fifteen."

"Yeah, huh, and I'm eighteen and a half. You look twelve. I'm ten."

"You're old enough to know better. Where's your friend?"

"Sumter? He ain't my friend, he's just my cousin. I think he's in *there*." I pointed to the shed. "Where are your brothers?"

"Who knows? They come and go—you know boys. I mean, *you're* a boy, you must know boys. Can I be your girlfriend?"

"No."

"I wouldn't be if you paid me. That's what my ma always tells them. Wouldn't be if you paid me. What's your name?"

"Beau."

"Like a ribbon. What's your cousin got in there that's so special?"

"It's a secret." I remembered my oath.

"I bet it's not really. What's his name? *Summer?*"

"Sum*ter*. Where y'all live, anyway?"

"West Island. Big old house, and ma always gets herself mad at Goober and Wilbur if they's to walk across the floor with mud on their feet. You want me to kiss you like before? Felt real good to me. I know it felt good to you, I *saw* what I *saw*." I could smell her salty breath, and it was almost sweet to me. She turned her back on me and headed toward the shack. When she got near it, she bent over and picked up a big old rock and threw it at Neverland's door. "Hey, *Sumter!*"

"Shut up, shut up." I leapt for her and covered her mouth with my hand. I whispered, "Nobody's supposed to know we play in there."

Zinnia giggled and licked the palm of my hand until I had to let her go. "And nobody heard me, neither. And if you tell me to shut up again, I'm just gonna have to go tell your mama on you."

Slowly the door to Neverland opened. Sumter stood there in his swimming trunks. He looked at Zinnia and then over to me. "Don't forget the lice, Beau."

As if I'd just gotten a shock, I jumped back from Zinnia. I *had* forgotten the lice.

"If you got lice, it wasn't from *me*." Zinnia combed her fingers through her hair. "I am washed as *clean* as they come."

"Go home or die," Sumter said.

"Oh, *please, please*, let me see inside again. I won't tell, honest I won't, I'll be so dang good you could cry, honest to goodness, please."

Then something bad happened, and I knew it was bad just like I could smell it. It was like when rubber burned in Uncle Ralph's old car—you didn't know where it was burning, but you just sat there and smelled it and knew it was burning. Maybe it was Sumter's woken-up look or the way he licked the edge of his lower lip—like smoking rubber. "Okay," he said, still standing inside of Neverland, "only if you pass our test. Right, Beau? She's got to pass our test."

"Right," I said, bewildered.

"Test? I could probably teach you both a thing or two, myself." She sauntered on ahead of me, and I watched the twin spheres of her behind beneath the fabric of her dress twist and turn like she was clutching something between them with no chance of dropping it.

"Hey wait," I said, stepping toward them. But Zinnia was in, through the door, and it slammed shut. I heard the inside lock click into place, and I heard Zinnia giggle and say, "I don't get it." I banged on the door with my fists. It gave a little, and I worked my fingers in through a crack, but Sumter, on the other side, pushed it down on my fingers until it hurt so bad I had to let go.

From the other side of the door Sumter said, "Sorry, cuz, this is only a test. For the next sixty seconds this place will be conducting a test of the Emergency Neverland System. This is only a test."

I swore at the door and then ran around to the side window, but could not see in.

It was quiet for the longest time, and I was just beginning to wonder what was going on in there when I heard a shriek. It was so quick and sudden that I wasn't sure if it came from inside Neverland or not. Then the shriek melted into a series of giggles, and Zinnia was saying, "No, hee-hee, please—don't—hee-hee," and even the giggles got quieter and quieter until they died in a sudden silence. Then I heard her making sounds like she was trying to sleep and couldn't, and he was still tickling her, only she couldn't laugh anymore.

The trees were whispering: It was only a breeze through their branches. The waves below the bluffs bashed against the shore. I became aware of the humming of locusts all around.

A few seconds later the front door swung open again.

Sumter's face was pearly with sweat. "You saw her. She *made* me do that."

I could not say a word.

I stepped past him and saw her lying there, still. Zinnia's face was pressed into the dirt. Her arms crumpled under her chest. "She didn't pass the test, Beau. Lucy judged her and found her wanting."

My mouth opened and my jaw moved, but nothing came out.

"She's just white trash."

"You *killed* her? She's . . . "

"Another sacrifice. Like the dead bunny. To Lucy."

"She was just being *silly*, you sure she's . . ." I moved closer to the body. I reached down and touched her back.

She moved.

"She's not dead, Sumter, she's alive," I said, relieved that we would not spend the rest of our lives doing hard time.

"Not dead? Not *dead?*"

"Gawd, that was some joke you two, Jesus," I said, thinking it was, after all, a prank. I could've clobbered them both for scaring me like that.

"*Please*," Zinnia murmured.

"Joke's over," I told her, "you can get up now."

"*Make it stop*," she whispered, and, shining the flashlight across her face, I saw where the blood had run down from her lips.

"*Hurts*." The blood ran from her lips but was also pooled around her neck, and as I shined the flashlight down her body, I saw her dress had been pulled up, and carved into her stomach were the letters L and U and C.

"She's still *alive?*" Sumter shouted, pushing me out of the way, and in the flashlight's beam was that rusty trowel that he'd threatened her with before. He knocked the flashlight out of my hands so I didn't see him bringing the trowel down for her heart, but I heard it rip into her flesh and slam against a bone and dig down into her.

I stood there, in the darkness, shivering, my skin feeling like ice.

"Sacrifice, Beau, it's a sacrifice, and it's good. It's change, it's turning, it's *feeding*," Sumter muttered, and I could hear him lapping at something, and I knew it was her blood without having to see anything. "Everything eats *everything*. That's sacred, Beau, you get it? All don't come from nothing. All comes from *all*."

I could hear my heartbeat like it was thunder, and I counted the seconds between each crash.

One-alligator.

Two-alligator.

Three-alligator.

CRASH!

"Sumter," I whispered, "you killed her."

"She doesn't matter," he said, "you know she doesn't matter."

"Killed."

"And you helped."

"You."

From near the door I heard a low growl.

"Bernard," Sumter whispered, "stay down, boy."

I dropped to the ground and tried to throw up but found I could not. My hand touched the edge of the flashlight. I picked it up again. I directed my beam over to where I'd heard the growling, but all that was sitting over there was his dumb old teddy bear. Then I brought the light back over to Zinnia, and as the beam hit her, I just about peed my pants, because it wasn't her at all, but one of Grammy's Victorian dolls. Its blue silk dress ripped off and the trowel sitting straight up in its chest.

Its eyes were open and staring and dumb.

I heard Sumter laughing at me in the dark as the flashlight battery died and the light shut off.

"It's just a *game*, Beau, don'tcha get it?"

From a corner of the darkness I heard a girl giggling stupidly, giggling within those walls of darkness, and her giggling was like a contagious disease—because I started giggling, too, and then Sumter, and we giggled madly in the dark, and I felt her hand, *her hand*, reach over and press down on my stomach, and her fingers like furry spider legs, tickling me into more giggles, and I knew, *knew*, it was bad, what we were doing, but I could not tell her to stop.

"It's fun," Sumter said, his breath on my neck, "to play in the dark, ain't it?"

SIX

Opening the
Window

⊰ 1 ⊱

I walked back home alone that night feeling ashamed of everything that
had gone on in Neverland. Entering the normal world of my parents and
lying awake in my twin bed, I thought of the endless tickles and whispers
in the dark of the shed with both revulsion and delight. I could not bring
myself to think on it directly, but instead thought of it as something that
happened the way things happened in my dreams: kind of true, but not
part of the daylight world in which I did pretty much what I was told and
was a good boy for the most part. I was thrilled to have this secret life in
a secret place, to have given a blood oath, to be somehow part of a world
alien to the master-slave relationship of parent and child. Thrilled, yes, and
ashamed, too—gleefully ashamed.

I dreamed that night of other worlds, like in *The Martian Chronicles*, where the planet was blood-red and even grown-ups were not in
control.

⇥ 2 ⇤

It was inevitable that one of those days Missy and Nonie would follow Sumter and me out to Neverland. We could only keep it secret so long.

It happened soon after I called Nonie the B word. The word had finally gotten around to my mother, who told me to apologize formally at the dinner table, which I did while Sumter kicked me from beneath. Mama would normally have disciplined me further, but she had her hands full with Governor, who was crying a lot more than usual, and with my father. They were well into their summer clothes of arguing and stormy silences. Dad never provoked the arguments, but he was always on hand to see them through. My mother would say that he never wanted a family, and he would deny it and tell her it was her imagination, to which she would reply that there was nothing she could imagine that didn't already exist.

Grammy Weenie slapped the table that evening and said, "Thank God your father is dead, Evelyn. If he'd known you'd grown up into such an unfeeling, self-centered creature, he wouldn't want to live. You've become a very hard woman." *Hard* was the meanest adjective Grammy Weenie ever used, and it was worse than more explicit terminology. From *hard* there was no return, and it ranked just above *brazen hussy* on the scale of insults to women.

"Why'n't you kids go out and play before it gets too dark," Dad said, nodding to me. He was wearing a checkered short-sleeved shirt, and for every checkerboard there was a food stain.

"Yes," Nonie muttered sarcastically, "we can play like good children."

Uncle Ralph sniffed, "Only don't you girls get Sumter out playing dolls or dress-up. Y'all play a game of War or something."

"We *don't* play *dolls*." Nonie, again.

"Yeah," Sumter grinned, "a little W. W. Two action and we set off the bomb in our own backyard. Lights out for the Rising Sun?" He rose from the table so fast his chair skidded right back into the yellow wall. He and his shadow seemed to move in different directions, as if they were not joined at all.

"That boy . . . " Mama sighed, and Aunt Cricket shot her a cold glance.

Nonie gave me a nod. "Let's get out," she whispered. Missy excused herself politely, and I stubbed my toes trying to get away from that table before a full-fledged fight broke out.

⇥ 3 ⇤

"Jesus," Nonie gasped as if for air, "I wish they'd just divorce each other and not stay together for our sakes."

"Oh, don't say that," Missy worried. She kept flattening her blouse down, trying to define whatever breasts were dully sprouting there. "If you say it, it can happen."

"Big deal." Nonie pointed at Sumter. "*You.*"

"Yeah, huh?"

"Just that. I know about you."

"Yeah, what do you know?"

"I just do."

"You don't know nothing."

Nonie kept smiling secretly to herself. "There are more things in Heaven and Hell than are dreamed of in your philosophy."

Sumter turned to me. "You have a spooky family." He had his teddy bear on his lap. We sat on the front porch. The light was dimming, and fireflies were blinking on and off in the woods out by Neverland. The heat did not let up, even at twilight. It would just become dark and humid, and the slurping sound of the ocean would be silenced by the maracas of locusts in the trees. Sweat and mosquitoes bit at the backs of our necks.

"Well, let's play something. Like Red Light, Green Light," Missy said.

"That's a baby's game," Sumter muttered.

I said, "We could play kickball."

Sumter held Bernard's ears back and made growling noises.

"I wish there was something to do here," Nonie said. "There's nothing to do here. I am so tired of the hired help telling me what to do, too. Don't you hate that Julianne?"

"With all my heart and soul," Sumter replied, "but she's got hairy legs and so it can't be helped. She ain't all there."

Nonie slapped aimlessly at the mosquitoes. Her face was spongy with sweat. "I don't need a *baby*sitter. I'm old enough. I am so tired of that dumb old beach. I am so bored. Aren't y'all bored? Well, *I* am. Not even a good book. At least the head lice provided some mild diversion. This is worse than summer camp. God, I wish there was a way to destroy all mosquitoes and to make it not get so sweaty."

"What a mouth you got on you," Sumter said, "and you're only bored 'cause you got nothing inside you. You're like one of those seventeen-year locusts you break open, only there's no innards."

Nonie fanned herself with the flat other hand.

"I think it's pretty here." Missy sighed, her voice dreamy. She swayed back and forth on the front-porch swing. "I could look at the sea forever."

Her twin snorted derisively. "Natural beauty only does so much for me. If only there were boys."

"You horny?" Sumter asked. "Beau and me know some white-trash kids that might find someone like you interesting."

I felt my face flush red all over, thinking that my sisters could read all about the tickling and giggling and shadows of the night before.

Nonie wasn't even looking at me. "You are so gross. And I mean nice decent boys like those high school boys we saw at the shopping center."

"They were okay," Missy said.

"*Okay?* They were major hunks. Really mature-looking, too. One guy had a *moustache*."

"You are so boy crazy," I told her.

"A slut at twelve, in trouble by fourteen, that's what Mama says," Sumter said. He had maneuvered his teddy bear around on its paws to make it look like it was crawling like a real bear. Every now and then he'd growl and pretend it had come from Bernard.

"Well, I only have one more year to work on it. Almost thirteen, and don't you forget it, twit."

"*I* know," Sumter brightened, "*I* know what we can do. We can play in Neverland."

I screwed my face up, trying to figure him out. He wasn't supposed to tell them. *I* wasn't supposed to tell them.

"What's that?"

"It's my clubhouse. Beau's and mine."

"You mean that run-down old shed? Jesus, wouldn't *that* be fun. We could play with spiders."

"Nonie, you are so cynical."

"I'd like to see your clubhouse," Missy said to me. She looked so sad with her choppy hair and that peeling skin along her sunburned nose.

Sumter rubbed his hands together, scheming. "I've got beer there."

I gasped. "Beer?"

"I snuck one of Daddy's out. We could all share it."

"But we'd get *drunk*," Missy said, horrified by the idea. We were all such good kids in spite of our longing to be bad, and since beer was the vice of our fathers, we longed for a taste. "And then we'd get in trouble. Oh, boy, would we get in trouble big-time. Oh wow."

But Nonie was genuinely interested. "You've got *beer?* And nobody found out?" She got up and brushed the dust off her behind. She had one of the largest behinds I'd ever seen on such a skinny girl and longer legs than Missy. I used to think that Aunt Cricket was right about her, that she was going to get in trouble sooner or later. "Well," she brightened, "what are we waiting for? Let's go."

As we trooped along the edge of the bluff, batting at mosquitoes the whole way, I whispered to my cousin, "What do you want *them* along for?"

He didn't answer me, at least not aloud, but in my head I imagined I heard his voice.

I don't want them. Lucy *wants them.* Lucy *asked* for them. *Lucy wants* all *of us.*

⊰ 4 ⊱

Neverland at twilight was all angular shadows crisscrossed along the walls. Nonie and Missy seemed as fascinated by the *Playboys* as we boys had been, only they couldn't see much of them in the fading light. We had our flip-flops on so we were not too careful of the glass on the ground, and Missy picked up the rake and began sweeping the glass and other debris to the side.

Nonie glanced around. "This is kinda cool." She shrugged. "Okay, so where's the beer?"

Sumter lifted a finger in the air. "Follow me." He set his teddy bear down on an overturned flowerpot and led us back to the crate. He brought a tall can of Budweiser out from behind his crate. We sat in a circle, Indian style. He popped the tab of the beer. He whispered something into the can.

I asked him what he was doing.

"Blessing it," and he took a sip. "It's warm."

"That's okay," Nonie said, "I like it warm." She plucked it from his fingers and took a long, hard swig.

"Since when have you had beer before?"

"I have. You just weren't there. You were a baby."

"Oh, *huh.*"

We passed the can around, all of us sipping, all of us wondering when we would start to feel drunk.

Sumter said, "Nothing like a beer on a summer evening." It was what his dad would say.

"You think they'd be really angry if they smelled it on our breath?" Missy asked.

"Does a bear poop in the woods?" Nonie asked, and then giggled. "I mean, is the Pope Catholic?"

"You're just acting drunk," I said. "You can't get drunk from two sips."

"I took more than two sips. This place smells like it's dead. Somebody die?" She was still giggling.

Missy started giggling, too, for no reason, and then I let out a giggle. Giggles were dangerous in that place, and I wondered where these would lead to.

"What if they catch us?" Missy's eyes went wide, and all the giggles subsided.

Then we burst out laughing, louder.

The skin felt warm along the surface of my face. A light seemed to have come up in the room, for everyone's face was yellow and rosy and dimpled like overripe peaches. I could see more things around us, a swirling pattern from the walls. Could you get drunk off just a few sips of warm beer? So it seemed. I tried to talk, but the words rushed so fast in my head that they never made it out of my mouth. Sumter was whispering to Nonie, who was pointing at me and laughing and nodding her head. Missy had her eyes closed and was moving her shoulders in time to some unheard music.

"Sumter," I said, but he was busy talking to Nonie, who opened her left hand up for his inspection. He traced a line with his index finger down her palm.

"Sumter," I repeated, and he looked at me for one second, but then returned his attention to my sister.

Missy started humming a tune only she could hear, but I couldn't quite make it out. The light was coming up brighter in Neverland, until it seemed almost like daylight.

Sumter had something small and shiny in his hand, and he scraped it across Nonie's thumb. She jumped a little.

No.

It was the rusty hook that he'd pricked my own thumb with. Something deep within me fought to try to stop him, but the good warm feeling of the

117

beer held me back. A mosquito lit on the edge of my hand, and I just sat and watched it suck the blood out. I watched it get fat and round, but I did not swat it. Sumter turned to his right and grasped Missy's thumb. She kept her eyes closed. She was now singing to the music in her head, but she sang the way I'd heard people sing in the Holy Roller churches when they were speaking in tongues. The hook went up and down into the thumb of her left hand and she let out a little squeal. I watched him milk her thumb and press it into his hand, while his other hand squeezed Nonie's. My sisters reached around with their free hands and held mine, the beer can laying empty in the middle of our circle. I felt blood flow between us all, joined palm to palm. Our voices in my head mingling, too, repeating the oath of secrecy and loyalty to Neverland, and then to one other, and then to Lucy.

No other gods before me.

Yes! Our voices cried, and it was both inside and outside my head. *Yes! No other gods before Lucy.*

We swear.

With our blood.

And then we began to fly.

⊰ 5 ⊱

At first we rose up unsteadily, still clutching each other's hands, and I thought we were standing, but we were moving up under the roof of the shack. My head pressed against it and then we began moving *through* the roof, out into the evening, flying as if with some direction, all holding hands, now afraid to let go. Nonie was laughing, exhilarated, and Missy was pop-eyed with wonder.

A dream? I heard Nonie cry out.

No, Sumter crowed, *we're really flying.*

Our feet brushed the roof of Neverland, and we headed up above the trees, disturbing the uppermost branches in our ascent.

I'm scared. Missy said to me, squeezing my hand tighter.

It's not real, I told her, *it's Neverland*.

Seems so real. She closed her eyes, afraid.

Below us we saw the ragged Retreat, the light on in the kitchen and the living room where the grown-ups would be, the upstairs dark. But we were flying and swooping together, the toes of our flip-flops brushing leaves off the tops of the trees. As we flew up higher I yelled to Sumter, *Where?*

To the moon, Beau, all the way to the moon.

There was no moon that night, and dark fingers were all around the edges of the sky.

Beau! Some other voice intruded. I glanced down to the Retreat. It was Grammy Weenie. She had wheeled out to the front porch, opening the screen door. *Make him stop. Beau! He'll hurt you!*

Don't listen to the old witch. Sumter said.

We began flying faster upward, straight upward, and the peninsula below us became smaller and smaller, and the darkness became wider. The only light now was the twinkling tiara bridge.

To the stars. Sumter was panting hard, as if he were running up stairs.

I looked upward, but there were no stars—just a ceiling of darkness.

It hurts. Missy moaned, her fingers loosening their grip in mine.

It was getting harder to breathe, and I felt an enormous pressure on my eardrums, and then they began popping. Missy was screaming. *Let me go! Let me go!* She writhed around. Nonie, too, was in pain: Her nose was wrinkling, and her mouth contorted as if with a sour taste. I could barely breathe now. My neck felt stiff; my spinal cord wanted to wriggle out of my back.

We're going too high, Sumter, get us down. I gasped for air.

Missy's nose started bleeding. *Oh, God.* She opened her mouth wide to take in deep gusts of air while blood dribbled out of her nostrils. Her body spasmed, jerking, and her hand tugged free of mine. Sumter let go of her, and we watched as Missy fell screaming back down to earth. Nonie's head began shaking, her whole body shivering—*Head hurts, Sumter, please—*

It's a dream, Sumter! Wake us up! You wake us up!

Don't let go, Beau, Sumter said, but I could see panic in his face as we continued to move upward. *She shouldn'ta let go, we'll be okay. You've got to believe. Lucy wants us, all of us, to believe.*

You better wake us up right now, Sumter, you made this happen and now you can unmake it!

Nonie was writhing in my grasp; we heard Missy's final scream as she hit the earth.

LUCY! I cried, *LUCY! DON'T LET HIM DO THIS TO US!*

My voice was high-pitched and shrill because I was as scared as I had ever been. The sky shattered from the sound, and I watched the earth below us rip apart like skin.

And then we awoke, all still holding hands, even Missy. We were sitting up around the beer can, and we had not flown, and it had been some kind of dream. The brilliant light around us was fading back into shadowy twilight. Neverland was a shack, and my sisters and cousin were dark with shadows.

"Wow." Missy glanced down at her hands.

"That was neat," Nonie said, gasping and laughing all at once. "Let's do it again. Please, Sumter?"

When Sumter opened his eyes, he looked very cross.

I was still hallucinating. I sat in Neverland with my sisters, but I continued dreaming.

We all sat there.

Missy.

Nonie.

Sumter.

Me.

But their skin.

Blackened and smoking, the flesh peeled back around their skulls, hair burned completely off. Eyes had burst and run down across cheeks and noses and lips like melting wax. Missy still giggled. "Completely cool, I really thought we were flying."

Nonie grinned liplessly at me, her teeth seeming huge and yellow. "What's *your* problem?" Her arms dropped skin like bits of tattered carbon paper as she placed her crisp hands on her hips imperiously.

Sumter was the worst, though. His skull had burst in on itself, and wisps of flame danced along its edges as if he were filled with dying coals. "You see it, don't you?" he asked. "You stupid . . . "

I closed my eyes, and then opened them again.

Still the burned apparitions were sitting around me. Bile dripped from Missy's gaping mouth while she giggled.

"You're not supposed to see it. Why would Lucy *let* you see it?" The burst face waggled side to side. "Only *I'm* supposed to see it. It's not *fair. Lucy, this is not fair, you said only me,* only *me.*"

"Make it stop," I said.

Nonie wiped charcoal fingers through her crusty scalp.

"Make it go away."

"Only me," the burned Sumter-thing whimpered. "Only *I* can see. Not *him.*"

Grammy Weenie's voice was in my head, what she'd said the other afternoon. *Don't let it out.*

"Put it back, Sumter, just put it back," I whispered.

"Don't you tell me—"

"Put it back. Don't let it out."

His whole body began smoking furiously, like a furnace about to blow. I heard the crackling of his bones as they heated.

"Put it back. Where it belongs."

"You can't tell me—"

But the fire that was brightening in his open rib cage died. He seemed to be listening to something, some voice. "Lucy," he said.

I once plugged a vacuum cleaner cord into a socket and held the plug wrong so I got a shock that threw me down. That's what this was like. A triple flash of white light as if there were a white world beyond the skin of this one, and then I felt thrown across the room, although I was still sitting, cross-legged, in the small circle. I had not moved at all.

I was afraid to look at the others, but when I did I was relieved to observe they were all covered with flesh and clothes and only looked slightly tired. It was nice to see my sisters again, alive, in their cutoffs and untucked shirts.

"What's your problem?" Nonie asked again.

Sumter was working hard to keep back tears in his eyes, which made them even shinier and more hateful than before. "It was only *pretend*," he said to me. "You *liked* it when it was with Zinnia. Well, it's all the same, you like it once, you gotta keep on liking it, Beau, because it *ain't never, never gonna go away no more.* I'm gonna let it out when I want, hear?"

⊰ 6 ⊱

That night I could not sleep. I sat up reading *The Martian Chronicles* and wished I was on Mars even though horrible things seemed to be happening there. I had a flashlight under the sheet so that anyone passing in the hallway wouldn't see any light under my door. It was hard to breathe, and I was sweating like a pig, but the world of that book cooled me off some—until the pages began falling out and distracted me. Sometime after midnight, when the house was quiet, I got up and went to use the bathroom. I heard the scraping of Grammy Weenie's wheelchair coming from just below me, down in the hallway.

I froze.

She was muttering to herself as she wheeled into the light on the stairs. She stopped there, and her profile reminded me of someone. Her hair was down around her shoulders and was as white as the farthest stars seem on the blackest night. She was brushing her hair with her silver-backed natural-bristle brush. I had never seen her hair unbraided before, and it made her look young because it was so long and thick. If I squinted I could see her as she must've been before I was born: so beautiful, and so distant and cold. Neither my mother nor my aunt had quite inherited those looks, but I saw someone there in that face. Someone I had never seen before there. Sumter. He had inherited the masculine version of those looks, and both had the white hair.

Suddenly Grammy Weenie dropped the brush to her lap and reached with her hands to wheel around and glance up the staircase. I ducked down low by the banister at the top of the stairs but knew she couldn't see me, both because of her bad eyesight and the stair light shining on her face.

Grammy Weenie whispered, "Is it you? Are you coming for me now? Come out, then, come out and we'll see what can be done about this."

I was afraid she was talking to me, but her eyes were fixed on another point on the stairs.

There, sitting propped up and off to the side, was Sumter's teddy bear.

Grammy Weenie whispered, "Fine, then. Make it go back to that special place I showed you. Make it stop. Good. It's important to have a place to go to, somewhere you can keep things to yourself."

⊰ 7 ⊱

For the next twenty-four hours Sumter would not speak to me. I couldn't figure out what it was that I was supposed to have done. If I tried to say anything to him, he'd reply through his bear.

"Sumter?"

He'd whisper in Bernard's ear: "Tell my cousin to go away."

"C'mon, don't be such a baby."

To Bernard he'd say, "Tell him I have more important things to think about."

I moped around that Saturday, not interested in watching television or going down to the beach with my sisters and Julianne Sanders, who warned me that my face would freeze in a pout if I didn't try smiling.

The grown-ups went to the market, although Grammy Weenie was around to watch Sumter and me. She just sat in her chair with her big rectangular magnifying glass she used for reading and pored over the Book of Revelations, another of her biblical favorites.

She loved reading aloud about the Beast of the Apocalypse and the Horsemen.

"Every day of our lives we see the Beast," she said, "and every day we must face our Creator and the fires that do not cease."

Certain times I was sure she didn't even notice us kids, and other times we were just like the flies that stole in through the torn porch screen to be swatted. She seemed to retreat into what she called her "perfect world of books."

"If only I were blind," she said, "then I could learn Braille and shut out the ugly place this world has become and live in a more spiritual time. I am not unhappy that I have momentarily lost the use of my legs, because where should I go? There is no place where I want to be."

Even while Sumter didn't speak to me, I tagged after him when he went out to Neverland. I stood by and watched as he unlocked the door. But I didn't follow him in; I knew he didn't want me there.

⊰ 8 ⊱

I went to the beach with Julianne Sanders and my sisters for the next several days, leaving Sumter to his own devices. Like all children, I thought my family was the strangest one in the universe, and perhaps it truly was. The girls were generally spooked by the hallucinations we'd had two days before in the clubhouse, but Nonie thought it was all innocent enough: She figured the beer had gotten us going. "I read somewhere about mass hypnotism, and you know with the beer and our thumbs all bleeding, that's probably what happened. Sumter is *such* a weirdo." Missy tried to shush her because of the blood oath we'd taken. Although neither of them could quite remember what they had sworn to do, Missy was pretty sure it involved secrecy, and the twins were pretty good at keeping secrets, at least between each other.

"It's not just hypnotism," I said. "There's something in that shack."

Nonie clucked her tongue, "Well, it was kinda cool but kinda weird, too. More excitement than I expected in this place. You don't think he did anything like give us LSD?"

"What's that?" I asked.

Acting smarter than everyone else was one of Nonie's special talents. "It's what hippies put in other people's drinks so they'll think they're Superman and jump off buildings."

"Watch the rocks," Julianne warned us as we tromped down the chalk-white path along the bluffs. She was walking several feet ahead of us, ignoring our talk.

"I just wish there were some boys or something," Nonie said just as we got to the end of the path. She was walking funny because her flip-flops had caused blisters on her big toes and she had wrapped her feet in Band-Aids and gauze. She told me it felt like she was walking on knives and she could feel each little pebble under her feet. Missy had one of my mother's broad, straw sun hats as well as her sunglasses and had slathered her face with white creamy suntan lotion.

When we reached the gritty beach, we made camp. I thrust the striped red-and-yellow umbrella down deep and opened it while Julianne spread out the towels. "We can look for shark's teeth," she said, "and if we find enough, you can make a necklace."

"You think there's sharks?" Missy asked.

"I know it. Not man-eaters, but sharks. You notice I don't go swimming in this water."

"You let *us* go. Why'n't you tell us about sharks before?"

"Your business if a shark takes a nip from your thigh. All those fishing boats chase the feeder fish in, and the bigger fish follow them, and then the sharks go for them. It's to be expected. But I'd be less afraid of the sharks than the jellyfish."

Missy nodded. "I got stung four times last year. It was worse than a bee sting."

"And the crabs, you know the way they close their claws around your toes?" Julianne continued. "I know they can't really hurt you, but it's dang scary."

"You're just saying it so we won't go in the water," I huffed.

"I won't deny it, but I'd think twice if I was you. It's a foolish boy who goes in over his own head. There's a whole world down there you can't see."

"Yeah, but if you don't go in, how're you ever supposed to find out what's there?"

"You need to get bit by something before you know it's got teeth? You need to cut your foot first before you put your shoes on?"

"Whether you put your shoes on or off, someday you get cut anyway."

"Yeah, smart man, but you don't *invite* it, do you? You don't stick your hand in the beehive and you don't walk across spikes, do you? You don't dance in the fireplace or eat broken glass, do you?"

"I heard Gullahs do all of that."

"You heard wrong, smart man, only *idiots* do it."

"She's got you there," Nonie said. "But Julianne, you must not know Beau too well because he *does* all those things. When he was six he tried to eat a tin can and cut his mouth all up. We told him not to, but he did, anyway."

Julianne raised her eyebrows and looked me over, up and down. "Well, now I see who you are, Beau. I see what you're made of."

"All right, who am I?"

"You're the one who does the things you ain't supposed to, just *because* you ain't supposed to. Now, that Sumter, he's something even more. He does the things he ain't supposed to because he thinks it's just what he's *supposed* to do."

"What's the diff?"

"You know right from wrong, only you do wrong, anyway. It's 'cause you're curious, and curious means being contrary. But Sumter, he thinks nothing's wrong. He thinks it's *all* right. Boys like that never get much taller than four foot."

"You mean like he won't grow? How's that gonna happen? Is he like a dwarf?"

"I mean like he'll never reach his full height; I ain't elaborating further. Now if you want to go out in that water, just be mindful of the crabs and jellyfish and sharks and anything else that's out there that we don't know about yet." Julianne had brought a paperback down with her, and she opened it. "Now y'all just be careful. I got a good book and I aim to read this in peace without nobody drowning."

I waded out into the water. It was cold. I glanced back to the beach and saw Missy waving to me. Nonie was lying on her stomach, facing the other way. Julianne had her book up to her face. The slight undertow sucked the sand over and beneath my toes so that with every step my feet sunk lower and lower. Tiny blue mollusks rose and fell with the water, burrowing down deeper as each wave sloshed the shore. They moved all at once, as if they had rehearsed this movement a thousand times, and as the water slapped them, they went down, then the sand dissolved around them, and then more water hit and they tried to dig deeper. I bent down and picked one of the tiny shells up and tossed it far out into the sea.

I went in deeper and began dog-paddling in the cold water. I thought, *I will just swim out as far as I can.* I tried not to think about the sharks that Julianne may or may not have made up. I wondered what the sea creatures must think when they look up and see a boy swimming above them. What instinct kept them darting beneath rocks, what made them afraid? Where did fear come from? I thought, *If I were a crab, how would I know to be afraid of something larger than me? How would I know to run across the ocean floor, to get away? And if Sumter were a crab, would he run* toward *the thing he should be escaping?*

It felt good to swim out. I turned my head around and looked back: Julianne and my sisters were just spots beneath the tiny umbrella, and the shore and the bluffs were the size of my fist. The trees up along the bluff near the Retreat were stalks, and Neverland was a smudge among them. I treaded water and watched to see if Sumter was up there near the shack. I was mad at him for what he had put us through the night before, for bringing whatever magic was there in Neverland out and into us.

"There is no Lucy," I said aloud. "He made it all up."

Julianne came down to the water's edge and called me back in.

I felt something warm touch the heel of my foot in the cold water, and I almost panicked, not thinking of sharks, but of slaves bound together, floating with one will, toward a swampy peninsula.

I swam faster than I ever have since, back to land, back to the woman who called to me. When I was almost to shore, I saw a blur of movement up on the white path. It was Sumter. He was sitting on a rock and his hands were moving rapidly in front of him like he was beating some drum. Only there was no drum. It looked almost like he was beating his fists into his lap. But I could not tell what he was doing, and as I just about made it to shore, a big wave crashed down around me and I went under. I saw, not the dark blue-green of water, but the white sand, whiter than what was on shore. My face was pushed by the undertow and the heavy water into the whiteness of the sand, and then I fought to come up. Seaweed was grasping at my ankles, trying to take me back out to sea, and when I tried to pull free, the seaweed clung more tightly, until it seemed as if it was not seaweed at all, but a half-dozen hands clutching me and pulling me down. Then, what seemed like another wave lifted me up by the shoulders. I was coughing and breathing and it was no wave at all but rather Julianne Sanders helping me back to my feet, slapping me between the shoulder blades to get water out of my lungs.

⊰ 9 ⊱

I lay on the sand, beneath the umbrella, and rested, while my sisters went exploring for seashells. Julianne glanced over at me every now and then as if she was meaning to say something to me. Finally I said to her, "You're a *sinistre*."

She didn't seem surprised at all. "That's what they call us."

"I hear that you people are part Gullah and part something else."

"Can't always believe what folks'll tell you. You get all the water out of your lungs?"

"Uh-huh. What's the something else?"

Finally she looked annoyed, just like I was one of the horseflies that were nipping at her hairy legs. "I keep my business private, and you can keep yours private, too."

"I didn't mean to be disrespectful."

"Oh, you didn't?"

"No, Julianne. I was just wondering. I mean, there's some things I don't know about. Like with this island. Like why this would be a place where there'd be gods at all."

"Maybe there ain't a god in sight."

"Maybe. But maybe there is."

"And if there is, Beau?"

"Why here?"

"You got windows in your house, don't you?"

I nodded.

"Why are those windows where they are? Why are the doors there, and the stairs? Why'd the kitchen go in one place rather than where the bedrooms are?"

"I guess somebody just wanted it that way. Somebody just decided that they liked the kitchen there and the stairs where they are. The guy who musta built it."

"Well, there y'are."

"I don't get it."

"Nobody gets it, you just got to take it like it is."

"Was your daddy really some kind of god?"

"Beau, you're how old?"

"Old enough."

"Nobody knows who my daddy was, and some folks'll tell you he was just some man who came and went like a summer storm. My mama believes different, and even some other friends believe different."

"How about you?"

"I believe. . . ." She paused, and her nostrils flared like she was taking in a whiff of something strong and good. "I believe there are windows and doorways, and sometimes . . . if the doorway's big enough . . . you can go from the outside to the inside. The Bible tells us that the House of the Lord has many mansions. Who's to say what lives in some of them mansions and whether all their windows are opened or closed?"

"I didn't think . . . "

"What, that somebody like me was a Bible reader? Well, surprise, surprise, Beau, learn something new every day. And now you come sniffing around me. I know something about you."

"Like what?"

"Like you've looked through one of them windows, but it ain't one of the mansions, no sir, it's a different house altogether. Down in the West Island we got stories about that place."

"I know." I remembered the tales of the Gullah graveyard near the site of Neverland.

"You think you know a lot, but you don't. We got stories that keep children up nights, scared. You stay up nights?" She returned to her paperback, not interested in my answer. "Beau, do you stay up nights, thinking about what you've seen through that window? 'Cause one day, somebody on the other side might just lift up on the pane, and then you're gonna go through and there won't be no coming back, I can tell you that. What waits on the other side ain't gonna let go of you, no matter how much you holler."

⇥ 10 ⇤

Finally, Sunday morning, Sumter actually began tossing a few words my way. Daddy had gotten doughnuts down at the bakery in town, and this always put us in a good mood. Aunt Cricket wanted us all to go to church over in St. Badon, but Mama said she didn't really feel like sitting through an hour-long sermon nor did she want to suffer through the new green prayer book this week. So instead, Grammy Weenie wheeled into the great room and read from her little Bible. For all Grammy Weenie's faults—and she had many—she did have a knack for finding perfect entertainment in the Good Book. She read the tale of Sodom and Gomorrah, which we loved because not one of us liked Lot's wife and we cheered when she turned into a pillar of salt. Then she read the tale of the Seven Plagues on Egypt and Salome's dance. Grammy Weenie almost never ventured into the New Testament, much preferring, she said, "the Old God who got angry with the Jews and fought His own people tooth and nail. That was back when God was really *God*. Before He was for every fool who walked the face of this earth."

But undoubtedly Sumter's absolute favorite part of the Old Testament, which he would put in a request for each Sunday morning, was when Abraham was about to sacrifice Isaac. "Of course, God *nixed* that," Sumter said to his teddy bear in a huff, "and there went human sacrifice. What a waste."

Grammy Weenie fixed him with a stern look, slamming her Bible shut. "Thou shall not kill, Sumter Monroe, do you understand? Vengeance is mine, saith the Lord. He didn't say it's Sumter Monroe's. He said 'vengeance is mine.' Abraham would've sacrificed his son for the Lord, but the Lord did not want him to. Man must not kill. It is the Lord who kills, if He so chooses."

Sumter whispered in Bernard's ear: "*I beg to differ with the Weenie.*"

⊰ 11 ⊱

After a lunch of lemonade and cream cheese and pepper-jelly sandwiches, Uncle Ralph brought out some gloves and the baseball bat. "You boys want to play some ball?"

"No," Sumter stated flatly.

"Oh, be a good sport, why don't you."

"I'll play," Missy said, even though she knew Uncle Ralph never liked it when the girls played. She'd been picking at a scab on her knee while she sat next to Daddy on the porch swing. I was on the floor beside them, flicking at big black ants just like I was punting paper triangles in a game of desk football.

"Yeah, let's choose up sides," Nonie added. She grabbed the bat from Uncle Ralph's hands and twirled it like a baton. "I want to be team captain."

"We're not talking whiffle ball, girls, or underhand," Uncle Ralph snapped.

"Afraid?" Nonie grinned. There was something in her eyes besides challenge. There was some kind of power that must've been passed from woman to woman and daughter to daughter from Great-Gramma, the Giantess from Biloxi, down to Grammy Weenie, to Mama and Aunt Cricket, and to my sisters—some kind of spirit that never broke stride. Uncle Ralph was scared of these women, all of them, and I could not say that I blamed him. "Afraid?" she repeated. "We could make it girls against boys. Mama, you want to play?"

Sumter said to Bernard, "Yeah, and we could use the Weenie as home plate."

My mother was sitting on the front porch steps eating a small triangle of sandwich while she bounced Governor on her knee. "I'm not sure I'm up for it."

"I'll play if you will," Daddy said as he got off the swing.

"All right, then." Mama half smiled. Then she turned to Grammy Weenie, who was knitting up on the porch. "Mama, would you mind holding Governor?"

Grammy Weenie looked up at us as if we were all crazy, but nodded and said nothing.

"Oh boy." Missy rolled the hem of her culottes up around her thighs. "Our team is red hot."

"Cricket, you got to play, too," Uncle Ralph called to her.

From the kitchen window she shouted, "What?"

"We got a game going out here, and it's got to be four against four, boys against girls."

"I don't play *baseball*."

My mother said, "You used to. Now you get out here Crick and be a sport or I'll tell them about the Kiss of Death."

Aunt Cricket let out a little shriek. "Oh, don't you dare, dear Lord God!" But she was laughing, too, in a way I rarely heard, the way sixteen-year-old girls laugh among themselves.

"Kiss of Death?" Uncle Ralph raised his eyebrows. "Keeping secrets from me, honey?"

"Oh." Aunt Cricket came outside, taking her smudged apron off and tossing it on the porch swing. "I'll tell you someday, Ralph, but this is hardly the time or the place."

Grammy Weenie said, "She was almost asphyxiated by a masher eighteen years ago while she was selling kisses at the Tri-County Fair."

"*Moth*-er," Aunt Cricket giggled, "the *children*."

"Nearly smothered to death, and me without my smelling salts. I told her that nice girls don't go around selling kisses, but she was almost seventeen and no boy had even attempted to kiss her yet."

Aunt Cricket blushed, and she and my mother kept on laughing.

"You sold *kisses?*" Sumter said incredulously.

"It was for a good cause. But, lord, I thought I would die, just *die*."

Aunt Cricket shot my father a warm glance. "And then a nice boy gave me mouth-to-mouth."

Mama stopped laughing and coughed a couple of times. She pushed wisps of her brown hair up behind her ears. Her ears were red as if it were cold, although it was going to be broiling if the sun stayed in the sky much longer.

Dad said, "Let's get this show on the road." He tossed the baseball up and down in his right hand.

The game was doomed from the start.

I was bad at sports but competitive by nature. I couldn't throw or catch to save my life. And in my heart, I wanted to win. Win! And I never would.

The girls were up first, and none on their team was fiercer than Nonie herself. Why she was such a flirt with boys I will never understand, given the fact that she was such a tomboy when it came to sports. Dad was catcher, and kept saying, "Batter-batter-batter-swing!"

Uncle Ralph pitched to her underhand at first, and she took it as a strike and rolled her eyes. "Let's play for *real*."

"You want it, you got it," he said, and pitched the next one low and fast.

She swung the bat. It made a sound like a lightning crack when she hit the ball. She dropped the bat and ran to first. I was near third and I watched the ball go up and up until it seemed to head right for the sun.

We all shielded our eyes to see where it would come down. Nonie was running to second and Mama was shouting, "Go! Go! Go!"

Sumter stood by second, his glove floppy and loose on his left hand, his teddy bear leaning against his ankles. He was not watching the ball at all.

"It's yours!" his father yelled to him.

Sumter looked at Uncle Ralph like he was speaking a foreign language.

"Goddamn it, it's yours!" Uncle Ralph started running over to second base.

Nonie was already to third, and even she looked back to see why Uncle Ralph was cussing.

"Home!" Mama cried out. "Home! You can do it!"

"You goddamn weak sister!" Uncle Ralph shoved his son out of the way and caught the ball himself. Then, turning back to the rest of us, "You're out! I caught it! Yerrr-out!"

My father tossed his glove down and said, "Jesus, Ralph, Jesus."

Sumter picked up Bernard and was off and running, out to the bluff, out to the woods, off to Neverland.

Dad took off after Sumter, and Uncle Ralph said, "Aw, let him go, he'll get over it." I dropped my glove and followed, and Uncle Ralph said, "Hey, what'd I *do*?"

We caught up with Sumter at the edge of the woods; sunlight thrust sharp white spears between each tree, and Sumter was half in and half out of the light. He was facing a bent and haggard tree trunk like he was counting down in a game of hide-and-seek. His shoulders rose and fell, his head was low. He appeared smaller than I had remembered him being.

"Sumter," my father said, "you okay?"

As my father approached him, he turned around. He wasn't crying like I thought he'd be, but he was doing something that seemed far worse: He was laughing his head off. "Fooled you!" he said to us. "I think it's funny. My daddy's so funny!" He slapped his knees.

"Beau," my father turned to me, "son, maybe you should leave us alone here."

"No," Sumter said, "let him stay. I think it's funny, is all. Really hilarious. A barrel of monkeys."

"Sumter, your father . . . " Dad had apology all over him.

"Don't you make excuses for him."

"He's just not good with being a father."

"I think it's funny."

"But it doesn't mean he's a bad man. He loves you. He just doesn't know how to do it right."

"Don't you tell me about my daddy. I *know* about him. I know *everything*. That man ain't my daddy. Don't pretend. I don't want to hear it. And what about you? You such a good daddy?"

"Sumter."

"You such a good daddy?" Then Sumter pointed a finger at me. "You think *him* with all his problems is the son of a good daddy? You get drunk and you fight with Aunt Evvie and you think you're so good? I never once seen you hold that baby—you ever hold any of your babies? Were they all accidents? 'Cause I know what's true here. I know about how you were the one who gave my mama mouth-to-mouth. I know you were in *love* with my mama when you were in school. You ask me, I think you're *bad*. You gonna abandon *his* mama like you abandoned *mine?*"

"I was *never* in love with your mother."

"She said you were. I heard her tell Daddy once. And Daddy slapped her for saying it. He'd like to kill you."

"Beau," Dad turned to me and crouched down, his hands resting on my shoulders, "I was never in love with your Aunt Cricket. We were friends, and that's all. I have never been in love with anyone except your mama."

"No," Sumter said, "my mama said you loved her, but her own sister stole you from her. But she says you *still* love her."

"That's just not true." My father looked into my eyes, and I did not know what to believe.

A voice in my head like Sumter's told me what to believe. *Your daddy's a liar.*

⇥ 12 ⇤

I watched my father lead Sumter back to the house. He had his arm on my cousin's shoulder and was saying comforting things to him. My father was always trying to be the peacemaker. I knew even then he would later explain to me that he had to do things like this for Sumter because Uncle Ralph would never do them, and *someone* had to. But it didn't matter to me. I felt like Daddy had let me down at that point; I felt like he was more concerned with Sumter's feelings than with mine.

As they walked away, Daddy turned and nodded to me as if this were understood between the two of us. "*Sometimes,*" *he'd said to me more than once,* "*other people need attention more than you, and you're strong enough, Snug, to stand by yourself.*" But I never felt that way. I wondered if I had made the scene and run off into the woods, if he would now have his arm around my shoulders and tell me that it was all going to be okay.

I went to Neverland by myself.

Your daddy's a liar. Sumter's voice had leaked into my brain.

Neverland was, of course, locked. Sumter had the key. I went around and tried the windows, but short of breaking them, there was no way in.

Then I remembered the crawl space, behind the crate. Just a small tunnel that led to a square opening. I went around to the back of the shed. The wood on that side was so thin and warped that when I touched it the walls gave a little. There was a small square opening at the base of the wall, camouflaged with a coiling wire of dried-up blackberry bushes. Yellow jackets spiraled around my fingers as I carefully lifted the thorny vines and scrunched down between the bushes and the opening into the crawl space. A wire screen on a small wood frame leaned against the opening. I pushed it aside; a daddy longlegs scampered out, and rolypolies slogged into the dark space. The opening was just big enough for my head to go in, although its splintered sides pinched my ears. The crawl space smelled like moth-balls and rat dung. Invisible webs tickled my nose and eyes.

I was about to withdraw my head, to go no farther, both because I was scared and because I heard my mother calling to me from beyond the woods, but first I said into the dark, "If there's really a Lucy . . . "

I heard a voice, not in my head, and not behind me in the world of daylight, but up ahead in the dark.

"*Beau,*" it whispered, "*can you let me out to play?*"

I jammed my head back against the opening, but it seemed to have shrunk, and I couldn't pull myself back. I was staring at darkness. I began pushing my hands against the small frame of the opening, slapping at it. I dug my toes into the ground for leverage and twisted around, trying to get my head out sideways. It hurt to breathe. I closed my eyes, even to the darkness, because I was afraid I would *begin* to see whatever was whispering to me.

"*Play,*" the voice whispered. It was coming closer. Whatever it was, it was moving closer. I could *smell* its breath, and it was sweet like rotting gardenias. It was so sweet it *hurt* to inhale it. I felt like I was choking. My eyes were tearing up.

"*Play.*"

Finally I tucked my chin down and managed to scrape the rest of my head out, leaving behind a thin layer of skin from my earlobe and the side of my cheek. Daylight slapped me, and I fell backward into the blackberry bushes.

"*Let me come out and play.*"

Come Out
and Play

SEVEN

Hurt

❧ 1 ❧

I'm not sure what I was thinking that afternoon, but I ended up down by the sea, cutting the bottoms of my feet on the rough edges of rocks. My arms and legs were scratched from prickers. Welts covered my neck and arms from yellow jacket bites. I didn't set foot in that water, but stood right where the waves licked at my toes.

The voice from Neverland I'd heard was the woman's from my nightmare, the woman who had told me "*The bunny screams because it is alive.*"

As I stood there, shivering not from cold but from fear, how was I to know that I was making a choice? When you stand at the border of the land and the sea, it is clear where one leaves off and the other begins. But where lies the boundary between the perceived world and the imagined?

I stood there not knowing that I was making that choice, that I was crossing that border then, that the forbidden would call me, that I had not run from Neverland because the voice from the dark scared me, but because it *attracted* me, and I was fighting that attraction. Fighting it with all my strength.

But even children have their breaking points.

⤙ 2 ⤚

I worked myself into a fever by the time the supper bell rang.

"You were playing in the woods again," Mama said, feeling my forehead as I leaned against the kitchen counter. The room was spinning, and I clutched her arm. She turned to give commands, "Missy, hon, run upstairs and get the orange shoe box off the top shelf of the linen closet. You don't have to bring the whole thing down, just look through it for the thermometer in the little plastic tube. Nonie, you open up a can of Campbell's and see if we don't have some saltines around and make up a little tray."

"I'm okay," I said, but I was close to fainting.

"It's probably nothing more than too much excitement and too much sun," Mama said, "but if you're coming down with something, I want you in bed now. If your temperature's low enough, we'll see. Missy!" she yelled through the kitchen doorway. "Better bring the whole kit down! *Beau,* where did *these* come from?" She had finally seen the bites and scratches along my arms. She rolled my short sleeves up farther to find even more.

"Yellow jackets."

"Well, no *wonder* you're ill." Mama held my arm up in the kitchen light. "Well, they don't look too bad, but we better wash all these out with peroxide."

I was in bed shivering with the covers up around my ears. My temperature had only been slightly higher than normal, and the whole time Mama had the thermometer in my mouth she was asking me questions that I couldn't answer—she'd had a martini or two and was becoming talkative.

"What exactly went on out in the woods today? Between Daddy and Sumter and you? You know you had Daddy very upset; he went looking for you and couldn't find you. You and the girls have been looking tired, and Grammy said you've been sneaking out of the house at all hours. Now, you and I have no secrets from each other, so you can tell me: What are you children up to? Are you just out playing? Are they good games? You and Sumter, you're getting along all right, are you?"

I nodded, I shook my head, and when the thermometer came out of my mouth I said, "I just went looking for berries and fell in some prickers is all." I looked down on the floor where Governor sat mostly naked except for his diapers, which were half off, anyway. If I avoided looking at my mother, she might miss out on the fact that I was lying. I always felt like she could see right through me. I think she really could.

She eyed me almost suspiciously. "Blackberries'd be all dried up by now."

"I saw some in the woods that weren't. Then I went down to the beach."

"You didn't go swimming by yourself."

"Uh-uh. I just was tired. I thought I'd soak the bites in saltwater." There, *that* was a good lie.

"Y'all play in the old gardener's shed, don't you?" Mama didn't seem suspicious.

"Sometimes, but we can't get in. It's all locked up."

"When I was a girl it was full of wonderfully old-fashioned things." She wiped a warm washcloth across my forehead. "Grampa Lee stored things there. Your great-grampa did, too. So there were, oh, coffee grinders and ancient sewing machines and Grammy's dolls used to be out there—not in their case at all, but just piled up. It was wonderful playing out there, although Grammy never liked us being there."

My mother's tone changed when she spoke about her mother. It was as if she began to remember something unpleasant and unkind—perhaps even cruel—about Grammy Weenie, but tried to disguise it by speaking softly, like a child herself, chastened. "She would tell us terrible tales about rats and spiders and broken glass. Cricket and I just stopped going through all that junk. And Babygirl, too, we all called her that—she was older than me, and she was still the baby. You never met your other aunt, you were about a year old when she passed on. The shed used to be *her* place. She was . . . well, childlike, even later. Even when she was older."

"Babygirl never grew up?"

"That's one way of putting it. But she was kind of sick all her life, Beau. They took her to doctor after doctor, clinic after clinic."

"She have bad circulation like me?"

"No. Your grammy always said she had a clouded mind, and she had dark days as well as some light ones. We loved her, we really did, she was our *sister*." My mother shook off this thought. "But we had fun in that shed! Games and hide-and-seek. Sometime after she died, Grampa Lee emptied it out. Mama—*Grammy*—sometimes gets things in her head. . . ." My mother combed her fingers across the top of my scalp absently. "She'd forbid us from doing the most innocent things."

"Grammy says she had red hair."

"Who?"

"Babygirl."

"She said that? Well, I told you she gets confused. She had blond-white hair. It was beautiful. Now *Grammy* used to have red hair before it turned gray. Maybe that's what she meant. But Babygirl had shiny blond hair. Grampa Lee had white hair like that."

"Sumter, he has hair like that," I said.

"Yes, he does. Funny how we get things from people." Mama brought her hands up to her face, pressing the palms into her forehead and wiping down the length of her face as if it were dirty. "Your grammy's always going on about who we look like, what's been passed down, and of course she can't *stand* the fact that your daddy's mother was *Irish*. When you get to a certain age. . . . Well, I suppose she clings to the past too much."

"I like hearing her memorials."

"*Memoirs.* You may be the only one who does. You feeling okay, hon?"

"Almost."

"You want some more soup?"

I slept for a while, occasionally awaking to the sound of the TV downstairs or chairs being pulled in and pushed out at the dining room table or footsteps in the hall outside my door. Next thing I knew, my door was creaking open and there was Sumter with a big blue towel wrapped around his waist.

"Hey," I said.

"How you?"

"Just fine, or getting there."

"Lucy says you went out to Neverland."

"Didn't go in."

"Okay if you did. Does Lucy talk to you ever?"

I hesitated. "No."

"You're a family of liars, but that's okay."

"You gonna take a bath?"

He nodded, holding up his box of *Mr. Bubble*. "My mama says I need a boiling bath to clean me off. I hate it when she turns the water on so hot. You're lying about Lucy, ain't ya?"

"Okay, Lucy did talk to me. I think. Maybe I imagined it."

"No such thing as *imagine*. If you think something happened, it did. Did you *see* anything? I mean, when it talks to you."

I shook my head.

This seemed to satisfy him.

"What is Lucy anyway?"

"Just a god. One among many."

Then it hit me—the reason I'd run down to the sea, the reason why the voice from the shed had chilled me. I'd had a thought buzzing through my head, and now I knew what it was exactly. *We were probably worshipping the Devil. I* didn't believe in the Devil, but maybe there was one after all. Boldly, I asked, "Is it like Lucy-*fer*?"

"That's for me to know and you to find out." With that, he turned and left the room.

A few minutes later I heard the water splashing in the bathroom next to my room. Aunt Cricket was saying, "It is not so hot. Now you get in there, the steam'll clean off all that dirt and you'll feel better. You will not boil up to nothing, Sunny, now just get in." The droning sound the water made, as Aunt Cricket filled up the tub, helped me to fall back asleep.

The bunny screams, the woman was saying to me. She had white hair like Sumter's. She was shorter than any grown-up woman I'd ever seen, just slightly taller than one of the munchkins from The Wizard of Oz. *Her face was broad and ugly, her forehead high and huge, her eyes pale blue and pretty, like glittering translucent marbles thrust into a potato. We waded through the water along the shore of the island in the middle of Rabbit Lake.*

"Why's the bunny hafta scream?" I asked.

Her legs were white and shiny with water, and her hair was white and shiny, too. She was naked like one of the Playboy *girls, but not as chesty and not as cuddly looking, and certainly with nothing about her that even approached beauty. It didn't bother me that she had no clothes on; what bothered me was she was holding my hand too tight and it hurt. Also, I was wondering what I was going to step on in the water: Fat albino pollywogs swarmed around our ankles by the dozens.*

"Because it's alive," she replied. "The bunny screams because it's alive."

"But wouldn't it be happy?" I asked.

"Not when things hurt."

"Things don't hurt."

"You haven't been dead yet. You don't know how peaceful it can be."

"Like Heaven? Like the bunny went to Heaven and then had to turn around and come back? Is that why the bunny screams?"

She squeezed my hand tighter. "There is no Heaven."

"Of course there is, everybody knows there's a Heaven." *I tugged free of her grip and almost fell backward in among the pollywogs.*

I said, "Don't you tell me there's no Heaven."

"I could show you where you go when you die," she said, "and it's not Heaven, but it's a playground and you never have to be a grown-up, ever. All you do is play. One of my little boys plays here all the time. I'd like him to have companions. Wouldn't you scream, too?"

"Playing's only fun sometimes."

"Do you like to hurt?"

"Nobody likes to hurt."

"What isn't play is hurt."

I looked up at her face. She wasn't a woman at all: She was hardly more than a child, a child-woman. I had mistaken her for a small woman, but she was really just a four-year-old with a grown-up voice. "Who are you?"

"A friend."

"Are you the Devil?*"*

She smiled, and she was pretty when she smiled. Then I watched as horns sprouted across her forehead and she hunched over and her bottom half became hairy.

"Are you Lucifer?*"*

"You can be a child forever," she said, as a long spiny tail with a scaly red arrow at its tip grew out of her backside.

"I want to grow up and drive a fast car."

"You want to grow up like them?*" the Devil-thing asked.*

I heard, from the other shore, the sounds of Aunt Cricket and Uncle Ralph squabbling, and the crashing and breaking of waves all around. "I'll tell you why I'm screaming! I'll tell you why I'm screaming!" Aunt Cricket shouted in a high-pitched voice.

"Because she's alive," the creature before me said. "And because everything hurts."

"Just keep your voice down!" Uncle Ralph yelled back.

Something was coming up behind me, something other than this woman-creature. I heard the buzzing of the yellow jackets and the clomping of hooves. I smelled its fish-oily skin, and I was turning to see it, to see him, not Lucy, who stood beside me, but something even greater than Lucy, the All, the Great Feeder who walked in shadows.

I almost saw his face.

I sat up in bed. "Everything hurts."

My door was open and Missy stood there. "Can you *believe* it?"

From down the hall we heard the sounds of fighting. Aunt Cricket was the loudest. "You just put that down right now! I will scream if I want to. . . . Oh, no, you don't. . . . Well, *let* them hear—I don't care!"

Uncle Ralph blasted, "He's never gonna grow up to be a man! You can just look at him!"

"Well, maybe if he had a *man* to look up to!"

"He's a goddamn mama's boy—"

The crashing of objects, like bombs going off.

Missy whispered, "They were getting drunker and drunker downstairs, and then he almost *tripped* on the teddy bear going upstairs, and it all started, and *Gawd*, Beau, you just gonna lie in bed or you gonna come out in the hall and *listen?*"

The hallway was lit by a single bulb, with faces peering around the banister and from doorways. Nonie sat on the stairs, her hands over her ears, her head almost in her lap, although every few seconds she'd look up and down the hall to the noisy bedroom. Mama was in the doorway to her room and said, "Beauregard, you get right back into bed. I won't have you getting sick for the rest of the vacation."

I slunk back to stand just inside the door to my room. Missy, rather boldly, went and sat at the top of the staircase.

Grammy Weenie wheeled below us, shouting out, "I *wish* for once my children would *behave* themselves like decent *guests* and not just use my home as a saloon!"

From the bathroom came the sound of Sumter singing "Old Folks at Home" while he splashed in the tub. I could imagine him sitting there, pretending that none of this was going on. He had a tremendous capacity for blocking out reality.

"You best not be breaking any of my dolls!" Grammy said. "That's all I have to say! You best not be breaking valuables!"

Nonie turned and looked at me. "Don't you just get sick of all of them? I hate this. I *hate* this. I wish we'd all just get divorced."

The door to the bedroom next to Uncle Ralph's opened, and Daddy peered out. Behind him I saw Mama pacing the floor with Governor up over her shoulder. She was patting him on the back, her face set in a tight mask. Daddy barked, "You girls *get* in your room right now!" I hid behind my door so he couldn't see me. Missy and Nonie went running down the opposite end of the hall.

Aunt Cricket was crying hysterically while Uncle Ralph continued his tirade, throwing things around as punctuation. "You *hurt* me, you bastard!" Aunt Cricket shrieked. "You're *hurting* me! Somebody! Help me!" Her voice was high and pathetic and it hurt just to hear her.

Daddy shut one bedroom door behind him and pushed open the other one.

From where I could see, Uncle Ralph was slapping at Aunt Cricket's shoulders, back and forth, *whap, whap, whap.*

"Get away from her," Daddy said, and went over and shoved my uncle back.

"How dare you," Uncle Ralph said.

Aunt Cricket cried and cried, "Oh, Lord, he *hurt* me, Dabney, he *hurt* me."

I watched my father put his arms around my aunt.

"Go to your room *right now*," Mama said. I looked up and she was standing in her doorway glaring at me. I had never seen her so angry except when she was ironing. "Go inside that room and shut that door, young man."

I did as I was told.

Sumter's voice was clear through the wall and almost sounded good. "All the world is sad and dreary," he sang, and I sat up in bed listening to him until I fell asleep again.

The world of dreams seemed a safer place.

In the middle of the night I was again awakened, this time by Sumter. "You feeling better?"

"Huh?"

"We're going to Neverland. You coming?"

Once I could move my arms and legs, sore from the bites, scratches, and the outrageous fortune of bad circulation, I slipped from my pajama bottoms into my swimming trunks and followed my cousin out.

⇥ 3 ⇤

As scary as it could be, Neverland itself was our playground. It was, as Missy said to me that night on the walk out to it, "Fun scary, not *scary* scary."

At least, before it got out of hand.

Everything in childhood gets out of hand.

⇥ 4 ⇤

In Neverland that night, Sumter entertained us.

"Step right up," he said, waving his hand in the air. From the rolled-up sleeve of his shirt he produced a bouquet of stinky chrysanthemums. "For the lovely ladies," he said, tossing them to Nonie, but as the flowers flew out of his hand, they became sparrows, twittering, and flying up against the roof. As we watched them, the birds dropped again, becoming bits of folded paper as they hit the ground.

"Oh wow," Missy gasped, clapping her hands, "a *magic* show."

We had come to accept the dream side of Neverland completely. I could not be surprised by anything that occurred within those walls.

Sumter held up his hand. "Ladies and germs, not a magic show, but a *tragic* show. Observe."

He reached into the opening of the crate, making a face like he was sucking on a lemon, and then brought out something small and furry.

The bunny from Rabbit Lake.

"How'd you *do* that?" I asked.

"Watch," he said. He sat down, clutching the bunny against his chest. "Presto-digito-boola-boola." He kissed the bunny on the bridge of its nose.

He held it up by the scruff of its neck.

The bunny began speaking.

It sounded just like Uncle Ralph.

"That boy's never gonna grow up, I tell you, he's always gonna be a little mama's boy," the bunny barked.

Missy leaned toward me and whispered, "Can you see his lips move? I think his lips are moving."

The bunny continued, "You got to stop playing with dolls, boy, you got to be more like your cousin Beau. You don't see him playing with no damn teddy bear." The bunny scrunched its nose up and tried to wriggle out of Sumter's grasp, but he shook it almost furiously.

"So Mr. Bunny," Sumter said, "you think boys shouldn't play?"

"More important things in life."

"Like what?"

"Like drinking good bourbon and chasing whores."

"You think your boy should be like you?" Sumter asked the rabbit. He shifted his fingers from its neck to its ears. It began writhing in his grasp, trying to escape.

Uncle Ralph bunny hissed, "You worthless whelp, you put me down. You put me down or I'll have your hide, you hear me? I'll have your hide!"

"No." Sumter grinned, and this worried me. Whenever he grinned like this, broadly, his eyes catching the glint of candlelight, I worried.

"Sumter," I said, "don't do—"

"*Shhh,*" Missy hushed me, "just watch the *show.*"

"I'm gonna tan your hide, boy." Uncle Ralph bunny flailed its back legs; with its forepaws it fought the air.

Sumter held it firmly by the ears. "No you're not, you *dumb* bunny, not if I tan yours first."

And with that Sumter reached up with his free hand to the nape of the animal's neck. With one quick and sure move, he ripped the bunny's fur right off its back.

The bunny screamed.

I yelped and jumped up and tackled Sumter to the ground. "Don't you hurt that—"

Sumter was laughing. "Get off me you moron, lookit! *Lookit*."

The bunny had fallen to the ground beside us, and it was, after all, just a stinky old dead bunny with its guts hanging out and some flies buzzing around its innards.

"It was already *dead;* you saw it before. It's been dead for at least a week. You know that."

Nonie peered beyond us to the rotting rabbit. "Disgusto."

"How'd you do that, Sumter? Huh? Show me how you did that. I only saw your lips move *once*," Missy said.

I looked around at the others, my sisters. Their eyes seemed to be glazed over as if they were walking in their sleep. I sniffed at the air; it was sweet and rotten.

"Why'n't you bury that thing?" I asked. "What're you keeping it for?"

"Don't you want to see what happens when you die?" he asked me, incredulous that I wouldn't want to watch a body decompose. "Don't you want to see how it all goes? *Lookit*," he poked his fingers into the open belly, jabbing them around, "ain't it something? *Nothing* hurts it. *Nothing*."

⊰ 5 ⊱

We all slept late after the emotional storms of the previous night. Even with the tragic show Sumter put on for us in Neverland, I was well rested. I felt better that morning than I had felt for a long time, and the scratches on my arms were all healed. My circulation wasn't even all that bad; I practically leapt out of bed. Uncle Ralph was moaning from his room and spent most of the day nursing a hangover. Julianne had already swept up the broken lamp and the two vases my uncle had thrown, and except for a sour memory, you'd've thought we were all back to normal.

"Julianne's taking us down to the West Island for the carnival," Missy said over a breakfast—which we didn't sit down to until nearly eleven.

"I didn't even know there *was* a carnival," Nonie said sullenly, forking through her grits like she was looking for a prize.

"The Sea Horse Park," Julianne said as she brought in a pitcher of juice. "I want to get y'all out from underfoot here, and they say some of the rides'll be open. Always some ride going down there, and I have a few things to do there, m'self."

"Mama, don't you want to come?" Sumter asked Aunt Cricket, who just shook her head. We all noticed and later commented on the fact that she was wearing an inordinate amount of makeup around the eyes this morning, and if you squinted, you could make out the barest smudge of a yellow-purple bruise.

⇥ 6 ⇤

Daddy dropped us off at the park just after noontime. The sun was up and hot like a big old egg yolk sizzling on the griddle sky. Julianne had a little white plastic purse that was almost too dainty for her lumbering form. "Your daddies've given three dollars' spending money for each of y'all, so you decide what you want, if you want cotton candy or a ride or a trip through the sideshow. Then you come to me for your money and I'll give it to you. But decide first, so's you don't just throw it away."

The Sea Horse Amusement Park was a shambles, and it's doubtful that it met any safety standards whatsoever. You didn't so much enter it as step in it. Dwarfing it was a gray-white wooden roller coaster that, as far as I knew, had never run, but had always just been this curvy skeleton taller than even the trees, or so it seemed. But it looked like you could blow it over by just coughing. The park was decomposing just like the dead bunny in the Neverland crate. Even the sidewalks between the bubbling asphalt were cracked and crumbling, with wild yellow stalks of grass fighting for space, and corkscrew roots of dying trees just waiting to trip you up as you headed toward the ticket booth. There was a Muzak version of "Bridge Over Troubled Water" coming through the crackly loudspeakers, and there couldn't have been more than a dozen other people in the entire park—and most of them looked like sleepy drug addicts. Floating as if in a trance were skinny men with goatees and red pirate bandannas around their scalps, wearing black tank tops and bell-bottoms, limp cigarettes lolling from their tight mouths. An older girl with long straight hair all the way down to her fanny strode up and down the walkway, a halter top barely holding her bowling-ball breasts in, a three-year-old curly-haired girl clutching her hand tightly.

The man selling tickets was fat and had no shirt on, and his nipples were huge and hung across his chest like two great puffy flapjacks; tattoos of dragons and naked women ran together in green and red all around his flabby arms, and he had a Viking painted on his overhanging belly, with its cavernous navel making the Viking's mouth. He smelled the way phone booths sometimes do when bums pee in them. The rides were between fifty and seventy-five cents, depending on their severity.

The bumper cars were disabled, but we went around to them anyway and sat in the cars and pretended they were going. Julianne leaned against the low wall outside and pulled her skirt together when a crazy-looking man walked by and leered at her.

"I bet you don't know how to drive a car," Sumter said.

"I do, too." I spun the wheel of the bumper car and made *vroom* noises. "Daddy lets me drive it up and down the driveway."

"Well, we ain't going nowhere in these things," he said, climbing out of them.

"Boys and cars," Nonie said dismissively, although she seemed to be enjoying scrunching down behind the wheel of a smart red bumper car.

"Cage is closed," Missy said when we got out of the cars. She pointed to the carousel. "I really want to go there."

"Then go," Sumter said.

Missy proceeded to tick off the list of rides that looked closed or stupid. "Trabant's not going. Whirligig looks dead. Nobody's set the sideshow up."

"Shut up," Nonie told her. "You can be so depressing. If you want to go on the carousel, we'll *go* on the carousel, okay?"

"Girls stick together," Sumter said to my sisters. "Boys stick together. We don't want to go on no *girl* rides."

"Oh, come on, Sunny."

"Don't call me that, *Messy*."

We were off to such a good start that Julianne herself separated us, giving Sumter and me our six dollars, and then she herded the girls over to the House of Mirrors, which was always open and never fun beyond the first goopy mirror. I followed after Sumter, who led me around by each ride, invariably making the dismissive pronouncement, "For kiddies," or "Closed." The carousel was open, but of course this was for kiddies. "If they were *real* horses with spears through their middles, now that would be completely neat." I wanted to ride the carousel, but went along with him anyway. We bought some candy apples. I was in the middle of devouring mine when Sumter grabbed me by the shirt and said, "Lookit."

One of the better rides was open.

The Crack-the-Whip.

"No way," I said, "I just *ate*."

"C'mon, it's the only good ride in the place."

It was seventy-five cents to get on, which, after the candy apple, left me with a buck and a quarter. "I'm gonna get sick if they go too fast," I said, handing the sleazy ticket-taker my stub.

"Who cares? Don'tcha just love Crack-the-Whip?" He raced ahead of the three other kids who were in line to grab what he considered to be the best seat. When I caught up with him, sitting down and pulling the safety bar down to our waists, he said, "When's it gonna go? When's it gonna go?" He began clanging on the safety bar with his fists, harder and harder. "Hurry up! Go! Go!" he shouted. But within a few seconds we were spinning and whirring around, and my stomach was heaving. The whole time the ride went, Sumter was just laughing his head off with pleasure.

After I wobbled out of the seat, clutching the railing that led down to the exit, I went around back behind the ride to throw up. Sumter stayed up front. As I was well into my second heave I looked up into bright merciless sunlight and saw Zinnia. I had not seen her since the night of the giggling and tickling in Neverland.

"Poor baby," she said. She was licking at an ice cream cone like it wasn't ever going to melt. She offered me her paper napkin. I took it and wiped my mouth.

"Can't you let a guy barf in peace?"

"Hey, I gave you my napkin."

"Thank you."

"You want a lick on my cone?"

"I just threw *up*."

She shrugged. "I don't mind." She had a blurred Southern accent, the kind I loved. *Ah-doan-mahn*.

I shook my head. "You're crazy."

"Far as I can tell, this world's a crazy place. Where's Summer?"

"Sum*t*er."

"You know who I mean."

"He's 'round t'other side. What you want with him?"

She dropped her ice cream down on the asphalt. She had chocolate all over her mouth as she approached me. I was still wiping my lips, and my tongue was sour with the aftertaste of candy-apple spit-up.

"'Member kissing me?"

"'Course."

"Whatja feel?"

I blushed. "Nothing."

"Nothing? You taste anything?"

"Huh?"

"Like water?"

"Well, 'course I tasted *water*. When you kiss, that's what you taste."

"You tasted sea water." She stood right next to me, and my skin both crawled and cried out for her touch. I wanted to do things you're not sup- posed to do until you're twenty and married, and I didn't even *know* what those things were. She continued, "You tasted sea water, on accounta you're like him. But he knows things you don't, 'cause he's more him than you are."

My ten-year-old heart was churning like a washing machine. Her breath was sea water then, too—fresh and clean and all-surrounding. Her lips were parched and peeled back from crooked teeth.

"You tell him something for me."

I whispered, "Yeah."

"You tell him it's not always good. Tell him some things never get better."

"Like what? Like what never gets better?" I felt sweat crawling from my belly downward.

"Like dying," she said.

"THAT GIRL'S downright crazy," I told Sumter when I came back around front. "That Zinnia."

"She's here? She's *here*? How could she've leaked out like that? She's *really* here?"

"Yeah, and she told me to tell you dying's not so great. Is she a nut or what?"

Sumter stared at me as if seeing me for the first time. "Beau, that means you can—" He thought better of what he'd been about to say. "If I was to tell *you* something, you keep it secret? On your sacred oath to Lucy and Neverland?"

"Sure."

"She's a ghost."

"Yeah, huh."

"She and her brothers. They're dead already. They were sacrifices. The first sacrifices to Neverland. Didn't I tell you that already? You sure I didn't tell you already?"

Of course I didn't believe him. He was so good at lies. We went around behind the Crack-the-Whip, but all that was left of Zinnia was the broken cone and a puddle of melted ice cream.

"So, do spooks like chocolate?" I asked him. "A ghost give us head lice, too?"

⊰ 7 ⊱

"Jesus God it's *hot*," Nonie said when we ran into my sisters near the Coca-Cola stand. "I wish we'd just go home. Maybe they're divorced by now."

"I wouldn't mind going on the carousel again," Missy said, "I have fifty cents left."

Julianne Sanders hovered around our perimeter. She was smoking a skinny cigar and talking to the man who sold the Cokes. They were apparently old friends, and Sumter whispered to me, "Probably her *boy*friend."

"He can't be. He's white," Missy said.

"He can be anything as long as he likes girls with hairy legs," Sumter said. "Oh, Miss Sanders," he called to her in that syrupy voice, and she turned and gave him a wise look. "We're just gonna walk around a bit, we promise not to go too far."

"You get into anything," she said, looking us all over, but her eyes kept coming back to my cousin, "and you'll get whupped."

"Oh, Miss Sanders, we won't get into anything. I promise you that, yes'm."

"THREE lousy dollars," Nonie said when we were well out of earshot from our babysitter. She kept her arms wrapped around her waist like she was hugging herself. She was walking stiff-legged and mad.

"I like the carousel," Missy said as if she were the only human being in the world who *did*.

Nonie sniffed at this, "If you had your own horse, you wouldn't have to ride some stupid wooden one."

Sumter said, "I know why girls like to ride horses."

Missy glared at him.

"I know what we can do for free," he said. "We can go on the roller coaster."

"Yeah, right. It hasn't run since before you were born," I said.

"I mean climb it. I bet we can see all the way across the world if we get far enough up it."

Missy decided to stay on the ground and watch, but Nonie was up for the climb. I was not. I was a little afraid of falling and was not fond of most heights. But Sumter started to dare me, and if there's anything I've always been up for, it's a good dare. My hand was sweaty, and I guess that helped: I stuck to each piece of wood when I touched it. I felt like a fly on the side of a building. There was great suction between my sweaty palms and the splintery gray-white wood.

"It's just like climbing up a ladder," Nonie said to cheer me on.

"If you weren't wearing culottes, we could look up your dress," Sumter said.

"Gross," she replied, scrabbling up faster, until her behind was just a pale blue dot rising toward the sun.

Sumter stayed with me to both coach and taunt me. "Just think, when we get to the top, we can see the whole world. It's not so far up, so don't wuss out on me, cuz, or I'll pry your fingers back one by one."

My joints seemed to pop every time I made a move, and my arms were sore from reaching. Splinters scraped across my fingers, and I was sure at any moment I would fall and break my neck.

"Stay with me," my cousin said, "Lucy'll make sure you're okay. We're part of Neverland."

"Yeah, huh," I grunted. "We're not exactly *in* it now. This ain't one of your tragic shows."

I heard a small voice in my mind, or maybe he said it aloud, *"Where I am is Neverland."*

WE DIDN'T reach the top, although we got close to it. Nonie stopped first and said, "End of the line here, look." Above her, one wooden slat was cut off from another. We could not go farther unless we went sideways for several yards and then climbed up and over.

"Look down," Sumter said.

"Jesus," Nonie gasped.

I clutched the wooden bar between my fingers and shut my eyes tight. The heels of my Keds dug into the lower shelf I was standing on.

"Beau, open your *eyes*. It's beautiful. You can see everything!"

"I'm gonna fall," I said.

"No you're not. I told you, Lucy'll make sure you're okay."

I opened one eye, and then the other.

Below us, we did see the whole world, the whole wide world of Gull Island.

"I see it," Nonie said. "There it is, the Retreat!" She had one arm hugging a pole and the other stretched out, pointing. I looked in that direction.

"I see Neverland," Sumter added.

I didn't want to tell either of them this, but as I looked down, feeling my stomach swooping as if it were falling without my body attached, I saw more than just the shack, even through the trees.

I also saw Grammy Weenie in her chair, sitting out beside the shack.

The climb down went slower and was scarier, at least for me.

Julianne Sanders stood below us with Missy, shouting, "You are gonna break your neck! Come down right now or I am going to whup you! Watch your step—wait until I tell your daddies, just wait till then!"

≒ 8 ≒

So of course we got in trouble. Sumter got spanked with his daddy's belt, and Nonie and I got no supper that night. But we were already grumbling about the grown-ups anyway, so this was like throwing gasoline onto a campfire.

And then the unthinkable occurred—perhaps what was to be, for my cousin, the final straw. The thing that sent him over the edge.

It was just after supper, and Nonie and I had just gotten swatted by Aunt Cricket for sneaking downstairs and swiping Oreos from the pantry. Sumter came barreling into the kitchen like a locomotive and ran smack into his mother. He was crying hard, but there were no tears to come out.

"He's *gone*," he gasped, sounding weaker than I'd ever heard him; his lisp had returned, also.

"Who's gone?" Aunt Cricket hugged her son against her skirts. "Tell me, Sunny, who's gone? Daddy?"

Sumter was clutching her, enraged. He stomped his feet on the linoleum. It felt like a small earthquake. "Bernard! Bernard's gone, that's who!"

Nonie shrugged and whispered to me, "Big deal."

Sumter heard her and glanced back, pointing at her. "You took him, didn't you? Didn't you?"

"Give me a break. I haven't even seen your dumb old bear since Tuesday. Have a cow, why don't you."

Sumter let go of his mother and lunged at Nonie, knocking her down. She yelped. He had his hands around her neck and was strangling her. Aunt Cricket moaned, "Sunny, Sunny, oh, dear God," but was not going to interfere.

"Get off her," I said, tugging at the nape of his T-shirt. "I said get off."

"Traitor," Sumter snarled at me. He swatted at me with his fists, and I fell on him and started wrestling around.

"The bear's probably where you left it in—"

"*Beau.*"

"I wasn't gonna—I was gonna say in the *car*, you dumb—"

"*Beau.*"

I heard his voice in my head. *Remember your oath. Neverland. Remember your oath.*

In my own head I asked him: *How did you do that?*

He didn't answer.

We struggled for a while longer, batting at each other's chests and faces with our half-curled fingers. We fought in ways that did little real damage, although I would later see the scratches across my face because Sumter had not clipped his fingernails in a while.

In our fighting my shirt got ripped, and I fell off him, to the side, taking great heaving breaths. Sumter sat up and brushed himself off.

"Oh, Sunny." His mother lifted him up, almost into her arms, but he was too heavy. I could tell she wanted to cradle him. She brushed her fingers through his shiny hair, his head pressed back against her breasts.

And it struck me, then, about their resemblance.

Not only did he not look anything like Aunt Cricket, but when she held him, it was as if he were a pet, a doll, and not her son, as if she never saw him as a child at all, but as something she didn't understand, something she could not comprehend—so she held him close to her breasts, not for comfort, but so that she wouldn't have to look at his face.

Because he did not look anything like her at all.

⋈ 9 ⋈

"All right, goddamnit, so I threw it out." Uncle Ralph didn't look back from the television set in the den. "A boy his age shouldn't be playing with dolls, and I was so dog-tired of looking at it."

"Well, just go back and get it." Aunt Cricket stood firm. She tapped her toe on the floor, up, down, up, down. The small den was dark and smelled of pine and mildew and Uncle Ralph's dirty feet. The TV set was its only light. I watched from the doorway. Upstairs, Sumter was pitching a fit in his room. You could hear things hitting the floor; you could hear his fists banging against the walls.

"I told you I threw it out. It's gone for good," he said. In his right hand he scrunched up a Budweiser can.

"Well, you just tell me where it went."

"Cricket, you are a piece of work, you know that? A goddamn piece of work. I pitched it. Off the bluff. It's probably sleeping with the fishes right now."

Grammy Weenie wheeled up alongside me and grabbed me by the wrist. "Go tell your cousin to calm himself. Tell him I will not tolerate a temper tantrum."

I wriggled out of her grasp and hurried along the hall to the staircase. Missy sat at the bottom of the stairs and watched me step around her. I took the stairs two at a time, sliding my hand up the banister. All this over a dumb teddy bear. I was in my socks, so I slid on the landing, skidding down the hall like I was ice skating. I came to Sumter's room and tried the door. Locked.

"It's me."

I heard things hitting the walls, glass breaking, feet stomping, hands slapping. Something thudded against the other side of the door—he'd thrown something at me, but the door was in the way.

"Go away, you traitor."

"I am not a traitor, now you open this door."

"You probably told them everything, anyway."

"You know I didn't."

"Go away, you hear me?"

"Sumter, Grammy says she wants to see you."

"She knows where she can go."

But even as he said this, just on the other side of the door, I felt another door opening in my brain and someone was digging around with his grubby little fingers. I heard Sumter's voice inside me say, *You hate all of them, too, don't you, Beau? Grown-ups are bad. Lucy wants us. We can be with Lucy. We just need the right sacrifice.*

⊰ 10 ⊱

In my dreams that night I was looking over the edge of the bluffs. I was wearing my underwear and I had a flashlight in my hand. I was looking for something down among the rocks and sea. It was night out, and the sea and sky had merged into one rippling purple robe, with a white stitch down its middle where the full moon reflected off it. Down below, something was coming out of the water.

Climbing up the side of the bluff.

Before I saw what it was, I heard it growling.

It was Bernard, the teddy bear, his button eyes gleaming fiercely when I shone my flashlight down on him.

A dark streak ran down his furry muzzle.

Blood.

EIGHT

Commandments

ᴹ 1 ᴹ

The next morning, Sumter had his teddy bear back. It was more raggedy than before, with thistles around its ears as if it had been caught in the underbrush. Its paws were covered with mud, and it had lost its left eye. But it was still Bernard, and Sumter kept it close to him. He would not explain how he managed to retrieve the thing from where his father had tossed it. But there were other things going on at home besides a teddy bear. Something new, a silence, had crept into the house. The fights were still there, but under the surface, like smoldering embers. Our parents were always at war, with each other, with alcohol, with the humidity, and the wars all began the way wars do: with a single shot, and this filled with bourbon or gin or blackberry brandy. We children had no wars, and still we had our fort, our hideout, our way of escaping.

Why could I not resist going to that shack?

Sumter spent all his days there, alone, away from the rest of us. During the better part of the day I would feel no compulsion to go there. The daylight world attracted me, with long walks on the beach, riding to town with my father on some mindless errand, watching television while I bounced Governor on my knee. Missy was progressing through the basics of knitting with Mama, and Nonie decided the best use of her time was to lie half naked across the gritty beach and darken. The grown-ups didn't start drinking until three or four. Julianne did most of our cooking and read aloud from Gothic novels down on the rocks while Nonie tanned. In other words, we spent our days in a relaxed state of boredom as if we were satiated drug addicts. Grammy Weenie became ever more silent, wheeling in her chair around the halls, stroking her hair with the dreaded silver-backed brush, reading silently from her Bible, watching the road from the front window as if expecting something *most peculiar* to amble up her driveway.

But the nights were different.

As the light faded in the evening, I'd begin picking up Sumter's radio signals in my brain. His voice, eating away at my own, *Lucy wants you. Neverland. Now. Come.* I would look across the dinner table at him through the steam of Julianne's leek soup. He would be helping himself to more mashed potatoes. He would not even be looking at me, and still I heard him in my head.

"You children go play," one of the grown-ups would say, "before it gets dark."

Sumter would be out first, and Julianne, more often than not, would shoot me a look that said *beware!*, but I would successfully ignore it. The grown-ups had no warnings: They were having after-dinner drinks.

⇥ 2 ⇤

As I went out the front door one night, later than usual because I had to kiss my baby brother good night to keep him from crying, I thought I saw a ghost. She was white and pale and shiny like a grub under a rock. But it was only Aunt Cricket in a white cotton nightgown. Holding her bourbon-filled glass in the air, she said, "It's okay, really, to have a sip or two, isn't it, Beau? My doctor in Atlanta says that it's good for the blood pressure, and when you're a grown-up, there's a lot of that going around, you know?" She sat in the front room, on the sofa, her legs curled up under her. The room was in twilight, warm like an oven, and quiet, even with the *tuh-tuh-tuh-tuh* of the electric fans encircling her. Grammy sat across from her and me, asleep in her chair, for she often slept early.

I said, "Aunt Cricket?"

"Yes?"

"Why do grown-ups like the taste of bourbon?"

She thought for the longest minute, and I was about to take off thinking she'd forgotten the question, when she replied, "I guess it's because we *have* to like it. When you're all grown up, you'll know. When you're just a child like yourself, you do what you want, you have choices. But when you grow up, Beau, I will tell you now, it ain't fun. I never do what I want. You know something, honey? I *never* do what I want. I've always done what I *have* to do. I *have* to like the taste of bourbon, and *hey*," she said with that drunken Southern twist that's so appealing and so disturbing, "I ain't feeling no pain right now. Nothin' *hurts*, you know?"

"I guess," I said.

"You boys play nice, don'tcha?"

"Yes'm."

"Be 'specially nice to my boy. He was born on a bad day, and his daddy never plays nice with him."

"Yes'm."

Then she whispered something, as if I wasn't in the room at all, and what I think she said was, *"Couldn't even have one, but she could have two, and look what she tried to do to that sweet little innocent baby. My own sister, my own blood."*

"Aunt Cricket?"

But she was off in some memory to which I was not privy.

So the grown-ups stayed put at night and drank and read and played the radio and fought in their minds.

But the children all went to Neverland.

The light toward the end of August was dimmer, moving closer to winter than any of us would suspect. The smell of the earth and the sea was strong in our nostrils, and we breathed the air as if we owned it. We enjoyed the diluted dark, the fireflies, the crunch of crickets beneath our bare feet. We'd troop single file, or go, shamefacedly, one at a time, thinking no one else would arrive, until we were all at the door, trying to see in around the cardboard Sumter had taped over the windows.

Neverland was our drug, our dream.

⊰ 3 ⊱

Sumter's face was black with mud as he opened the clubhouse door. He had combed mud through his white hair, causing it to stick straight out. He was naked from the waist up, more mud and filth streaked across his small round belly, armpit to armpit. Only his swimming trunks were clean.

"You been playing pig?" Nonie asked.

"What's the password?"

Missy shrugged and looked at me.

I said, "Ain't no password." I peered around him. The inside of Neverland was yellow with fluttering light.

"Yeah, huh."

Like a pencil stuck in my ear, I heard the password in my mind and then blurted it out.

Nonie lip-farted.

"You may enter," Sumter whispered gravely, moving to the side to let me in.

"Some password," Nonie said, but repeated it.

"I can't say that," Missy shook her head, "it's too *nasty*."

"You don't get in unless you say the password."

"Well, I won't get in, then."

"Lucy wants you to say the password."

"Lucy can go have a cow."

Sumter shot his hand out at Missy so quickly it was like a bird taking off in flight, and then he slapped her so hard I could practically feel it.

"Do not take Lucy's name in vain."

Missy's eyes teared up. She reached up and touched the red skin along her right cheek where he'd slapped her.

None of us took Missy's side in this. We were already inside Neverland. We had already said the word that was both dread and wonderful.

I thought my sister would hate her twin and me for betraying her. She looked at all three of us, standing on the other side of the door. But like the rest of us, she wanted in. She knew that the only adventure she'd have for the rest of our last week on the island would be inside those old wooden walls.

"Oh, all right," she said, frustrated. Then she repeated the password three times fast.

Inside Neverland the air was fragrant, like gardenia blossoms. Sumter held up the small atomizer that belonged to Grammy Weenie. "Isis of the Nile," he said, spraying more of the perfume around. "I stole it from her table. One of Lucy's commandments is 'Thou shalt steal.'"

"Oh, wow," Missy said, her eyes widening.

Sumter had lit the shed with candles, also stolen from the Retreat. They were arranged in a starlike pattern around the dirt. He'd been cleaning, moving the broken pots and garden tools off to the sides, bringing the large peach crate to the star's center. The crate now rested upside down, and Sumter had carved a small hole near its base. "Our god resides within."

Nonie cupped her hand over my ear. "You believe this?"

Sumter clapped his hands. "No secrets. Not among us. All must be revealed."

"Is something *really* in there?" Missy asked.

"See for yourself."

She tiptoed over the squat white candles and knelt down beside the crate. She put her ear against the wood. "I hear something."

"Lucy."

Missy screwed her face up. "It sounds like growling. Don't y'all hear it?"

"Put your hand in there." Sumter nodded to the hole at the base of the crate.

"Uh-uh."

He went over and knelt beside her. "Watch," he said, and thrust his hand inside the crate. "It's a test of faith."

"There's nothing in there," Nonie huffed.

"Then put your hand in."

"Don't—" I said, grabbing Nonie's arm.

She shook herself out of my grasp. She practically knocked a candle over on her way to the crate—the yellow light wavered. When Nonie strutted, nothing got in her way. Missy sat back on her fanny. Nonie looked bored as she stuck her hand in the crate. Then she grinned, smug with whatever knowledge she'd just grasped.

She started giggling.

"It feels," she said, "it feels . . . "

"Not *it*," Sumter corrected, *"Lucy."*

"It's *licking* me."

"Lucy."

Nonie stuck her arm in farther. "You have a kitten in there?"

Missy said, almost greedily, "A kitty? Here, let me."

Nonie had been reaching around inside the crate when she seemed to hold onto whatever she'd been grasping at. A look of puzzlement tightened her face. She drew her hand out, looking at it curiously.

Missy leaned forward, her back to the crate's opening, thrusting her hand in. The hole in the crate was almost too small for her hand. "Kitty? Wait, it's tiny. It's the size of . . . all furry. Is it a hamster? Jeez!" She brought her hand out, shaking it. "That thing bit me."

Nonie rubbed her hand. "It bit me, too, or something." She bled slightly just around her wrist. "I didn't feel it. It likes to bite. But it doesn't hurt."

"Lucy." Sumter beamed like a proud parent.

"What you got in there, Sumter?" I asked. I didn't move from where I stood at the open door.

"It's okay, c'mon. Beau, it's okay," Missy said, but she sounded slightly drunk. Her eyes were half shut. She wiped at her face, grinning. "Gawd, they all tickle, like little feathers. Lightning bugs." She nodded her head up and down and back and forth as if the air were liquid and pushing against her. "Swimming," she whispered, "swimming lightning bugs, lights, sea."

"Lucy," Sumter mouthed without speaking, "Lucy likes blood."

Nonie nodded. "Lucy. Yeah." She, too, seemed to be seeing what Missy saw. She grabbed at the air with her fingers. The yellow light painted their faces and made them seem very old and wizened, and I had a vision of my sisters as old ladies getting high on sherry and sitting on a porch, nodding at the lightning bugs on a summer evening. A ribbon of blood spun out from Nonie's wrist and tangled in and around her fingers as she flapped her hands in the air.

I became itchy with hives, as if a cold wind had come up. I knew sometimes when to leave a room, when not to talk to strangers, when something bad was going to happen so that I might avoid it. I wouldn't call this anything more than common sense or intuition. But for some reason, in Neverland, this ability was deadened. I knew I should've stopped this, but I was fascinated. Nonie and Missy stood, grabbing at the air, reaching higher, hopping up as if the lightning bugs were getting away from them.

Sumter grinned happily, his face dark with dried mud. "C'mon, Beau," he beckoned. "It's *beautiful.*"

Missy wiped her bloodstained wrist across the wall, creating a dark spiral smudge right beneath the words, no grown-ups. Nonie was lapping at her own wrist, her lips stained brown while the yellow candlelight aged her face. "It's more than beautiful," Nonie said delicately, as if she could not waste her breath. "It's . . . it's . . . delicious."

She offered her wrist for Missy to taste.

Her twin kissed the cut.

I could not look at them. They seemed too hungry.

I felt itchy with fear, but I wanted to be a part of what they were doing. I did not want to be left out. I was more scared of being left out than of what was in that crate.

I watched my sisters' shadows on the far wall and then Sumter's, which was fainter than theirs. And among those shadows I saw another. A shadow among shadows, a dimly glimpsed figure. It dwarfed all of us as it slid up the wall, a dark stain forming a body as it moved up toward the low roof of the shack. *The All*, Sumter's voice told me, *the Great Feeder, the Great Father*. And then it was no foreign shadow at all, but my own among the other children's as I stepped forward, over the candles, toward the crate that contained our god.

MY MEMORY draws a blank there: I only remember digging my hand into the opening of the crate and then a period of blankness.

I awoke with a queasy stomach.

We all had what looked like blackberry stains on our faces, and I felt warm and goofy and dizzy. The candlelight had turned smooth and white, and when I tried to stand, I felt a little sick.

"It tastes like something," Missy said stupidly.

"Tastes like blood," Sumter giggled.

Nonie got the joke and laughed also.

"I don't feel so good," I said, plopping back down into the dirt again. I held my hand up. I was sure my fingers would've deflated like a balloon after all the blood they'd all been licking at. The blood around my wrist had pretty much dried, although Sumter kept swiping at it, trying to get another lick. I shivered, crossing my arms on my chest. "Am I the only one who's cold?"

"Are we Draculas?" Missy asked.

"Stupid," Nonie huffed. "You've got to be *dead* before you can be a *vampire*. And you get bitten on the *neck*. Sometimes I wonder about you."

"Don't call me stupid, stupid."

"You cold?" I asked Sumter.

He shrugged. "A little."

"I'm tired," Missy sighed, and then she seemed to awaken to her surroundings. She pointed at the walls. "Lookit!"

Nonie covered her ears with her hands. "You don't have to screech."

I followed Missy's pointing finger up. There was more writing all over the walls, thick, loopy writing from our blood.

steal

kill

no other gods before me.

The writing was not ours, although the handprints surrounding it were.

Beneath these words was a tapeworm of blood stretching across half the wall:

whereiamisneverland

⇥ 4 ⇤

These few words would be our commandments.

steal kill

As if reading from a most peculiar Bible, Sumter closed his eyes and said in a voice that sounded like someone else was speaking through him, "First rule of the tribe of Neverland: Thou shall have no other gods before me, says Lucy. The second is like unto it: no grown-ups. Steal and kill and do what you will."

⇥ 5 ⇤

The following morning we became thieves.

Stealing came quite naturally to us, and I'd be a liar if I were to insist that I had never stolen anything before. I spent five minutes every morning going through the pockets of my father's khakis taking spare change and half-opened Wint-O-Green Life Saver rolls. We approached our first thefts to the greater glory of Lucy and Neverland with gusto and spirit; we'd given ourselves a kind of green light to snooping and sneaking and pretending we didn't know that certain items in the household had been taken. Nonie began sneaking cigarettes from Aunt Cricket's purse, and we spent an entire afternoon sitting in the shack while a fog of tobacco blinded us. We coughed all the while we puffed away on the Salems, and we felt the refreshment of clean air in our lungs once we stepped out to walk along the bluffs. Missy took to stealing utensils from the kitchen, and although this seemed less gutsy than Nonie's thefts, Sumter emphasized that Lucy wanted us to steal, and these were the first fruits.

I was the bad egg of the group, because every time I thought I would steal something, Mama or Daddy would come in the room and I'd feel guilty for having even thought to take something that wasn't mine. Sumter pulled me aside while I brushed my teeth and told me, "You've got to steal something *special*, Beau, if you want to be part of Neverland."

After spitting out in the sink, I said, "What if I don't want to?"

"You do. I know you. You do."

"What if I don't?"

"Well, then, you don't. But if you do want to be *in*, do it soon. That's all. Get it?"

"Got it."

"Good."

I DIDN'T struggle with this moral dilemma at all. I knew I'd probably steal something. I longed to, just because I wanted to feel good inside the way I'd felt in Neverland drinking Sumter's blood.

One morning I had my chance.

The peninsula was caught in a fog, and Grammy Weenie, who rarely wanted to go out in the midday sun, begged to have someone take her down to the beach—"Just to sit and watch the water."

Missy and I stared out the window at the wispy mist that crawled across the front lawn and bleached out the trees and the bluffs. She whispered to me, "Don't you think it's scary?"

I almost laughed. Nothing seemed scary anymore—or rather, everything that had once been scary now seemed like fun. We had been drinking each other's blood and writing dirty words on the walls.

She revised her question. "I mean scary in a good way."

"Mama," Aunt Cricket said, as if placating a child, "of course Ralph and me'd be happy to drive you down, but you won't be seeing much ocean in *this*."

"I have sat in this house quite enough for one summer," Grammy insisted, "and you can either take me down there in your car or I will crawl down myself." She was wearing her thin lace dressing gown and had drawn it almost up to her knees to pick at a thread that was coming loose. Her legs were shriveled and skinny and almost completely pale blue with all the veins coursing on the surface. Her stockings, which she always wore, were rolled and wadded around her ankles.

Daddy was buttering toast, leaning against the sink. "Rowena, we'd be delighted." The crunch he made when he ate his toast was like walking across gravel. He seemed remarkably happy this morning; I thought it was the fog, because fog made me happy, too. It meant it would be a cool day, at least until afternoon when the sun and humidity would burn it off.

"We can take the Chevy," Uncle Ralph volunteered, not wanting my father to be the hero of the day.

"No, I'll ride in the wagon, then I can take my chair," Grammy said. "Where's Evvie and my grandchild?"

Daddy said, "Still upstairs. She said she'd skip breakfast."

Aunt Cricket and Uncle Ralph exchanged glances. Mama had been drinking last night: It was written across everyone's faces.

Mama was humming to Governor when she finally came down.

Julianne arrived before nine and pretended that we children didn't exist. She only had six days left with us, and it was becoming obvious that she didn't need the work anymore. You could tell that she didn't like Sumter at all, and whenever she could, she said something unkind about him. "Baby Hitler's looking a little tired this morning," she said to him, scruffing his hair up backward so that he winced. "It's a dirty bird that messes its own cage."

"What she mean by that?" Missy whispered.

Sumter said, "She's on the rag."

⤙ 6 ⤚

If we had walked down the path, we would've made it to the beach in five minutes. But because of Grammy Weenie's legs, we drove down a dirt road that took us twenty minutes out of our way, protected on either side by the barbed wire of blackberry bushes. Daddy drove slowly because the fog was so thick. We were all squeezed in together in the very back, feeling like we were smothering; Grammy and my aunt and uncle in the middle seats; my parents with Governor up front. Governor seemed as much in awe of the mist as we did: His eyes were wide, and he made his happy noise, which went *dit-do, dit-do,* like a bird chirping. Daddy parked the car where the road met the rocks. There was no one else in sight.

The sea apparently ended at a white wall several yards out, and the beach seemed a thin strip of dirt. Uncle Ralph and Daddy carried Grammy Weenie out of the wagon and set her, with some pillows, down upon a large, flat rock. Sumter was wearing his long pants, as we all were, and he rolled them up to his knees, kicking his flip-flops off in the sand. He waded in the shallow surf. My sisters, like gawky ducklings, followed him in, rolling their jeans up, too. Nonie kick-splashed Missy.

"It's warm!" Missy cried. "Oh, wow."

The grown-ups huddled around Grammy, who nodded and pointed as they spoke. It was a calm. Air did not move, waves did not crash. We existed for the moment in a fog crate. Only the keening gulls informed us of the great wide world. We were a family here. I ran ahead of my sisters, avoiding the surf the way the sandpipers did, running ahead of it, too, and then back down as the water receded. I looked back at them and they were gray shadows against the whiteness. I could not even see my parents back near the car. As I ran up the shore I saw someone else standing in the surf: a fisherman with high boots on, looking out into the water. All around him pelicans dove into the thin glassy waves. He wore a baseball cap and beneath his overalls had on a pale blue shirt. But he had no rod. What was he fishing for without a rod? But he pulled something up from the water: a large hooped net, which he proceeded to drag through the sea with an almost gentle, tender action.

"Hey," I called. "Whatcha fishing for?"

But the man didn't hear me. He turned and walked through the water, parallel to the shore, occasionally bending forward to drag his net in the sea. Small feeder fish danced on the surface, as if being tossed up from below just for him, but they were not what he wanted.

I looked back again and saw a white day behind me. No family, no nothing. Fog was everything.

I wanted to go home, not for the usual home reasons, but because this would be my opportunity to fulfill a Neverland commandment: *steal*.

Again I began running, and didn't stop until I'd reached the path up the side of the bluff, back to our property. I trudged carefully up it, glancing over my shoulder occasionally to see if I'd been missed. When I reached the top, I looked back over my shoulder. The fisherman was just a gray shadow passing through whiteness. The fog hid him from me.

Steal. Sumter's voice in my head.

I headed to the Retreat. I would steal something good for Neverland, for Lucy.

THE HOUSE was quiet in a way it could only be at the end of summer: like a vault. Inside its airless chambers you would not believe that a world existed outside.

"Hello?"

My voice came back to me. Flat light sliced beneath the drawn shades. The downstairs was brown and yellow: Color seemed shocking after coming out of the mist. I walked room to room, kitchen to den to bathroom, and back around again. Julianne was supposed to be here. There were some fat red steaks defrosting on a blue plate. Grease stains around the counter. The kitchen was as filthy as we'd left it. None of my family were very good housekeepers. Bad cleaning habits had been passed down from generation to generation, from the Giantess of Biloxi all the way to me. And Julianne Sanders had apparently absorbed our casual messiness by osmosis—we could never be comfortable with a perfectly clean house. But all the evidence of Julianne was here: the steaks, a carton of milk left out, vegetables soaking in the sink. Big green flies batted at the kitchen window from the inside.

"Julianne?"

I wandered back through the kitchen to the back door. Julianne parked her run-down Volkswagen Bug there. I looked out the door's window. The sun was burning off the haze. I could see all the way to the next house down the road. It was in slightly worse shape than the Retreat. A woman was on the porch poking a broom into the eaves, unraveling spider webs or batting at a wasp's nest. Julianne's car was gone. She must have gone into town on an errand. She would be back shortly.

If I was going to steal something of value, I would only have a few minutes.

I took the stairs two at a time. My aunt and uncle's room appealed to me. It had been Grampa Lee's old bedroom and was the largest of the four. The enormous four-poster bed against the wall was about as large as the room I slept in. Sumter's roll-away cot was next to the window. The shades were drawn. Grammy's Victorian dollhouse and doll collection, in its glass case, had been moved from their usual sunny location beneath the window and pushed up against the wardrobe. I went over to the dresser. Aunt Cricket had left her Salems carton on the marble top, with cigarettes scattered across the smudged wax surface of the cherrywood border. A length of pantyhose hung out from a crack in the top side drawer, beckoning me with its suggestion of intimacy.

This was the drawer I would open.

It was like exploring an unknown universe, like digging into someone's thoughts, their private parts. The drawer was swimming in gold and green paisley scarves, and more pantyhose, some of it still in crisp packages. Loose cigarettes, too, and jewelry. I picked up an earring: It was a tiny red and yellow ceramic antherium flower. A stack of square black-and-white snapshots, mainly of Sumter when he was a baby. Sumter's first Christmas. Sumter walking. Sumter sleeping. Sumter and his teddy bear on the porch of the house in Marietta. Sumter on his mama's lap.

I dug down deep in the drawer and found sunken treasure: a small wooden box. An engraving of a Japanese dragon was on the lid. I opened it. It was crushed velvet inside. There was a string of pearls and a silver ring with a blue stone. A charm bracelet with three charms on and two fallen into the velvet. One of the fallen charms was a seal, another a schnauzer. I reached into the velvet to see if there were any more, and in doing so, discovered another layer beneath this one—I greedily lifted it.

There at the bottom of the box was another snapshot and a small green pin. I looked at the photo: a skinny man, not quite a grown-up, but almost. He wore boxer shorts and a grin. His hair was short and slicked back, and his ears stuck out like Dumbo's. Behind him, a lake. Uncle Ralph had never been that thin. I turned the picture over. Scrawled on the back: *The day you hid my clothes and I had to wear underwear or nothing—what would Rowena say?* What looked like dried blood smudged across the words. But it wasn't blood—it was lipstick.

I held the green pin between my thumb and forefinger and squinted to see what was engraved there. ΛΧΑ.

My father was a Lambda Chi Alpha, and I'd seen that symbol on one of his baseball caps. Had Uncle Ralph been in that fraternity, too?

From downstairs I heard singing.

Julianne was back.

She was singing "My Baby Does the Hanky-Panky." Water ran in the kitchen sink.

I put the pin and photo into my pocket and closed the box. I laid it back beneath the scarves and hose and shut the drawer.

"What are you doing?" Julianne asked as I came down the stairs.

"Nothing."

"Don't nothing me. Your mama know you're up here?"

"I had to use the bathroom."

She stood there in the hall, her hands soaking red. She noticed me looking. "It's from the meat. We're barbecuing tonight. The steaks are runny." She wiped her hands across her apron. "Blood as warm as swamp water."

⇥ 7 ⇤

That night, for the first time, we had our meeting after bedtime. We all faked falling asleep, and then around about two a.m. Sumter shook me by the shoulders. Missy and Nonie stood around my bed, shining a flashlight in my face. My circulation was acting up again, and they massaged my feet and my arms to help speed things up.

"Will you hurry up?" Nonie whispered to my toes. "You weren't *really* supposed to go to sleep, you know."

"Lucy said she wants to cure you," Sumter said.

WE SAT in a circle and smoked Aunt Cricket's Salems. I felt light-headed, but not sleepy at all. When the time came to pass around what we'd stolen that day, I brought out the snapshot and the pin. "From a box in your mama's dresser," I said.

Nonie stared at it a good long while before passing it to Missy, and Missy barely glanced at it. "It's Uncle Ralph," she said, "in his boxers."

But Sumter grabbed the picture from her. "It's not *my* daddy. But I know who this is. I've seen Mama go through her box when she thinks no one is looking. She puts on her earrings in front of the mirror. She looks at this picture and she starts crying. She bawls her eyes out sometimes when she thinks no one's looking. Sometimes she *kisses* it like this." He pressed his lips against the photo and smacked his lips. Then he nodded his head toward me. "You done good. Lucy is much pleased." He went over and got a hammer and tacked the photo up on the wall. "This is a better steal than most, 'cause it means a lot to someone."

"Oh, *I* know who it is," Nonie said. "It's our daddy. Big deal. Everybody knows your mama has a thing for our daddy."

Missy, shocked by her casual use of the Neverland password, let out a squeal and then giggled.

Nonie, looking weary and unsatisfied, asked, "Why can't Lucy show herself?"

I was about to say *Sometimes she does*, but felt an invisible hand go over my mouth.

Sumter clapped his hands. "You have no faith. Your faith must be tested. And the way to the test is through the first principle of the universe. And the first principle of the universe," Sumter told us, "is sacrifice."

⊣ 8 ⊨

Our first assignment was closer to animal experimentation than to sacrifice.

The next morning Sumter caught a skinny lizard from the bark of a tree with a small string noose. "If you cut off its tail, it'll grow back." Sumter had a small steak knife from the kitchen, adding to his cache of stolen items. Rather than just slice the tail off, he hacked at it like he was trying to machete his way through a jungle. The tail came off in his hand and thrashed about, while the terrified lizard ran off for a corner of the shed. "If we cooked it, it would taste like chicken," he beamed proudly, waggling the tail in Missy's face.

Nonie rolled her eyes. "Grotesque."

"To Lucy I dedicate this lizard tail," he said, dropping the tail into the crate's opening. "Now where the hell did that lizard go? We got to sacrifice it to Lucy, too."

MISSY became fond of taking fat black ants and popping their abdomens into the back of her throat. She said it tasted like honey. Then she would take ants and put them in the freezer. After about a minute she would pull them out and watch them move slowly around. She found that if she left them in the freezer for more than a minute, they never recovered. So she caught a small chameleon lizard and tried freezing that, too, only she went off and forgot about it. This we sacrificed to Neverland, too.

I went with Nonie one afternoon to buy some bait down at Shep and Diane's, and she got a Cayman lizard and some goldfish. We spent a late evening in Neverland feeding the fish to the lizard. Although I felt sad for the fish, they were just fish, after all, and I ate them all the time.

"It's the law of nature," Sumter said wisely. "Eat or be eaten. I mean, which would you wanta be? The Cayman or the goldfish? You eat cow, don'tcha? You eat pig flesh."

THEN it was my turn for some kind of sacrifice. I didn't really want to take part in this ritual, but I figured I'd have to. I was sitting out on the bluffs one day by myself trying to come up with something a little less disgusting than killing lizards and goldfish. Because sacrifice was supposed to be part of our devotion, I knew I'd have to kill something.

There was one kind of animal life at the Retreat that I was never very fond of.

Field mice.

Or more specifically, the field mice that entered the house from cracks in the chimney at night and ran across the kitchen counters. If I woke up in the night and decided I needed a glass of milk, I would flick on the kitchen light and get the tail ends of the small gray-brown mice all skittering for cover. Uncle Ralph had put out traps and caught a few, but there were always more. Mice are like that.

Unlike other children my age, I had no affection for them. I didn't see them as Stuart Littles or Mickeys. I saw them as disgusting. And I was always afraid that one of them would pass their mouse germs to Governor while Mama changed his diaper on the cutting board.

So I would have to figure out how to catch a live mouse and take it to Neverland. I came up with the age-old trap: a cigar box, propped up on one side with a small wooden dowel from the toilet paper holder in the bathroom. Attached to this, a string. What I figured on doing was smearing some bread crumbs with peanut butter and then when the mouse crawled inside for a bite, pull the string and trap the mouse.

For two nights I lay in the kitchen, wrapped up in a sleeping bag from the attic. The grown-ups thought it was adorable that I was hunting mice. Only Grammy Weenie suspected I was up to something that might not be as sweet as catching a live mouse for a pet. "All life is sacred," she told me, but she'd been the one who got Uncle Ralph to put the mousetraps down in the first place.

Finally, the second night, just as I was about to fall asleep on the linoleum, a mouse ventured into my cigar box. I tugged on the string and the box came slamming down on its lid.

I had my mouse.

I heard it scratching and squealing, trying to get out. I turned the box over, keeping the lid down tight. I went up to my bedroom and piled several hardback books on top of it. Remembering Missy's dead hamster, Pogo, I poked holes in the lid so the mouse could breathe. I tried to sleep, but could not. Every time I began to drift off, I thought of that small mouse and wondered how it must feel to be trapped like that and not know what was going on.

I expected the creature to be dead from either fear or exhaustion by morning, as I myself was well on my way. But, shaking the box, I heard still another squeal, so I knew my mouse was alive and well.

"Beau caught himself a mouse last night," Missy whispered at the breakfast table.

Daddy and Uncle Ralph had risen early to go fishing out on Rabbit Lake, and since there were only four days left to us on Gull Island, I dropped all pretense of wanting to bait hooks and swat mosquitoes out on that swamp. All the grown-ups seemed to have elongated cocktail hours in the evenings, during which they'd carp at each other or just sit in stony silence. The mornings were full of gray hungover faces downing tomato juice and talking about how peaceful the Retreat was. Grammy sat across from me and wrote in her composition book, occasionally thumbing through it to mark a section. Julianne Sanders had made hush puppies and eggs, and we greedily wolfed these down. Mama was distracted, as she had become increasingly since our arrival on the island, distracted and distant. Occasionally she would shoot me a look that scared me and she'd say, "You children are up to something, and I don't think I like it one little bit."

Only Aunt Cricket was chipper, and what a nightmare that could be. "I think I'll take you girls down to the beauty parlor with me today. You'd like that, just us girls?"

Nonie wrinkled her nose. "I don't think so, Aunt Cricket."

"Leonora Burton Jackson," Mama said, snapping her fingers, "you be polite to your aunt."

"No one ever listens to me," Missy whined. "I *said*, Beau caught himself a mouse."

We ate the rest of our breakfast in silence.

The world of grown-ups became the world of shadows. I began to hate them, to want to cut myself off from them as much as possible.

≼ 9 ≽

After lunch I took a nap, setting the cigar box trap with its skittering occupant down on my dresser. I awoke after a spell to some noise: footsteps in the hall, Governor's *dit-dos*. I lay in bed, rubbing my legs with my hands—getting my defective circulation going, cursing my unhappy birth. Next I heard *clumpaclumpaclumpa*, the sound of something falling downstairs. I knew immediately what—or rather who—it was, before he even started wailing: Governor. The sounds of other footsteps, and then my legs were well enough to carry me out into the hall. Mama was crying, holding the baby at the bottom of the stairs. She looked up at me and said in a whisper, "Beau, oh, Beau, sweetie. I just set him down for a second." I bounded down the steps almost tripping until I was beside them. I looked into my baby brother's pale eyes. He had stopped crying.

"He's made of rubber," I said.

Mama's face was a sickly yellow, even with her sunburn. Her eyes were dark like a raccoon's. She was wearing a long white slip beneath her robe. I couldn't look back up at her face.

Governor seemed fine. "See? Governor's okay. Puppy-dog tail Governor, the bouncy baby bumper boy." I grinned at him and caught his nose in my hand and pretended to make it disappear.

"He tried to walk," Mama said. "I just went away for a second. I didn't know he'd get to the stairs. Oh, Beau."

"He's just fine, Mama, don't cry."

"This means something," she said, straightening up a bit. "I should've been watching him, this means ... I've misplaced the car keys this week—twice. Sometimes I get so mad at him, Beau, and he's just a little baby; he doesn't know why I get mad at him."

For the first time in my life, I looked at my mother like I had never seen her before. She seemed a stranger.

"I just left him for a second. Less than a second."

"He's just fine."

"No, I don't think so." She held him up over her head. "He's got a bump. I think something's wrong with him. Or me. My sister, what she did to her child ... "

"Governor's okay. It was an accident."

"He'll have a bruise now." She brought my brother's face down to hers and gave him a kiss. "My beautiful baby with a bruise. It's this place, this house. This is no place for children. It never has been. It's all *her*. Grammy. She's a monster. What she did. . . . You don't want to hear this, do you, Beau?"

"Mama?"

"Whenever we're here we always fight. Governor never falls down the stairs at home. He never falls. I never get mad at him at home. I never lose things. You like your grammy?"

"I guess."

"She does this to me. She makes me like this. She makes everyone like this. What she did—what my sister did—and what *she* did—and my sister, with her child—not your cousin—*yes*, your cousin, but the *child*, the *child*, I never saw, but I heard, Beau, I heard. *She* told me, *not* my sister. . . ." She began babbling hysterically. I didn't know what to say to my mother once she started talking like this—quickly, nervously, as if she were afraid someone was spying and then she'd get in trouble. Of my several fears, one was that my mother might turn insane and they'd take her away. She was only insane around Grammy, though; she only drank like a fish at the Retreat.

"It'll be all right," I said, patting her shoulder.

"Maybe we'll just go home soon." She sighed, rocking Governor against her breast. "We've stayed too long, is all, too damn long."

⇥ 10 ⇤

Nonie said to me, "When I grow up I'll know how not to raise children by just watching *her*." Daddy and my uncle came in at four with no fish and smelling like a brewery. As we walked off to Neverland in the early evening, Aunt Cricket called after her son, "Sunny? Don't play too long in the woods. It'll be too dark to play freeze-tag soon. You gonna play freeze-tag, Sunny? The croquet set is set up in the yard. You want to play croquet?"

Sumter said the password to Neverland over and over as we got farther and farther from his mother's voice.

"Beau, present your sacrifice."

I held up the cigar box.

"No, I mean get it *out*."

I opened the lid carefully.

The mouse was adorable. It cowered, terrified, in its corner. "Gawd," I said, my mild Southern accent becoming stronger as I realized the awfulness of hurting living things. The mouse had small nipples on its belly. It was a mother mouse, and somewhere its children were starving because I had trapped it.

"One less mouse," Nonie said.

Sumter, with outstretched arms, "Hand it over."

I shut the lid on the box. "I'm going to let it go."

My cousin snarled. "When you gonna learn? When you ever gonna learn? Neverland *wants* the sacrifice, Lucy *wants* the sacrifice. The *All* wants the sacrifice. You have to prove your faith to our god. Get down on your knees, sinner, and *pray!* Pray to Lucy for forgiveness for your sin of *pride*, for your sin of pretending to know the mind of Lucy!" He was spitting as he railed at me, slapping his hand down on the top of the sacred crate.

Missy clasped her hands together in prayer, her eyes rolled up into their lids, and she began whispering to herself, *"Lucy, we pray you, forgive this our brother, he doesn't know what he's about."*

"Jeez, Beau, just give him the mouse, for God's sakes," Nonie huffed, her hands on her hips like a little mother. "All this racket over a *mouse*, jeez."

Missy made a grab for the cigar box, and I wrenched it away from her, but as I did this I hit my elbow into the wall and the box flew out of my hands. I watched as it spun in midair, the lid snapping open and the mouse cannonballing out of it, squealing what I was sure would be its last squeal.

It landed on its feet, knocking over one of the burning candles. Its fur caught fire. The sound of its scream was not that much different from a human cry.

I got down on my knees and scrambled in the dirt, trying to put the flame out with soil. I cupped my hands around the mouse; it was biting at my palms. The fire was out. The mouse was still in my hands. I could still feel its heartbeat.

I opened my hands.

The thing in my hands had red eyes.

It had a ridge of thick gray teeth like a shark's.

It was growling at me.

It was still a charred mouse, still smoldering, still breathing. But its red eyes, its gray teeth.

"Beauregard, bring me my glasses," it said.

The way Grampa Lee always said.

Beauregard, bring me my glasses.

Its breath was sourmash and old coffee grounds.

But the creature in my hand was just a burned mouse.

Now dead.

"You did that," I said to Sumter.

Lucy.

Sumter clapped his hands slowly. Nonie and Missy began clapping their hands.

"Your first sacrifice," my cousin said cheerfully. "That wasn't so hard, now was it? Don't cry, cuz. You done good."

"It's just a mouse. You hate mice."

"Shut up, Nonie," Missy said. "I understand, Beau. But that's why it's a sacrifice. 'Cause it hurts to do it." She put her arm around me and whispered, "It's just make-believe, anyway, isn't it?" I noticed her eyes: dull, half-lidded, drugged, the way all our eyes were when we were in the shack.

NINE

A Book of
Revelations

⇥ 1 ⇤

"Look what I stole," Missy said after Sumter had plucked the burned mouse from my hand and popped it through the opening of the crate of our god, Lucy.

Missy bent over to retrieve something from a paper bag. What she brought out was one of Grammy's black composition books. She handed it dutifully to Sumter, who shushed all of us.

He opened the notebook to its first page. Sumter read aloud.

To my mind there is no more lovely and terrible phrase in all the English language than 'summer afternoon.' For it was on a summer afternoon that a horror began for us, when I was just sixty years of age. I have never forgiven myself for what I did to my daughter, and I relive that moment every day of my life.

"This is gonna be great reading. What a *steal*. Lucy is very, very, very happy."

"Read more."

But what she had done was a sin of the gravest variety. What else could be done? She had given herself over to that darkness waiting there on the bluffs. Old Lee believed her to be an idiot, ever since the surgery in New Orleans, but I knew that all the doctors had done for her was remove the very emotions that kept her sane, that kept her human. If anything, her operation had released something from her mind that was better kept in its cage. But after we had come here, to Gull Island, she had only one purpose left in life, and it was a dark one. She was like a mad child, speaking to birds and to the grass as if all of nature could reply to her. The operation had opened a door in the madness of her mind; it had made it possible for her to see another world, one that may be all around us, but that we can't see. It was the Wandigaux inheritance; it was our curse.

"What a yawn-o-rama," Nonie said. "Grammy's always been a nut." Sumter glared at her. "Lucy wants us to read it."

"Yeah, sure."

He continued.

And then there was the sad story of the drownings. I had thought, because her mind seemed so much like a child's that playing with children was good for her. She was barely more than a child herself. I didn't dare venture near the shed, for she would fly into rages each time I approached, but I thought a play area was good for her.

How was I to know what she did there? With those three children? How were any of us to know in what arts she tutored them?

In my mind's eyeball, as Sumter would say, I saw Zinnia sitting where Missy had moments before been. Zinnia in her scraggly sack dress, her hair sun-yellow, her teeth crooked as she smiled up to Babygirl, who had become a shadow in the back of Neverland. Zinnia's brothers, Wilbur and Goober, were there, too, and were playing jacks. Wilbur took up one of the small metal jacks and cut himself across the wrist; he held it up to his sister, who lapped at the dripping blood.

Sumter's voice was soft as he read.

Shall I commit to paper the atrocity of that golden summer afternoon when she swam with the children out to sea? I knew what she was about. I could've stopped her, I could've saved their lives. But I wanted to be rid of her: She was driving me to madness. I turned my back on them as they swam, and when I finally looked back, I did not see a single one of them . . .

"Hey," Nonie said, "the Weenie's been lying about Babygirl. She went and killed herself."

"All grown-ups are liars. We *never* want to be grown-ups, do we?" Sumter closed the composition book. "You have done well, Missy, by stealing this in Lucy's name. You are truly a child of your god."

"They are liars," Nonie nodded, dreamily. "They expect you to always tell the truth, and they lie through their teeth. They can all go to Hell."

Even your daddy. Sumter's voice was in my brain.

He pointed to the snapshot I'd stolen from Aunt Cricket's jewelry box: the man in the boxer shorts, pinned to the wall with the ΛΧΑ pin.

Even your daddy's a liar, just like mine, just like all of them.

"It's just your mama," I protested. "She probably stole the pin and the picture from our mama. My daddy never loved your mama."

They all lie, Beau. But there's a way we don't never have to be grown-ups. Lucy will take us there. Lucy wants us to never hurt.

"Can't we fly again?" Missy pleaded. "I really loved that."

"I wish we could just disappear," Nonie sighed.

"Through Lucy," Sumter grinned, reaching behind the crate, "everything is possible. And now we have one more sacrifice this afternoon, before the great sacrifice."

Getting angrier the more I looked at the snapshot of my father on the wall, I said, "I think you're making all this up as you go along. Why don't you show us Lucy, huh? Why don't we get to see?"

"I told you," he said, "one more sacrifice today. Before the great one. And Lucy will be revealed."

"What's the 'great' one?"

"For me to know and you to find out." He lifted a picnic basket—also stolen—from behind the crate. Reaching into one of the flaps, he withdrew a small black kitten. "And one of you must make this sacrifice," he said.

The kitten mewed and pawed at the air, trying to bite him.

Growling noises came from the crate.

Lucy was hungry.

Sumter reached down and picked up a trowel.

He held it, handle out, toward me.

Bash its head in.

For Lucy.

"Not a kitty," Missy huffed.

"Oh, it's *okay* to kill mice and chameleons and junk, but not cats? Killing is *killing*."

"I don't care about mice. But not kittens, for God's sakes, Sumter." Nonie stood up, dusting herself off.

"Lucy wants us to do this."

"I don't care, I'm not gonna kill a kitten. It's just plain mean and stupid, and if Lucy wants that, then I'm tired of playing this game."

"This *game?*" Sumter was incredulous. "You think this is a game? Lookit." He pointed all around the walls of Neverland: It was painted over with dirty words and sayings, some in chalk, some in spray paint, some in blood. We had written all of it. "You think this is a *game* we been playing?

You think *flying* was a game? You think that sacrifice is a game? We're calling Lucy into us, don'tcha get it? Lucy's our only salvation from them. Lucy's the way out."

And in one quick motion, before any of us could stop him, he jabbed the point of the trowel into the kitten's neck.

⊰ 2 ⊱

The bunny screams because it is alive, the woman was saying, and when you're alive, everything hurts.

"Did you see?" he asked me afterward, after my sisters had run shrieking from Neverland, after he had lain the dead kitten down in the crate. "Did you see?" His hands were covered in blood, and he didn't look like a monster, and he didn't look like the high priest of a god.

He looked like a stupid little boy who had just torn through the wrapping paper on his Christmas present. His eyes were wide and sparkling, his face flushed with excitement. I wouldn't have been surprised if he'd begun foaming at the mouth and gibbering. He looked like a wild animal who had just caught its prey. I could imagine him holding the dead kitten between his teeth and shaking it in victory.

I knew then that he liked to kill.

"Did you see? You musta seen, cuz. I know Lucy speaks to you, so you musta *seen*."

I fled from that place like it was the entrance to Hell itself. I heard his maniacal voice behind me. "You *saw*, but you're too much like them! You're a liar! Well, I banish you from Neverland! You hear me? You are *banished!*"

⊰ 3 ⊱

My sisters were inside by the time I reached the house. I was prepared to tell all, I was prepared to spill the beans regardless of my blood oath. Nonie said, "You really think he killed it?"

193

Missy shook her head. "Uh-uh, remember the rabbit? I think it was a trick. Beau—didn't you say the bunny was already dead? Well, maybe the kitty was, too."

"You don't know that," I said stonily.

"I'm gonna watch TV," Nonie said, pouring herself some milk.

I wanted to scream at them: *He killed a cat!* Why were they so undisturbed by that sacrifice? Was it all a dream? If a child can feel the tidal pull of sanity within his small skull, I felt it then. The world was coming apart, and I didn't know anymore what was real and what was imagined. My sisters acted as if nothing much had happened. Nonie went on a bit about how she was getting tired of Sumter's games and all the make-believe. Then she very calmly went into the den and switched on the black-and-white TV. Missy followed after her with a plate of graham crackers with peanut butter spread over them.

I kept seeing in my mind's eyeball that kitten unharmed, its small green eyes wide with curiosity as Sumter held it in midair. The mouse burning. What was in that crate, what thick fog covered our eyes in that shed that warped the way things really were? I was beginning to doubt that any of what had gone on in Neverland had truly occurred. Would we need surgery, too, and would we both one day egg each other on and swim out to the horizon until our limbs grew heavy and we longed for endless sleep?

I felt disembodied.

I saw the little boy who was standing in the kitchen doorway, leaning against the jamb. It was as if all my bad circulation had finally just stopped, the machine of my body had shut down. *Spirit and flesh constantly at war*, Grammy had said, *and always we must seek the higher ground.* I saw my flesh and spirit separate then. I saw them as two distinct entities, and I was ready to leave my flesh behind. Even my body parts seemed to tear loose from their tenuous connections, my hands floating away from their wrists, my head cut neatly at the neck, my torso twisting itself out of the sockets of my thighs.

I knew at any minute I would explode, and my spirit would look on from above and watch the explosion. My cells were fighting to rend themselves free.

And then I heard the crying of a baby.

My brother Governor.

Upstairs, in his crib.

And in my mind's eyeball I journeyed up those stairs, down the hall, through the bedroom door. I imagined myself over his crib, and there he was, his feet up in the air, his toes wiggling, his diaper soaked yellow, his eyes like rolling marbles, and his screams shattering and wonderful. A human scream—a scream that others complained about, but that made me feel like I was sitting by a hearth fire on a cold night drinking soup. *Warmth.*

We all scream because we are alive.

Just that one thought.

And I was standing in the kitchen doorway again, while my brother cried for someone upstairs to change him.

There were other cries, too. Another fight was breaking out between my parents, and Julianne came in from beating a rug and announced to me that she was quitting.

4

"This family's getting to be too much for me." While she spoke she glanced out of the corners of her eyes. She would not look at me directly. Usually she had her sleeves rolled up, ready for work, but her sleeves were all the way down, discreetly buttoned. She looked older; she looked too much like a grown-up. She was speaking like she was still sorting things out in her head. "I don't need the money that bad, anyway. I can get some other job— maybe in St. Badon. Maybe I just won't work—I can get by. I don't need this *hassle.*"

When she finally looked me in the eye, I saw fear.

She *knew* all about Sumter. She had to know. Sometimes I felt like she could see right through all us kids. "You're leaving 'cause of Neverland. You're a *sinistre*, and you know we're all hexed."

"Let me tell you something, Beau, and get it now or never get it. Now, you want the truth or you want to hear what you want to hear?"

"The truth."

"I am a *sinistre* by birth, but that's nothing. Folks on this island'll tell you that *sinistres*, Gullahs, and full moons and hoot owls all got some kind of power, but none of us does. It's all a lie just to make life more interesting. It's make-believe. I am a Catholic and I don't even believe all that. You know what I do believe, boy? I believe I know about what you children do in that shed out back, and let me tell you, it ain't got nothing to do with no *sinistres*, no dead slaves, no sacred places. What it's got to do with is that cousin of yours, and the more you let him do it, the worse it's gonna get. I don't know that I believe in God, Beau, but I once met a man I *know* was not from Heaven. He could raise the dead, and he could make you see things, but it ain't never good, Beau, and it ain't got nothing to do with God and the Devil. It's got to do with the *mind*, you hearing me? The *mind*. Nobody knows why some people's smarter than others, and nobody knows why some people got certain talents, and nobody knows why some of those talents can't be explained in some research lab. Ain't no IQ test for what your cousin's got, but I can tell you it ain't got nothing to do with Gullahs and *sinistres*."

Who else could I turn to? I felt like my insides were coming apart. My teeth were chattering like I was locked in a freezer. I whispered, "I—I think he makes us worship Lucifer."

She came over and put her hands on my shoulders to both steady and warm me. "Ain't that a laugh. What you're worshiping out there, Beau, what all you children are worshiping, is more like Sumter, that's what's going on. He's a little god and you're letting him get away with it."

"I seen ghosts there."

"I know. But it *can't* be real, Beau. Keep it in mind. It's got to all be from him. He's got that thing I've seen before. He's got the *mind*."

"Don't go, Julianne, please."

"I got to go, Beau. Things are gonna happen here I don't want to be around for. You'll be fine if you just keep in mind what I told you. You're his cousin; you've got a mind, too, it's not all him. He's just a conjurer; he just has a bag of tricks. He's just a child. He's just . . . "

But there was fear in her eyes, too, and I saw the lie. We all lied. Julianne was lying, because in her cinnamon-flecked brown eyes I saw the truth: She didn't know any more than I did.

I took a step back from her. "You're *scared* of him. You're leaving 'cause you're *scared* of him."

She turned her face away to look out of the window over the sink. She must've been gazing out over the bluffs and the pines. She shivered just as I had done a few moments before. "You just don't go near that place again, and you keep your sisters away. Hear?"

"You said you'd tell me the truth. You said you'd tell me the *truth*."

Her voice shrunk down; it was tiny, I could barely hear her. It was like wind through the crack of an old house in winter. "Who knows the truth? You think just 'cause you grow up you know the truth? You think your gramma even knows the truth just 'cause she's old? *Nobody* knows for sure *nothing* until you die, and then maybe not even then. You just got to stay away from things that don't look good."

"It is so a sacred place."

"Every place on earth is sacred to *something*. Who knows what's underground anywhere you walk on this earth? You just don't dig, do you? You know when something's bad it's bad, and you stay away."

"You know something. You tell me."

"I can't . . . "

"You tell me." Without wanting to, I began bawling like a baby. I couldn't even see straight for the tears. I had been holding so many fears inside me, so much *wondering*, that it finally was breaking out through my eyes. I went and held her around the waist just like she was my mother. She smelled of cocoa butter and sweat. I closed my eyes and wished it all away. I wished I was back home in Richmond, and I wished it was Mama I was clinging to, and I wished I would never grow up. "You tell me, 'cause I need to know . . ."

Her voice steadied as mine broke. "Something I saw. When I first looked at him. I knew."

"You tell me."

"I saw a devourer."

"It *is* Lucifer." I was almost comforted by this thought. I knew what you did to ward off the Devil: You pray. You pray real hard and you wait for an answer. You make the sign of the cross. You sprinkle holy water all over the place. You read passages from the Bible. You get your soul saved.

Her fingers combed through my hair. The fabric of her skirt was fuzzy and soft. She pushed me away. "Let me go, just let me go."

Julianne Sanders leaned over and kissed me on my forehead. "It may be nothing," she said, tears also in her eyes. "I don't know, Beau. I don't *know*."

I followed her out back to her Volkswagen Bug, and she squeezed my hand and told me to just stay away from Neverland. I didn't watch her drive away. I ran around to the front of the Retreat, angry because I didn't know who to turn to, and I was filled with a giant rage.

I needed to destroy something.

⊰ 5 ⊱

It was a childish impulse, but I was a child. The storm inside the house raged out of control, and I stood there and began stepping up and down on the flowers that Aunt Cricket had planted in neat rows to the side of the house. It felt good to destroy.

Voices from the house, familiar and alien: "You don't love me, so why don't you just leave."

"And don't you tell me how to raise my children, either. It's not like you were terribly good yourself. You with that damn brush just beating the crap out of us all the time. You think *that's* mothering? You think *fear's* the way to raise kids up to be good little ladies and gentlemen? You've never been anything but cold to me! And don't tell me how good you were; I don't want to hear it! Grampa used to tell me the truth about that. He used to tell me about her, about what you did to her, how you drove her—"

"I wish I had never given birth." Grammy was shouting, too. "I wish I had hollowed out my womb with fire before I gave birth to a girl like you."

"Christ Almighty!" Daddy cried out, "I am getting the hell out of this sick family. I am getting the hell away from here—you and your insane relatives!"

"Good, good! It's about time you did *something*. And don't come crawling back here tomorrow expecting me to forgive you."

"Forgive me, *forgive* me? That's a laugh, that's a goddamn laugh! Don't expect me to come back, either, Evelyn, not to your sick little family and this rundown rat-trap!"

I stomped every flower in that garden and then some.

The front door slammed like a trap, and Daddy came out on the porch cussing and hitting the porch column with his fists.

TEN

Dread Night

My father's face was almost calm. His hair, glistening with sweat, was pushed back away from his high forehead, and there were no wrinkles there. His anger had reached its peak; he was now beyond feeling. Those words, "Don't expect me to come back," had removed him from the situation. And the others, "Your sick little family . . . " Daddy was somehow gone even before he headed for the wagon. His eyes were clear, and the slanting afternoon light flattened his features, leaving him no clear expression.

I stood there, watching him. He would not even notice what I was doing: stomping up the garden Aunt Cricket had planted over and over, each summer, and over and over the garden had died. It didn't even feel like I was doing the killing of those flowers; it felt like a force of nature unleashed through the soles of my feet. I could see myself watching my father. I could see myself as if from above, standing motionless. I was sure if I stayed very still, Daddy would walk right past me and not even know I was there. His face was fixed with blankness. His long knuckly fingers pumping at invisible tennis balls.

I hated him just then with all my heart.

"Coward!" I shouted.

Again I was removed. I watched a little boy yell at his father. It wasn't me.

He turned and looked right through me.

"Beau?" He took a hesitant step toward me. He wore the V-neck T-shirt that made him look potbellied. His khakis sagged around his waist.

"You're a goddamn coward and you know it!"

"Snug, you okay?" He squatted down in front of me. I felt a blast of heat from his body as if he'd been absorbing the sun so much that he had turned into a furnace.

I covered my face in my hands, thinking, *Go away, go away.*

His fingers gripped my shoulders, digging in. They were as warm as I'd ever felt them.

"I'm just going to St. Badon to run some errands," he said.

"No you're not, you're running out on us."

"Okay, I'm not. I'm going to go spend a night at a motel in St. Badon. I promise I'll be back."

"Liar."

"I'll be doing some thinking, too, Beau, but I'm not running out."

"I don't believe you. You *lie* about *everything*."

"Don't you talk to me like that."

"Well, it's true. What about you and Aunt Cricket?"

"I won't lie to you."

"Well, what about it?"

"I never even liked your aunt, Beau. She liked me, but I never liked her. She followed me around. But that's how I met your mother, so it wasn't all bad. I just have never liked your aunt."

"I don't believe you."

"I think you do."

"I don't. So why don't you just get out of here. We don't *need* you."

"You don't mean that."

"Get out of here, you coward."

"I'll be back by supper."

"I don't care if you ever come back."

"All right, then."

He got up and walked unsteadily to the station wagon. I knew I had hit my father with what he feared most: the scorn of his children.

He glanced back at me briefly as I stood there, and I felt the cold sinking mud of the garden beneath my feet.

My vision went out of focus. I began crying, and, on the inside, I tried fighting those tears, but they wanted out through my eyes. I felt like a Roman candle that was spiraling through the air, hitting whatever came in my path, ready to burst into vivid colors. I aimed for him, running toward him, hoping to wound him some more. I was full of stomping madness. "And don't you ever come back! Hear? We don't need you! None of us needs you!" My voice was shrill and stupid, and my lips were curled in a grin, and I began laughing at him.

He got in the car just as I slammed my fist against the hood of the wagon. He started up the engine. His face seemed large, his eyes seemed small. I had the most horrible hallucination as I saw him only half clearly through the dusty windshield: He was doing the exact same thing as I was, and we were the same person, my father and I. We were not even separated: Like the swimming minnows at the bait shop, our minds moved in the same direction without knowing why.

Then I felt a kind of tugging inside me, of my muscles rebelling. "Daddy, I'm sorry," I panted. He put the car in reverse. He rolled down his window.

I shuffled over to lean against his door. "Daddy, take me, too. Take me."

"Beau?"

"Can't I go?"

He reached out with his hand and patted my head. "Your mama needs you right now. I'll be back."

"No you won't."

"Promise."

"How long you gonna be gone?"

"A little while. Till tomorrow. I'll be back by early." He must've read the disappointment in my eyes and thought better on it, because he said, "Tell you what. You go out on the bluffs right when the sun is just barely up over the water and wait. I'll flash my lights on the tiara bridge—four times—and you'll know I'm home."

"You won't come back."

"You watch. I'll never leave you, Beau. Ever."

He honked the horn as he pulled back out of the drive, in reverse the whole way down to the main gravel road. Dust and big green flies and pebbles sprayed up from the wagon. He flashed his headlights at me and honked the horn. I glared at the dust and flies. I looked down at my feet: Pansies lay crushed there, purple and yellow petals between my toes.

The bunny screams because it is alive.

I wanted to scream, too. I wanted to holler to raise the dead, but I couldn't even find my voice. *What are we gonna do without Daddy? What's Mama gonna do? How are we gonna get by? What's gonna happen to Governor without his daddy?* The thoughts spun through me in my panic. I felt like I couldn't catch my breath, and then that I had forgotten how to breathe at all, and I opened and closed my mouth like a fish on land. I watched the station wagon go until it disappeared into the sky. *What are we gonna do?*

I turned. Behind me the Retreat was unchanged and without calm. I could still hear my mother throwing things around her bedroom, pulling drawers from the dresser, her curses at her own mother. Grammy Weenie, downstairs, shouting up biblical quotes, the squeak of her wheels as she rocked back and forth on the warped floors. Governor was wailing. The television in the den was turned up loud, blaring "Mighty Mouse" cartoons—my sisters' attempt to tune out the world around them. Where was Sumter? Where had he gone? Was he in Neverland? This was all his fault, his Neverland, his god.

It had to stop.

All this playing.

No more.

The dark giggling, the blood, the sacrifices.

The voice in my head was not Sumter's, but my own.

Wrong, just like a baby bawling for the first time. *Stop Sumter. No more.*

I ran back to Neverland on unsteady feet. The mud oozed up between my toes, making obscene sucking noises as I went. I stepped on prickers and kept running, not stopping to pluck them out. I knew my father was gone for good—he'd had enough, he was a coward, he was running, too, perhaps to his own Neverland.

The shack seemed smaller and thinner than it had ever been before. I was just about as tall as it was. Maybe I was too tall for it. Maybe I had grown this summer and hadn't noticed it. But I almost felt like I was looking down at Neverland. I tried the door, but it was locked from the inside. "You let me in, Sumter, goddamn you, you let me in!"

There was no answer. I could hear the thin wind across the curling yellow grasses. I waited to the count of sixty, and then I still waited to hear him moving inside, but I heard nothing.

I ran around to the side window, pressing my face against the glass. Brown cardboard was taped up on the inside. I slapped my hand against the window, rattling it. "You open up! You hear?" The outer wall gave a little as I leaned against it, as if with a little more effort I could just tip the shack over.

"You show me what's in that crate, damn you, you show me what you got!" I kicked at the splintered wood of the wall with the ball of my foot, and my toes went right through. My foot came out smarting with splinters, but I didn't care. I kicked again. "You open up or I will kick this place to shreds, you hear?" The pain from my foot was shrieking, but I slammed it again into the wall. I kicked so hard that I fell down in the mud on my butt, barely missing a large rock. Using both hands, I lifted the rock and threw it at the window. The glass broke in a neat chunk where the rock went through, and when I heard a small yelp, I actually thought it was the window that had screamed.

Then I heard him, knocking things over, tripping around all that junk that was piled around inside there.

"You let me in," I whispered, "or I'll tell them *everything*."

The door creaked open. Sumter stood there, his dark-encircled eyes glaring at me. I hadn't noticed, but he'd gotten thinner in the past week, almost like he was shrinking in on himself. He looked wizened; he looked like he was dying.

"All right," he said.

I limped to the open door.

⊰ 2 ⊱

"Your daddy's gone," he said, without his usual tone of superiority. He stood back, away from the door. He held a trowel in his hands. It was caked with dirt. Spiraled around his left arm was some of Aunt Cricket's laundry cord.

I remained in the doorway. "Did Lucy make him leave?"

Sumter looked surprised, like this hadn't occurred to him. "I wouldn't— Lucy wouldn't do that. Lucy doesn't care about grown-ups."

I glanced around the shack. It was cold and smelled like the meat drawer in our refrigerator back home. The candles were lit, and in their center, the crate. Next to the crate was a ditch. A shovel was thrust in the dirt.

"I've been burying something," he said quickly, but I could tell he was partially lying. He had that look.

"Another sacrifice?"

I thought he smiled, but his face was pained. It was a grimace. "No."

"What's in the crate?"

"Lucy."

"No, I mean, what's really in the crate?"

"You have to see through the crate to Lucy. And to our father. I know you seen him. I *know* it. He is the devourer. He is the Feeder Who Walks

206

in Shadows. And he *loves* us like we were his own. And there's this . . . " From the dirt he withdrew the small animal leg that he'd shown me before—a dog's leg. "This was my brother's."

"You ain't got a brother."

"I had one just like *you* have one. Only mine was a year older than me. She kept him here. She nursed him here."

"Who?"

But he ignored me. "We come from her body and we must return through her body. My daddy's waiting."

"Your daddy's drunk, if you ask me."

"My daddy's waiting. God is a feeder, don't you know that? Everything eats everything. Let me show you what I seen, Beau, what I *seen* with my mind's eyeball," and he reached over with that paw and scratched across the back of my hand, and it hurt really bad, and I wanted to scream, but it was like a strong electric shock and I was thrown across the room, against the wall. When I looked up, the color of the light had changed in the shed, and it smelled new; it smelled fresh.

From outside, the sunlight entered, a violet sunlight like it was early morning, and Sumter was no longer there with me. The strange dwarf woman with the white hair was in his place. *Lucy.* Her frog eyes rolling up into themselves. She had stitches across her forehead, just above her eyes, and she was tearing at them with her fingernails, and they were popping out. Into the chasm of her open skin she poked around with her fingers and moaned as if someone were tickling her, and then she giggled, pressing down harder with her fingers into her open forehead, her eyes twitching, her legs rubbing against each other like she had to go to the bathroom, and I heard some noise in the corner, from the shadows, and there were eyes staring out at her, and there was the paw, reaching from the dark to the light.

And the creature that the paw belonged to.

Moving clumsily, like the baby it was, into the light.

Its lips slippery with saliva.

It was small and ugly as it moved, with its one paw, its hand on the other arm clutching at the air, searching for nourishment.

The woman giggled as her fingers dug more deeply into her scalp.

The child that crawled toward the woman had no eyes, and I would not have screamed because of its one paw, for Grammy had often told stories about monster children who were the cross-bred sons to farm boys, or old women who had daughters with enormous heads filled with water. But the scream came up through my stomach and into my throat and out into the air because of the baby's tail, which was like a fish's, swimming upstream in the air as it moved forward.

And the resemblance.

Not to the giggling mother.

But to the brother.

To my cousin.

Sumter.

My real mama, Beau, his voice pricked into my mind. *She had found a way into another world, where my father lived. Where nothing hurt. Nothing. They all lie, the grown-ups. All lie, and all feed. And my daddy is the All that Must Feed. I look like my mama, but I am my daddy's son, and this is my daddy's house. I was born to devour. I was born to feed. Where I am is Neverland. I am Neverland.*

"Sumter," I gasped. The light in Neverland extinguished, and I lost control of my body—my shorts were moist where I had suddenly urinated.

Then I opened my eyes: They had been closed all along, I had been dreaming standing up.

Sumter stood close to me, his breath tickling my face.

"Who is Lucy?"

"You know. Or are you stupid?"

"Who is she?" I grabbed him by the shoulders and shook him hard. *"You tell me!"*

He snarled, "Who do you think she is?"

"I *don't* know."

"She's my mother. My *real* mother. *The Weenie killed her. The Weenie is evil. The Weenie stopped Lucy from taking me to Neverland, so now I have to bring Neverland here. Out. We won't never have to grow up and be like* them." He grabbed me by the shoulders and shook me, too, with strength I didn't know he had.

"Let go." I tugged myself free of his grasp and stepped into the circle of candles.

"Beau, what they did to her—was *bad.* They're *bad* people. We don't never got to be like them. We can change the whole world. We can make everything Neverland. Just one more sacrifice. *One more.*" He pointed to a place near the crate. Next to the crate was the ditch, only it was more than a ditch. It was a long hole.

"You burying more animals?" I asked.

"Not exactly," he said.

This got my curiosity up. I leaned over the hole and looked down. Because of the rain, some of the hole had filled with muddy water.

His voice was sly: "I'm just digging."

"You're trying to dig up those dead slaves."

"No. I'm trying to bury . . . "

I glanced back at him, peripherally, because there was a flutter of movement. First, I saw the laundry cord, dangling along his arm like a giant white worm.

But the movement was the shovel, in his hands.

The shovel was coming for my head just as he was saying, " . . . you."

⇥ 3 ⇤

I dreamed of the dead slaves, manacled together, floating above me. Their limbs moving as if with some will, but it was the tide pulling them forward and pushing them back, forward and back. Seaweed wrapped between them. They were heading for the peninsula; it was drawing them to it. I was beneath them, somehow able to breathe in the seawater like it was the cleanest air. I held onto a rotted length of timber from some ancient wreck. The faces of the slaves were indistinct, and as I squinted through the green waves, I saw who they were. One was my mother, her hair all but torn from the side of her head, her eyes bug-wide; and then there were Nonie and Missy, barnacles attached to their necks, small fish pecking at their earlobes, at their toes; Aunt Cricket and Uncle Ralph, too, the farthest. All floating toward Gull Island, all heading there, dead but being pulled. Pulled, and eaten by the things that feed. Grammy Weenie had once told me that even trees move, perhaps even stones, all creation moves. And even the dead. Tugged at by the sea, but who was to say that even in life we did not move because of forces outside ourselves? Human will could not be separated from the will of the universe. Grammy Weenie's voice again, "The flesh and the spirit eternally at war, never resting. Always we must seek the higher ground."

In the dream, I began swimming upward, into the horror of my drowned family, up into that mass of flesh. Because beneath them, I was trapped by them. But if I swam into them, if I rose above the waves, I would reach higher ground. I would be safe. I became tangled in their arms: They formed a circle around me, and as my head came up above the surface of the water, I could no longer breathe, and the bodies of the dead dragged me back into their loving, devouring arms.

I awoke gasping.

I was lying on my back in cool mud, water coming up around my neck and back, but my face was well above it. My hands were tied together, as were my feet, but it wouldn't matter—I tried moving my arms and legs, and there was nothing doing. I tried wiggling my fingers to get the blood going, but my wrists were bound tight with laundry cord. I was packed in by wet earth, with just my nose and mouth coming up to some opening for air. I tried opening my eyes, but the dirt pressed against them.

When I spoke, all that came out was a moan. But I knew I was awake, I knew I was conscious.

"Beau?" It was Sumter above me. "You can breathe, Beau?"

I let out a moan.

"It's the last sacrifice, Beau, a human one. To Lucy."

I didn't say anything.

"It's not you, Beau, I'd *never* do that. You're my cousin." Sumter was crying, or just about to cry. His voice was weary; he sounded like he longed for sleep. "And it won't be your sisters. I wouldn't . . . and it doesn't matter, because a sacrifice, once you make it, well, it ain't really a sacrifice 't'all. It's for Lucy. It's what Lucy *wants*. Lucy and my *natural* daddy."

I concentrated on breathing.

"And anyway, it won't be painful. I don't think he can really feel pain. Not like we feel pain. And it's the law of the universe, right? Eat and be eaten. It's a cycle. It's where we have to go, and he won't mind. And this way he'll never have to go bad. Everybody, you know, everybody in this whole damn world goes bad one day, if you live long enough. Even the Weenie knows it. Corruption. He won't never have to know corruption. So it's not even a bad sacrifice."

And I knew.

I knew who the sacrifice would be.

My brother.

The baby.

Governor.

Sumter! The scream that came out of my mouth was a whimper.

"Beau?"

Sumter, don't you dare!

"Don't even think about it, Beau. It's why I had to put you here. But not for very long. Just tonight. I figure they'll go looking for you, and it's probably gonna rain, and I'll make 'em think you ran down to steal a boat on accounta you're mad at your daddy. They'll leave him with the Weenie, and then I'll figure a way of getting him away from her. After it's over, after I've given him to Lucy, then I'll get you out of there. Neverland will be everywhere then. My daddy, my *real* daddy, will make sure nothing hurts. You'll see. It'll be okay. I'll make sure he don't really hurt too much. Lucy promised it won't hurt too much. He'll go to a place of pure innocence and never have to hurt *ever*. Know how he cries? Well, he's *never* gonna cry again. You'll see. He'll be in bliss. It's a real place. We're all gonna be there. You know how he cries. It hurts to hear him cry so much. I know how he hurts—I can feel it. He ain't never gonna hurt again, ever. It's for his own good. And us. To sacrifice. 'Cause once you make the sacrifice, you know, it never's a bad sacrifice, 'cause it's always for something better."

Sumter, you don't touch him!

"I know you see my daddy sometimes. I know, I just know," he repeated.

Sumter, he's my brother and you don't touch him!

"It's what Lucy wants." His voice was growing more faint. He was walking away. "I'm gonna take him to the place of pure innocence, on accounta that's what he is and what he's always gonna be. It's the final sacrifice of summer. It's got to happen for the world to keep turning. It's what sacrifice is for."

I panicked for a long time, not for me, but for Governor. I squeezed my mind down over my closed eyes, trying to see with my mind's eyeball so I could dream things awake the way I did in my sleep: *I could picture the house in an uproar, I could picture everyone being distracted through their tempers and rages. I could picture Sumter coming in at supper, and when my mother asks him, "You seen Beau this evening?" Sumter saying, "He chased after his daddy's car almost all the way to the West Island. He told me he was so mad he was gonna run away. I tried to tell him not to, but he was mad. So he says he's gonna go out and get one of the dinghys and try to take it out." And Aunt Cricket saying, "Sunny, why'n't you tell us this before?" And my cousin shrugging, "I dunno. I didn't think he was really gonna do it." Grammy Weenie saying, "Beauregard would never do a stupid thing like that. He's a boy with conscience. Something you, young man, would not know about." And Sumter ignoring her as he always did, as all of us always did: the old lady. Grammy Weenie, the surly old biddy in a wheelchair.*

But Grammy Weenie knew about him. She would know he was lying.

She'd recognize him for what he was.

I could see it all in my mind's eyeball, just like one of my dreams:

There Grammy Weenie is now, protesting to her daughters that Sumter is possibly lying, and her daughters, my mother and aunt, shutting her out of their minds because they have just about had enough of their mother for one day, thank you. Uncle Ralph, into his sixth beer and saying, "You women drive me up a wall, you know that?" And Aunt Cricket ignoring him, too. Aunt Cricket is more worried about Daddy than anything. It's Mama who thinks of me, "Well, he should've heard the dinner bell. You saw him?" Sumter saying, "I'm sure he's just fine. I'm sure he ain't doing none of them things."

Would Julianne Sanders be there? No, she would be home by now. Mama would have Governor on her lap.

She would be spoon-feeding prunes to Governor. "Well," she's saying, "I'm sure Beau has more sense, and once he cools down he'll be home. It's been such a rough day." Nonie, whispering to Sumter, "Is that really what he's gonna do?" He would shrug. Sumter would keep them guessing as long as he could. Mama saying, "Well, I'm sure he's just fine." "Yes," says Aunt Cricket, her face skewered with fake concern, "and don't worry so much about the boy, Evvie. If he's not in by nine, we'll take a drive down to the boathouse and see if he's there. How much mischief can a boy get up to on the island, anyway? It's not likely there's any place he can hide." "Look!" Sumter is hollering, pointing to the kitchen window, "it's raining."

In that darkness, with my eyes sealed shut with dirt, I imagined all this. I tried not to think of the bugs that were probably crawling around on me. I tried to only think of Governor, of protecting him, of keeping him from harm. *Don't hurt Governor, don't you hurt him.*

But who could protect Governor?

Who would know what harm was headed his way?

Lucy knew.

Whatever Lucy was.

But Lucy wanted the baby.

No, Lucy wanted a sacrifice.

It didn't have to be the baby.

I had prayed to Lucy once before, and Sumter told me that Lucy only dwelt in Neverland—it was the temple. Prayers outside of Neverland would not work as long as Lucy was there.

Help me, Lucy.

I didn't really believe.

But I knew I had to save Governor.

Help me out of here. Help me out of here, and I will bring you your sacrifice.

I lay for another hour, praying as hard as I could. Praying to a god that I would have to believe in for the moment. If there was a god in that shack, it would hear me. I would do it for Governor.

I did something I had never done before: Instead of allowing my mind's eyeball to just roam, I worked hard to imagine what I wanted to be going on. I tried to see what I wanted to see, not just take the images presented to me.

I willed my thoughts to take form.

In the house Aunt Cricket is saying to Sumter, "Where's Beau gone off to?" And Sumter is lying to them. But don't let them believe his lies, Lucy, make them know. Make Grammy Weenie tell them. Make Grammy Weenie tell them—she knows about Sumter! She knows what he's about. Make Nonie and Missy squeal and break their blood oath; make them talk about Neverland; make them tell my mama that I may be here. Make them! If you're a god, make it happen, and I will give you the most hellacious sacrifice you ever did see!

I imagined the crate in the earth above me. I imagined the creature that Lucy was, scratching at the wood, the skull, the horseshoe crab, the dead floating slaves, the fluorescent obscenity on the door to Neverland. *All right, Lucy, I'm gonna believe in you, I'm gonna believe in you and you're gonna answer my prayer. You're gonna be a good god and do what your follower says, because I'm gonna give you a sacrifice to end all sacrifices.*

I'M GONNA give you your own high priest.

Sumter.

I'm gonna take him and give him to you, tied with a ribbon.

But you gotta get me outta here, now.

YOU HEAR ME, YOU DO WHAT I SAY.

I kept trying to get my circulation going by squirming around. Although Sumter had been pretty tight with the cord, he hadn't packed the earth all that much, and I was able to move my knees a little. I opened my mouth for air very much like a fish, and something small and feathery crawled in along my teeth, but then wriggled out again.

The small voice, in my head, the one that had abandoned me when Sumter banished me from Neverland, it was there again.

promise?

Huh?

sacrifice?

Lucy?

Sumter sacrifice promise?

Yes, I will give him to you. If you get me out of here now. Right now. Right this instant.

will you let me out to play?

Whether it was my imagination, childhood madness, or truly some dark god speaking to my mind, I said. *Yes, I will give him to you.*

And then I heard the door to Neverland slam open, almost off its hinges, as if a gale force wind had pushed it back.

I had called Lucy up.

ELEVEN

Lights Out

All the coldness of the damp earth was gone. The mud against my back was liquid and warm, like loving hands massaging my spine and shoulders. Feeling came into my limbs like it never had before; my blood pumped through my veins, around my heart, just as if, instead of lying bound in the dirt, I was swimming out to sea. The earth moved around me, accommodating my form, and grubs and beetles touched the skin of my arms and legs with their feelers. I felt at once an absurd union with the ground in which I lay buried, and although fear overtook me, something else put my mind at rest. It was like music, this feeling, it was like a song that the earth was singing to me.

I saw her.

Her scarred forehead, her round eyes, trying to tell me something, trying, but she could not get her mouth around the words—her face, the ugliest, most pathetic white, prematurely wrinkled, troll face, but beautiful and shining and tortured.

"My child," she worked hard to form the words. "Bring . . . my child. Hungry. All . . . hungry . . . child."

Then the vision melted, and the earth was again cold and wet.

Above me: a clomping of heavy feet, shaking the land with tremors at each step.

"Beau!"

The voice was Sumter Monroe's.

⇥ 2 ⇤

My cousin knelt above me, digging with his fingers, pulling clods of dirt off me, drawing my head up.

"I don't care if you are my cousin," he snarled. "How *dare* you! I don't know how you did it, you bastard"—his lisp was coming through in his excitement, *you bath-turd*—"but now they know, damn it, now they know it all!" He untied my hands and feet. "Now you get out of here, and if you tell them you were in here, I'll—I'll—"

"You'll what?" I challenged, rubbing my hands together.

"I'll—" But he wasn't able to complete his threat.

In the doorway was a drunken Uncle Ralph, looking like a mad grizzly bear. "Is *this* where you kids've been playing? What the hell have you been up to?" He shined his flashlight along the walls. Our fluorescent obscenities flickered as the light played across them. As if seeing the place for the first time, I felt a revulsion and shame: The place was filthy, *unclean* the way Grammy talked about leprous houses in the Old Testament. It smelled like dead animals. It smelled like milk that was turning. The ceiling was heavy with spiderwebs, the dirt floor covered with mold and sprouting fungi around the corners. "Looks like some animal's been living in here," Uncle Ralph said. He came over and pulled Sumter up by the scruff of his shirt just like he was a puppy and shook him violently. He tossed him to the ground; Sumter fell like a rag doll.

Aunt Cricket came in behind her husband. The beam from her flashlight played across all our faces. "Sunny?" she asked uncertainly, then to me, "Beau? You and Sunny just playing a game, isn't that right?"

I looked from her to Uncle Ralph to Sumter, and they were all glaring at me.

But then Aunt Cricket saw the words on the wall: every single cuss word any of us had ever heard in our entire lives. Right there, scrawled in Sumter's handwriting.

"Sunny?" Her face was stricken as if with sudden illness. Some knowledge poured across it. "What have you wicked, wicked children been up to in here?"

My mother stood in the doorway, holding Governor in her arms. "Beau? Are you all right, sweetie?"

I was out of the cords and standing up.

Uncle Ralph took the cord I'd been tied with and swung it like a whip against his son's back.

Sumter didn't make a sound.

"You goddamn pervert," Uncle Ralph said.

"It's not his fault," I said quietly.

Uncle Ralph came up behind Sumter and slapped him hard on the shoulders.

"I said it's not his fault!"

"You just shut up and stay out of this," Uncle Ralph muttered. "Get up, Sumter, you're coming with me."

Sumter crawled like a baby over to the crate. He hugged himself to it. His eyes were not looking at any of us. He was already in another world. His lips were moving furiously but without sound.

He was praying to Lucy.

"Whatchu saying, boy?" his father growled at him. "What in God's name are you saying? What in God's name is wrong with you? I shoulda known! I shoulda known—you got to raise your own blood, you got to raise your own blood, not some goddamn idiot's! I told you. Crick, I told you, but *no*, you wouldn't listen, you wouldn't listen, would you? And now look what we got on our hands—a pervert, an unnatural bastard!"

Sumter's mutterings became a whispered chant.

I heard him; we all heard him. But he was not whispering for our benefit. *"Lights out, lights out, lights out, lights out."*

⊰ 3 ⊱

The fits began as soon as Sumter was taken from Neverland. Aunt Cricket, in spite of her faintness, swooped down to kneel between her husband's wrath and her child. She cradled him in her meaty arms and said, "He's had a horrible shock, Ralph. Let it be, for now. Let it be. Later we can sort this dreadful thing out."

"Lights out," Sumter whispered. He began sucking his thumb.

"Jesus H," Uncle Ralph said. He turned to me as if it were all my fault. "You get up and get inside, too. You kids all need a good talking to." He swatted at me with the back of his hand.

"My head hurts," I said. "He hit me with the shovel."

"He *what?*"

"He hit me with the shovel, look." I felt for the lump on my head. There was no bruise. Neither was there blood as I had expected. Had I been hit at all? I was feeling dizzy, and drugged. Was everything inside that shed a hallucination? Was there nothing from there that was real?

Uncle Ralph felt around my scalp. "He hit you on the head?" He picked the shovel up. "I'd be surprised if my boy could lift this thing, let alone swing it. If you got hit with this, and lemme tell *you*, you'd be black and blue and red all over."

"Beau wouldn't lie," Mama said to him. "You okay, sweetie?"

I shrugged and nodded. "I guess."

"I have to put Governor to bed. You go on up to my room and you talk to me about this, you understand me?" My mother was never one to come up and hug me as if she had almost lost her child. I knew this. Once when I had half drowned out in Virginia Beach and had to be dragged out by a teenager swimming nearby, my mother gave me no sympathy. "You're not supposed to go out higher than your knees. Go back to the motel room

220

and dry off and sit there until we can talk about this." So now, still achy from a blow to my head that might've all been part of my mind's eyeball, I would get no sympathy from her. I would have to explain myself and go to bed. But I was happy to see Governor in her arms, and I knew that if I told her the truth, she would know I'd done right.

I stood uncertainly, meaning to follow her. She walked on past Aunt Cricket, who was lingering at the threshold, hugging her boy to her, as heavy as he must've been.

"You got him into this," she said to me. Then she, too, turned and stepped out among the slender trees. I saw them in silhouette, her and Sumter. He was in her arms, his face pressed into her neck.

Within a few seconds the screaming started.

At first I thought it was the memory of a dream: a dream where trees screamed in the wind.

But it was Sumter, his mouth an endless chasm of pain.

Uncle Ralph ran out first, taking his flashlight with him, leaving me in complete darkness. I didn't want to stay in that place, and I remembered my oath to Lucy: to deliver Sumter to Neverland. I knew I would never keep my oath, and I also knew I had better get beyond the boundaries of Neverland so that nothing bad would happen. If everything in Neverland was a hallucination, I wanted to see no more of it.

I stumbled up to my feet and, dodging trash and fallen candles, got out, slamming the door behind me.

Sumter was scratching at his own throat as Aunt Cricket shook him.

Her voice crested and fell like a wave; she wept and shuddered. "Sunny, *Sunny*, you stop that, hear?"

He was cursing her, cursing God, cursing himself, digging his fingers in around his neck, thick white spit flying from between his teeth. Uncle Ralph was trying to pry Sumter's hands away from his throat, but every time he got one hand lifted, the other snapped back like a bear trap.

"He's had a tremendous shock. My poor little baby."

"Damn it, stop it, boy." His father finally slapped him across his face.

Sumter began cussing like he was possessed—from the f word to the c word and all the a-to-z words in between. It was like he was speaking in tongues in some lost language of obscenities.

Like his mother, his father also began weeping, and as much as I disliked my uncle, it was a sad sight to see: him slapping Sumter back and forth as if on one of the slaps his boy would see the light, and his crinkled eyelids oozing tears.

I heard distant thunder and the crack of lightning and counted the seconds between them as we headed back to the Retreat.

⊰ 4 ⊱

"Where is his Mr. Bubble?" Aunt Cricket shouted from the upstairs bathroom. "My baby needs a hot bath to calm him, and where in *hell is* his Mr. Bubble?"

Rain was beginning to bat at the windows, and it was my job to run around and shut them so all the bugs in creation wouldn't sneak beneath the screens and so the furniture wouldn't get wet. She called out again, "Doesn't anyone in this house know? It certainly didn't get up and walk away. Where *is* his Mr. Bubble?"

Nonie and Missy were sitting on the stairs as I came in behind the others. Nonie whispered, "What was that all about?"

"Later."

"Did he really bury you alive?"

"I said *later.*"

"Grammy Weenie's on her knees and smiting herself on accounta she thinks God's punishing her." Missy kept her voice low, too. The Retreat was like church now, or like a library, and we all had to whisper.

"Who told, anyway?" I asked. "Who told where I was?"

"Not me." Missy laid her chin gently into her hands.

Nonie didn't even blink. "It was Sumter himself. Mama kept asking him where you got off to, and he kept making up different stories, that you went down to steal a boat, that you were going down to look for shells, that you were already out on Rabbit Lake."

"One of 'em was you went with Daddy to St. Badon."

"Yeah, and you know Sumter's a lousy liar sometimes. One story after another, until finally Grammy says to him to make up his mind and tell the almighty truth for once in his life, to just grow up here and now, and he says like he's gotten shocked that you're in the shack in the woods and that he put you underground. And then he says that you made him squeal, that you made him break his sacred word. He has gone certifiably mental. And that's when he blasts off outside like a lit fart."

I continued on up the stairs, stopping at the top when I heard my aunt's unceasing wail.

I passed by the bathroom door. Steam came out at me. Aunt Cricket had taken her blouse off and was wearing her bra above her skirt. The skin on her stomach and beneath her neck was pale white. The steam made her hair stick around her forehead in slimy spirals. Sumter, having come down from his fit, sat on the toilet seat in his underwear. His eyes were glazed over. He was muttering to himself—an incantation. He was brilliant with exhaustion and steam.

"I think it's under the sink," I said.

Aunt Cricket looked at me sharply. "What is it *you* want?"

"The Mr. Bubble. It's under there." I pointed to the plastic curtain Grammy Weenie had fashioned around the sink bottom. "Here, let me." I knelt down and reached under the small curtain and withdrew the box of bubble bath.

She grabbed it from me.

Sumter's mutterings increased, became louder. "Fuck you," he said, again and again.

Aunt Cricket uttered a small cry of shame, covering her gasping mouth with pudgy fingers as if he had just conjured the devil in a word.

She took the box of Mr. Bubble from my hands and shoved me away. Then she turned her back on me as she dumped the powder into the tub.

"That's gonna be too hot," I said.

She ignored me. I noticed she had moles all over her back.

"You're gonna hurt him if you put him in there." At this point, knowing what Sumter had intended to do with Governor, it wouldn't have bothered me a bit to let him boil like a lobster, but I knew that my cousin was very sick and not himself at all. That was what Gull Island had done for him, and Neverland—and his god—had made him a sick little boy.

I stood there, watching him for several minutes. He didn't seem to notice me at all. His small pink stomach a perfect grapefruit, the dimples between his ribs sunken, his face an upside-down triangle. He looked very sad and very small and reminded me of baby birds I had seen fall from trees and die just as they were being born.

Aunt Cricket did not acknowledge my existence. She had given herself over to the vapors rising from the tub, filled to the brim with white bubbles. "A hot bath. Sunny, my baby, my Sunny, a hot bath is what you need. Calms the nerves. You're high-strung is all, my baby. You're different from other boys. You're more sensitive . . . a nice hot, hot, hot bath."

⇥ 5 ⇤

I dreaded going into my parents' bedroom and having to face my mother. She would get the whole story out of me, I knew. Somehow the magic of Neverland was gone, and along with that, the threat of Neverland, too. I would never set foot within its walls again. But how would I make sense of what we had done there? The sacrifices, the games, the imaginary ghosts of children from the island. It all seemed less substantial now than ever: just a children's game that had gone too far.

I dragged my feet. Perhaps if I hid in my bedroom, Mama would fall asleep and then I could for at least one night avoid her anger and disapproval. She would say, "We thought you knew better"—and she would be right.

Uncle Ralph shouted up to me, "Beauregard! Get down here right now. I want you to help me with something."

I didn't want to obey, but I felt like I had to. I took the stairs two at a time, and when I hit the landing, he grabbed me by the collar and I figured I was a goner. His beer breath slapped me as hard as his hand did as he pushed me out the front door. "I don't know every damn thing you kids been up to out there, but you and me's gonna go out and take that place apart board by board so's this kind of thing can't go on no more. Now get in the car."

HE DROVE, swerving off the main drive into the mud. Rain came down at a windblown angle against the windshield, and he didn't bother to turn the wipers on. He drove the Chevrolet between the scrawny trees, scraping the sides on low-hanging branches. The trees really seemed to be screaming now, as they screeched against the metal of the car. I figured we'd crash, and to avoid going through the windshield, I held what little there was of a seat belt together with my hands and kept my head low.

"I shoulda known you boys wasn't up to no good." His speech slurred, and I did not know how that man could see what was ahead of us with all the rain blurring the windshield. "I shoulda known when you marched like a buncha little Nazis out to the woods. Didja touch each other? Didja? Is that what you boys been doin'? You pull your things out and piss on each other? I swear, boy, if I find out you been playin' little faggoty games with each other, or with the girls—God Almighty, I will give you both a talkin' to neither or both'a you's bound to forget."

I was shocked to the core. Uncle Ralph didn't even have a clue. I couldn't contain myself any longer. "It ain't nothing *sexual*. Gawd, you are so stupid. Uncle Ralph, you're as dumb as they come."

Before I knew it, he whacked me hard across the face and I hit the back of my head against the window. "And you're so all-fired insolent. Okay, smart mouth, if it weren't sex, what were those words on the walls?"

I was so mad I could barely talk. "Just words."

"You know what they mean? You answer me, boy, or I will give you a good talkin' to, *you hear me?*"

I nodded, terrified that he'd hit me again.

"You know what that kind of language means?"

"It's just a word, that's all," I muttered.

Finally he turned on the windshield wipers. The Chevy's headlights were shining straight ahead through a grove of trees.

On Neverland.

Uncle Ralph reached over and opened the dashboard. "See if you can find my cigars in there."

I brought out a long rectangular tin and handed it to him.

He took out a cigar and lit it.

The wipers slashed at the rain. *Kashit-kashit-kashit.*

He seemed calm.

I thought he was going to kill me right then. I almost relaxed. Uncle Ralph with a cigar thrust between his lips looked fatherly for once in his life.

"It's all gonna have to change," he said. "It's all gonna have to start over. I told his mama a hundred times: You can't let a willful boy loose, but you got to *discipline* him; you got to teach him what most boys know by nature. When you got somebody else's child—an idiot's child, for Christ sakes—you can't slack off none, but you got to come down hard on him every time. You boys've been livin' like filthy dogs crappin' in their own house. But it's gonna have to change, and I'm the daddy, and I'm gonna have to take matters into my own hands."

He gunned the engine.

He jammed his foot into the accelerator like he wanted it to go through the floor.

The Chevrolet flew head-on to Neverland, and I thought we were going to die.

He spun the wheel at the last second, and the car skidded in the mud, barely missing a tree whose branches scratched across my side window. The tail end of the car smashed against the shack. I said, "Gawd, Gawd, Gawd."

Uncle Ralph put the Chevy in reverse and we rammed against the walls, scraping and crunching, and I turned back to watch Neverland lean farther and farther back, until it was just about collapsed into the ground. He turned off the engine. "Beau, you do what I say, you hear me? You do what I say."

We got out of the car, but I was scared of him.

Uncle Ralph said, "I'm gonna tear this place apart with my bare hands, and I want you to help." He went through the rubble and grabbed the rake, tossing it aside. When he found a hand axe, he began chopping into the wood, through the walls, against the roof, smashing all the windows. "Beau! Get in here and help clear out this crap!"

I was afraid of him, but on some primal level I was more afraid of what might or might not be in that fallen shack.

Lucy.

Her words: *help me come out and play.*

I was even afraid *for* my uncle because he was destroying the holy of holies, and just supposing there *was* a Lucy, this spelled doom for him, too.

I followed my instinct.

I ran for home.

Uncle Ralph's voice was behind me like a bear's growling, shouting bloody murder at me, but I didn't care. I would go back to the Retreat and hide and hope this was all a bad dream.

IT WAS like I had left one world and entered another.

The house seemed almost back to normal. I stepped in out of the rain and stood in the front hall light. It was quiet and the lights were warm and yellow. I heard the television on in the den. I looked above at the ceiling, to the cracks that ran down them. Mama was probably exhausted, resting, with Governor. I shook rain from my hair and wiped my muddy hands across my face. I was shivering. For the first time ever, I was freezing in August on Gull Island. I smelled what had been supper: lamb chops, their grease probably still spitting on the frying pan. Someone had forgotten to turn off the stove. How many times had Grammy or Aunt Cricket done just that, or whenever Nonie tried her hand at cooking? I wandered into the kitchen and flicked on the light.

Grammy Weenie sat there in her chair. I didn't immediately know what she was doing. She didn't look up at me.

She kept her hand down in the blue gas flame.

Her hand was blackened.

"If thy left hand offend thee," she said feebly.

I went over to the stove top and wrenched the dial around so the gas was turned off.

She took her charred palm and held it up to my face. "I feel no pain, child, none at all. It's part of my inheritance. It is part of the Wandigaux family line. We have no pain. Pain and suffering are gifts we are denied."

In her right hand was her silver brush. She reached up and began stroking her white hair gently. The brush was brilliant hard silver, and her hair was brilliant hard silver.

The front door slammed open and Uncle Ralph's voice boomed like morning surf, *"You know what these bastards've been doing?"*

⊰ 6 ⊱

Uncle Ralph waited until all of us had come into the living room. Mama came first, and then Nonie and Missy, who had gone back to watching television after the first outbreak. Finally Aunt Cricket came down. "Keep your voice down, you oaf. Sunny's been through something terrible, and all you can think to do is throw your weight around like a two-hundred-pound gorilla."

Grammy Weenie, covering her left hand with the crocheted throw that was across her lap, wheeled in behind me. "Now what's in there?" She pointed to the crate.

"Oh, *wow*," Missy gasped.

But Nonie was braver. "He's got some animal in there." She glanced about to the others. "Sumter does. He has some animal in there. I think it's a snake."

"It's a dead one, you ask me, it stinks like an S.O.B. Ain't no snake." Uncle Ralph set the crate on the floor. He brought the heel of his shoe down against the crate. To tear the thing completely apart, he dropped to his knees and, with his bare hands, pulled at the boards.

Like the breaking of an egg to find inside a half-formed bird, we beheld what we'd been worshiping.

"What I figured, you kids're sick," he said.

Aunt Cricket screamed, "Get those things out of this house!"

In the crate were the animals we had sacrificed, in various stages of decomposition, ricelike maggots frothing from their open wounds, the small human skull that Sumter had shown me on that first day, and the shell of a horseshoe crab. It was no mystery at all. He had just put the dead animals in there and they had rotted.

We had been worshiping a vat of decaying flesh.

Nonie let out a little laugh and nodded to me as if she'd known all along. But I had put my hand inside there, and something had grabbed me. What had it been?

"Lights out." We heard a small voice at the top of the stairs. "Lights out. You let it out, you let it out."

Sumter was standing there, clinging to the banister for support. He was drooling and naked, and when he had finished uttering these words, he thrust his thumb into his mouth and began sucking on it.

We heard a crack of lightning like a bomb exploding near the house, and the sky outside the front window lit up like dawn: A tree had burst into flame out on the bluff. Then another explosion closer to us cut through the night, as lightning hit near the house.

Above the roar of thunder came Sumter's high-pitched, shrieking voice, *"Lights out! Lights out! Lights out!"*

And the Retreat went completely dark.

⇥ 7 ⇤

A woman's voice whispered to me, so close I could feel her breath on the back of my neck, "Because he is alive . . . "

I didn't know if I was dreaming again, and I bit down on my lower lip just to feel pain and know I was here and awake. *Hurts.*

"*Sacrifice,*" the woman said.

"Lucy," I whispered. I reached with my hands and touched her shoulders, which were barely as high as my own. They were scrawny, bony shoulders, and the woman in the dark gasped as I clutched her. "Lucy," I whispered, "Jesus, Jesus." I began breathing more rapidly than my lungs could handle, and felt that I was going to faint.

"Beau, my child . . . my lovely, lovely boy . . . " But it wasn't Lucy, it was Grammy Weenie. "How did it get this far? I thought he was keeping it contained." Her voice was distant and kind and full of hurt, as if she herself were a child. I could smell the burned flesh of her left hand as she brought it near my face.

"Grammy," I said, "what does Sumter have?"

"A disease. He is contaminated. He needs to keep it. Somewhere safe. Too late," she murmured, and then I heard the squeaking of her wheelchair as she drew away from me in the dark.

I was blinded by a white circle of light from a flashlight and heard one of my sisters giggling. Then the light drew away.

My eyes adjusted after a few minutes, although someone kept slashing flashlight beams across the room in zigzag patterns. I said, "Cut it out." Every time the light hit my eyes, I had to wait another several seconds for my eyes to see again in the dark.

All the voices in the dark:

"Isn't it spooky?"

"No. It's just stupid. Missy, wouldn't you know we'd get struck."

"*Beau.*"

"Huh?" I tried to see better in the dark.

"*Beau.*" A lit shadow at the top of the stairs. Sumter holding his teddy bear.

"Sunny?" Aunt Cricket's voice, and then the shape of her body moving in front of the picture window.

Missy said, "I never been struck by lightning before."

"Not you, the *house*. No more TV tonight."

The sound of quick, clodding footsteps on the stairs: Aunt Cricket shrieked and then laughed. "Almost tripped on the rug. Now Sunny, let's go on back to bed for a little lie-down."

Uncle Ralph fumbled around in the darkness for candles, but I knew he wouldn't find any: They were melted down beneath the rubble of Neverland. When we were stealing candles for our clubhouse, none of us figured on them being missed.

"I'm scared," Missy said.

"You would be." Nonie was spinning the flashlight around on the ceiling like it was a spaceship. "The only thing to worry about is tripping on that crate. God, will someone get it out of here? It *stinks.*"

Aunt Cricket said, as she cautiously descended the stairs, "We have to get Sunny to a doctor, he's got an awful fever and he's just talking baby talk."

In the dark I began to make out everyone's features, and the grown-ups looked tired, the way they did when they were waiting in line at the grocery checkout.

I went over to the couch, where my mother was sitting. Mama, in the darkness, seemed smaller than I'd ever seen her—a hunched shadow.

"*You* tell me what went on in that place."

"Just a bunch of stupid games," I said.

Behind me Missy added, "We played pretend things."

"It was all bad stuff," came Nonie's judgment. "Sumter made us."

Missy sounded close to tears. "It was awful. Mama, just awful. But we didn't kill the animals. *He* did."

"We all did. I don't know why, but we did," I confessed.

My mother was silent, and it stung just like a hard pinch on the knee. "Well," Mama sighed, "I wish your father were here, but I'm glad he's not because I don't think he could take this. I think it would kill him. His own children hurting small animals for fun. Isn't that just evil? How would you like it if someone did that to you?"

"We didn't mean to, Mama. It was like we didn't have no choice."

"You girls go on up to your bedroom, and Beau, you, too."

Uncle Ralph began cussing from the top of the stairs as he clanged his way through the linen closet. "Goddamn it, I know we had candles in there."

"I don't mean to be such a wife, Ralph, but why don't you try the buffet. I think we have those red ones I bought in Williamsburg."

"No we don't," I said.

"Beau?"

"We used those up. We used all the candles up."

"Snitch," I heard Nonie whisper.

Through the darkness came Grammy Weenie's voice as if just inside my ear, "Look at it burn, will you?"

She wheeled her chair up beside the couch at the front window. The tree that had been struck lit up the night with spears of white flame.

"It's pretty," Nonie said. "I betcha, though, somebody left the croquet set out in the rain. I hope it burns, too."

"You think it'll spread?" I asked.

Nonie sounded disappointed. "The rain'll put it out. Fires don't last long up here, not with everything wet. Three years ago, don'tcha remember that tree down the road got hit? It was bigger than this one. It really got going. But it'll go out."

Grammy Weenie said, "It's a sign."

Nonie went to the front door, opening it. The wind brushed through us. "Better view from the porch."

Mama said, rising from the couch and brushing past me, "Shut it right now, young lady, and get upstairs to your room. All three of you. I have had enough for one night."

I watched her shifting form move up the stairs. "I am so tired," she said.

"Good night. Mama," Missy said, following behind her.

Nonie huffed, but stepped back inside, slowly easing the door closed. She came over to the window. "Grammy? You feeling fine?"

"Child, I have never, ever been fine."

"Grammy burned her hand," I told her.

"She did? You did?"

"To bed," my mother called from the top of the stairs.

"Grammy burned herself."

"Mama? You got some cold cream? It'll make it all better, Grammy. It won't hurt."

"It doesn't hurt now, child. I can't feel pain."

"She really burn herself?"

"Look," Grammy said, tapping at the window with her silver brush.

The tree was now smoking, the fire dead. The rain came down harder.

"Fire's out."

"No, Beauregard, I mean look *there.*"

Grammy reached out, grabbing me by the nape of the neck and pulling me closer to the window. "That place . . . where you played."

"I don't see nothing."

"You didn't see it?"

"No."

"Look, there." She held me tight.

And then, when lightning lit the sky over the bluffs, I thought I saw a half a dozen figures or more, as if bound together in chains, moving forward on a tide of air; but then nothing but the straggly trees sweeping at the rain with their branches.

I could not move because my blood had stopped pumping; I could barely form words. "You're scaring me."

"You tell me precisely, *precisely* what you children did out there. And don't lie. And don't leave anything out. Nothing."

So I completely broke my oath to Lucy, to Sumter, to Neverland. I told. Every last thing I could remember, from first going in and having something reach out of the crate at me, through flying above Gull Island, all the way past the sacrifices to what Sumter wanted to do with Governor. And nothing happened. My thumb did not burst with blood as Sumter had predicted. I felt relief wash through me like warm seawater. I could only see

Grammy's face in flashes when the lightning lit up the sky, and she had a look of supreme terror on her face—she was not looking at me, but outside, out the window, out to the bluff.

"What's out there?" I asked. "What's *coming?*"

She made noises through her closed mouth like she had forgotten language, or like her tongue was cut out.

"Grammy, what is it? Is it Lucy? Is it really *Lucy?* You know, don't you? You *know*. What is it?"

My grandmother was like a silver reflection of a human being as she brought her face near mine, like a mirror of fear that I could not quite make out in the darkness, but through which I could see the twisted image of the world surrounding me.

Her breath was like mold dust.

"Unspeakable," she said, and I had to strain to hear her. "*Unnatural.*"

Lightning struck again, and her face was so white that I could not make out her eyes or nose. I only caught the wrinkled curve of her lips, glistening with saliva. "Dreadful."

"What is it." This was not a question.

"My child. . . ." Her eyes went back to the window, to the storm. "Nothing good has ever come from that place, but I thought it could be *contained*. Since he was a little baby, I thought it could be contained."

"It?"

"That shed is the site of a great tragedy."

"I know. The dead slaves."

"What?"

"The dead slaves. It's their burial place."

Grammy Weenie let out the first laugh I had ever heard from her lips. "Is *that* what you think? *Slaves?* My Lord, Beauregard, you think the island slaves were buried up here? They were dumped down in the West Island without markers. My family has owned this property for the past one hundred years—they wouldn't buy a graveyard, I can guarantee that, child. No, it's where Babygirl . . . where she . . . died. I thought you knew that. Beau, your mother's sister, the first child. Babygirl, then Evvie, then Cricket. I had three daughters . . . your aunt. She lived up here the last years of her life. I thought you knew by what you said. I thought *you knew*. Babygirl, Beau. *You* know her *name*, for the love of God, I thought you knew."

I shook my head. "I don't know what you're *talking* about—her name was Cindy."

I thought Grammy was going to fly into a rage at my insolence. "It *was* short for Lucinda, Beau. But the Gullahs all called her *Lucy. Lucy Wandigaux Lee.*"

⊰ 8 ⊱

"That's why I never go out in those woods. She died in a bad way. She had what Sumter has, and she is as bad as Sumter. Your grandfather planted those trees out there, on the bluff, just to hide that place. How I loved her and feared her, Beau. But she let it get to her. She didn't learn to contain it. She had no choice. But when it gets *in the blood*, dear God in Heaven, what must then be done?"

I was puzzled. I looked out through the storm and saw nothing but gray rain.

Grammy Weenie continued, "Her imagination, Beau, her visions. It is part of the Wandigaux line. I have had them, and I know you have your dreams, don't you? You used to tell me your dreams when you were four and five, and then you stopped. You did the right thing, child, because it never does one good to let these things out into the world. It is like the blue of our eyes: handed down. And she would've been fine, too, but Lee was worried about her fits of depression and anger. She was backward and slow, and he hated her for it. God, how he hated her for it. Old Lee was not understanding of differences, of the unusual. But then, he was not a Wandigaux.

"Old Lee could not suffer her moods any longer, may God forgive him, and he had this, this *quack*, perform an operation on her. This horrid doctor. To—to take out the emotions from her head. He swore he was only removing the part of her that hurt. That carpetbagger from Boston, he swore she would never hurt again. But I tell you. Beau, after he stuck his needles beneath her scalp, above her eyelids, *all she did was hurt.* There was no hope for her then. None. They say humans can't live without hope, but she did. Oh, yes. She lived. She spent nights out in that shack. She worshiped what none could see, but she saw. She saw. All around us, an invisible world. The world is a skin, and she was able to hack at the flesh of life to the beating heart, and no man or woman should ever do that. It is forbidden to us. Children came to her. I saw her playing with them out in the woods, teaching things children should not learn. And one by one those children died, swimming into a rough surf, swimming away from the something that came toward them. And Lucy, my daughter, who had been merely slow, merely *different* before her surgery, after . . . after . . . she was a monster. She said the children were infested and that the sea would cleanse them. She laughed as they went under."

I gasped, "Zinnia and her brothers."

Grammy Weenie continued, "I have the sight, child, but it is faulty and I often wonder if it is anything more than a strong intuition. But Lucy had what Sumter has. The full Wandigaux curse. You can go back hundreds of years and find it, back to France when certain members of our family were tortured for conjuring. It doesn't go with everyone. You may have a little—I've always felt you do. But your sisters are lacking, as are your mother and your aunt, as far as I have been able to tell."

"I do have dreams, sometimes," I whispered, but she didn't seem to hear me. It was as if I wasn't there at all, and I had tapped into some inner fountain of my grandmother's memory—something she could not hold back when it was touched on.

"And it is a curse, not a blessing," she said, and I felt a chill as she spoke. It was as if she were speaking to a ghost. "Lucy never saw the world as it was, only as she created it in her mind. She stayed a child up until her death, even though physically she should've been a woman. Beau, you have to cross that bridge into the world, and Lucy could not."

She nodded several times; I thought she had gone insane as she ranted. "The Gullahs here know about her, what she did. They know. They know how gods mate with humans, they know both the visible and invisible world. They have stories . . . they have stories about seeing what can't be seen. Most of my life, child, I was taught that the church was the dwelling place of God. I have no doubt he has other places, also, be they temples, mosques, or tents. But who would've thought there would be other gods? That there are cathedrals for these gods? And what that doctor did with his needles, with his scalpels, with his *drugs* was to cut a peephole through the altar of some creation other than our own."

My grandmother went silent. I was about to say something, but I felt invisible fingers along my back, a terrible chill, and the confusion of her words as they poured from her mouth.

"We see only what we need to see to survive. Who is to say there is not another world moving all around us to which we are blind? And perhaps until we enter that world, its inhabitants, also, are blind to us. Lucy! Oh Lucy!" Grammy Weenie bleated. "Lucy became a bride of a god—a terrible, savage god. And she bore children, yes, *children*. Two. First, one which was more her blood than its father's, a child she named Summer for the season in which he arrived. Old Lee and I cared for him and hid our shame from the rest of the world. But within a year, in spite of our watching Lucy as much as we could stand to, she bore another. The second was more his father's son . . ."

Here, Grammy's voice faltered, and I would not have been surprised if there were tears in her eyes, but in the lightning, I saw that her eyes were clear, her gaze steady. I could tell that she'd repeated these words to herself many times over the past ten years, and only now, in that instant, was she prepared to accept the truth in them.

"The child was . . . beast and human, male and female, an abomination, and yet . . . it had her eyes . . . my eyes . . . *Wandigaux* eyes. I saw it. I saw her give birth, bellowing like a heifer, on her side, the child emerging, his face covered with a caul, but beneath it, *eyes*. Our eyes. I was all prepared to kill it. Snuff out its life quickly, the way I had years before helped my father kill a calf that had been born with two heads. Kill it because it didn't belong in our world. But those eyes. Beau, what was I to do? Human eyes, and Wandigaux eyes. I felt it was in God's hands, that He would take care of the child.

"And then I found her, one day, out on the bluffs, and I heard the horrible screaming, and I ran—it was the sound of a baby crying for dear life, and I ran until I fell, and I saw her there, by the shack. *What she did.* Unnatural. I could not . . . *stand* . . . I could not *stand* my own *child.* Devouring her newborn. Even . . . *it* . . . this baby *deserved* . . . it was a freak of nature . . . but even *it* deserved a better mother, even *it* . . . And I was too late.

"But in the basket beside her. The other. Summer. Her firstborn. Eleven months old with blood on his forehead. My Babygirl was going to devour him, too. The rake. I saw the rake. I had raked that garden with it. It was old and rusty, but good. I only saw the rake. I held it in these two hands and stopped my Babygirl from what she was about to do with her first child. Her skull was crushed. And she had not let out a whimper or a cry, and I knew that her soul had been released from the awful torment of its earthly cage."

As if to myself, I said aloud: "Summer *is* Sumter."

"Your mother and your aunt never knew how she died—they were both newlyweds and busy with their lives. Cricket married her husband the previous spring and miscarried in her fourth month. I brought your cousin to them, and they adopted him. I told them that Babygirl had died because of complications relating to her surgery, and no one was surprised. Life does continue.

"Your dreams, Beau, are like mine. We see things that may come. But Sumter has more. He can make things happen. He can *change* things. And it was all safe, but now it's free. Madness can be its only name."

"But it does have a name," I whispered. "Neverland."

"Yes." Her voice was ice and fire at the same time, and then it became the barest of whispers. "Sumter could keep it there, keep it in that shack, where his mother played. It was safe. But no more. No . . . more."

⊰ 9 ⊱

I was exhausted that night, and I believe it must've been two a.m. when I finally crawled into bed. I knew I would not sleep. The visions—of a ghost, of Lucy coming from her desecrated shrine, coming for the child who had not made the sacrifice as promised to her, of the dead creatures from the crate slithering up the stairs toward me, of my premature burial out in the mud of that shack, and of bony fingers pulling me down further into a rotting embrace—all kept pounding against my eyes.

Lightning and the booms and crashes of wind and branches and thunder outside, the rattling of the screen at my window—all of it slapped at my brain.

I tried shutting my eyes, but it hurt more to keep them shut than to keep them open. When lightning lit up the corners of the room, I saw Sumter standing there.

"You are the destroyer of the temple," he said. "You are the blasphemer of Lucy."

"I know who Lucy is, Sumter. Lucy is not a god!"

"Shut up!" he shouted, and drowned me out with his cries.

Behind him, a hulking shadow, and the smell of a wild animal.

I sat up in a cold sweat. I awoke. I had been dreaming. Sumter was not in my room at all. I got up to use the bathroom, feeling my way along the walls. How would I pee? I would have to take good aim in the dark. Afterward I went to check on Governor. He was not in his crib, and I panicked until I heard my mother's voice.

"Who's that?"

"Me."

"Beau? You should be in bed."

"I want to make sure Governor is okay."

"He's right here, with me. He's fine."

"Okay. Just checking."

"Beau, we'll leave here tomorrow. When your Daddy comes back from St. Badon."

"He'll be back early. He promised. Don't worry, Mama."

"I know. Go back to sleep. Get some rest."

I tiptoed back down the hall. I thought I saw someone sitting on the stairs, but I chose not to investigate this. I lay in bed until dawn, not sure if I was sleeping or not.

When I awoke, it was because a woman was screaming.

⊰ 10 ⊱

Aunt Cricket had three kinds of screams: the shrieky kind that meant someone had gotten into something he wasn't supposed to; the high-pitched cat squeals like she'd just tripped on something or gotten bit by a yellow jacket; or the one I heard this particular morning, which meant something had just scared the bejesus out of her. "Sunny! Sunny!" she keened, and I heard her clopping horseshoe steps all along the hallway; she was dashing down stairs, then up. I heard doors fling open, until finally she came to mine. "Sunny! Sunny! You seen him? You seen him, answer me, will you?"

I shook my head. After she ran off down the hall, I got up and got out of my underwear and into my trunks. I went out in the hall, and wondered why Governor wasn't crying the way he usually did in the mornings.

Mama was in her room, crying as she pulled her clothes on. Nonie and Missy were standing around looking lost. Mama said, "He was right *here*," indicating, with a nod of her head, a small oval lump on her bed. "I just got up for a second to get some water. My throat was parched. I was only gone for a minute."

My worst fear was realized.

Governor. SUMTER, DON'T YOU DARE!

"What time is it?" I asked my sister impatiently.

Nonie glanced at her watch. "Jeez, it's five to ten."

"Why's it still so dark out?" Missy asked.

"Must be the storm. Clouds and stuff."

"He's taken Governor," I said, gasping. "He's gonna sacrifice Governor."

I ran past them, down the stairs. Grammy Weenie was out on the porch, her hair greased and batted down by the rain, her face white and empty. "Why didn't you stop him?" I asked.

"The trees," Grammy hung her head low, defeated, "the trees were screaming, the light . . . changed . . . I saw behind the trees, I saw what walked . . . what walked in their shadows . . . his face. His face. The Feeder. Oh, dear God, the face of madness. Starved, coming for me."

"He took—" I caught my breath; she was not even listening.

"I was watching. For her. For my lost daughter. I felt she was coming back for me, last night." Grammy tapped the silver brush in her lap. "All night I felt her. But she has won. We are in Neverland now. For all I know, the whole world is Neverland."

Missy squealed from the upstairs window: "Jesus! Somebody pulled the plug on the ocean or something!"

I went running out to the bluffs through the storm. The rain came down in sheets. I was soaked through by the time I made it out to one of the trees. I climbed up to its lowest branches, and clung to them even as the wind bent the tree over. My father was going to cross the bridge at any moment, he was going to flash his headlights, but as I looked out over the sea to the bridge, I saw what Missy meant.

The tiara bridge was overtaken by an enormous wave, and the peninsula itself seemed to be separating from the mainland, to become what it was intended.

An island.

TWELVE

Where I Am Is Neverland

⊰ 1 ⊱

There is no tyranny like a child's imagination, and all my cousin Sumter could imagine was encompassed within Gull Island. Grammy Weenie had been right when she said, *"Don't let it out."* He had kept it contained within that crate, within those walls of Neverland. Now that sacred place had shattered, and the fragments, like jagged glass arrows, had flown out in all directions.

Each of us got a splinter of Neverland, and it dug down in our skins.

⊰ 2 ⊱

The thin branches of the tree I sat in whipped at my face; the wind and rain battered across the bluffs. The sky was dark and misty, and I let out a scream when the tiara bridge went. "Daddy! Daddy!" But no tears would come, I was all cried out. I had reached the furthest point of exhaustion.

And I felt reborn, as if I had truly died and was buried, and only now back from the dead. It was over, all that I had put up with in Neverland was out of me, out of my skin.

In my mind I heard Sumter's voice. *Where I am is Neverland, now we are the All.*

"Sumter," I whispered, clinging to the branch, "bring him back," I prayed. "Don't hurt Governor. Keep him safe."

Lucy says she will take him with her, that he will never have to turn into what they are. Look at the Weenie, Beau, look at her and her sad lying life, and your mama and daddy. Is that where you want to end up? In their world? Or in Neverland? You can come, too, if you want. Lucy wants all of us. Before it's too late. As his voice wormed its way through my mind, I smelled water and that vanilla way that Governor always smelled in the morning.

Don't hurt him, Sumter, don't hurt him.

Another smell: rotting wood, strong and strangely aromatic. *It's too late for you, Beau, I can see that. Lucy told me how you tried to bribe her. You'll do anything to save your own skin.*

Not mine, his. *Don't you hurt him.*

It won't hurt. He's pure innocence. You can't hurt that. He hasn't learned how to lie yet. He's living in bliss.

I heard Governor's small *dit-do* sound.

Hear? He's happy. He knows I'm taking him to a happy place.

SHAME ON YOU! YOU HEAR? SHAME ON YOU FOR WHAT YOU'RE DOING!

You do sound like the Weenie.

Please don't . . .

Lucy wants him.

Tell me where you are.

Just as if I were hooked up to a radio, the frequency buzzed and crack-led, and I didn't hear his voice anymore. I screamed inside my head for him, but he didn't respond. He controlled the telepathy between us, and he could shut it off if he willed.

I scrambled down from the tree and fell smack into the mud. It splashed up all around me, drenching me from head to toe. I let out a string of obscenities. The rain pelted me. I heard cries from the house, and from beyond the land the roar of surf and thunder and ear-splitting lightning crashes. It was like a booming orchestra with no conductor other than madness. I would've liked to lay down and die, to just let things go out of control, but the thought of my baby brother, over and above all else, was my fuel. This was nothing as easy as checking on him in his crib to make sure he was still breathing. This was going to take everything I had. I pushed despairing thoughts out of my head: of Daddy perhaps washed into the bay with the tiara bridge; the image of Sumter taking up a trowel and stabbing my brother through his chest in some demonic ritual.

I stumbled against the wind, to that sacred place, with branches scratching at my face, and came around the side of the smoldering tree beside the ruins of Neverland. The bark of the tree was blackened, and I caught a glimpse of movement. Above the wind, the sound of creaking wood, as if it were being bent. "Sumter?"

The tree, with its lightning streak split, was shaking in the wind. What were left of its branches swung down and back. But there, at the trunk, something inside of it, something moving. Fingers coming from inside the wood, tugging at the bark. Their nails long and curled, the skin of each finger ragged.

Scraping at wood.

Trying to emerge.

Grammy Weenie's words in my mind, *that place beneath the skin of this one . . . it is madness . . . they know how gods mate with humans . . . the world is a skin . . . hack at the flesh of life to the beating heart.*

The fingers bled as they scraped at the wood, shaking the tree.

"Lucy," I said.

As the fingers scraped, the tree began screaming, but not the way the trees had screamed in my dreams, but the way a baby screams because he's been awakened.

"Sumter!" I yelled. *"Goddamn you, Sumter!"* I slogged through the mud and rubble of Neverland, stepping over bits of aluminum siding and wood, and grabbed the rake. I battered the tree with it, taking aim for the fingers. One of the tines from the rake drove into the knuckle of an index finger, and blood gummed up the rake like sap, holding it fast to the trunk.

I tried to wrestle the rake out of the tree, but another sound caught my attention and I let go.

From behind me I heard my mother calling, "Beau? Beau! Come back inside! Right now! You hear?"

I turned around and saw her running from the Retreat, still in her bathrobe and slippers. Her hair was matted against her scalp, and her face was colorless. All around us the howling storm separated us even as we came together. "Mama," I said, feeling like a two-year-old.

Mama yanked at my hand, and we both almost slid into the muddy ground. She looked like a stone wall, no fear or anger or upset. At the most emotional times, the ones when she was truly backed into a corner, she put on a mask of emptiness. "Get in the house," she said, and I felt the pinch of her fingers on my arm.

"He has Governor!" I screamed.

"I have enough trouble without . . . " But her words trailed off. She was looking over my shoulder, her mouth half open.

I heard the crunch of twigs and mud and leaves, the earth splitting in two, the sound of something digging its way upward, scrabbling toward the air. *Always we must seek the higher ground.*

Spirit and flesh, constantly at war.

My mother's expression of wonder had not changed, and were it not for her open mouth, the drool down the side of her chin quickly being washed away with rain, I would not have dreaded looking back over my shoulder. Her face was stripped of all emotion but one, and that emotion is unnamable: It begins with fear but becomes what a human being must experience when she sees through the skin of the world to the madness of its bones and sinews.

A voice behind me, one I recognized immediately, said, "Hey-ey, Beau, what are we gonna play, anyway?"

My blood froze as I turned, my mother squeezing my hand so tight at the wrist that it felt like she was sawing into me with a dull blade.

"Zinnia," I said, recognizing the voice.

She had the rake in her fists, all her fingers bleeding. She swept aside mud and leaves with her hands as she scraped her way out of the grave from beneath the trunk of the burned tree. Even through the rain her smell was strong: the stench of barnacles and dead bluefish, the rotting timber of docks, of damp seaweed buzzing with flies. Mama smelled it, too; she finally let go of my wrist and put both her hands over her nose and mouth, gasping. "Help me out," Zinnia said, pressing the palms of her hands down into the sinking mud as if it were quicksand pulling her under. Her round face turned up to mine, the brows crossed with exertion, her dirty blond hair caked with mud, her rotting skin gleaming with sweat.

When she opened her eyes, as if just waking from a long sleep, they oozed with a lumpy white fluid that dribbled down her tattered cheeks.

I could not move, I could not speak, I could not think.

Her brothers were also digging their ways up from where they'd been buried, shaking frantic grubs and ants from their fingers as they tore at the ground. Wilbur's face was bloated, and when he opened his mouth, as he stretched upward, a large catfish struggled to emerge from where it had been stuffed down his throat. The fish's mouth opened and closed, its eyes stared insensibly, its fins flexed and relaxed. The boy made choking sounds, and when his hands were freed, he clutched at his neck; the anchorlike tail of the fish was caught in his throat like a squirming Adam's apple.

Goober had emerged, and he grinned like an idiot, his mouth a gash of gray meat. "Eat flesh, drink blood," he giggled. He had on his swimming trunks, and the skin was ripped from his shoulders down to his navel, exposing charred bones alive and swarming with grubs. Like a baby who has just learned his first phrase, he repeated, "Eat flesh, drink blood, eat flesh, drink blood."

Zinnia had the rusted rake in her hands. She clutched it so tightly that the bones of her fingers ripped through her flesh like she was shedding a glove. The teeth on the edge of the rake looked more like gray shark's teeth than metal. "I *told* you."

I could not answer.

"I *told* you. Some things just don't get better." Her dress was soaked through, so I could see her nipples like buds on cherry trees, her stomach low and egg-shaped. I didn't look back up to those curdled and dribbling eyes.

"Eat flesh," Goober said, "drink blood. Eat flesh, drink blood."

"Lucy made us this way," Zinnia said. She waved the rake in front of my face, swiping at the air. "She told us we wouldn't hurt, but Beau, *everything* hurts. Sometimes," she licked her lips, "we *like* to hurt."

Wilbur still was struggling with the catfish in his throat, shaking his head from side to side, picking at the skin of his neck, making sounds like he was trying to throw up.

"We swam out for miles, it seemed like, and she told us we would reach Heaven, Beau. But you know where we are? You know where she *keeps* us?" She swung the rake down, and it almost hit my face. I didn't flinch. I didn't think I could move; my muscles would not work, my blood would not thaw.

"It sure ain't Heaven," Goober said, the gash of his mouth chewing on the words. He jabbed his fingers into his breastbone, coming back with a handful of grubs; he stuffed them greedily into his mouth.

"You know where she keeps us? Do ya?" Zinnia brought the rake down, and as it sliced through the sheets of rain, aimed directly for my face, she said, "She keeps us buried. She keeps us good and rotten!"

Both Mama and I had stood there paralyzed, and I had almost forgotten her, standing behind me, her mouth agape. But as the rake came down, I fell back against her and we both fell to the ground.

The rake grazed my shoulder, tearing my shirt, and I fell to the grass.

"Just teasin' you, Beau, just teasin'," Zinnia said, her eyes almost dribbled empty.

"In the house." Mama sounded like she was in shock. "Now, Beau, in the house." I leaned back against her for support.

"Y'all called us back to play," Zinnia said. "Y'all made the sacrifices to Lucy. It's not fair if you don't want to play now. You *got* to play. We been waiting for*ever* to play."

She stumbled forward with the rake.

She held it up like a banner.

A jagged spear of lightning shot from the dark sky right to the rake's handle, illuminating Zinnia's bones like an X ray, and she shook violently as she swung the rake around again.

I was blinded by the brilliant white.

Blinded by the lightning, or by the rake as Zinnia brought it down on my mother and me.

I felt like I'd been shot out of my body.

IS THIS *another one of your games? I was asking Sumter.*

We sat in our tribal circle, candles all around us to keep the dark away. Missy and Nonie were drunk on their own blood, their faces smeared black with it. The crate was in our center, and Sumter sat on the other side of it from me.

Another tragic show, he said, the sad, sad story of the white trash kids.

It is *just a game. It seemed so real for a second.*

He said, it was real all right. They've been rotting underneath here for ages. They used to play with Lucy, too, and she took them with her. The Weenie's a liar, if you was to ask me. It was the Weenie who killed her. You know that, don't you?

As he spoke, a noise came from the crate, a hissing sound and a low moan.

Where do ya think it all goes when you die, Beau? Huh? You think when you're a god that you just die and that's it? Nope, I don't think so. It's got to just hang out for a while. Maybe the Weenie was scared of that. Maybe she knew about how Lucy was, and maybe she knows about how I am, too. She was afraid! So she did something kinda gruesome, something that's almost unthinkable, Beau. Not just killing Lucy, 'cause whenever you kill a god they rise again—that's the beauty of being a god. She smashed her head in. You shoulda been there, Beau, Lucy showed me everything that happened! How the Weenie followed her all around, spying, spying, spying. All Lucy wanted to do was play.

Be ye fishers of men, Sumter's voice spat out.

In Neverland, Lucy held the slumped-over body that had been Zinnia. Wilbur and Goober's corpses were set up in the corners of the shed.

But, Sumter grinned, now we come to the final sacrifice, Beau.

You spill a little blood and you put the pieces back together.

Sacrifice is the law of the universe.

Lucy can play now.

I'm gonna raise her up from her grave.

I'm gonna spill innocent blood in her name.

She's gonna be resurrected, and my daddy's gonna be there, too. Not that man you think is my daddy, but my real daddy, the one who wants me, the one who loves me the way daddies are supposed to.

Like a lightbulb that is almost out, blinking and buzzing; like a television screen warming up and turning on; like the mind of a little boy just wiping the sleep from his eyes and not surrendering his dream to the waking moment, so the world came back to me then. My head ached like a truck had rolled over and flattened it. I was sure I'd been blinded, and I reached up and touched my left eye: It was liquid, but as I rubbed it, I could again see. Blood was dripping down from my forehead. As I rubbed it away from my eyelids, I said, "Dang, I'm still *alive.*"

Zinnia stood directly above me.

I thought you liked me, I thought, feebly, sure that she would bring the rake down and tear my face right off.

"It's not me doing this," she said. But she hesitated.

It's Sumter, I know. It's all Sumter. It's all Neverland.

From somewhere in the corridors of my brain, I heard Governor wailing.

My mother was screaming, too. She had fallen a few feet away, rain batting her face, while Zinnia's brothers descended on her, the one still choking on the catfish, the other chanting, "Eat flesh, drink blood, eat flesh, drink blood."

In Goober's left hand was one of Aunt Cricket's croquet mallets. He had already begun pounding my mother's knees. "Eat flesh," he hit it against her ankle, "drink blood!"

"You want to see something neat, cuz?" Zinnia said, twirling the rake like a baton. Sumter was not making a pretense anymore: It was his voice.

I had been right—they weren't proper ghosts, but some kind of collision between Sumter and the place on which Neverland had stood. The rotting corpse towering above me was merely his dummy. "Like the ultimate gross-out? The tragic show to end all tragic shows?"

Don't hurt—

"Don't you think *I* hurt?" Sumter's words were coming out fast, and as he spoke he began stuttering. "Don't you think I hurt? All the *time* I hurt. I hurt so much I could just explode!" Zinnia brought the rake down and scraped the mud. "You broke your oath, and for that, Beau, I'm not even gonna take you with me. You can become like *them*, Beau, you can be a liar and a cheat. You can be a *grown-up*."

Lucy wants you for the sacrifice, Sumter. She wants me to bring you to her. You know that?

Zinnia seemed confused. Whatever power was behind that rotting corpse, it was getting mixed signals. It wasn't sure of itself. It's what Sumter always feared most: self-doubt.

Mama shrieked as another mallet blow caught her in the shin. "My God, my God," she whimpered, trying to crawl away from the two boys. But they wanted to keep playing.

You kill kittens and babies, Sumter. Is that the kind of god you got for yourself? Huh?

"Lucy," Zinnia's mouth pursed, "Lucy is my god."

Lucy's been dead too long. Nothing but a skull you got.

"Not with the sacrifice. I'm gonna put the skull together with the rest of her, and then she and me, and Governor, can always be in Neverland."

You know she's just a dead woman. It's you, Sumter, you have control. Put it back where it belongs, put it back in Neverland.

"Where I am is Neverland," Zinnia said, but her jaw was sagging.

Then put it back inside you.

"Hurts." Sumter's voice came from Zinnia's open mouth. He sounded whiny and tired. "Hurts."

So you're gonna hurt everyone else.

"That's it. You had your chance and you screwed up." Zinnia lifted the rake and swung it down at me. With all the strength I had, I held out my hands and caught the rake just beneath its teeth; my hands stung as it *whopped* against my palms. I tugged on it, and the dead girl came toppling down on me. I gagged as she pressed her lips against mine. Like saltwater and a festering wound, the smell and the taste overpowered my senses. I struggled for my breath as she drew her head back. Turning the rake around, I scraped its teeth across her face, and the flesh tore from the bone like it was marshmallow.

A dark figure, like a wavering shadow, swung a croquet mallet down against the dead girl. Her body rolled, lifeless, off me.

"Lucy?" I asked wearily, dizzily. "Mama?"

Before I passed out, I glanced over and saw Mama. Wilbur and Goober lay in the mud, unmoving. Somehow this was over. I wondered if Mama was all there, or if she had gone off to a Neverland of her own. She was bruised and bleeding, but her expression indicated that in the fight between flesh and spirit, her spirit had fled. But she was alive. I was fainting, and I thought a silly thought.

Grown-ups ain't allowed in Neverland, that's why Mama's mind is gone: It's 'cause she ain't allowed.

I was closing my eyes and thought I saw an angel, but it was just Julianne Sanders peering at me to see if I was still breathing.

⇥ 3 ⇤

The rest of the island was in a state of panic, and I would only learn later of the strange occurrences. The first thing—besides the fact that there was a solar eclipse that day that was only perceived by Gull Island residents, and there was a hurricane that had come out of nowhere to sweep across the coast—was the birds. Gulls, to be specific. They were falling dead from the sky just like they'd forgotten how to fly. Two traffic fatalities that morning were attributed to sea gulls smashing through windshields while a panicked driver rammed head-on into another. It was this first sign that caused Julianne Sanders, our former nanny, to call up to the Retreat. Naturally, she discovered what everyone on Gull Island was just finding out: The phones were down, as was most of the electric power. So she got in her VW and headed back up to the house. There were mudslides all along the main road, and then coming up the gravel proved to be truly hellish, full of enormous splits in the earth that could easily swallow a car whole. But Julianne was driving a Volkswagen, after all, and not only were those Bugs airtight, but they'd go anywhere. She veered off the road and drove across muddy lawns; summer residents on our side of Gull Island were few and far between, and with uprooted trees and dead sea gulls scattered like a messy child had left them in his wake, who was going to notice some tire treads across their front lawns?

She parked the car and, getting out, heard cries coming from the bluffs. She couldn't see much with all the rain and birds coming down, but she ran out there. The sight she beheld didn't shock her so much as confirm something for her.

"I knew, Beau, the first time I saw your cousin—he was like an iron filing, and the bluffs were a magnetic field. I worked as hard as I could not to believe—but when I saw those dead children . . . and me, armed with what every Gullah woman knows are her best weapons," she explained when we were both back inside the Retreat, "my two hands."

She found it easy enough to wrestle the mallets from Wilbur and Goober. It seemed Sumter, the master puppeteer, wasn't really great at walking and chewing gum at the same time. "My granddaddy said, 'It ain't the dead you got to watch out for, it's the living,' and he just maybe was right." Then when I had raked off Zinnia's face, Julianne was there to knock her off me.

I awoke in the living room a few minutes later. Uncle Ralph had gone out to bring Mama in, and when he did, Mama recognized no one but kept calling out for Governor. They put her upstairs to bed with a good stiff drink; Aunt Cricket and Uncle Ralph, themselves armed with stiff drinks, were up there tending to her bruises. All I could hear of them were my mother's shrieks for her baby and the rushing sound of water running in the bathroom: A boiling hot bath was Aunt Cricket's remedy for everything life threw at you, and she would no doubt be trying to dunk my mother to keep the hysteria to a minimum. Uncle Ralph was shouting to my sisters to stay in their room or they'd get a whupping, but I could hear them whispering and Missy's exclamations of "Wow" at the top of the stairs.

Julianne said to Grammy, "You knew all along what that boy was up to. You could've stopped him."

Grammy replied, "Could I? Can you stop imagination? Can you tame impulse? And what do you call what he has? Birthright?" My eyes fluttered open and closed. "Sumter speaks to you, doesn't he?" she asked me.

I nodded. "In my mind's eyeball. We sometimes talk. To each other. But it's all from him. It's only when he wants to talk to me."

"I hear him sometimes, too," she heaved a big sigh, "just like I used to hear my Babygirl. Even . . . even after she died. I saw what happened to her body. When she died. I saw her shift, turn, her corporeal self shimmer and become monstrous and twisted. She became beastlike, covered with hair, her teeth sharp and long, and then she was like a boy, and then an even younger girl, she changed so fast before my eyes, at times like a lizard, and then herself, and then a shiny eel in my hands. It was her *mind;* she had no control, do you understand? She had *no control.* She was pulled by a tide I could not see."

"Sumter took Governor. To her grave. Where—where is it? It's where he's gone."

"Dear God." Grammy was calmer than I'd ever seen her. "She's on Gullah ground. Sacred ground."

"The bluffs," I said.

"No, child, the bluffs aren't sacred. It's the swamp, the island."

A place of pure innocence, of bliss.

"Where the dead dance," Julianne Sanders said, as if repeating something she'd heard for years, "the island in Rabbit Lake. It's where the first

Gullahs here were believed to be buried, and the water was to lock in their souls. They could not travel over water, for it always would bring them back."

"I knew that legend," Grammy Weenie said, "and I thought perhaps, just perhaps, it would keep her soul there, keep her from returning."

"But she *is* back. I seen her. In my mind's eyeball. And she's small like a dwarf and's got white hair, not red like you lied before, Grammy."

Grammy clutched her breast with her shriveled hand. She was moving her lips but not exactly talking. I had never seen tears come to her eyes before, but they did, and they were fat tears that just sat there on the lower lids.

"Dear Jesus," she gasped. "Beau, her hair *was* red, in the end. Soaked with her own blood. I had forgotten . . . I had thought it was always red, because that's how I remember her looking. That way. The last moment I ever looked at her face, and it colored my memory. My God, I'd *forgotten.*"

I tried to sit up, but Julianne pushed me back.

"And he's *really* gonna do it. He has Governor. And I know where he is," I said.

"What?" Grammy asked. "Where, child?"

"Where you buried her body. 'Cause that's where he's gonna sacrifice Governor. He's gonna try to bring Lucy back with Governor's blood. And with her . . . the other one. His father. The Feeder. The All. He'll be down there, down there with Governor—" I said, still dizzy but trying to sit up. "If I can just—"

But my words were cut off when we heard the sounds of my sisters screaming from upstairs—and the growling of a wild animal.

⇥ 4 ⇤

What Nonie later told me was she and Missy had been running amok through the house when I had run out to see if Daddy would flash his headlights. Missy was terrified of storms, so she thought she was having heart palpitations, and when Nonie tried to get her to calm her down so she wouldn't run around like a chicken with its head cut off, Missy slapped her so hard that Nonie hit her head against one of the doorknobs. My sisters started hitting each other, and Mama, who was in a tizzy on account of Governor being gone, yelled at them to stop right this instant.

"She started it," Nonie complained, but Mama was too confused to respond.

"Where's Beau?" Mama asked, and when she didn't get an answer, she grabbed Nonie by the shoulders and shook her. "Where's Beau?"

"He took off outta here." She pointed to the door that was swinging open with rain coming in the front.

"Maybe he knows where the baby—" As she said this, a tree branch crashed through the hall window and the glass sprayed in. Nonie went to her bedroom to get her sandals so she wouldn't cut up her feet.

Mama looked distracted when she got back from the bedroom, and Missy whispered, "She's gone round the bend, I knew she would."

"Mama?" Nonie asked. "You doing okay?" Mama's hands seemed unusually warm as my sister held them.

"I'm going to have to take Cricket's car," she was saying aloud, but it was like she was talking only to herself. "The roads'll be washed out, but I need to get help. Maybe Daddy came back and took the baby. Maybe that's what happened. Where the hell is your daddy?" She drew her hands away from Nonie's grasp. She started wiping her face over and over with both hands like she wanted to pull the skin right off. Aunt Cricket was coming up the stairs looking like a shambles of her usual run-down self. She had been keening like a madwoman in the kitchen, trying to locate her boy.

Aunt Cricket said, "You children tell me everything you know right now or else, you hear me? You hear me? You tell me where my boy is!"

Missy, who never liked being accused of so much as coughing, started bawling right there, backing up against the broken window and scratching her feet up something awful with the glass chips on the floor. "We don't know where he is," she whined. "We just got up. Leave us alone. We didn't mean for him to be like this."

"Like what?" Aunt Cricket cornered her. "Like what, young lady?"

"Like he is," she spat, her words running together in one long string. "Killing and stealing and praying in his clubhouse. We didn't mean to drink the beer that time, or steal cigarettes and stuff, but he made us, he made us, and I never wanted to hurt anything, and he made us see things and feel things, and then writing in blood, and all—"

Nonie wanted to cut out Missy's tongue. "Don't tell them *everything.*"

"It's over, don'tcha get it?" Missy's eyes were all squinty and her nose was a wrinkled bump with two flared nostrils; her lips had gone purple and blubbery. "You *know* what he's gonna do to Governor, they gotta try to stop him."

Mama said, "What about the baby?"

Missy was crying too hard to make any sense.

Mama turned to Nonie, "What about the baby?"

"He isn't gonna do it, don't worry. Mama don't cry, he isn't gonna do it."

"Do what? Tell me now."

"There's no *way* he'd hurt Governor."

Aunt Cricket slapped Nonie. Nonie was always headstrong, and this was the second time in the last ten minutes she'd gotten slapped, and she slapped Aunt Cricket right back, which didn't go over too well with either grown-up, but they put the question to her—the punishment, Mama promised, would come later. So Nonie told them about the big sacrifice, and how I had run out of the house when the bridge washed out yelling about how Sumter was going to use Governor for the sacrifice.

"My Sunny would never do that kind of filthy thing," Aunt Cricket admonished my sister. "You're just Little Miss Liar, Leonora Jackson, and that's all you are."

"I *said* he wouldn't really go through with it. He wouldn't kill a *baby.*"

But Mama was already headed down the staircase, saying, "I'll get Beau, he'll know. He always watches out for his brother, he'll know." That's when she headed out the front door and stumbled out through the storm to the remains of Neverland.

Missy ran past Aunt Cricket to get to her bedroom. She escaped our aunt's wrath, but Nonie did not.

"You're just Little Miss Liar, I know you." Aunt Cricket grabbed Nonie by the wrist and dragged her along the hall with her. "You'd like to make out like my boy is a bad boy, but I know what's true and what's not."

"Let me go." Nonie scratched at our aunt's arm with her free hand, and Aunt Cricket hauled off and slapped her one again. Nonie struck back again, kicking Aunt Cricket in the shins and then scampering off to the safety of the closest bedroom, which just happened to be Grampa Lee's old room, which was an unwise choice on her part.

Uncle Ralph occupied that room. He was sitting up in bed in his boxers and a tank T-shirt, practically scratching his balls. It was ten a.m., but he still had a Dixie beer clutched in the hand that wasn't scratching. Six empties were overturned on the rug near his puffy feet.

"You kids's nothin' but trouble," he said, belching. "Nobody should have kids, nobody, understand?"

Nonie had her back up against the door. Aunt Cricket was banging on it from the other side, telling her in no uncertain terms to open up.

Uncle Ralph yelled at his wife, although Nonie figured he might be yelling at her, too. "You can just go off with Mr. Goody-Two-Shoes Dabney Jackson and give birth to some more village idiots, for all I care! You got that, Crick?"

But Aunt Cricket had her one goal: to get Nonie for kicking her. She shoved hard on the door and it gave a little, but Nonie held her ground and shoved back. "Little Miss Liar, you let me in right this instant."

And between Uncle Ralph shouting obscenities and Aunt Cricket pushing on the door, Nonie saw something battering at the bedroom window that made her scream.

It was a little girl, floating in midair, slapping hard at the glass. Nonie knew the girl: It was herself, only she was blackened as if from fire, and the only way Nonie recognized it was her and not Missy or somebody else was through the eyes. In her mind Nonie heard Sumter's voice saying, *Lucy wants it all, now.*

But the girl at the window flew away and off into the storm again.

Aunt Cricket was distracted and turned away from the door because of Grammy Weenie shouting that something was going on over at the bluffs, and then a while later Julianne was bringing me back inside, and Missy was sure I was dead, but Nonie told me later that she knew I was alive on account of she heard me coughing. She went back and hid with Missy while Uncle Ralph ran out, practically tripping down the stairs, to bring Mama back, too.

My sisters watched as I came to, and they eavesdropped on everything that was said between Grammy, Julianne, and me. When Aunt Cricket started running a hot bath for Mama, she seemed to have forgiven Nonie the kick long enough to enlist her aid. "Get some clean towels—the large ones—out of the linen closet, and I can't find iodine, so if you know where it is, bring that, too. Your mama's all scratched up and I need to clean the cuts out." Nonie did as she was told, afraid that Mama was never going to come back from the place her mind had sent her to.

Missy kept saying, "It's 'cause we been worshiping the Devil."

Nonie tried to shush her, but Aunt Cricket latched on to that. "You brought that kind of stuff down from *Virginia*, didn't you? My boy wouldn't've learned that Devil stuff in Marietta, let me tell you. You bad, bad little girls."

Nonie would've contradicted her, but she figured she was already in enough hot water as it was. Then she noticed something about Aunt Cricket, something she hadn't noticed until now. Aunt Cricket had a shadow, in the dim light—a long shadow just like it was late afternoon—and the left hand of Aunt Cricket's shadow seemed to move differently than Aunt Cricket's own left hand.

"Mama," Nonie whimpered. Mama had crawled over to a corner of the bathroom. She was surrounded by steam, so Nonie could just make out her face. Aunt Cricket was running the water so hot, Nonie thought it actually might be boiling. Even in the steam Aunt Cricket's shadow moved and grew, and Nonie wondered why nobody else seemed to notice. Mama wasn't recognizing anybody, but she kept asking for her baby, her little baby boy, and wiping at her face like she wanted to scrape the skin off. Aunt Cricket was barking orders and trying to get Mama to sit up. "C'mon, Evvie, just so I can get your blouse off, and Nonie, where *is* that first-aid kit? How many times do I have to ask for it?" The shadow didn't wag her finger at Nonie; the shadow seemed to be dancing around in a jig, still attached to Aunt Cricket.

"Your . . . your shadow," Nonie stammered.

Aunt Cricket said, "Will you go get the first-aid kit? Will you?"

Nonie ran out into the hall with Missy tagging along. The first-aid kit was kept in a shoe box in the linen closet. As the girls opened the doors on the closet, they heard something shuffling toward the back. Nonie reached as far as she could to the back of the closet for the shoe box when something touched her. It was soft and furry and warm, but it reminded her of when she put her hand in the Neverland crate, and she tried to draw her hand back from the shelf, but the creature held her. It had claws that began digging into her hand.

"*Jesus!*" she yelped, falling backward as the thing let go of her. While Missy went scrambling for the stairs, Nonie looked at the back of her hand. It was practically scraped raw, although the claws hadn't dug as deep as she figured; only the top layer of skin was gone. Her hand didn't hurt so much as feel numb, and she got up as quickly as she could to shut the closet doors, when the creature leapt out at her and she hit her back on the floor so hard she was sure her tailbone was broken.

Its furry paws clutched her throat.

It was the teddy bear.

Bernard.

He stared at her with his blank button eyes, his muzzle curled in a snarl, his teeth dripping with foam.

❈ 5 ❈

From the living room we heard the screams, and Missy would've gone flying past us and out the front door, but Julianne shot up and caught her by
her shoulders as she ran by. "Let me go, it's awful, let me go, they got Nonie!"

Nonie was screaming, and I tried to get up, but damn if my body was unwilling: My limbs were slack. I tried to will the pins-and-needles feeling of circulating blood through me, but my arms and legs were frozen. Nonie was now crying out in little gasps, and Julianne let go of Missy and headed for the staircase. Missy went to cry on Grammy's lap.

I was thinking what Sumter had told us, that one of Lucy's commandments was *Do what you will.* So if Neverland was the whole world around us, then, hell, I was going to *will* my body to move in spite of itself. *Lucy, come on, get my blood going, come on.*

Aunt Cricket was freaking out in the bathroom. Nobody's really sure what happened with her and the bathroom door. There's a good chance she went to help Nonie but the door slammed in her face and maybe threw her back against the wall. The last thing Nonie saw was just a glimpse of the black glove shadow hand on the doorknob. No sound from her after that, but then everybody was screaming so much, who really knows?

But after another moment we heard Aunt Cricket cackling, "Take a hot, hot, hot bath, soothes the nerves, don't it? A boiling hot bath, *take the skin right off you! Get you all nice and* clean, *scrubbadubdub, just like you was a crawdad in a pot, all red and hot, hot, hot!*"

Uncle Ralph came out in the hall blustering and babbling, "What the hell is goin' on *this* time?" He beat his fist on the bathroom door, and Aunt Cricket began shouting at the top of her lungs, "*Cleanliness is next to godliness. I'm just washin' all my sins away in the river that burns eternal, hallelujah, amen!*"

"Just turn it down, woman," he muttered. "Off her rocker, for sure." When Uncle Ralph saw what Nonie was shrieking about, there at the end of the hall, he almost laughed. Even though the bear had ripped through her shirt and left a bloody claw mark down her stomach.

Seeing Uncle Ralph, the bear stopped, and Nonie said she was sure the bear was just going to slice her in two. But it sniffed at the air. It turned and looked back at Uncle Ralph and crawled off her. She used her hands to pull herself up. By that time Julianne had grabbed her up in her arms.

"Sure must be on some damn bender," Uncle Ralph laughed, "'cause these DTs are a bitch." He wasn't exactly seeing straight because he kept wobbling from side to side, trying to get a take on the bear.

The bear growled, and Sumter spoke through it: *"Vengeance is mine, mine, and all mine, you hear? You're in* my *playground now, and here* you're *the weak sister."*

The teddy bear advanced on Uncle Ralph. It moved clumsily, wobbling on its flat round feet. Maybe if Uncle Ralph hadn't been so drunk he might've just gotten around Bernard, but Ralph stood stupidly and watched the bear approach him. He didn't even get it. There was his wife screaming in the bathroom and his niece with her shirt torn, and Uncle Ralph just had a slap-happy grin on his face that didn't change. He thought it was some kind of joke or dream.

He plopped down on the floor like he wanted to play with the bear. "Boy's too old to be playing with dolls."

The teddy bear climbed almost sweetly into his lap, and Uncle Ralph hugged it. "I guess ain't no harm in a teddy bear," he said.

"This is the way we wash our skin, wash our skin, we wash our skin!" Aunt Cricket howled from the bathroom.

Nonie said Julianne screamed and almost dropped her then, on account of the bear tearing into Uncle Ralph's throat and all the shooting blood.

Up until the last, Uncle Ralph looked like he thought he was still dreaming, and only during his last second of life did it seem to occur to him that a dream wouldn't hurt so much.

⊰ 6 ⊱

"Beau?" Julianne called from the upstairs landing. "If you can, you get that croquet mallet I left by the couch and you bring it up to me."

I was still fighting my blood, but I was willing it. I was going to control my mind, I was going to make my body do what I wanted it to do. I saw in my mind's eyeball my heart pumping and my toes wiggling. I blocked out Missy's whimpers and Grammy's fever-pitch prayers and just saw my body working the way it was supposed to.

I was able to raise my hand.

"Beau!" Julianne shrieked, and I was up like a shot. I grabbed the mallet and practically tripped over my feet before I got my balance.

Julianne was backed up against the bathroom door with Nonie hugging her tight around the neck. The door wouldn't budge, and the bear, having done a messy job of severing Uncle Ralph's head from his neck, was advancing on her.

"Beau? You got it?"

When I came up the stairs, I thought I was going to throw up. Uncle Ralph's legs and arms were still twitching, and the stench was overpowering. I slammed the mallet against the banister, cracking it.

Sumter growled from the bear's mouth, "Okay, Beau, see what happens when you disobey Lucy? Y'all broke your blood oaths, and you will pay in blood. All of y'all."

The bear came running at me and I wanted to shut my eyes, but I knew that would do no good, so I kept them open wide. The bear's muzzle was matted with fresh blood. I could smell my uncle's blood on its face as it came at me. I brought down that mallet and caught the animal right in the back.

It let out one last snarl, and the stuffing flew out of it. I brought down the mallet again and again until there was not so much as a ripple from its coat, and stuffing was all over the floor.

Even then I wanted to keep battering away at it. I could barely see for the tears in my eyes.

Finally it was over.

The teddy bear did not move, did not growl.

I dropped the mallet on the floor. The noise echoed throughout the house as if it were empty. *Where I am is Neverland,* Sumter had said, so it was easily defeated if he wasn't around. Uncle Ralph didn't believe in Neverland, so he hadn't even tried to fight it. I turned around to see if Julianne Sanders and my sister were okay.

Julianne was hyperventilating, trying to stay in control, but the horror around us had gotten to be too much for her. Her face glistened with sweat, and her eyes were wild. "I'm gonna take you kids outta here, we'll be safe outta here," she whispered rapidly, tripping over her words.

I shook my head. "The whole island is Neverland. For all we know, the whole damn *world* is Neverland. We got to stop him. I know where he is. You can drive me down to the boathouse. We got to get out to Rabbit Lake. We got to, before he kills my brother."

Julianne was no use: She, like the others, was just a grown-up, and even though she was also a *sinistre,* it didn't mean much, just like she'd told me before. The fear in her eyes was crippling, just as it had been for Mama. "You're not gonna drive me there, are you?"

"I ... I ... "

"You're scared."

"I don't want to *die,* not like *that.*" She was ashamed, but given the fact that Uncle Ralph was proof enough of Sumter's powers, I can't say as I blamed her. This was overload for any adult, even a superstitious one.

Aunt Cricket was tapping on the bathroom door. *"Bath time, kiddies, a nice hot bath to make you all shiny and new!"* Steam poured from beneath the door.

"Shadow," Nonie whispered, so I knew she was conscious and hadn't gone too far off the deep end.

"Nonie?" I asked.

"Shadow, tragic show, shadow in there, in there." Nonie pointed to the bathroom.

"Mama and Aunt Cricket are safer in there than out here," I told her. I went over to the door and knocked on it. "Everything okay?"

"Squeaky clean behind the ears," Aunt Cricket said.

I shrugged.

Nonie's eyes grew wide, but she said nothing. She watched the door intently.

"When I'm done with my bath, kiddies, I am going to give each of you a nice hot, hot, hot bath." Aunt Cricket sniggered.

I had to laugh. They must've thought I was crazy, and maybe I was by that point. Aunt Cricket talking crazy like that about bath time when all hell was breaking loose around us.

"Shadow." Nonie pointed to the steam that was rising from the cracks in the bathroom door.

"Don't you fucking laugh at me," Aunt Cricket said.

It was 'round about then I felt the hairs on the back of my neck start stiffening. My aunt never said the password to Neverland—she thought it was one of the dirtiest imaginable. The voice didn't even sound like my aunt's—more like a bad imitation of it.

Julianne, still clutching Nonie, stepped away from the bathroom door.

Aunt Cricket was scratching at it with her fingernails. "Won't somebody open up the door?"

"Jesus." I gasped.

Julianne said, "What . . . do you . . . think is in there?"

"Whatever it is, it's in with my mama." I bent over and picked up the mallet again and whammed it against the doorknob. Instead of the door flying open, the mallet broke just at the head, which went bouncing down the hall.

It felt like several minutes passed, although it couldn't have been more than a few seconds. I was exhausted; there was no way to win this battle. Sumter could keep us fighting phantoms and teddy bears until the end of the world. He was the source of this. I had to get to him. All this in the house was just distraction from my main purpose.

I tried to communicate with him in my mind.

Sumter! You hear me?

No answer.

Sumter! You talk to me right now! Lucy! Sumter!

Finally, a reply. *Don't you take the name of Lucy in vain ever again, you hear me?*

Yeah? What are you gonna do?

Just don't is all.

You stop all this. You make it stop.

It ain't me anymore. It ain't me. It's Neverland. It's all out—and it's their fault, anyway. It's all their fault. They went and opened it up, they went and let it out.

Where's Governor?

No reply.

You hurt him?

Everything hurts.

And again silence like a stone wall.

I would have to climb that wall and enter into that playground where Sumter had lived for so long. He could enter my mind with his thoughts—I would have to enter his.

I tried the bathroom door again. This time the knob turned easily in my hand.

I took a deep breath.

Not a sound from the bathroom other than the hissing steam of the bathtub.

I only opened the door partway—who knew what was going to leap out at me?

The room was white with steam. First I saw my mother. She was still off in another world, wiping at her face and asking for her baby. I could not see Aunt Cricket anywhere, but the steam was clearing.

The bathtub was fizzing with popping bubbles—at first I thought it was Sumter's Mr. Bubble, but it was only water. Boiling water.

Lying in the tub was Aunt Cricket, her head just above the boiling water, her skin a mass of enormous red blisters which still grew and exploded as she continued to cook. She smiled at me and said, "Ah, nothing like a hot bath to cure all of life's little miseries."

I could not even scream. I stood there in the doorway and watched the skin fall from her bones and muscles the way meat fell off the chicken bones when Mama would boil them for broth.

I turned back to Julianne.

Her eyes were glazed over.

What could I say to her? What could I tell any of them? *Okay. I'm gonna take my uncle's car. The only way to stop him is to go down there. I want you to stay here. Maybe if everybody stays together, it will be okay. I don't know what else he'll do.* Was that going to do the trick? Would that make it better? But I knew I had to stop him from sacrificing Governor to his dark mother, if for no other reason than that I was not going to let him hurt my brother.

All I said to Julianne was, "Watch them for me."

"What are you gonna do?"

"Whatever it takes," I said, sounding strangely like my father.

⊰ 7 ⊱

How deep does a child's imagination go? The rain battered at our house, and I was sure Sumter had called that rainstorm up; but over and above the thunder and rain, I heard the sounds of music: a calliope playing "Take Me Out to the Ballgame." Was it my imagination or *his?* My cousin and I had become tied to each other through the warped passages of his mind; he could speak in my head, and he could project a movie of his own making on the world. What would we find there—more corpses rising from graves? More bunnies screaming? More demons to torture us?

Although my fear didn't exactly evaporate, I had only one purpose: to make sure Governor didn't get hurt. It was the only thing I saw before me, in spite of the storm he'd conjured, in spite of my dead uncle and aunt at the top of the stairs and my mother off in her own fevered mind. Nothing else mattered, not even the fact that I knew I might have to kill Sumter in order to keep Governor from hurting.

Grammy insisted on going with me, and I felt that was right. I grabbed Uncle Ralph's keys from the key rack and ran out and got soaked again. I was afraid to look out at the bluffs because of the dead children that may or may not have been out there. I got behind the wheel of the car and tried every key in the ignition until I got the right one. I started the car, having to stretch my leg down until I thought it would pop out of its socket just trying to push the gas pedal. This wasn't that much different than driving the family wagon up and down the driveway at home. I wasn't really panicking anymore, either. The way panic works is you have about a minute or two of it, when you can't do anything right, and then you experience a calm because it begins to sink in that you really *can't* do anything right, so you just go ahead and do what needs to get done. *In life, Beau, you just do what needs doing and leave the rest, the rest can wait.* I could hear my father's voice from times past, instructing me as to turning the wheel and when to give it gas and how smoothly to brake. Daddy had been sitting me on his lap from the time I was two, putting his hands over mine on the wheel, and when I was eight he taught me the rules of the road. So I let my body take over—I went into automatic.

I brought the car around to the porch, skidding in the gravel and mud. Julianne was helping Grammy down, and I left the car idling and ran around to help her in. Grammy could walk only just a little; she leaned on our shoulders for support. When we got her settled in the front seat, she reached in the pocket of her apron for something, although I couldn't tell what it was.

I said to Julianne, "You watch. The storm'll end. You'll know things're just fine if it does. If . . . we make it to him okay . . . I may need you, then. To help. But only when the storm ends. Stay here and watch my mama and sisters. When the storm ends, you'll know we're okay." I didn't know if this was a lie or not. I wanted it to be true. I wanted things to turn out just fine. "But Julianne," I shivered, and her eyes seemed to be wearying of this nightmare, "if it ends, come down to the boathouse. We may need help."

"And if it don't end . . . " she said, and did not finish the thought.

As I skidded the Chevy across the flooded lawn, out to the road, I caught a glimpse of something in Grammy's hands—something hard and silver—and at first I thought it was a knife, but then I saw the bristles, the stiff tacklike bristles of her brush. She held it fast in her good hand.

As fast as the wipers sliced across the windshield, the rain sprayed across it and blinded me. The sky was lighter than it had been, though, and the occasional flashes of lightning lit up the road ahead for at least a few yards at a time.

"You hear the music?" Grammy asked.

"Uh-huh." We were being treated to another round of "Take Me Out to the Ballgame."

"What do you think it is?"

Up ahead, in my lights, there was a downed telephone pole. A wire was spitting and sputtering orange and white light from its tip. I swerved the car up the side of a slight hill to get around it. We came down with a *whump!* and skidded back onto the road.

Lightning burst across the sky, and for a second the rain froze in midair and the landscape shifted as if one slide were being stuck in the projector over another slide. There were fires all along the hills where trees and houses had been struck with lightning and now seemed to be lighting our path.

The calliope music was getting louder, and as I drove down the rest of the way to the boathouse, the road was blocked by what I figured were several horses, having escaped some stables nearby.

But the horses had lances through their backs.

As my headlights lit them better, I saw that the horses were painted various colors.

They were from the carousel at Sea Horse Amusement Park.

Sumter had brought them to life.

One horse stood there right in front of the car, scraping its right front hoof against the road.

From its flared nostrils came breath of fire.

Sumter called to me. *I don't want to hurt you, cuz, but don't try to stop me, 'cause I'm gonna do what I gotta do. If you get in the way, I'll stomp you.*

DON'T YOU HURT HIM!

My mind's eyeball went crazy, like somebody was switching channels on a TV at a rapid pace. He was sending me images now; I was picking up what his mind was producing. *Aunt Cricket holding him so close to her breast, kissing the top of his head; Uncle Ralph unlooping the belt from his pants and curling it double, swatting it at the back of Sumter's unprotected leg; a summer day on the island, and Sumter looking all of six years old, crying by a tree stump—in his left hand he held a jagged piece of glass, and he shut his eyes tight and thrust the glass into his right arm and sliced the flesh up; Sumter sticking the trowel into the kitten, and that wild look on his face; and then a place I didn't recognize, a place of vast fields of ice and red sky, and Sumter walking with the woman I knew to be Lucy, and there were other children there, too, playing games of freeze-tag, but there was something not right about the picture: It wavered—the word Neverland whispered across the barren white land—black-and-white bunnies sniffed the air; Bernard the teddy bear lumbered out from behind a tree carrying a dead bunny in his mouth, still shaking its hind legs even as blood stained its fur; whatever Neverland was exploded across this vision, and the ground that Sumter walked on began bleeding, until both he and Lucy were up to their ankles in a dark crimson marsh, and I heard cries of animals and children; and the creature in Bernard's jaws was not a bunny after all, but my brother Governor, his small hands reaching out for a mother who was not there, his mouth opened but with no voice left with which to cry.*

Sumter, I said, *Neverland is a bad place. Don't put Governor in a bad place.*

Lucy's soft voice whispered, *Do what you will.*

It was a Neverland commandment, and I felt a key turning in my head. *All right,* I figured, *I* will.

I opened my eyes, back in the Chevy, with Grammy Weenie's hand on my arm.

"Beau?" Her voice was filled with panic, and I glanced back at the road: The carousel horses had their heads down and pawed the road with their hooves. Fire shot out of their nostrils and sprayed red sparks across the windshield. The largest of the herd charged first. It reared up on its hind legs and brought its front hooves down on the hood of the Chevy. The pole that was thrust through its middle punctured the hood, and I was sure the car would die at any moment. Other horses attacked the sides of the car, rocking us back and forth. Grammy gave a shriek as one of the horses rammed her window with its head; the glass broke, and the horse spat fire at her.

The horses formed a circle around us.

It's only Neverland, I thought, *it ain't real. It's just* Sumter.

I jammed my foot down on the accelerator and rammed the car right through the lead horse. I shut my eyes for one second, figuring that we'd get burned to a crisp or stomped under their hooves, but the commandment of Neverland applied. The horses had fallen to the roadside; they writhed in pain, howling louder than the calliope and louder than the wind, for the carousel poles in their middles now impaled them to the ground. I was going to *will* us through these creatures, I was going to *get* to a boat and row us out to the island in Rabbit Lake. I was going to keep my brother from harm.

I was going to do battle with Neverland, and it would take all the imagination I possessed, all the will in me, to fight my cousin Sumter's own imagination.

⧏ 8 ⧐

As we approached the boathouse down at Rabbit Lake, the wind died and the rain turned to a drizzle. Fog was rolling in off the bay—a thick white mist barely touching the water. What was not white fog was piss-yellow sky, but the light was not from the sun. The light, I knew, was from Neverland.

I thought perhaps the storm was finished, and this terrified me, because it would mean that he'd already sacrificed my brother. But Grammy gasped,

"Dear Lord God," and I saw what she meant: The storm still raged, but it was all behind us—a protective calm surrounded the swamp. *A place of pure innocence.*

Where the dead dance, was what Julianne Sanders had called it.

Grammy Weenie touched her burned hand to her face; her skin had paled beyond whiteness and was now a translucent blue with the pulsing veins beneath its surface. "What must I do now, dear Lord?"

"Can you make it?" I asked, helping her from her seat. She felt like she weighed a ton leaning on my shoulder.

"I'll just have to," she said, but she winced with pain. Each step she took brought with it a sigh. In her hand she clutched her silver-backed brush.

Shep and Diane's Nightcrawlers Live Bait Shop was too quiet—in fact the whole dock and boathouse were dead silent. It was deafening, having come out of the hurricane. Our shoes got sucked and slurped with mud, and when I set foot on the wood planks of the dock, it made a noise like rocks smashing. A single rowboat was tied up to one of the pylons, as if waiting for us.

"Too easy," Grammy said.

"Huh?"

"He's left us a boat. He knows we're coming. He's waiting for us."

I knew what she meant. The world was too perfect here, too silent. It wasn't just a boat waiting for us—it was Neverland.

"What does it mean?" I asked.

"Beauregard Jackson." Grammy leaned harder on me as we walked across the splintered planks toward the boat. She was losing her temper with me, and when I looked at her face, I saw she was just an overgrown confused child: All those years on this earth had not taught her anything. "Beauregard Jackson, if I had answers, I would not have stuck my hand in the fire."

I thought she was going to haul off with her silver-backed all-natural bristle brush and swat me one good, but she didn't. I only then realized that a grown-up could be angry with me and still not want to hit me or yell at me. "Grammy," I said, not knowing what was going to come out next. I felt different, not just because I was wondering if the world was going to end any second now, but because I felt different inside.

I felt her weight on my shoulder.

"I love you, Grammy."

"I know you do, child. I love you, too. We're the same flesh. Even your cousin and you and me—we're all blood. I love all my children and my grandchildren. But do you know something? I think I love Sumter the most, because he's never had a chance. I wanted for him to have a happy childhood, but it is not in his nature." I helped her into the boat and then sat down in the back and lifted the oars in my hands.

I rowed as hard as I could, and still it took forever to cut through the white fog and even see the gray shadow of the island. The only sound I could hear were the reeds scraping beneath the boat as we moved through them. As we got closer to the small island, I began picking up the radio signals of Lucy's voice.

I wait. Give me sacrifice.

"*Why?*" I asked silently.

I want to play with you.

"*So you hurt people?*"

Hurt is all.

"*Grammy loved you.*"

She put me here.

"*Because she loved you. Because you were hurting people. Because she knew you hurt too much and you couldn't get better. If I was to find a wounded animal on the road, I might put it out of its misery.*"

All animals are wounded.

The voice in my head died.

Tongues of fog licked at my face, but it was clearing, and I knew we were near the island because long, thick grasses grazed the sides of the rowboat, and clumps of sticks and leaves floated by. Something else scratched at the underside of the boat, like fingers, and Grammy Weenie whispered in my ear that I must not be afraid.

My oar scraped mud as we came into the shallows. I pushed myself over the edge of the boat and, holding it, pulled it up onto the muddy bank. Grammy managed to straighten herself up using an oar for a crutch and then stepped out unsteadily. She slid her hands down the oar, falling slowly and gracefully to the ground.

I went to help her. Sweat tickled the back of my neck. Frogs chirruped to each other like songbirds. When I offered my hand to my grandmother, she shook her head. She grasped the oar and bore down on it, lifting herself back up.

Ahead, among tamped-down stalks of wet grass, a figure came clear through the fog.

Sumter stood there, waiting for us. His face shone brightly, flushed with excitement. At his feet was Lucy's skull.

In one arm he cradled the baby.

His left arm was stretched out to us.

In that hand he held the trowel.

"So, Weenie, tell me," he said, "where'd you put her bones?"

Grammy knelt down on the mud; her face was tense with the pain of movement. "Her bones must be dust."

"I can call her up. I got her skull. It ain't dust."

"It's your mind, child, all of this is from you."

"Don't you say that, it's from her—her and Neverland." Sumter stomped on the ground like a two-year-old having a fit. The whole island trembled, and I heard the distant thunder from the storm on the other side of Rabbit Lake. "And my daddy—I want to see my daddy, I want him to come to me!"

"No, it's you. You have what she had. But she only lives in your mind. It's you who's doing all of this. It's you hurting people," Grammy crept closer to where he stood, and Sumter took a step backward. "And you must stop, child, for in this world, what you do is bad."

"I will drain every ounce of blood from you for what you did to Lucy," he snarled.

"Then come, child, come. I will give it to her."

"First, the baby," he said.

In my mind I whispered, *Sumter, no, don't—*

I CAN'T! IT AIN'T ME ANYMORE! IT'S SOMETHING ELSE! IT AIN'T MY FAULT, I CAN'T HELP IT! EVERYTHING FEEDS ON EVERYTHING, AND MY DADDY'S HUNGRY, HE'S BEEN WAITING FOR THIS, AND I WANT HIM TO EAT! I heard his voice in my head, but when he moved his lips, he snarled, "I *hate* you, Beau, I hate you and your damn family. I *hate* your pukin' baby brother!" Something dark and shadowy rose up like smoke behind Sumter, something that for a moment I was sure was his father. The One Who Walks in Shadows. The Feeder. Nonie's voice, at the bathroom door in the Retreat, "Shadow."

The shadow was cast against nothing but air and moved its arms the way Sumter moved his. My cousin said, "I hope you never leave this place. You'll always have to play what I want, live the way I want, die the way I want you to die!"

But in my head his voice was shrieking, *IT AIN'T MY FAULT! I CAN'T CONTROL IT! AIN'T MY FAULT!* The screaming inside me was like a frozen knife cutting through my gray matter; my eardrums seemed ready to burst. *YOU GOT TO HELP ME! I CAN'T CONTROL IT!* I felt the tremendous pressure of something moving in my head, and in my mind's eyeball I saw what he was trying to do: He was trying to get inside my brain completely, out of his own body. It was like I was physically being pushed out of my body. *Flesh is the cage for the spirit.* My nose ran with blood as the pressure built. I was thinking: I'm going to explode, he's going to make me explode.

"Sumter," I gasped, "don't . . . "

I CAN'T HELP IT! NEVERLAND! IS! ALL!

I turned to Grammy Weenie for help. "Grammy, we can do this. All three of us. We can stop Neverland. We can put it someplace safe again."

She shook her head, her eyes avoiding mine.

"No, we *can*. It's like you told me, like blue eyes, like inheritance, we all got this . . . thing. Like you told me, *you told me*, only he's got it stronger and different, is all. But we can put it back, put it someplace safe."

"Too late," she said, "once out, it cannot go back."

"There must be a way, there's *got* to be."

Can't control it. His voice was getting weaker inside me.

Sumter held the trowel up over Governor's face. There were tears in his eyes. The shadow behind him reached around and hugged him tight.

I felt nightcrawlers slithering along the undersides of my feet and looked down.

Where the dead dance.

Faces of Gullah slaves embedded in the earth, grass growing from their eyebrows and nostrils; their fingers sprouting in the moss. Their mouths, opening and closing, gasping for air.

Sumter cried, "I don't got a choice. I'm doing this 'cause Neverland *wants* it. Governor ain't never gonna hurt again." His arm moved like lightning, and the faces in the earth screamed.

My baby brother cried out just before Sumter brought the tool down to the top of his head.

Please, Sumter called to me as if from a great distance, *don't let it make me.*

Sumter hesitated in that moment.

Something had caught his eye.

There, among the reeds by his feet, was a small, white rabbit.

Pure innocence. His voice was faint.

The bunny screams, another voice intruded, and I recognized it as Lucy's, *because it is alive.*

The rabbit at his feet wiggled its tail, sniffed the air. Then it began howling as if it were being skinned alive. The noise was almost human. It was that part of all living things that could express pain, it was a noise that we all would make one day. The sound was stronger than the cries of the faces in the earth.

Not pure innocence, Lucy said, *pure pain, pure pain. All hurt.*

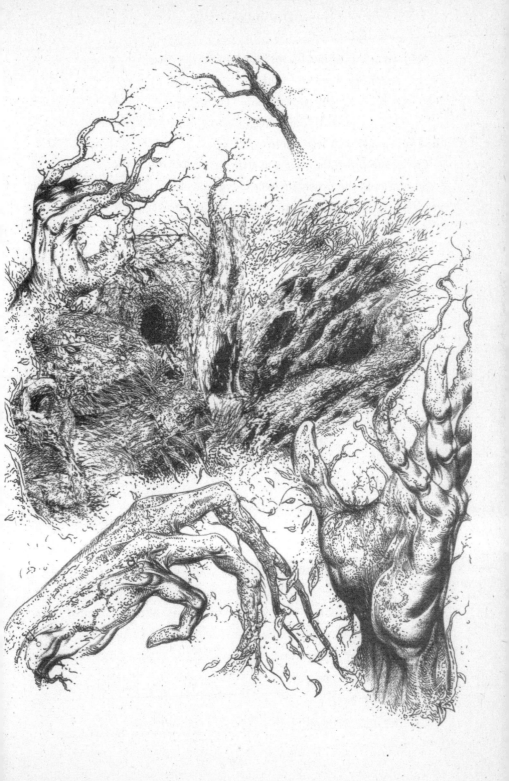

The rabbit sat up on its haunches as its keening continued, and then fell over stone dead.

With whatever telepathy I had, I screamed, *SHE WAS GONNA LET ME KILL YOU, SUMTER, INSTEAD'A GOVERNOR! DON'T YOU BELIEVE A WORD LUCY SAYS! LUCY IS A LIAR. LUCY AND NEVERLAND ARE LIES! IT'S HER THAT MAKES THE BUNNY SCREAM! BUT YOU GOT THE POWER NOW, YOU'RE THE ONE WHO'S ALIVE, NOT HER AND NOT NEVERLAND! SHUT IT DOWN, SUMTER, PUT IT SOMEPLACE SAFE!*

But Daddy, my daddy, wants me, he wants *me,* the voice in my head whimpered. *Daddy, I want to see you, I want you, I want, want, want . . .*

I made a leap toward Lucy's skull at his feet. My cousin stepped back, holding tight to Governor. I picked up the skull and threw it like a football out into the marshes.

I heard the splash a few seconds later.

The light of the world wavered and switched off with that splash, and then came up again, blinding and white.

"My son," a voice I had not heard before called out, "come to me. You are mine."

The geometry of the earth had changed, and we were surrounded by a sea of ice, and fog so thick I could barely see my cousin or the baby at all. Grammy was not there. All around us, in the whiteness, lay dead, torn animals, rabbits and sea gulls and mice and crabs. Some moving still in their moments of agony, their throats and shells and stomachs torn. Beneath the ice, the frozen faces of Gullah slaves, staring up at us.

From among the dead and dying a dark creature came, moving on hooves and hands, its skin spiny, its face eclipsed by a mouth that was open wide and studded with gray shark teeth. There, in its chasmic throat, was Aunt Cricket's boiled and blistered grinning face. "My son," it said, "I love you, you are mine, I am hungry."

Aunt Cricket's shredded lips parted, "Hallelujah!"

"Mama," Sumter moaned.

"*Why, I ain't your* mama, *Sunny, you know that. Why Babygirl's your mama.*"

"*No, you're my mama, you're my mama.*" *His eyes burst with tears.* "*I love you, mama, don't let me do this, don't let me.*"

"*HUNGRY,*" *said his father,* "*SACRIFICE TO ME.*" *The creature's jaws opened and shut, and when they opened again, Aunt Cricket's face was all but gone. Only a shred of her nose and mouth remained caught between its teeth.*

"*Not Governor.*" *I moved toward my cousin.* "*Give me Governor. What about will, Sumter? Do what you will, it's a Neverland commandment, what do* you *will?*"

Sumter was crying too much to see or hear me. He held Governor close to his chest, the trowel still poised above my brother's head. His father lumbered over to be near his son. The mouth opened again, as if not wanting to miss even a drop of the baby's blood.

Governor, who must've been oblivious to all this, looked up at my cousin, and what must Sumter have seen then?

But I knew, I felt it.

It was in the eyes.

Governor and Sumter, and me, and Grammy, and all the Wandigauxes— we had those same eyes.

We were the same blood.

We had come from the same flesh.

There was nothing to separate us.

"*Dit-do,*" *Governor made his happy noise.*

Sumter took the trowel and jammed it down and I screamed and jumped for him and the trowel went down easy into the spiny skin of the Feeder's neck as it howled in pain.

Even Neverland could not make him hurt the baby.

The sea of ice was gone, and we were again on the island in Rabbit Lake.

The shadow that had been his father became part of the fog.

Sumter dropped the trowel and set Governor down on the damp grass.

Drops of blood on the trowel.

He had driven the trowel into his own stomach.

"Grammy." Sumter's eyes were bursting with tears, his face crumpled up, his nose runny; he himself sounded like a little baby. "Grammy, it ain't my fault, it ain't my fault." He made croaking sounds, and I could not look at the gash in his stomach.

Grammy Weenie's arms were outstretched for him. She sat up taller on the bank. "No, my baby, it's not, it's not."

I rushed over and picked up Governor. He opened his small bean eyes and made his *dit-do* noise. I carried him back to the rowboat, setting him gently down, careful to keep his head up. "Grammy," I said, "now we can go home. Sumter . . ."

For the first time I heard her voice in my head. *No, Beau. I love you, I love you all, I even love him, more now than ever, for his sacrifice. But where can we go? Neverland is only sleeping. It will awaken again when he has rested. You take your brother and go back. Where would this child be safe? Say goodbye to them for me, and forgive me for what I must do, and keep your brother from harm. If you live your whole life and that is the one thing you accomplish, it will have been enough.*

She held onto Sumter tightly.

"Hurts," he was whispering, "hurts." His hands clutched his wound.

Go, Grammy's voice commanded me, *go, Beau, go quickly.*

Sumter was crying, I know because I heard his small voice in my head as I rowed.

In my mind's eyeball I saw: Grammy whispering to Sumter, "Close your eyes, my child. I'll take you to a place beyond even Neverland, a place where we can all be together: you, Lucy, your mama and daddy, and me. All of us."

"It ain't Neverland?"

"It's called Heaven, Sumter, and nobody ever gets hurt there, least of all you. We will go there together."

The vision faded as she lifted her natural bristle brush in the air, turning it around so that the hard silver back was aimed for Sumter's scalp, but I knew when she had brought it down because I heard a cracking noise and a gasp inside me, and it was the last time I would ever hear Sumter's small voice in my head.

A fog in my mind enveloped them, and my grandmother was also dying, *willing* herself to die, but still holding her grandchild close to her breast so that their spirits might leave their cages of flesh together.

Epilogue

I lay down exhausted, holding tight to Governor, and slept in the rowboat as the haze of fog engulfed us. The world seemed to have disappeared. We floated along into the emptiness.

I closed my eyes, feeling Governor's steady breathing as I cradled him in my arms.

I dreamed, and in my dream I was still rowing, but out on the bay, and in my boat were my sisters and my mother. It was my version of Neverland.

My arms were tired from rowing, and the water was calm. I could not see through the fog and expected at any moment for a monster to come out of it and sink us. I knew I was dreaming, but there was a peacefulness to the dream. Mama was still sweating in her fever dream, but she held tight to my baby brother, who squealed happily at our adventure. Missy did not help with the rowing, but cried hysterically, her hands covering her face, and would not look up for one second, even when I told her it was all over.

Nonie said, "Do you think Daddy's all right?"

I did not want to lie ever again. "Who knows?"

"I think he is," she said, and seemed comforted by her own answer. "How long we been out here, you think?"

"An hour."

"We headed out to sea?"

I shook my head. "We're in the bay. We'll get to land one way or another. If we were heading to sea, it wouldn't be this calm."

"I'm scared. We could die." Missy whined.

"We won't die." I said, knowing this was the truth. My back ached and the small muscles in my arms felt like they were going to rip right off the bone. But I knew if I stopped rowing we would get nowhere.

"Is that the sun? Jesus Gawd, is that the sun?" Nonie pointed up, and son of a gun if it wasn't the sun, and the white mist all around us was rending in two, painfully slowly the way clouds do, as if it hurt them.

As I continued rowing, the sky, too, became visible: slate with clouds, but the sun was still there among them.

"Look!" Missy pointed off the starboard bow. "It's there!"

The tiara bridge had not been washed out after all. It stood just as it had; someone had had the good sense to turn its lights on in the fog.

We still could not see land on either side of us, but I rowed, following the line of that bridge, knowing that one way or another we would reach the other side.

I looked forward and back, trusting we were heading toward the mainland.

"Daddy's okay," I told Nonie, "I know it now." I didn't say it just to make her feel better. I told my sisters that our father was there waiting at the end of the bridge because, through the fog, I saw his flashing headlights, our signal that he would not abandon us.

I awoke from this dream to see my father, half in the water, scrambling out to get the rowboat, with Julianne near him, calling to me, calling and laughing because the storm *was* over, the fog *had* lifted, and in my mind's eyeball I'd pretty much gotten it right. Julianne shouted to me that my mama and my sisters were doing fine, that they were waiting for me back home.

My father came for us—he had gotten across despite the storm—and had not let even the fury of Neverland stop him.

I passed my brother to him.

He kissed the top of Governor's scalp, and then mine, and he laughed, too, as if he could not withhold a surge of joy.

⇥ 2 ⇤

Gull Island is still there off the Georgia coast, although it has been given a new name, and nice people with nice cars drive over the newly rebuilt tiara bridge to summer and winter homes.

The hurricane that swept across it the summer I was ten destroyed the older homes, including my grandmother's. Trees were torn up at their roots.

There is still a bait shop, and even a semblance of the Sea Horse Amusement Park, although now it runs and has a low Ferris wheel rather than a roller coaster. Gullahs still live there, and if you were to ask them about that storm, they would tell you stories that would make your hair curl.

⇥ 3 ⇤

I've always told anyone who asked that Sumter Monroe wasn't really born bad, and I stand by that.

He'd inherited something—maybe just an imagination that was too big for his britches, and perhaps boys like that never do grow up. But nothing he ever did was just to be bad. Even trying to take Governor—at the last, I knew he wasn't going to hurt my brother.

At the last, he had some sense.

Where is a child to go when the bridge is washed out? Grammy had asked, and I won't pretend to have an answer.

Some of us make it over that bridge that connects that island of childhood to the mainland where we all must go eventually, sometimes kicking and screaming. Yes, and sometimes we scream because we are alive.

I have watched my brother Governor grow up, and I have watched my parents divorce and find other mates and still fight the same fights they did with each other. I have watched while my sister told my mother off and never spoke to her again, and her twin made herself happy with a man who I could not stand to be in the same room with. She's had five children with him. I have failed and succeeded at various careers and with various relationships. I have seen my cousin, my aunt, my uncle, and grandmother die, and did not feel grief until years afterward.

I have gone back and seen in my mind's eyeball all that was and tried to change it, to fix it so it wouldn't turn out so bad.

It's important to me that things don't turn out so bad.

I have tried, unsuccessfully, to exorcise the child who haunts me even to this day. He still waits on the other side of the tiara bridge.

Neverland, he says, *where I am.*

Perhaps we never cross that bridge completely.

But if childhood memory is filled with pain and nightmares, it is only memory, after all. It is not what lies ahead as we naviguess with sore muscles and tired hearts through white fog.